a Stories of Faerth novel

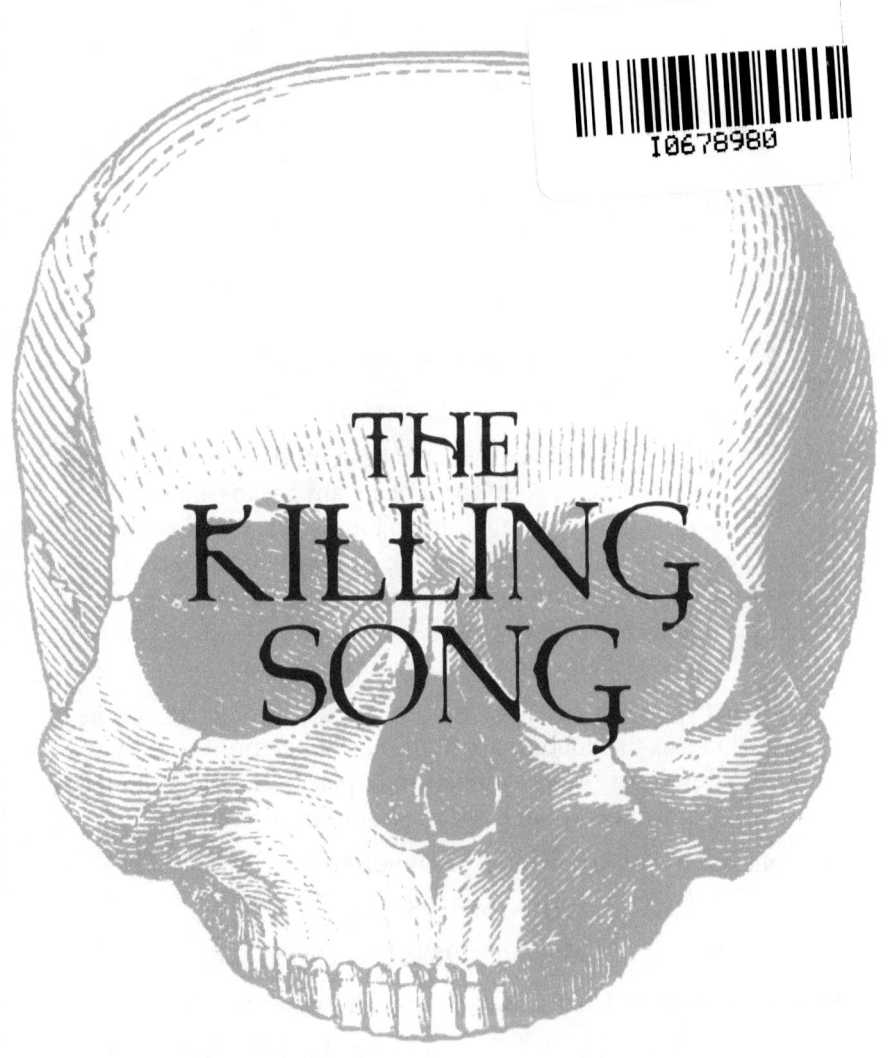

# THE KILLING SONG

## Felix Graves

ISBN: 9798987144947

eISBN: 9798987144930

Edited by Charlie Knight (cknightwrites.carrd.co)

Cover Illustration and Design by Fay Lane (faylane.com)

Interior Formatting by Adik Graves

Map Illustration by Lilly Lockwood
(ko-fi.com/lillylockwood)

Vintage Illustration of Skull (1843) by John Lloyd Stephens

# CONTENT NOTICE

The Killing Song is a dark fantasy horror novel and contains scenes and topics that may cause distress for certain readers. Please exercise caution when reading. For a non-exhaustive list of content warnings (does contain spoilers) please check the last page of the book.

This story is dedicated to those who have looked injustice in the face and burned with anger. The ones who have watched it and wept, feeling helpless at the horrors in this world. The ones who have bravely and continuously opened their hearts to their suffering communities and fostered love, safety, and connection. The ones who have survived the hatred inflicted on them, and the ones who have not.

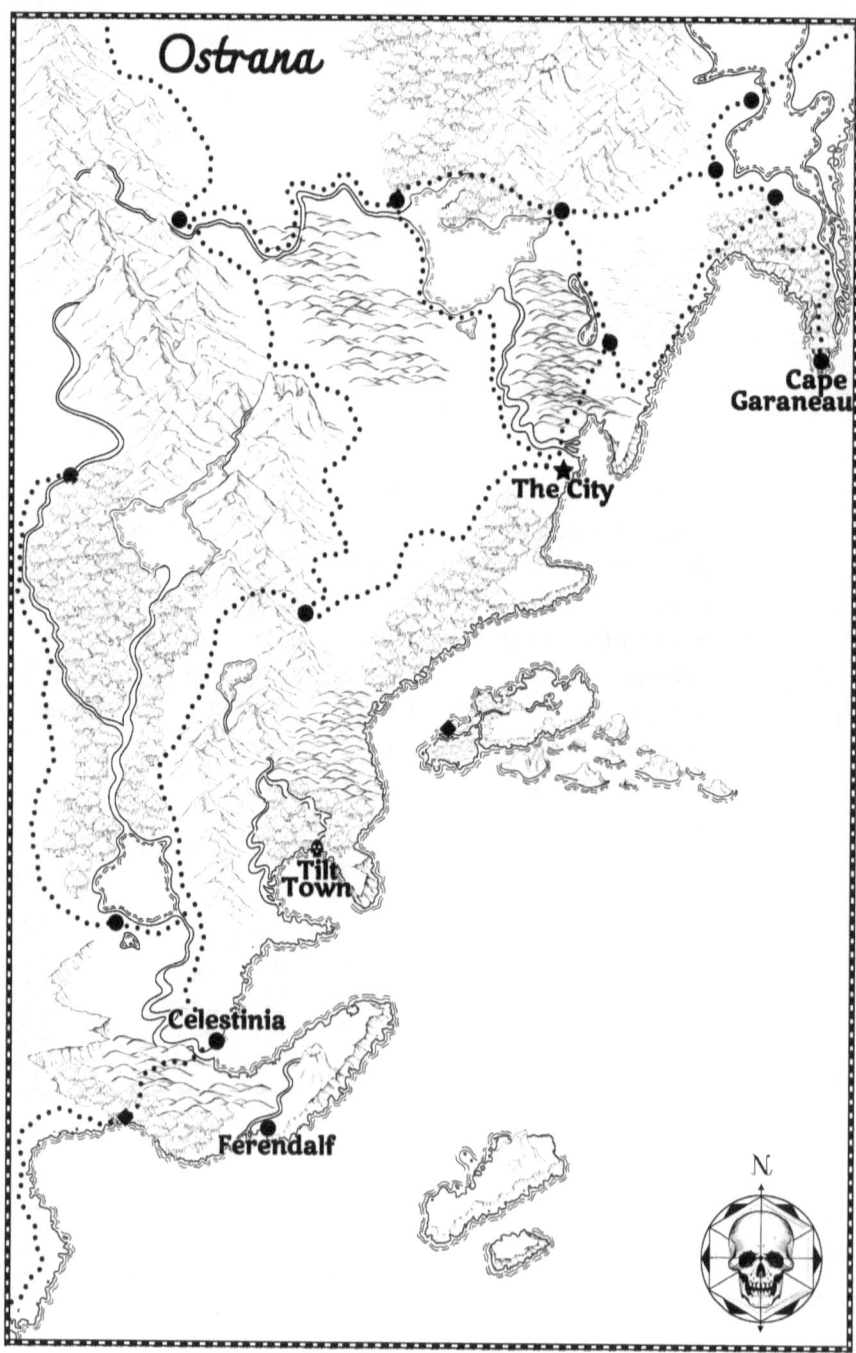

# CONTENTS

# FOREWORD

The year was 2019. My first child had just turned one year old. And my friends in my various online communities were talking about ICE and the camps that were being set up on the Mexican border. They were talking about the forced sterilization via mass hysterectomies in the camps. How children were being ripped away from their parents, locked in cages, and never seen again. How so many people were dying from the brutal conditions. And how no one was doing anything about it.

It all felt hopeless. It felt like the people who could do something didn't care, and the people who cared had no power to do anything other than keep trying to draw attention to the injustice in the hopes that something would be done to stop it all. I was reminded about how the U.S. had rounded up other races in the past for the audacity to try to live in the land of the free.

I remembered that this country has never been a safe place for people like me or my kid. People who have brown skin, or features not commonly associated with European whiteness. People who look "foreign."

At the time, a bunch of my friends were talking about protests, both planning them and taking inspiration from the past. Since it was Pride Month, we were of course discussing the Stonewall riots. How sometimes violence IS the answer.

I thought about Faerth, my own make-believe faerie world, and how the different faerie races would interact. Would this kind of horrific racism exist in my world? And I realized that yeah, it probably would. I don't think there exists a place where people don't persecute others for being different. And when one group of people is seen as a threat? We were seeing the effects of that in real time on the border.

I thought about how this was being done legally. How the people in charge were corrupt. How they bred and cultivated evil against their fellow humans. How the country you were born in or the color of your skin shouldn't dictate how much humanity you're allowed to have, how much compassion you were allowed to be treated with.

I thought about how, if sometimes violence is the answer, if sometimes the "good" law-abiding people are evil, that maybe the "bad" guys are the only ones who would actually step up and do something.

And so this book idea was born. This story, in which a small band of pirates on one single ship are the only faeries fighting against the kingdom that's rounding up sirens to put them into internment camps.

I hope this book makes you sad. I hope it makes you think. And, most of all, I hope it makes you angry.

# NAMES AND THEIR PRONUNCIATIONS

- Romada: roh-MAH-duh
- Neiara: nee-YAH-ruh
- Injago: en-YAH-go
- Yaya: YAH-yah
- Ceta: SEE-tuh
- Fayne: fayn
- Otandar: OH-tun-dar
- Delaini: duh-LAY-nee
- Rehka: RAY-kuh
- Imber: EM-bur
- Atar: AH-ter
- Anavi: AH-nuh-vee
- Eetan: EE-tun

# A BRIEF DESCRIPTION OF FAERIES

- **PIXIE/PIXIES:** winged humanoids with long pointed ears
- **WATER NYMPH/WATER NYMPHS:** hairless, amphibious humanoids with blue, green, or purple skin, dorsal fins, gills, and webbed feet, hands, and ears.
- **ELF/ELVES:** humanoids with pointed ears
- **SIREN/SIRENS:** humanoids with pointed spines and pointed ears
- **MERFAE/MERFOLK:** hairless half humanoids with a dorsal fins, an eel–like tail, tendrils on their heads, and webbed hands and ears. Skin can be any color.

For full, in-depth descriptions of each faerie race, including their physiology, social hierarchies, and religions, please check the Glossary at the back of the book.

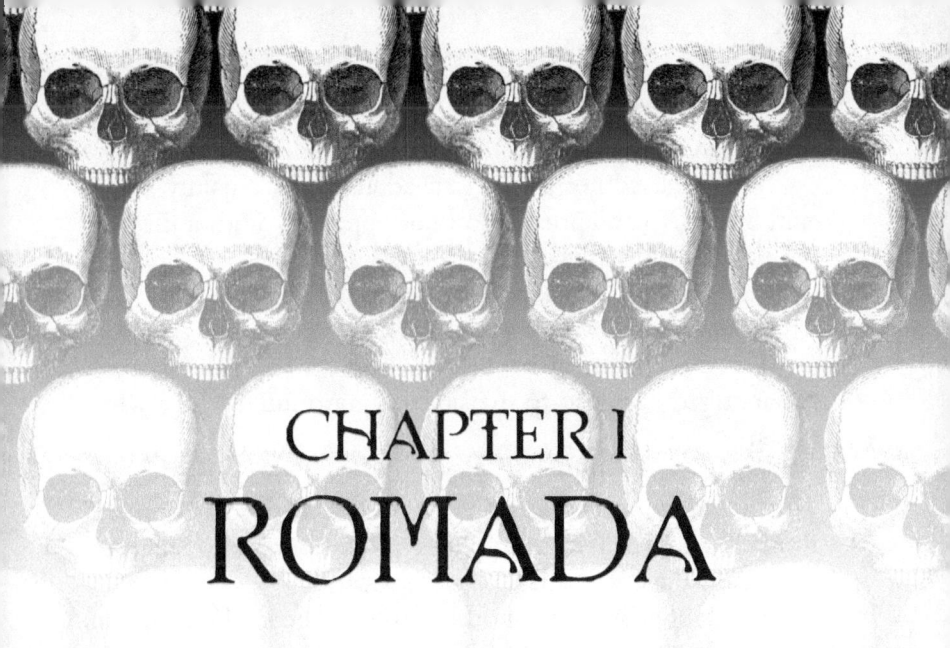

# CHAPTER I
# ROMADA

**ROMADA SAT ON THE SUN-DRENCHED PATIO, A** breeze ruffling her fins and the taste of a fine ale on her tongue, and watched the gorgeous fem-fae walking toward her. Neiara held a drink in each hand as she glided across the tiled patio with all the grace of a dancer. When she looked up and met Romada's gaze, a wicked grin curved her full lips.

"Hello, darling," Romada crooned once she got in earshot.

Neiara sidled up between Romada and Injago to settle into her seat at their table. Her leg brushed up against Romada's as she asked, "Miss me?"

"I always do." Romada leaned over to brush a kiss against Neiara's temple. The answering side-eye glance beneath lowered lashes prompted a warmth to creep across Romada's cerulean skin. Her head fin shivered in spite of the day's heat as Neiara reached over the table to hand Injago his drink.

"Many thanks," he said, grabbing the glass and taking a hearty quaff of amber beer. If the curve of his lips didn't bely

1

his contentment, the hum that followed confirmed it.

Neiara raised her glass of mead and took a dainty sip. A thin line of foam appeared on her upper lip. With a flick of her tongue, it disappeared.

Pulse racing, Romada's head fin twitched again.

*I can think of better uses for that tongue.*

The thought must have been plain on her face because Neiara tilted her head to the side and murmured, "Like what you see?"

"Get a room," Injago groaned, rolling his eyes at them both.

"If we had stayed at the inn where I *do* have a room…" Romada waggled her brow ridges. Neiara burst into laughter, but Injago gave Romada a playful scowl.

He shrugged, taking another sip of his beer. "Don't come with me next time."

Romada snorted. "Like I'd let you go out alone!"

It wasn't that she didn't trust him, but Injago was a magnet for fun, and nothing would make her ever want to skip out on that. Even back at the Orphan Center as a young orphan—the only water nymph there—she hadn't wanted to miss out on the shenanigans that were sure to ensue wherever he went. The fact that Injago had all but adopted her as his baby sister all those decades ago had just as much to do with her never leaving his side as him feeling protective of her.

His fangs glinted in the midday sun as he threw his head back and laughed. "Probably for the best. But hey, it's not every day you hear of a nice new establishment that actually allows pirate customers. We always end up at the same rundown places. Isn't this better?"

That was hard to deny; whenever they came to Celestinia for some much-needed relaxation, they frequented the same tavern and inn. Pirate code dictated that they keep all illegal activities out to sea, but that didn't mean that most business owners were willing to trust them, especially after a rogue pirate ransacked a fishing village a few decades back. When he was questioned about abiding by the code, he had shrugged and said they were more like guidelines. It would have been funny if it wasn't for the fact that all pirates had since been viewed with disdain and suspicion throughout Ostrana. The downside of long-lived species: they knew how to hold a grudge.

To Injago's credit, it *was* nice to see more of the quaint seaside town, and this particular bar had a patio in the middle of an outdoor plaza—the perfect place to unwind and enjoy their vacation.

Neiara clicked her tongue, grabbing Romada's attention again. "Looks like you could use another drink."

The dregs in Romada's glass had her agreeing with a chuckle. "What would I do without you?"

"Have a sober vacation?" Neiara smirked at Romada and delicately snapped her slender fingers in the air to signal the willowy elven barmaid at the other end of the patio. "Another glass of ale for her, please." Neiara's language switch from Pixish to Elvish was quick and flawless.

"Right away," the barmaid said in the nasally voice of a native Celestinian. Her long blonde hair fluttered behind her as she ran off, and she returned a moment later with the drink.

"Many thanks," Romada said, digging out five coppers and handing them over. She brought the glass to her mouth; the heady scent of hops flooded her senses as the first crisp sip of golden ale washed over her tongue. It took effort not to immediately gulp half the glass.

"Better?" Neiara asked. The twinkle in her emerald eyes said she already knew the answer.

"Immensely."

Romada leaned back in her chair, taking in her surroundings. Palm fronds waved high above her, and to her right, crowds of faeries bustled this way and that through the dust-paved plaza. A pair of merchants sold street food at a stall across the way; the smell of spices mixed with charred meat floated in the air, tickling Romada's nose and reminding her how long it had been since breakfast.

She dimly noticed Neiara and Injago start to gossip about Ceta. Romada didn't even bother feigning attention; Ceta was a pain in her fins and had been ever since she realized Romada didn't want to be her friend. As captain, Romada wasn't obligated to have anything other than a professional relationship with anyone on her crew, but Ceta had gotten it into her head that after Romada promoted her to quartermaster-in-training, they would end up being best buds.

Ignoring the conversation, Romada looked toward the entrance of the bar. The interior was a mass of shadows with swaying pinpricks of light from the lanterns hanging from the ceiling. Along the outside wall, a massive, gilded mirror was displayed. It wasn't currently on, so instead of a broadcast, all she saw was the reflection of the plaza. Bored of it, she looked past Injago's animated face to see an inebriated masc-fae elf. He wore loose pants that billowed in the soft breeze and an obnoxiously sequined vest over a yellow shirt bright enough to rival the sun. Peering over at their table, he stepped closer as if trying to place them.

Whether it was their painstakingly out of place attire—plain leather and linen clothing stood out compared to the quintessential Celestinian fashion featuring brightly colored and intricately embroidered cotton outfits—or the weapons they openly displayed, something he saw caused his face to contort with what was clearly disdain as he rushed over to them.

"Pirate filth! Scum of the sea!" He brandished the half-empty bottle of liquor in his hands at them as though it was a weapon.

Romada's ire kindled in an instant, and she shot him a scathing glare. Land-lovers had never shown much respect; thanks to the pirate code, they thought they were safe so long as they stayed on solid ground. For the first time, Romada considered breaking the code, if only to put the fear of pirates in him so that he would leave them in peace.

Neiara shielded her face from his view and whispered, "Should we get out of here?"

Too livid to answer, Romada placed a hand on the hilt of her dagger and made to move. Before she could, Injago stood and spread his gossamer grey wings wide.

"What were you saying?" he asked, a dangerous glint in his eyes.

The elf gulped and squeaked, "Don't care for the likes of you being around here, stinking up my favorite bar."

"What, you don't like pixies?"

Romada suppressed her laughter at Injago's antics, and her fury deflated as swiftly as it had appeared. His ability to feign naivety and deliver deliberately obtuse replies during confrontations was second to none.

The elf bristled, his hand curling into a fist. "You know that ain't what I meant. Got nothing against pixies. It's pirates I can't stand."

"And what are you going to do about it?" Injago's voice was silky and yet threatening.

Quaking, the elf turned his back on Injago and grumbled as he walked off. Either he didn't care that they heard, or he thought he was too far for them to hear, but the next word that came out of his mouth had Romada clenching her jaw and Neiara on the verge of tears.

"*Vreksesh.*"

"Oh, I can't wait to retire already!" Neiara snapped, smacking the iron-wrought surface of the table with the palm of her hand. "We are not honorless vultures!"

"I'm sorry, *deshani*," Romada said, reaching for Neiara's hand and bringing it to her lips. "I know this isn't the life you dreamed of."

Injago snorted. "Like dancing for coppers was her dream life?"

Romada narrowed her eyes at him for bringing up her past, but Neiara nodded.

"He's right. This isn't my dream life, but you whisked me away from one that was much less exciting. I chose you, Romada. I don't regret one single minute."

"Not even the hours of seasickness?" Romada teased.

Neiara knocked her shoulder into Romada's with an exasperated sigh. "Okay, yes. I regret every single minute of seasickness."

"So do we!" Injago quipped.

"No one asked you!" Neiara pouted, crossing her arms.

Romada's eye was drawn to the barmaid as she fiddled with the mirror. Flipping through a couple channels, she eventually settled on what looked like a documentary on the dangers of merfolk. As if merfolk needed help spreading more fear about them.

"Well, I agree," Romada said, turning back to Neiara. "I can't wait to retire. I'm done pirating. A century is a long time to be in this line of work." And it was no place to raise a family.

Injago gave a noncommittal hum. "I'm having the time of my life, Rome. Though I wouldn't mind taking over for you so you can retire."

"Yes, we know you're dying to be captain." Romada smirked.

"You'll get your ship one day. And we'll get our clifftop mansion." Neiara let out a wistful sigh.

"Hopefully sooner rather than later," Romada said.

After five decades together, Romada was eager to start a family with Neiara. Pirating was definitely an adventure, but she was ready for something new and just as exciting: parenthood.

With a dissonant screech, the mirror changed to the sight of an elf wearing an ill-fitting black suit and standing before the royal palace.

"Oh, great. The news." Injago slumped in his chair.

Romada shushed him. Black clothes on the news meant only one thing: a death.

The news-fae had short, curly hair and pale skin that looked sickly in the bright light of the mirror filming crew. A crowd had gathered behind them at the palace gates, obscuring most of the golden statues and flourishing gardens one would normally see when walking past. Bright red Elvish script flashed over the elf's face that read, '**Breaking News**.'

The elf took a deep breath before speaking in a quavering voice. "It is with immense sorrow that I pass on the news that the crown p-prince has died."

Romada blinked in surprise. A royal death? That hadn't happened since before she was born.

A hurried whisper offscreen led to the elf stammering, "C-correction: the prince has been m-murdered. The prince succumbed to a stab wound he received last…late last night. Guards arrived at his room after hearing screams and saw what appeared to be a siren fleeing his chambers."

Neiara stiffened. "Rome…"

"I know," Romada said, her voice coming out rougher than intended. She grabbed her drink and started chugging. Time to go.

"What this means for the already t-tenuous relations between Ostrana and siren immigrants remains to be seen. This has been a royal update from the palace."

A low keening began to spread throughout the plaza as the elves around them mourned their prince. The atmosphere, earlier so light, suddenly felt oppressive.

"Let's get out of here," Romada said, grabbing Neiara's hand and hauling her to her feet.

"Looks like everyone else has the same idea," Injago said, pushing in their chairs.

And he was right; faeries of all kinds—sirens, pixies, water nymphs—were making a mass exodus from all properties within the plaza, weaving through the elves who wailed and beat at their chests. The resulting crowd crept along slow as fog toward the exit at the far end. Romada hesitated to jump in; she didn't trust anyone to be pressed up against a group of pirates and not pull any tricks.

A sobbing elf exited the bar, knocking into Neiara. He must have spotted her pointed spine because his pale face went red with rage, and he screamed, "Thornback!" The siren slur flung in her face was followed by a bottle thrown at her feet. With a resounding crash, it split into pieces, flinging drops of alcohol and shards of glass. The elf swayed and leaned against the wall.

Glaring daggers at him, Romada reached over and tugged Neiara's hood over her head, hiding the delicate points that began at the base of her skull. She pulled Neiara close to her side, putting herself between the elf and her girlfriend.

The sound of glass shattering erupted overhead, and Romada looked up to see a broken window falling from above—along with the body of a faerie.

"Shit!" she shrieked, pulling Neiara back just in time to avoid being sliced or crushed.

The faerie, who Romada could now see was a siren, landed heavily on the ground, their pointed spine visible through a long tear in their shirt. A shadow fell over them as an elf in a green jumpsuit leapt out of the window, landing beside the prone body. Raising a leg, she drove the heel of her boot down hard into the body of the siren.

"Damn spike!"

Romada's blood ran cold as she started to grasp how perilous the situation was. If the elves surrounding them were throwing slurs and physically attacking sirens, how would she be able to keep Neiara safe? With the recent surge of siren refugees fleeing from the neighboring kingdom of Zerean, tensions between the native Ostranan elves and the newcomers were at an all-time high. Still, she never would have thought to witness outright hostility between the two.

More and more emboldened elves switched from keening to wielding slurs and fists against the sirens in the crowd. With each sharp word and dull thud, Neiara shrank against Romada, growing smaller and smaller as though she might be able to disappear.

The edge of the frenzied crowd pressed up against the patio, pushing the pirates back against the bar. The panic of the masses was an intoxicating nectar Romada had no choice but to consume. Her heart raced through her chest as she searched for an escape. She looked behind herself. Where was Injago?

A hand flashed in her vision, snaking past her to hook onto Neiara's wrist and wrench her away.

"Injago!" Romada cried out, hoping he was close enough to help.

Jumpsuit Elf gripped Neiara by the arm, pinning her to the wall while the drunk elf from before held a piece of glass as though it were a blade.

"Hey!" Romada yelled, tapping Jumpsuit Elf on the shoulder. When she turned, Romada drew back her fist and slammed it against her nose.

Howling, she released Neiara and fell to her knees. Drunk Elf glanced between her and Romada, clearly unsure of what to do.

Romada grabbed Neiara and pulled her away. Someone brushed up against her opposite side, and before she could panic, she heard Injago's low voice in her ear.

"I've got her."

"Get her out of here," Romada ordered. She felt them leave her.

"Water nymph bitch!" Jumpsuit Elf snarled, getting back to her feet. "I'm gonna teach you a lesson."

"Oh? A lesson in racism?"

"You think you're so clever," she said, a vicious gleam in her eye. She bent to grab a piece of glass, tightening her grip on it; blood welled up as it bit into her hand.

Drunk Elf let out a cackle, his full focus on Romada. The elves lunged forward, and Romada hissed as a shard sliced through her arm. She knocked Drunk Elf onto his ass in retaliation.

"Hurts, don't it?" Jumpsuit Elf grinned at her.

Romada didn't dare glance down to see the damage. Instead, she reached for the dagger at the small of her back, unsheathing the blade and brandishing it. "You want to dance? Let's dance."

The wild look in Jumpsuit Elf's eyes intensified as she feinted to the left; Romada jumped forward, closing the space between them, and sliced through the veins in her opponent's neck. A gurgle of blood escaped the elf's lips as she pressed her fingers to the wound, as if feeble hands could stop her life from draining away. She slumped to the ground just as Drunk Elf got back on his feet.

Romada crooked a finger at him, daring him to attack.

He hesitated, but before he could move, the barmaid appeared behind him and slammed a tankard over his head. He crumpled to the ground without so much as a peep, eyes rolling into the back of his head.

"Thank you," Romada said, sheathing her blade.

"Wasn't you I was saving," she said with a look of utter disgust.

*Elves.*

Feeling safe enough at least to turn her back, Romada twined through the crowd, pushing and shoving until she exited the plaza. Outside, the streets were in a similar state of upheaval. Elves all over were making sirens feel their pain. Romada contemplated jumping in to help some of them, but the need to find Neiara and make sure she was safe overwhelmed her. She could think of nothing else.

She slunk through West District, keeping mostly to the alleys. Once she reached Central District, the scene changed. Faeries were scarce, hiding in their homes. Shops stood silent with curtains drawn. The streets were all but deserted. There wasn't any evidence of rioting—no broken windows, trashed shops, or bodies of beaten faeries. Central district seemed to be a perfect safe zone.

When Romada rounded the corner, and the inn came into view, a squeal echoed in the street: she had been spotted. Neiara took off running toward her, Injago hot on her heels.

It was then that Romada finally felt the burn of pain in her arm; she looked down to see blue blood dripping from the cut and seeping into her pant leg. Grimacing, she pressed a hand to the wound, making a futile effort to stop the bleeding.

"Oh no," Neiara said, sucking in her breath at the sight. Tears sprang to her eyes.

"I can't even feel it," Romada lied, cracking a smile as she swayed on her feet. A look into Injago's grey eyes revealed roiling anger.

"I should have stayed with you," he said, a nearly imperceptible shake in his voice.

"Seriously, I'm fine. Once we stop the bleeding, I'll take a nice, long bath. And until then, I just need a drink, okay?" They gave her identical looks of uncertainty, but she mustered her best smile. "Oh, come on! I've had way worse than this!"

Injago sighed. "Okay, fine. One drink, and then a nap."

"Deal."

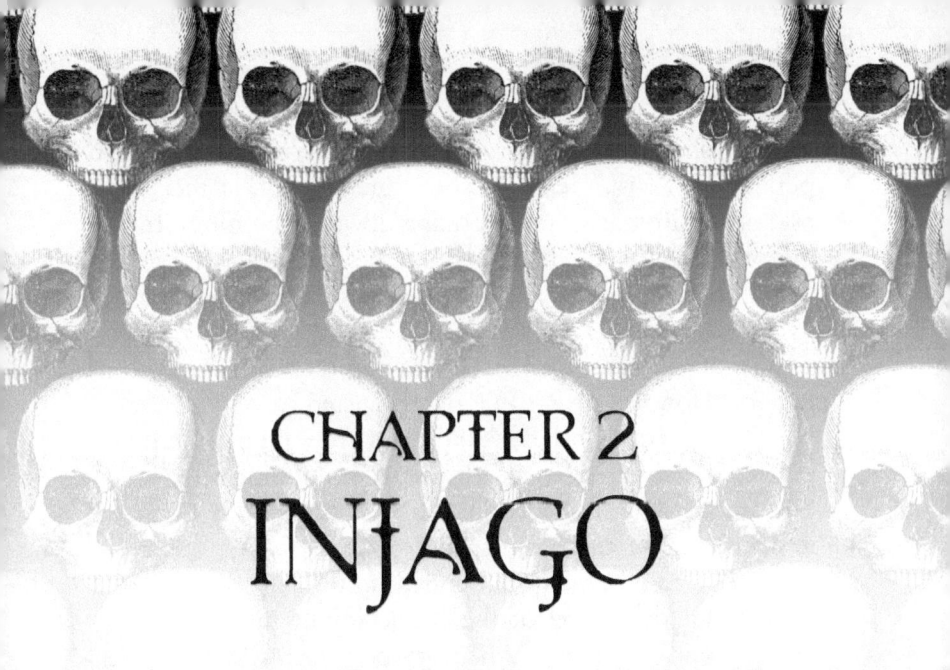

# CHAPTER 2
# INJAGO

**THE CRACKLING OF FIRE FROM THE HEARTH**
dominated the inn's dining room. Despite every table being
packed, the scant number of hushed conversations created a
somber atmosphere. The only crew member missing, as far
as Injago could tell, was Yaya. In fact, he hadn't seen Yaya at
all since breakfast. His patience grew thin as he watched the
staircase and struggled to keep his mind from creating scenarios
in which his best friend was lying in an alley somewhere, their
blue skin broken and bruised. Whenever Injago's eyes grew
tired of staring into space, he alternated tracing the whorls in
the wooden tabletop.

Romada and Neiara sat across from each other, talking in
low voices about Romada's fight. Injago couldn't quite make out
their words, but when he looked up, Neiara's eyes were bright
with tears. Either she was feeling overly emotional from the
day's stress, or Romada was describing something worse than
what she had alluded to earlier.

A flash of movement at the top of the stairs had Injago perking up; Yaya, the only other water nymph in their crew aside from Romada, stood looking down at the room. Injago grinned and waved a hand over his head. With an answering wave, Yaya made their way through the small crowd of pirates over to the table.

"Yaya!" Neiara smiled at them as they sat down across from Injago. "How are you? You look exhausted."

Their normally bright skin looked grey and dull, and their eyes had dark circles beneath them. Everything about their posture screamed exhaustion; even the perpetually perky fin in the middle of their bald head drooped.

"I tried to take a nap but ended up tossing and turning. I couldn't get the images of the attacks out of my head."

"Did you get caught in the riots too?" Romada asked, turning in her chair to face them.

"I decided to come out and join you, but by the time I arrived in the Western District, faeries were already in a rage. I saw a few sirens being beaten to a pulp... I couldn't have stopped it if I had tried." They hung their head, dark eyes trained on the tabletop.

Romada patted their back. "We got caught in them as well. Thankfully, we made it out okay."

Yaya eyed the bandage on her forearm, the stain of blue indicating the length of the wound. "Not unscathed, I see."

"You should have seen the elves after I was done with them."

"I bet they didn't even know what hit them," Yaya said.

A quick smirk lifted Romada's lips before she turned back to Neiara, reaching for her hand across the table. "I'm just glad Neiara was safe."

"All thanks to Injago," Neiara said with a smile in his direction.

"Yes! My hero." Romada gave him a matching smile.

A deep heat flamed Injago's face as he raked a hand through his curls, lost for words. He hadn't expected praise. What did one even say in this scenario? He looked around the room for inspiration and spotted a lone water nymph sitting at a table in the corner. The water nymph caught Injago's stare and gazed back at him with an odd look in his eye as if he knew him.

"Looks like dinner is served," Yaya said, drawing Injago's attention back to the table.

After already parsing out food to most of the other tables, a busty siren barmaid headed for theirs, bearing a platter in each hand. One was laden with a roast, and the other piled high with steaming potato wedges. The scent of herbs and spices flooded Injago's nose, and his mouth began to water.

"Here we go," the barmaid said, depositing the platters between Yaya and Injago. As the barmaid bent down to place the platters on the table in front of him, he was confronted with the swell of large breasts barely contained by her top. He felt a twinge in his own chest and a burn in his ear tips. Too late, he realized she had caught him staring.

"I'll be right back, darling," she said with a wink before she turned and headed back to the kitchens. He was positive her hips were moving a bit more salaciously than they had on her way out.

Romada snickered, having seen the exchange. "Poor Inja, always accidentally enamoring the fem-fae."

"Well, with a face like his, he's bound to," added Neiara.

He shot her a glare, but she wasn't looking at him anymore. It wasn't his fault he had such a pretty face. And it wasn't his fault that so many fem-fae threw themselves at him despite a lack of interest on his part. He had known since childhood that he was only attracted to masc-fae. Rome was lucky her butch looks kept most masc-fae from flirting with her. As for himself, Injago didn't have much more he could do to look as masculine as possible while also trying to deter unwanted advances from fem-fae. Binding his chest was one thing, but how could he change the bones in his face?

When the barmaid came back, this time with pan-fried greens and buttered bread rolls, he did his best to avoid her gaze. The scent of freshly baked yeast and melted butter hit him, and, to his mortification, his stomach let out a growl loud enough to disrupt every conversation in the room. The barmaid burst out laughing, and she wasn't the only one. Something about everyone laughing, even though it was technically at him, was a relief. Even Yaya chuckled, though they politely attempted to hide it behind their hand. Seeing them look so much more relaxed than a minute ago lifted his own spirits, and he couldn't help joining in as well.

He glanced back up at the barmaid, who still lingering at their table in front of him. No longer laughing, she instead kept steady eye contact with him and very slowly bit her lower lip.

"Everything looks incredible! Many thanks," Romada said in a rush. The barmaid turned to flash her a smile.

"You're very welcome, darlin'. Anything else you want from me?"

Despite Rome's best attempt to save him, Injago once again had the barmaid's full attention. He glanced around helplessly—anything to stop looking into her big, brown eyes—before blurting out, "Plates!" His voice was much too loud, so he gave her what he hoped was a convincingly casual smile and repeated, quieter, "Some plates would be lovely. Thanks."

Her expression slowly dropped, and then she nodded, finally looking away from him. "Of course! Right away." Injago couldn't help noticing that her rosy cheeks had darkened several shades as she hurried away.

"Plates!" Romada mimicked in a loud whisper.

Injago sighed, slumping back in his seat. "I thought she'd never leave! What was I supposed to do? Proposition her right here? Throw everything off the table and, and…" He trailed off with a scowl as Romada and Neiara started giggling at him.

"Well, I don't think you'll have to worry about seeing her again," Yaya said, gesturing back at the kitchen entrance. In place of the busty barmaid, an elven child came trotting out with a stack of plates so high they obscured his view.

"Whoa!" Injago said, jumping out of his chair to help him before the plates all came crashing down. Together, they handed plates out to the crew and the couple of random non-pirate patrons, including the brooding water nymph in the corner.

Snagging the last plate for himself, Injago sat down at the

table and began to help himself to some roasted potatoes. His appetite piqued as he noticed the caramelized onions and fresh herbs mixed in.

"Want some?" Yaya asked as they carved the meat into thick slices. Injago eagerly held out his plate in answer.

"Catch," Romada said before lobbing a roll at his head.

He had just enough time to duck his head before the roll hit the center of his palm, releasing a small puff of air and coating his fingers in melted butter. "Thanks," he drawled, glaring at her as he licked his fingers clean.

"Even with the riots, I'm glad we got a chance to come here," Neiara said, pushing some greens around on her plate.

"We need a nice break before we go on our next adventure," Yaya said with their mouth full.

"Oh, yes! The map! Oh, holy moon, can you believe we finally have the map to that abandoned mine?" Neiara's voice grew higher in pitch with every word.

Romada nodded, her face animated. "I can't wait to see what we find."

"Hopefully, whatever it is will be enough to build that dream house and retire, yes?" Yaya asked.

Injago glanced up in time to see the lone, lurking water nymph run into the barmaid on his way toward the exit; he knocked her into the wall, causing her to spill a tankard of liquid all over herself. She shook the empty tankard at him as he slipped out the door.

"Yes! The house! Rome, tell me about the house again," Neiara squealed.

Romada sat back in her chair, eyes locked on Neiara, who leaned so far forward she was practically on the table. "It's going to be up on a cliffside overlooking a lagoon. We'll be able to walk down to the water and fish right from the dock. We'll catch fresh fish every morning for breakfast."

Neiara and Yaya listened with dreamy expressions. Injago didn't understand why they never tired of hearing about the house. He was eager for them to build their dream house, truly, but he was also the only one who still wanted to pirate after it was built. They had all agreed that he would take over as captain of the *Guardian* and bring his plunder back to the family.

"The far wall of the main living room will be all windows, so we can always look out and see the ocean and the sunset every night. We'll have so many rooms! A room for us, a room for Yaya, a room for Inja, and a room for each kiddo."

Neiara bounced in her seat, her plate of food forgotten.

Romada's expression softened. "One water nymph and one siren, just like us."

"What about a pixie too? I'll help you teach them how to fly," Injago added.

"Oh, gods. A pixie baby. Flying around the house! Can you imagine? That's too much for me," Neiara said.

Injago stuck his tongue out at her. "We aren't *that* high maintenance!"

"Sure you aren't," Romada said.

"And you're still set on adopting from our old Orphan Center?" Injago asked, turning to Romada.

"Absolutely."

"Delaini will be so happy to hear that. You know how often she pushed for us to come back as adults and adopt."

It seemed like Romada's face held a flash of anger at the mention of their old orphan manager, but it was gone so quickly, Injago couldn't be sure. A wry smile spread across her lips.

"Exactly. Every orphan deserves a home. Anyway, let's talk about tomorrow! What are our plans? Anywhere special in mind for outings?" She ran a hand over her bare scalp, looking at first Injago, then Yaya.

Injago exchanged a look with Yaya. Romada wanted to make plans? As in, stay in Celestinia, even after what happened?

"I really want to look for some new books, but I'm scared," Neiara said in a small voice.

As she should be. Who knew if more siren attacks would occur?

Romada reached over to caress Neiara's hand. "I didn't see any evidence of rioting or violence here in Central District. So long as we stay near the center of town, we should be fine.

There's an open-air market a couple blocks from here that we can check out."

Neiara perked up. "That sounds like fun."

Injago pursed his lips but stayed silent. Far be it for him to be the one to burst Neiara's bubble of tentative happiness. He would speak to Romada in private about his misgivings.

Stretching her arms over her head, Neiara yawned.

"Tired, *deshani?*" Romada asked.

Neiara nodded sleepily.

"It's been a long day. Get some sleep, you two," Yaya said as the couple stood up.

"Night, boyos!" Romada called out over her shoulder as they headed for the stairs.

Yaya scoffed at the state of Romada and Neiara's plates and gestured at the untouched food. "If I had cooked this meal, I would be offended."

"Hush, Yaya. This isn't your kitchen or your food. We all know your cooking is divine," Injago assured them. "It was a tough day for us all. Why don't you get second helpings to make up for them?"

Yaya's eyes widened, and they licked their lips. "I guess some more potatoes wouldn't hurt...and another roll. And this roast is delicious!"

Injago laughed at the enthusiasm with which they scooped food onto their plate before he quieted, remembering his worries. Staying in Celestinia was dangerous, but every town in Ostrana might be the same. He didn't think any of the crew could have predicted the amount of hatred shown by the native Ostranan elves. Who knew they had so much hate in them?

He wondered how many sirens had died. How many would have been tended by a local healer? And how many more of them had been turned away? He sent a quick thank you to his god, The Harvester, for assisting him in keeping Neiara safe. There was no telling what Romada would have done if Neiara had been hurt. Having Neiara out in the open was asking for trouble. Neiara may be the lover of a pirate captain, but she was no pirate. She was a liability.

"What's on your mind?" Yaya paused their eating to look at him. "You've got steam puffing from your ears."

"Just worrying about Neiara. We shouldn't be staying in Celestinia. I need to convince Romada to leave."

Yaya raised a brow ridge. "You know how stubbornly optimistic she is. You think she'll listen to you on this?"

"I'm her quartermaster. I aid her in all decisions."

"Yes, but this is a well-deserved vacation you're talking about. The crew deserves this. We deserve this. And Romada sure as the moon wanted to make sure Neiara got a break from the constant seas."

They had a point. It had been over two years since the last vacation; the entire crew needed a break.

"But our safety?"

Yaya took a bite of their roll and chewed carefully before answering. "We'll all be there. The three of us should be more than enough protection for Neiara. She'll be fine so long as we stay in Central District."

Injago didn't agree but wasn't sure how to convince them. He was often told he worried too much; was this one of those times? "I'm still going to bring it up to her tomorrow," he said, taking a bite of his now cold potatoes. The thick oils coated his tongue, weighing it down.

Yaya shrugged. "Good luck."

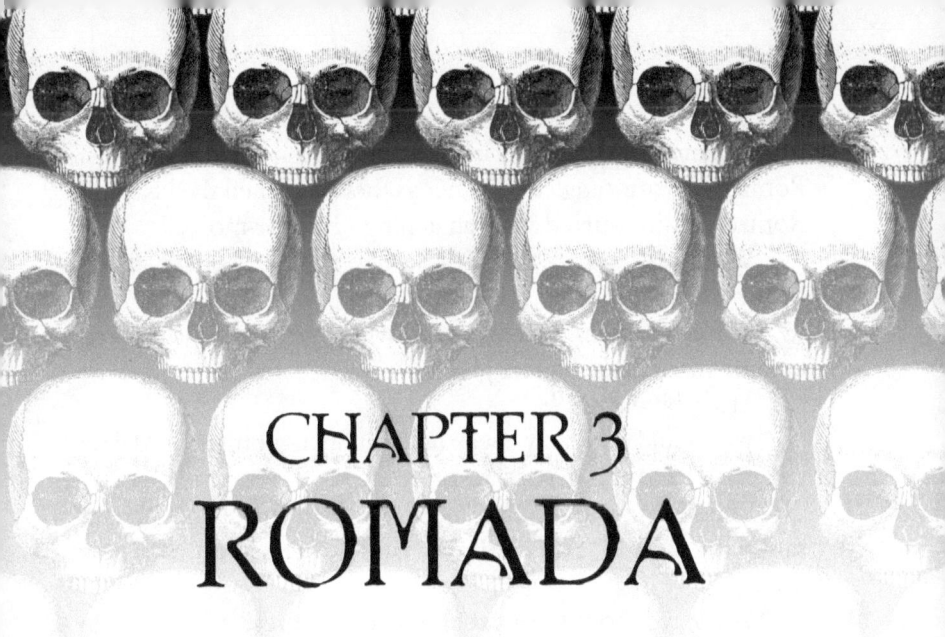

# CHAPTER 3
# ROMADA

**SUNLIGHT PEEKING THROUGH THE SLATS IN** the curtains tugged Romada awake. The pressure of Neiara's arm across her chest was a comfort that had her wishing she could succumb to sleep once more. She shut her eyes tight and laid still, to no avail. With a sigh, she rolled over to face the love of her life.

Neiara's usual umber skin was a deep red in the glare of the midmorning sun. Her freckles, pinpricks of darkness, dotted every inch of her body. Lips parted slightly as she breathed with a slow rhythm, her chest steadily rising and falling. Romada brushed a wayward curl from her face, and with that brief touch, Neiara roused, eyes blinking before focusing on Romada's face. A smile tugged at her full lips.

"Hello, beautiful," Neiara murmured, stretching her arms above her head.

"Mm, good morning, *deshani*," Romada said, leaning over to graze Neiara's lips with a kiss.

Neiara arched her back in answer, pressing her chest against Romada's. Arms tangled together as they deepened the kiss, and Romada's loins stirred with an aching need for more.

"What are your plans for the day again?" Neiara asked, breathless as she came up for air.

"Before or after I've had my way with you?" Romada quirked up a brow ridge as Neiara giggled.

"After, obviously."

"We should definitely check out that open-air market. Maybe you can pick out a new scarf or book."

"I need a new scarf like I need a hole in the head," Neiara said with a grin. "You spoil me. But I can't say no to a new book."

"You have more books than you do scarves!"

"That's true. But the scarves I can wear over and over again. The books...I mean, I *can* read them over again, but it's nice to find new stories."

Romada shook her head in amusement. Having only ever read a couple books for pleasure in her life, she didn't understand Neiara's fascination with them. But Romada was always willing to fund the obsession.

"I'm starving," Romada said, jumping out of bed. "Where are my pants?" She found them thrown over a chair along with her halter top—little more than a leather rag with strings—and shoved her feet through the pant legs before looping the halter strings around her neck and loosely over her dorsal fin.

When she turned around, Neiara was staring at her, a slight smile gracing her lips as she watched.

"Like what you see?"

"I would have liked it a lot more if you had pulled those pants up a little slower."

Romada shook her backside at Neiara, earning another giggle.

"Let's go eat," Romada said, crawling back on the bed for a kiss.

"Mm, I'm so tired though. Bring me a coffee?"

"Of course." Giving in to the urge to pleasure her lover,

Romada tugged the sheet down from Neiara's chest and placed her mouth over one pert nipple. A slow circle with her tongue had Neiara gasping, and Romada tore her mouth away before she started something she wouldn't be able to finish.

Romada was starving in more ways than one, but food would have to come first. Snatching up her coin purse, she strode to the door.

"Don't forget my coffee!" Neiara wailed.

Romada blew her a kiss and shut the door.

Downstairs, Injago and Yaya, along with a handful of the crew, were waiting on breakfast. Injago gave her a baleful look and chugged his coffee—no doubt laced with rum, knowing him. Yaya didn't meet her eyes and stared out into space. If Romada had to guess at the reason for the less-than-warm reception, she would have placed money on the two having a disagreement. It didn't happen often, but when the two fought, the entire ship's atmosphere became tense and awkward.

"Hello, friends," Romada said, eyeing the two of them. "Good morning to you as well."

"Morning," Injago choked out.

Romada rolled her eyes, reaching for the pot of coffee. After pouring a cup for Neiara, she glanced around the table for cinnamon. Not finding any, she went to the kitchen.

The voluptuous siren barmaid from the night before fanned her face as she stood over a glowing stove, frying eggs in a giant pan. She flipped them one by one with quick flicks of her wrist, a new sizzle joining the cacophony of cooking noises with each plop.

She noticed Romada then, standing with uncertainty in the doorway. "What can I get you, darlin'?" Her voice was husky and soft but Romada was focused on a drop of sweat slowly trailing down her cheek.

When she repeated her question, Romada blushed and asked for cinnamon, which the siren found after rummaging through a drawer of spices. She handed it over with a cheery smile, then watched in horror as Romada dumped some into the coffee.

"It's how she likes it," Romada explained, stirring the powder in.

The barmaid shrugged and started piling eggs on a platter. "Breakfast will be out soon, darlin'."

Muttering thanks, Romada placed the jar on the nearest counter. Armed with the proper ratio of cinnamon and coffee, she went back upstairs only to find a snoring siren. Chuckling, she left the mug on the nightstand and headed back down for breakfast.

"Romada, we need to talk," Injago said as she entered the room.

Romada raised a brow ridge and sat down. "Alright."

Injago looked over at Yaya, who shrugged and looked down at their mug.

"Okay. Well, I think we need to leave. Today." Injago's emphasis on the word 'I' had Romada side-eyeing Yaya, who stared down into the depths of their coffee like it was the most fascinating thing in the world.

"Uh-huh." Romada leaned back in her chair, an arm slung over the back. "And why would we leave? We've still got a few days left to relax. Not to mention, the other half of the crew still needs to get their time off. We need to resupply as well."

Injago huffed. "That's beside the point. Neiara is in danger. This town clearly doesn't have any love for sirens. I thought you realized that. I'm just worried about her," he finished, trailing off.

Romada wanted to blurt out that he worried too damn much about absolutely everything, but she bit her tongue and contemplated her next words. "I appreciate your concern. And I appreciate you saving her yesterday. But we will be fine."

"But—"

"I said we will be *fine*, Injago."

He bristled at her use of his full name and opened, then shut, his mouth, clearly at war with himself on what to say next.

Yaya finally spoke up to say, "We should trust our captain, Inja."

Injago shook his head vehemently. "If I had known that

she would be this stubborn, I should have used loaded dice and become captain because at least *I* wouldn't put my crew in danger."

Romada stood with fury alight in her eyes, but before she could do something she knew she would regret, Yaya stood up and put a hand out to her.

"We all care about Neiara. Injago is speaking rashly because he is worried. But Romada knows what she's doing. She will keep Neiara safe."

Injago didn't look convinced, but he sat in silence as the barmaid came out and started laying out platters of food on a table against the wall. Heaping portions of fried fish, fried potatoes, fried bread, and fried eggs had Romada's stomach growling. Shaking off her anger, she walked over to grab a plate and started shoveling piping hot food onto it.

The next few minutes were filled with the sounds of utensils scraping across plates and small noises of appreciation as everyone dug into the meal. Romada paused for a moment to savor the crunch of the potatoes, the flakiness of the fish, and the richness of the still soft egg yolks. Injago seemed to be in a confused state of bliss, his brows furrowed but his eyes glazed with what she would only call pleasure.

Romada glanced over at Yaya to see them holding a fork of food up to their face, inspecting it. She wouldn't say it to their face but the barmaid was every bit as good of a cook as them. Turning her attention back to her own plate, she punctured a yolk and watched it run over her potatoes.

She nearly choked on a forkful of those potatoes as the front door slammed open, hitting the opposite wall. A pair of elven guards—one tall and stick-thin and the other short and portly—barged in. Their hands held manacles, and their faces bore a look of contempt.

"You!" The tall one shouted, pointing at the siren barmaid.

She blanched as they came up to her. A sob tore from her throat as they wrenched her hands behind her back.

"W-what did I do?" she asked as they clapped the manacles around her wrists. "Please! What did I do?"

Her cries cut through Romada's heart, but she sat still as a statue, watching the scene unfold with frozen terror gripping her limbs.

"Shut it, spike," the short guard snarled. "You're being taken to a siren holding camp. For everyone's safety." He said the last sentence out to the room as if proclaiming his act of service to everyone else.

Romada's grip on her fork threatened to snap it in two, and the force of Injago's stare bored holes in her skull, but she still couldn't move. She couldn't risk drawing attention to herself or—gods forbid—the upstairs rooms.

*Oh, holy moon, don't let them search the rooms.*

"I didn't do anything!" the barmaid yelled, wrenching herself from side to side, to no avail.

No one else moved. No one dared to even breathe.

The short guard shoved her through the doorway as the tall elf turned to everyone else and tipped his hat. "Have a fine day now," he said before closing the door.

The dining room sat in stunned silence for a second before Injago stood up, his chair scraping the ground with a shrill screech.

"Do you see now?" he asked. His soft voice was thunder rolling through the stillness of the room.

"Everyone back to the ship. Whoever isn't there in ten minutes gets left behind." Romada spoke with quiet authority as she stood. After seeing Injago nod, she bolted up the stairs and slammed the door open to find Neiara sipping her coffee. She blinked owlishly up at Romada.

"Hi."

"We have to go. Now."

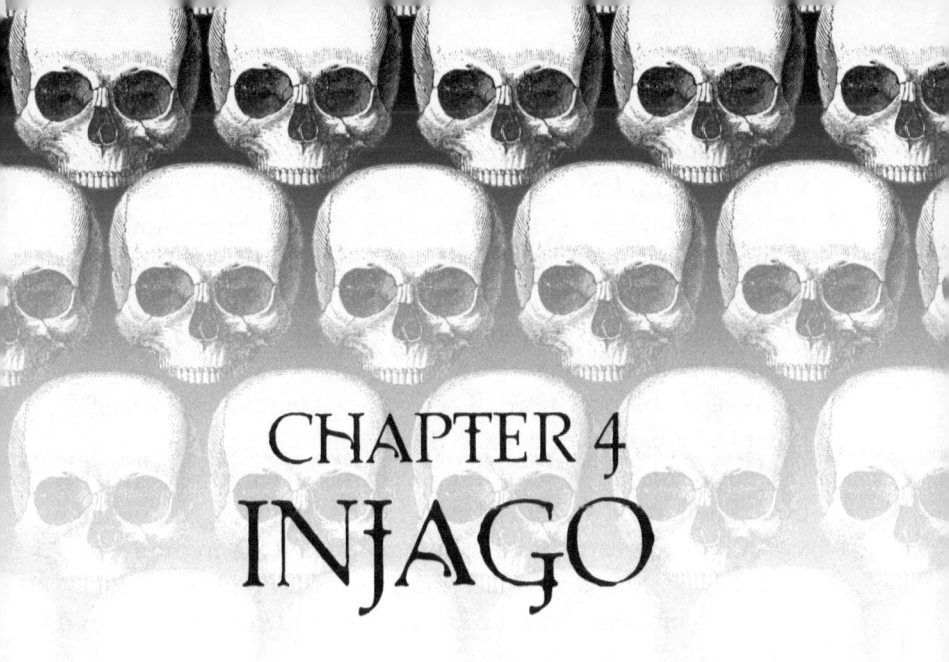

# CHAPTER 4
# INJAGO

**RUNNING THROUGH THE STREETS YIELDS** nightmare after nightmare. Countless sirens being pulled from their homes and businesses in shackles. Siren after siren begging for mercy. Guard after impassive guard locking them away.

Where were they all going? What would happen to them? And, more importantly, would the crew be able to escape in time?

Injago's breath came in short puffs as he jogged toward the pier. Romada and Neiara were far in the distance, running at breakneck speed through the alleyways. Neiara was practically being dragged along by Romada, which Injago couldn't help but notice wasn't all too different from how the guards were treating the other sirens. Even with her hood up and a scarf wrapped around her neck, why had none of the guards thought to stop her and check her spine?

Perhaps they were too engrossed in their tasks at hand.

The sun was still low enough in the sky that the alleys were blanketed in relative darkness, a boon for the crew as they slipped through. Injago emerged from one into bright sunlight in time to see a guard carrying a wailing baby. Disgust twisted his features as he held the baby as far away from his body as possible. The blanket around the tiny body slipped down, revealing a pointed spine.

Injago's blood chilled. They were taking babies as well? What had a baby ever done to deserve imprisonment?

"She needs me!" a fem-fae cried, hands shackled behind her back. She lunged for the guard—to do what, Injago couldn't say. A second guard raised his leg and kicked her in the small of her back. She landed face first, tears falling into the dust. Injago ran into the next alley. Her cries echoed in his mind even as they faded from his ears.

At the far end of the long alley, a pair of guards attempted to stop Romada and Neiara. Drawing her dagger, Romada slashed at the guard reaching for Neiara and whirled past. The other guard drew a loaded crossbow from his back and aimed at them as they ran.

Injago leapt into the air, using his wings to propel himself forward, and threw his dagger at the guard. It hit him where his neck met his shoulders. Injago landed and bent to grab the dagger as he ran past the two now-dead guards.

The gate to the dockyard came into view, and Injago picked up the pace. Yaya and the rest of the crew who had come ashore were hot on his heels. Romada and Neiara jumped into a rowboat right as a guard reached them. Romada's grin was too wide, showing too many teeth, but the guard nodded and started heading back toward the dockyard entrance.

"Whoa there! Where's the fire?" he asked, seeing Injago and the rest of the crew running pell-mell through the gate. His hands stayed perched on his belt, though not on the hilt of his weapon. A warm smile brightened his face and lit up his kind eyes.

Injago didn't trust him.

"My boss took us off shore-time early," he said through

gritted teeth in what he hoped resembled a proper smile. "You know how that goes."

"Oh, I do! Are you lot sailors?" The guard looked them all up and down.

Injago couldn't believe a guard would ever mistake them for anything but the pirates they so clearly were, but he laughed and slapped Yaya's arm as though this was the funniest joke he had heard.

"Sailors! No, we're humble fishermen," Injago said, wiping away imaginary tears of mirth. "No fancy jobs here."

"Ah. Well, are there any sirens among you?" The guard did a quick scan of the crew, noticing wings on everyone but Yaya—though their blue skin was an obvious marker of being a water nymph—and waved them all by. "Get on back to work then! No use angering your boss." He winked at Injago as though they were fast friends and walked on, whistling a little tune as he went.

Injago resumed his trek toward the rowboat, albeit at a slower pace.

"What was that about?" Romada spoke under her breath once Injago climbed aboard.

"Just checking for sirens," he answered, voice low. "Why didn't he notice Neiara?"

"He's pretty gullible. He thought we were sailors."

Injago chuckled as he helped her untie the mooring line from the dock, and Romada's mouth quirked up into a tiny smile in reply.

"You there!" A pair of guards had rounded the corner and were heading straight for the rowboat, hands already on their weapons. Injago knew they wouldn't be so easily fooled.

"Row, dammit," Romada hissed before turning to smile and wave at the guards. "What seems to be the problem?" she asked as the rowboat began to move away from the dock and toward the *Guardian*.

"We need to check your spines! Halt!"

"We are none of us sirens!" she called back as the distance between them and the guards grew. "Have a fine day!"

"Get back here! Stop!"

One of the guards broke from the group and sprinted away, no doubt toward the guard shack just outside the dockyard. As Injago and the crew continued to row, a stream of guards came pouring out of town. They jumped into another rowboat and began to pursue the pirates.

"Should have burned that," Injago said, gasping from the exertion.

Romada grabbed an oar and began rowing beside Injago, setting a new, grueling pace for the rest of the crew. "Faster," she grunted, even as they all put their backs into it.

They went faster.

Injago checked the progress of the guards and saw six of them in a boat, bearing down on them. "There's six of them and ten of us. We can take them."

"I'd rather not," Romada huffed.

They made it to the *Guardian* a few minutes later. Ceta, ever helpful, threw down a rope ladder to get everyone aboard faster. Half of them used the built-in hand and foot holds, while the rest used the ladder. Neiara was first to climb on deck, with Injago and Yaya coming up last.

"Loose the sheets! Weigh anchor! Let's get this ship moving!" Romada shouted.

Once on deck, Injago and Yaya turned to heave the rowboat back up into place using the pulleys. It crept into the air, swaying from side to side and dripping rivulets of water. For a moment, it blocked the view of the guards, and Injago let himself believe they had given up the chase.

With another heave, the boat lurched into place.

"They're still coming!" Ceta called out, her voice shrill with panic.

As Yaya and Injago finished tying off the ropes holding the rowboat in place, the guards got close enough for everyone onboard to hear their curses.

"BLOODY PIRATES!"

"In the name of the Crown, STOP!"

Injago jumped to the helm and landed beside Romada. "We

need to row," he said, glancing at the depressingly limp sails.

"Then give the damn order!" Romada yelled, spinning the wheel to point them out to sea.

"Aye," he said, leaping down to the deck. "Let's row, everybody!" Taking the steps two at a time got him down belowdecks to the rowing stations with enough time to grab a crossbow off the weapons rack. The bolts weren't huge, but a few strategically placed shots at the hull of the rowboat could have them slinking back toward land. Attacking the guards themselves could end things quickly, but fleeing the law was a completely different level of illegal than killing guards. Romada wouldn't be pleased to have a bounty added to their heads.

Taking aim through a porthole, Injago almost didn't see the blitz being pulled out of a holster. The guard raised it and aimed at the ship.

"BLITZ!" Injago screamed, and everyone scrambled for cover. Not that it would do much good. The energy beam from a blitz could leave a hole wide enough for the damn rowboat to fit through.

Which was plenty big enough to sink the *Guardian*.

With a new target in sight, Injago pulled the trigger. The bolt sank into the guard's shoulder, and useless fingers dropped the blitz over the side of the boat, where it was lost to the sea. A cheer went up on deck, and the oars slid into the water as the boat reached the ship. With a vicious twist, Injago rammed his oar against the boat, shoving it away and shattering the oar in the process.

The wind must have caught the sails because, in that moment, the ship lurched forward, speeding away from the guards. Breathing a sigh of relief, he gave the signal to stow the oars before heading up to the deck.

"Injago!" Ceta collided with him, eyes wide, wings fluttering behind her. Her body vibrated with nervousness. "Something happened last night."

"Okay…" Great, now he was nervous, too.

"There was a break-in last night. A water nymph was seen leaving the cabin, and before we could catch him, he dove over the side and never surfaced. I don't know if he took anything. I...I *hope* he didn't take anything."

Water nymphs made excellent pirates, what with being able to breathe underwater. It was one thing to have wings and fly away from an enemy at sea; it was another thing entirely to be able to simply vanish into the all-obscuring depths of the sea, never to return. And unfortunately for Ceta, the only two water nymph crew mates who could have caught him had been on shore leave. Injago sighed and pinched the bridge of his nose. Romada was *not* going to be happy about whatever had happened in the cabin.

"Is that it?" Injago asked, his voice coming out harsher than he intended.

Ceta blinked up at him once before nodding.

"Thank you for telling me," he said in what he hoped was a soothing voice. His stress levels were through the roof, so to speak, but he needed to watch his temper. There was no point in lashing out at the crew.

"Wish we had caught him," Ceta murmured as she stepped out of his way.

*That makes two of us, then.*

As soon as Injago's head popped up above the deck, Romada signaled for him to take the helm and then raced for the cabin. Did she already know?

No, she was probably worried about Neiara. There was no way Ceta would have told Romada to her face that she failed to catch an intruder. He would give Romada some time with Neiara before heading in with the bad news. Hopefully, whatever had happened in the night wouldn't have any lasting effects... but his gut was telling him something was very, very wrong.

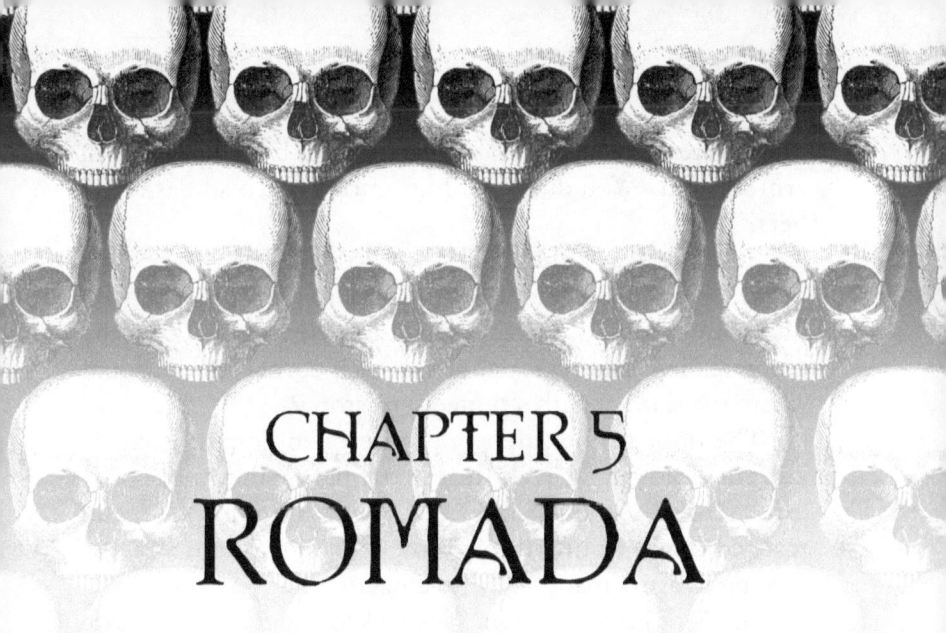

# CHAPTER 5
# ROMADA

**ROMADA BARRELED INTO THE CABIN—SEND-**
ing the door swinging behind her and smacking into the wall—
and saw Neiara huddled in the corner of the canopy bed, a
pillow pressed to her head. Her tear-stained face peeked out,
and she let out a sob.

"I heard the blitz warning!" Neiara cried, launching herself
off the bed and into Romada's arms.

"Shh, it's okay. Everyone is safe. You are safe." Romada buried
her face in Neiara's hair, inhaling the sharp scent of her citrus
curl lotion. The smell was nearly as relaxing as the embrace.

"I know, I know," Neiara said, shaking in Romada's arms
for a moment before twisting to look up and press her lips to
Romada's jaw. The midday sunlight through the gauzy curtains
threw strange shadows over her face, rendering her half there
and half gone.

Romada felt queasy at the sight but returned the kiss, lightly
pressing her lips to Neiara's.

33

"You're okay, though?" Romada asked, holding Neiara at arm's length. "You didn't get hurt during our mad dash over here?"

"Just because I stumbled once doesn't mean I got hurt, Rome," she chided. "Actually, I wanted to ask you something. Did you leave that open?" Neiara turned to point past the commanding oak desk and at the back corner of the room where the safe sat with a potted fern atop it.

The door to the safe stood wide open despite Romada knowing for a fact that she had shut it before they took shore leave. Blood thundering in her ears, Romada stomped over and reached down to rifle through the contents. The map—the fucking treasure map!—was no longer there.

"Shit! It's gone!" Fuming, she kicked the edge of the safe and instantly regretted it. Hopping on one foot, she glared at the safe—as if it was to blame for the theft—and unleashed a string of curses at it. To no surprise, the safe stayed as map-less as it had been for who knew how long. Since neither the kick nor the profanity was actually helping, she opted for attempting to take several deep breaths to steady herself. But how the fuck does one breathe when their life's work has up and vanished? Also, her foot really fucking hurt.

*Note to self: do not kick the safe.*

"Knock, knock," Injago said, tapping on the open cabin door. Neiara and Romada spun around to stare at him. "Wanted to let you know that someone broke into the cabin last night."

"Yeah, I figured that out," Romada said through gritted teeth. Planting both feet on the floor, she pointed at the derelict safe. "The map is gone!"

"The map? *The* map? Our map is gone?" His mouth hung agape, and his beautiful grey wings cocked as though he would fly away.

"Yes, Inja, *that* map is gone." Romada crossed her arms so she wouldn't be tempted to start breaking things. The delicate inkwell on her desk was practically begging to be thrown against the wall. So was the tiny succulent Neiara had gifted her for her last birthday.

"What do we do?"

"What about our contact in Tilt Town?" Neiara piped up, looking between the two simmering siblings.

Romada inwardly groaned. Why did it have to be Tilt Town? Anywhere but Tilt Town. The last time she had visited...well, she hadn't exactly left on the best of terms with their favorite barkeep.

"That could work. If anyone would have heard of our map being put on the underground market, it would be Otandar." Injago noticed Romada's expression and smirked.

*Must not have hid my grimace well enough.*

"Okay, fine. Tilt Town it is. Please set a course," she said with a sigh.

Injago nodded and pulled the door shut behind him, giving them some privacy.

"I was so scared for you," Neiara said, coming up and nuzzling into Romada's arms. "What would I do if anything happened to you?"

"Nothing happened, *deshani*. I'm safe. You're safe. And we'll continue to keep you safe."

Neiara pursed her lips, looking at the floor.

"What is it?" Romada asked, tilting Neiara's chin up with a delicate touch.

Neiara avoided her gaze. "It's... I don't know. I feel bad. For all those sirens."

"I know, love. But there's nothing we can do but make sure their fate doesn't become yours." Romada rubbed Neiara's arms to warm her up; she was still shivering and had prickles all over her skin.

"But what about them? They didn't have anyone to keep them safe. They didn't know to run. Is that their fault?"

Romada pulled away from her, frowning. "Of course not. Why is this something you're even thinking about?"

"Well, what are we going to do?"

"About what?"

"About the other sirens, Romada! We can't just stand by while sirens, my species, are being locked up like animals." Neiara's lower lip trembled.

If this were any other moment, Romada would have swept Neiara into her arms and carried her to bed to make love and distract her from these horrible thoughts. But she doubted that was the right course of action in this particular case. She would have to use her words instead. Which was...frustrating.

Instead, she stared at Neiara in confusion. "What can we do? Darling, I love you. I would do anything to keep you safe. But faeries we don't even know? They're nobody to us!" Romada winced as the words left her but knew she couldn't take them back.

"Glad to know that's how you really feel," Neiara said, still staring at the floor.

Romada wanted to scream. "Why are we fighting about this? We are free and safe, and that is what matters. Your safety—that's all that matters. We can't save the others." Romada reached over and held Neiara's unresponsive hand in hers.

"Okay."

"Please don't be mad at me," Romada begged.

Neiara pulled her hand away and crossed over to the bed, sitting with her back to Romada.

"I'm not mad. I'm disappointed."

Like a punch to the gut, her words hit Romada and sent her reeling.

*Disappointed...*

Neiara had never expressed disappointment in her before.

"I'm bloody starving," Romada choked out. "Want anything?"

"No."

"Fine." Hot tears burned the corners of her eyes as Romada left the cabin.

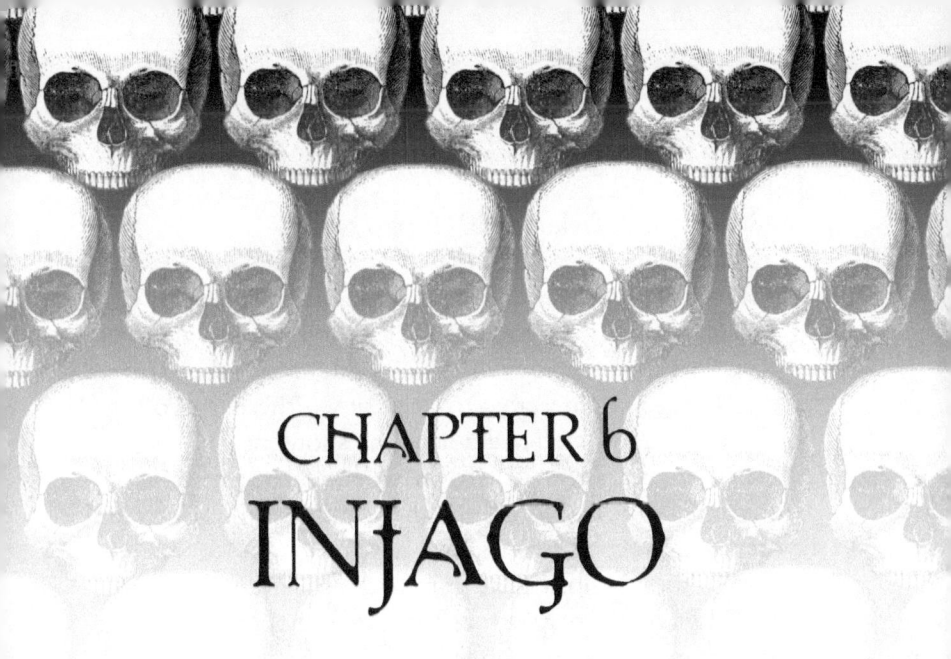

# CHAPTER 6
# INJAGO

**THE CABIN DOOR SHUT WITH A CRASH, AND**
Romada came into view on the deck. She stood silent for a moment, staring off into the distance, before turning and heading up the steps to stand beside Injago at the helm.

Injago studied her. She radiated unhappiness in the tense set of her jaw, the redness of her eyes, her pursed lips. Her head fin twitched every few seconds; after the strained silence became too much for him, Injago spoke.

"Copper for your thoughts?"

Romada grunted and turned away slightly, flattening her head fin with a stroke of her hand.

Injago waited a moment more. "Talk to me, Rome."

"I don't need a second person disappointed in me right now, okay? Just drop it." Romada turned on her heel, leaving Injago wondering why on Faerth Neiara was disappointed in Romada. What had happened in the cabin after he left?

"What was that?" Ceta asked, coming up the other set of steps.

"Romada isn't feeling well," Injago said.

*Bottling up her emotions instead of talking things out. Again.*

Ceta gave him a conspiratorial look. "Is she ever?"

Injago shot her a glare, but she ignored it, unrolling their map of Ostrana onto the oak table beside the wheel. Moving various bottles on the table to hold down the edges of the parchment, she pointed at a dot on the shoreline.

"If we are heading to Tilt Town, we should be clear to make a straight line there. No islands in the way. If the winds are favorable, it'll take us two to three days."

Injago took a moment to admire the calligraphic lettering of Tilt Town on the map before answering. "Sounds good. The sooner we get there, the better."

"I'm so sorry for not having a better watch last night. This is all my fault." Ceta grabbed a bottle of spiced rum and took a swig.

"It's not your fault. We were talking about the map in the inn last night... I can't help but think that the water nymph I saw there is the same one who stole our map." Injago sighed and ran a hand through the curls lying on his forehead.

"So it's your fault!" Ceta hiccuped and handed the bottle over, but Injago waved away the offer. "Well, that makes me feel better."

"We should do a better job of setting up watches, however," Injago added. "A little more caution can't hurt."

The stairs creaked behind him, and he turned to see Romada sidling up the steps with a look of contrition.

"Take the map back," Injago said, dismissing Ceta.

"Aye, aye," she said, placing the rum back on the table and carefully rolling up the map.

Injago grabbed a random bottle and took a hearty drink, hoping for a buzz. The sweetness of the port didn't lessen the sting down his throat, and he wished for some water to wash it down. He had never been a big wine drinker, but they were all out of beer and hadn't been able to replenish before they left Celestinia.

He offered the bottle to Romada, who accepted it without a word. She stood there, holding the bottle's neck in a death grip.

"I didn't mean to snap at you," she said in a small, rough voice.

"I know." Injago didn't expect any more of an apology than that, and she didn't offer one.

Romada visibly relaxed and took a sip of the port before handing it back. It was still over half full, so Injago took another drink before putting it on the table. His head was starting to feel a little lighter.

"You know, maybe if you opened up a little more instead of bottling everything up, Neiara wouldn't be disappointed in you." Was the alcohol loosening his tongue? He couldn't believe he had said that out loud. Anticipating a rebuttal, he glanced over to see a purple blush creeping over her blue skin.

"It's nothing like that. I share everything with Neiara. That's the problem."

Injago felt a pang of jealousy but quickly repressed it. He didn't want to cause Romada to stop talking, to stop opening up to him. When they were orphans back at the Center, they only had each other. Romada told him everything. But as adults... It hadn't taken long for Neiara to replace him as confidant.

"Neiara's disappointed because we aren't doing anything about the other sirens."

"What about them?" Injago raised an eyebrow.

"She wants us to rescue them," she answered, rolling her eyes.

"What, rescue all of them? That's impossible."

"I know!"

"Not to mention absurd."

"Right? I just... I don't know why she thinks that's something we would even do. She knew what she signed up for by joining us. We aren't heroes."

"The opposite," Injago said, laughing. His heart felt strangely light as he realized he and Romada were speaking ill of

Neiara—for the first time ever—in such a casual manner. Neiara, the faerie who could do no wrong. He wasn't sure Romada had ever expressed anything even remotely negative toward her. "We're bloody pirates! We don't rescue anyone."

A wave crashed against the hull, causing the ship to list. Romada and Injago shifted their weight in tune with the ocean, standing firm.

"Anyway, she's disappointed." Romada sighed and crossed her arms.

"There's only one faerie I would go to the ends of Faerth to rescue, and that's you, Rome."

She turned and grinned down at him. "Yeah?"

"That's what big brothers do." Romada snorted at that. "Older brothers, then," he amended.

"Ah, so it's a familial obligation then." Injago scowled at that, but Romada ruffled his hair and laughed. "I don't need rescuing. I'm fully capable of handling myself."

"Of course you are. But if you ever need help, you know I'll be there."

"I know," she said, her voice soft. Placing her hands on the sturdy banister, she gazed out over the ocean.

"Copper for your thoughts?" Injago asked again.

Silence, for a moment. Or, as much silence as there could be aboard a bustling ship surrounded by waves. When she did speak, her tone was wistful. "There's nothing more beautiful than the open water."

"Not even Neiara?" he teased.

She smacked his hand. "You know what I meant."

"Sure. Don't worry, I won't tell her."

"Ha! How kind of you."

A splash reached his ears, and they both turned to face starboard, looking for the source. Romada gasped.

"Merfolk!"

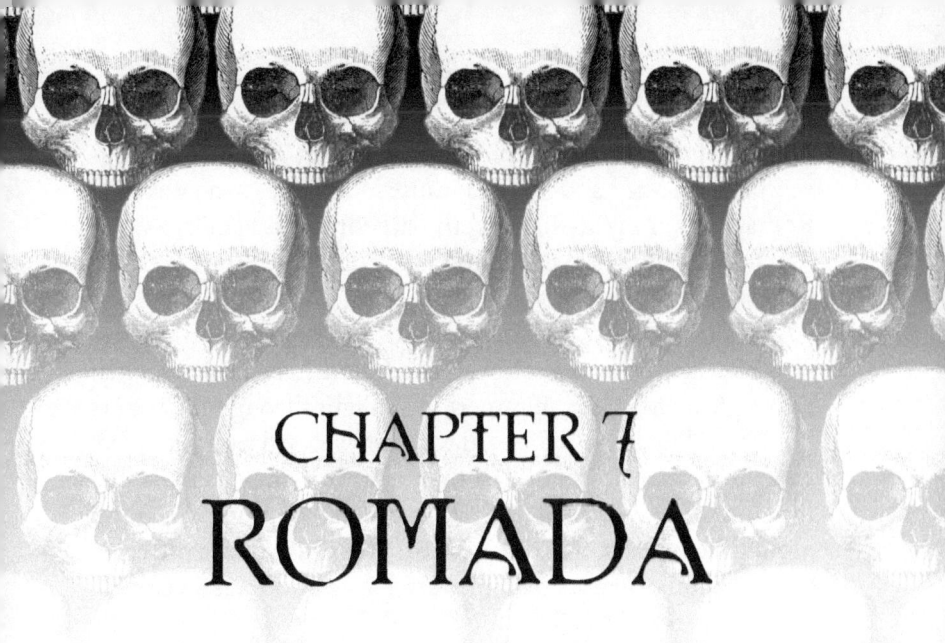

# CHAPTER 7
# ROMADA

**ROMADA LEAPT STRAIGHT DOWN FROM THE** helm to the main deck, calling out, "Someone grab Yaya!" Excitement pounded through her body as she stripped the boots, weapons belt, and clothes from her body.

"Someone said merfolk?" Yaya said, their head popping up from the hatch. A smile split their face from finned ear to finned ear.

Romada grinned back, practically tasting the salt on her lips already. She climbed atop the hand-carved mahogany banister and prepared to leap.

"Let's go!"

Shoving off, Romada soared through the air, wind whipping her fins before plummeting to the ocean below. The hard surface slapped her face, leaving her breathless as she sank before she flexed her gills and felt the familiar and comforting sensation of liquid flooding her lungs. A stream of bubbles fled her mouth, clouding her vision momentarily as she searched her surroundings for the merfae pod. Right on cue, a gorgeous merfae with a red and gold tail came into view. Fayne waved at Romada, their razor-sharp teeth bared in a feral smile.

"Friend," they said, shaping the words with their webbed fingers.

"Friend healthy?" Romada asked with her own fingers.

"Yes. Happy and healthy. Glad friend here in sea." Their scales gleamed in the shimmering sunlight through the waters.

Propelling herself forward with her webbed hands and feet gave Romada a glorious burst of speed. She spun, enjoying the thrill of being encased in the ocean, cradled by her goddess. All around her were stunningly beautiful merfolk, each a different combination of colors than the rest. Fayne's pod was a veritable and infinite rainbow.

Romada pointed up at the surface, gesturing for Fayne to follow her. She breached, knowing the merfae was close behind her, and purged the water from her lungs. A burning sensation filled her chest as she gasped and readjusted to breathing air.

Yaya surfaced beside her and Fayne, coughing up water as well. Only Fayne made a smooth transition, seamlessly switching to breathing air as though they were born to it.

"Fayne!" Romada cried. "I'm so glad to see you!"

Fayne clapped their hands in glee, the long red tendrils on their head undulating around them with the movement of the ocean waves.

"We could use some good luck if you wouldn't mind escorting us," Romada added. Merfolk were indeed dangerous in their own right, capable of incapacitating their prey with a single venomous bite. For pirates, however, they had always been seen as symbols of good fortune. Romada could never decide whether that said more about pirates, the merfolk themselves, or everyone else.

"You go where?" Fayne's hands twined around their words.

"Our map was stolen, so we are heading to Tilt Town to see if our underground contact knows anything about it," Romada spoke as she tread water, keeping her head and gills just above the waves.

"Treasure?" Fayne looked from Romada to Yaya, concern on their face.

"That's the one," Yaya piped in. "Someone stole it when we were anchored in Celestinia."

Fayne bared their fangs. "Who dare?"

Romada shook her head. "Doesn't matter. We'll get it back. Our dreams aren't crushed yet."

Fayne looked thoughtful and then nodded, tendrils flailing with the motion. "We follow you."

"Thank you! With your luck on our side, we'll have swift winds and be there in no time."

Fayne swam around Romada in a lazy circle, flicking water at her face and eliciting a giggle.

"Come. I show something." Diving below the surface with a flick of their powerful red and gold-mottled tail, they disappeared.

Romada glanced at Yaya, who made a noncommittal sound before they followed Fayne.

After blowing all the air from her lungs, Romada sank beneath the surface and gulped water through her gills. Fayne and Yaya were a short way below her, but with strong strokes, she caught up within seconds.

Down they went. Down, down, down. Romada swam behind Fayne, their gills leaving a trail of bubbles for her to follow. Down, down, down. The light from the sky began to flicker like a doused candle. Romada's eyes struggled to adjust to the limited visibility at the bottom of the sea.

What little sunlight managed to filter to their depth illuminated the outline of a ship, a wreck cradled by the ocean floor. Romada admired the three masts—though the mizzenmast sported a crack midway down—and the beautifully sculpted merfae on the bow. Fish swam in and out of the portholes and hatches, bright flashes of color against the backdrop of the murky behemoth. The back end of the ship hovered over the opening to a trench.

Romada started to swim toward the hatch in the deck, eager to search the trove for treasure, when a thought hit her.

"Sharks in ship?" Romada asked, her fingers twitching around the last word.

Fayne shrugged.

Of course, Fayne had no fear of sharks or anything under the sea. Their tail was more powerful than a shark, able to be used as a weapon, and their teeth were just as sharp and lethal to boot. The razor-sharp claws made any fight even more unfair.

"I protect you," Fayne said.

Yaya and Romada exchanged a glance before Romada said, "We follow you."

The trio swam for the hatch and made their way belowdecks. Rotten wood hung from the ceiling, allowing weak rays of sun to pierce through like spotlights to aid their sight. Romada found a hatch to the cargo hold and reached for the handle to pull it open.

A behemoth of white and grey sprang from the opening, smashing the hatch to pieces, and lunged for Romada. She twisted like an eel, narrowly avoiding the shark's rows of jagged teeth. With a watery squeal, she lurched back and slammed into Yaya, who grabbed her and wrapped her in an embrace.

Quick as a flash, Fayne latched onto the great white and pumped their venom through the tough skin. The shark spasmed, its tail wreaking havoc on the waterlogged interior of the ship before it succumbed to Fayne's deadly bite.

Romada worked to calm herself. Her heartbeat galloped through her chest; the sound blocked out everything else. She shut her eyes, placing a hand over her chest, and steadied her breathing.

Yaya tapped her on the shoulder, and she spun to look at them.

"Fayne look in ship first," they signed.

Romada nodded and then realized Fayne was nowhere to be found. Opening her mouth to shout, she remembered she couldn't speak underwater without air. Biting her tongue, she swam forward toward the damaged hatch.

Fayne popped up beneath her, waving her forward. "Safe ship," they said.

Together, they made their way down into the cargo hold. The ship had settled on the ocean bed at an angle, so everything had shifted to one end. A pile of trunks lay beside a warped painting of a palace. Popping one of the trunks open, Romada ran a hand through ruined silk dresses. They were slippery to the touch, like kelp. Shutting the trunk, she moved on to another and found a pair of silver goblets. She waved Yaya over and handed one to them. Yaya grinned and clinked their goblet to hers, and they both let out a stream of bubble laughter.

Finding nothing else of value, Romada decided to leave. Swimming back the way they had come, she passed the floating corpse of the shark and gave it a vicious kick on her way out.

Once outside of the wreck, a glow began to creep into Romada's vision. She twisted around in time to see a huge deep sea merfae glide past the shipwreck. Their back had a multitude of glowing tendrils attached along their spine, and in their arms they carried an octopus like a pet, caressing it's head. The octopus was twice the size of Romada and she shivered as she watched the two giants pass by. Beside her, Yaya was in a similar state of awe.

Right as the fluke of the merfae's tail came abreast of the shipwreck, they twitched, knocking the ship into the trench it had been perched above. With a colossal explosion of bubbles, the entire thing sank again, lost to the depths.

The merfae continued past them, not even bothering to notice their existence or the fact that it had knocked over an entire ship. Not for the first time, Romada was thankful deep sea merfae never came to the surface. The glow faded swiftly as the merfae disappeared into the distance.

Turning toward the surface, Romada angled herself toward the far-off shadow of a ship. The *Guardian* had moved quite a bit during their adventure, so she adjusted her course to meet it. Bursting up from the water and flinging droplets of water from her fins, she heaved, sucking air into her lungs while simultaneously coughing up water. Her exits were anything but graceful. Yaya and Fayne popped up beside her.

"That was incredible! Did you see how big that deep sea merfae was?" Romada asked as she wiped salt water from her eyes.

"They could have crushed us in one hand," Yaya said, eyes wide.

"Deep merfolk gentle," Fayne interjected.

"You're probably right," Romada said. Her stomach chose that moment to let out a growl, and Yaya laughed. "I'm starving. You didn't happen to cook already, did you?" she asked.

"What, after we were so rudely denied a hearty breakfast? Of course I did," they scoffed, though their humor faded as they no doubt remembered the scene at the tavern.

Romada gave them a small smile before turning to Fayne. "See you later?"

Fayne nodded and dropped below the waves.

Romada always felt lighthearted after a swim with merfolk, especially with Fayne. They had been visiting her ship for over ten years, and she looked forward to spending the next few days with them and their pod.

Maneuvering over to the carved hand and footholds, Romada climbed out of the water and heaved herself over the banister. She sank to the deck, legs weak, and sat for a moment, watching Yaya struggle to get onboard.

Their face contorted as they hauled themself over the railing, causing Romada to break out in laughter. Sitting beside her, Yaya chuckled, legs shaking just as much as hers.

Romada looked up to see Ceta staring at her like she had two heads.

"What a pair we are," Romada murmured, hiding her smile behind her silver goblet.

Yaya held out their matching goblet as if making a toast. "Come on," they said before standing on newborn legs. "Let's go eat."

With food in mind, getting to her feet was easy, and she toddled behind Yaya all the way to the galley.

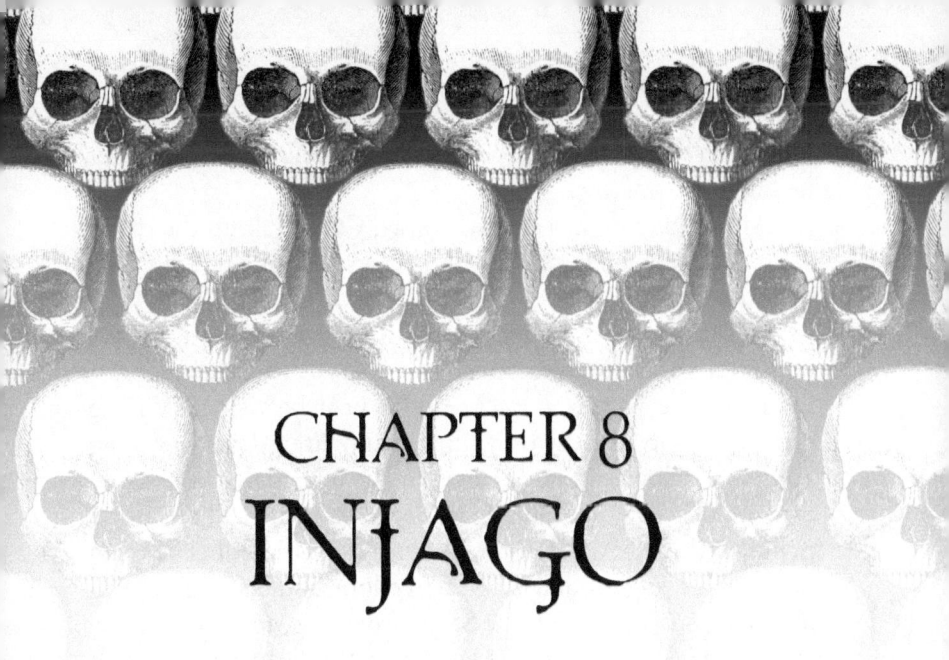

# CHAPTER 8
# INJAGO

**DUSK FELL SWIFTLY ON THE OCEAN. ONE**
moment, the sun hovered over the horizon; the next, stars
appeared overhead. After using them to find his way-
point, Injago locked the wheel in place and made his way
to the deck where the crew had gathered for the evening
performance.

Neiara was going to Sing.

Wearing several layers of silk scarves over a tiny black dress,
Neiara stood before the dim entrance to the cabin as if it were
a stage and the deck an amphitheater full of throngs of adoring
fans. Perhaps it was. She wore a dazzling smile as she looked
out over her attentive audience.

Injago wondered sometimes whether she regretted leaving
her life as a paid performer to join a ragtag group of pirates.
She had been admired, adored, never wanting for anything.
And he would see the moments her eyes met Romada's. They
would gaze at each other with a tenderness and longing that

he couldn't help being jealous of. And without ever asking her, he knew the answer.

After plugging her ears with wax, Ceta took up the drum, settling it between her knees. She began beating out a slow yet hypnotic rhythm.

Closing her eyes and tilting her head back, Neiara opened her mouth and began to Sing.

Injago's eyes glazed over, and his heartbeat slowed. Time came to a stop, and the only thing that mattered was her Song. She Sang of love and acceptance, and he felt it in his bones. She Sang of heartache, and his chest began to cave in. She Sang of riches, and his hands felt the coolness of gold coins slipping between his fingers. She Sang of freedom, and his heart soared like a dragon in the wind. She Sang of dancing, and suddenly, he was clapping, feet a blur. He laughed so hard that tears flowed over aching cheeks, and his legs began to cramp, but he danced and danced until her Song ended.

And just as suddenly as he had been ensnared in her enchantment, he was freed from her control. He looked around at everyone, heading spinning; someone laughed, and then everyone joined in, merriment ringing across the ship. It was a relief to be in control of his body again. Being ensnared by a Song felt like being intoxicated. Coming to with a free and clear mind always left an uneasy aftertaste in his mouth, a cloying sweetness that coated his throat. Almost a nagging feeling that something bad had happened.

But he trusted Neiara…or rather, he trusted Ceta, and she always observed everyone free of enchantment during the Song, saved from Neiara's voice by the wax plugs in her ears. She had never given him a reason to suspect something had gone amiss.

But there was always that leftover feeling. That buzz of warning. And the only way he could get rid of it was to laugh, so he did. He wasn't sure if everyone else felt the same, or maybe they laughed because they felt joy at being enchanted and then released. He had never asked anyone. He wasn't sure he wanted to know.

The drumbeat continued, steady as always, and after a moment to allow the laughter to die away, Neiara began to sing. It was a simple and normal song, sung in Pixish and free of any enchantment, and one they all knew by heart: a pirate shanty. Most of the crew joined in, their voices merging with Neiara's as they clapped their hands and stomped their feet.

Romada made her way over to him, settling herself on a barrel beside where he stood.

"My favorite part of it is watching her, you know?" Her eyes couldn't have been stuck faster to Neiara's dancing form than if she had plucked them out and handed them over for safekeeping. As if she would die if she looked away.

He nodded, though he didn't agree. He watched Neiara to make sure she didn't try anything, though he knew he wouldn't be able to stop her even if he tried. He watched because…he worried, just like he worried about everything. He watched because he had to, so maybe his watching wasn't all that different from Romada's at all. "That Song chilled me to the bone, and yet I'm burning up from all the dancing."

"I know what you mean," she said, fanning herself. Sweat coated her forehead, the drops shining in the lantern light.

"Are you excited to go to Tilt Town?" he asked, knowing the answer.

Romada grimaced and groaned. "Not. At. All."

"What, upset you can't go to your favorite bar anymore?"

"Hey, it is *not* my fault that Erdanto's mirror broke! That pixie threw me into it. If anything, I was just as much of a victim as he was."

"Except Erdanto didn't provoke a pixie into throwing a water nymph at his brand-new mirror," Injago pointed out.

"You—! My poor fins! You saw how bad my back was! I did not deserve to be thrown out of that bar, and you know it."

Injago snorted as he recalled the look on her face as she had flown into the mirror. Her fins and back had indeed been a bloody mess, but it was her indignant face as she argued with Erdanto about her own honor that stuck fast in his mind.

"I can't believe we got banned for that," she huffed.

"No, no. *You* got banned. Not the rest of us. I, for one, will be enjoying a beer and ice cream float at Erdanto's when we get to Tilt Town."

Romada's mouth dropped open in astonishment. "What— How— You—"

Injago struggled to keep a straight face at her sputtering.

"I can't believe you!"

Giving in to the laughter, he grabbed her in a headlock and gently ruffled her head fin. She grappled with him, spitting curses before biting his arm.

"Yow! What was that?"

Romada bared her fangs at him. "I win."

"Fine, you win. I won't go to Erdanto's."

She beamed at him, blue eyes sparkling. "We'll find a new bar."

"A better bar!"

"Exactly!" She gave a happy sigh, rubbing her gills. "I'd be lonely without you, Inja."

"You act as if you could ever be rid of me."

"Overbearing much?" She punched him in the arm.

"That's what big brothers are for, if I recall!" Words from a tiny water nymph, smaller than him at the time, a century past. Words thrown at him with tears as he was sent out into the world. Without her.

"I know," she said.

Neiara's voice rose over the crowd in a love song, her eyes locked on Romada. As if entranced, Romada hung on her every word, eyes smoldering. The tension between the two of them was palpable, cutting through the crowd and making Injago feel itchy.

"Get a room!" someone yelled as the song ended.

"Have a good night," Injago said as Romada got to her feet and began moving toward Neiara like a pin to a magnet.

"Uh-huh," she said, her eyes and ears for Neiara only.

Neiara's face glowed in the lantern light, a beacon for Romada. Reaching out, she grasped Romada's hand and led her into the darkness.

Injago tore his eyes away and focused on the rich black of the ocean's surface. When would he find that? When was it his turn to be loved?

"Injago, you want first or second shift?" Ceta's soft voice came from his side, and he turned to her. Her large brown eyes looked up at him, and he fell into their depths for a moment. What would it be like to be attracted to her, to someone who was also attracted to him? Could mutual attraction ever be his? What would that feel like? What would it feel like to…kiss her?

She must have sensed his need—his desperation—because she reached a hand out to caress his face—*oh gods, it burns*—and leaned in. For a second, he almost gave in, almost allowed himself to taste her. For a second that lasted a lifetime, he watched as her lips moved to his, saw her breath mingle with his, saw his face reflected back at him from her shimmering, dilated eyes.

Disgust twisted his face as he realized what he was doing, and he shoved her away. "What the fuck, Ceta?"

She held up her hands to placate him, tears in her eyes. "I'm so, I'm so sorry! Oh gods, I just… I thought—"

"You thought that I could want you?" His words came out like poison.

Her jaw dropped as she stared at him. "I…"

"Go to bed. I'll take first watch." He stomped past her and up the steps to the helm, checking the lock on the wheel and adjusting his heading. When he looked down at the deck, Ceta still stood in the same spot, arms hugging herself. He thought he heard a small sob, and then she ran for the hatch and disappeared belowdecks.

He shook his head and looked back out over the ocean, wondering why he had almost kissed her. Was he that far gone? He was no doe-eyed virgin; he had had countless nights of passionate sex with many handsome masc-fae. And yet, when he woke in the morning, it was always to an empty bed. He was attractive enough for a romp but not enough for love, it seemed. At least insofar as the faeries he found attractive were concerned. After all, he wasn't like them. His body had swells and curves where theirs had none, though he did his best to bind his chest into the "right" shape, and his legs hid a cunt rather than the cock everyone expected. In the dark, in an alcoholic frenzy, a hole was a hole. No one bothered turning him down once his clothes were already off. As for staying after… No one bothered saying why they left. He knew why.

And yet Romada… She hadn't been looking for love when she met Neiara. She had been drunk and saw a pretty dancer, and that dancer saw her, and it was love at first sight. Happily ever fucking after. His chest crumpled as he contemplated how unfair that was. He glanced down at the entrance to the cabin and wondered what it was like to make love to someone who loved you, someone who wanted to stay with you even after the alcohol wore off and the sun came back up

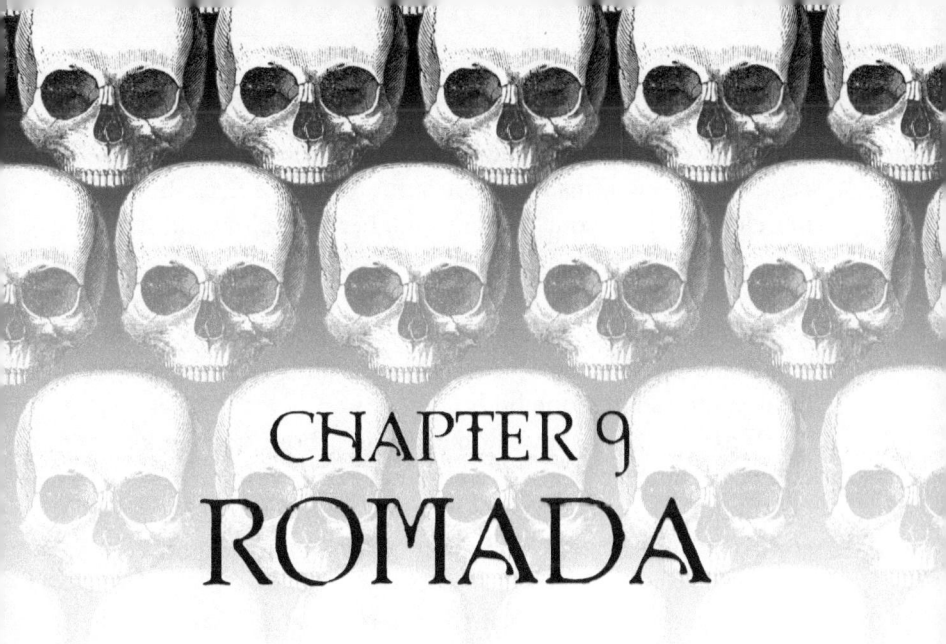

# CHAPTER 9
# ROMADA

**NEIARA HELD ROMADA'S HAND, GUIDING HER** into the depths of the cabin. The moonlight filtering through the curtains yielded a modicum of visibility, rendering Neiara as a shadowscape of curves. Romada held her breath as Neiara first drew off her scarves and then slipped out of her tight sheath dress; beneath was a dainty brassier cupping perfect breasts and a tiny strip of lace playing at being proper underwear.

Blood rushed through Romada, an urgent fire, as she stepped into Neiara's embrace and breathed in nutty coffee, the spice of cinnamon, and the sharp citrus of her curl lotion.

Though the darkness hid them, Romada still pictured the countless freckles covering every inch of skin, and she yearned to kiss each one, to taste them on her tongue. Instead, she tilted Neiara's head up and locked her mouth onto hers, nipping Neiara's full lower lip before whispering her name.

Neiara smiled, her fangs winking in the dying light. Deceptively strong arms looped around Romada's neck, holding her close. "I love you," Neiara said, her voice low and husky. "I don't want to fight."

"We aren't fighting, *deshani*," Romada murmured against her temple, pulling Neiara even closer. She wanted to feel her heartbeat, feel the breaths rising and falling in her chest as though they shared one body.

Neiara smiled against Romada's collarbone, trailing kisses up her neck. Each one stoked the fire between them.

"I remember the night we met," Romada gasped, trying to control her breathing. "You reminded me of it tonight."

"Oh?"

"Your eyes... It was as if they were glowing."

"Ah, my famous green eyes," Neiara said, fluttering thick lashes.

"Mama always said the one with green eyes would capture my heart."

Neiara laughed, a sad, hollow sound. "You didn't have a mama."

"Okay, fine. Delaini said that. Once, I think." *Delaini said a lot of things.* "Or maybe those were words floating through my dreams."

"Mm, I like the idea of me haunting your dreams before you ever actually saw me." Neiara gave Romada a tight squeeze and then pulled back to look up at her, her eyes glittering emeralds. "What was I wearing? When you saw me?"

"Mm. That green scarf of yours. It's why I noticed your eyes; it matched them so well. I was smitten at first glance."

"I still have that scarf," Neiara said in a conspiratorial tone.

Romada tweaked her nose. "I know, love. You should wear it."

"Right now?"

"Mm. And nothing else."

Neiara paused, and Romada wondered if she was blushing. Even in the dark, Neiara got embarrassed about being seen as desirable.

"It's not like I'm wearing much now."

Romada tugged at the edge of the brassier. "There's still too much left to the imagination."

Neiara laughed again, throwing her head back and exposing the hollow of her throat. Quick as lightning, Romada placed a kiss there, enjoying the velvet feeling of her skin and the slight quickening of Neiara's pulse beneath it.

"Alright. Just for you," Neiara purred.

Romada released her, and Neiara walked to her chest of clothes, digging through it. A moment later, she straightened and pulled the aforementioned scarf around her shoulders, draping it over her chest and back. Turning to Romada, she unfastened the brassier and dropped it to the floor. The lacy underwear followed.

Romada's mouth watered. Dark nipples were just barely visible beneath the scarf, and Neiara's triangle of hair was a dense coppice beckoning her to bury her face between her lover's thighs. Romada longed for—no, she *needed*—Neiara's musk to envelop her. With a finger, she motioned for Naira to come to her as she stepped backward to the bed. Eyes never wavering from Romada's, Neiara stepped forward, hips swishing from side to side, her thighs rubbing out a soft song in the silence. It might as well have been a siren Song, the way it grabbed hold of Romada and wouldn't let go.

The back of Romada's knees hit the edge of the bed, and she fell onto it, landing in a cloud of silks and furs. Neiara reached her within moments—the wait was an indomitable eternity.

Neiara straddled her then, the parting of her legs releasing a heady scent. Romada breathed it in, closing her eyes as Neiara rubbed a hand down the back of her head, her fingers stroking the delicate webbing of Romada's fin as Romada gripped the edge of the bed for dear life. She couldn't stop the hungry shudder when Neiara's mouth closed over hers.

Pushing Romada onto her back, Neiara began to undress her, pulling her pants off with slow, wandering fingers. Romada reveled in the sudden feel of skin on skin. She fondled a breast through the scarf, its silkiness heightening the experience. She ached to place her mouth over the nipple, to tease and suckle, but Neiara gently removed her hand and pinned Romada's arms to the bed. Acknowledging the unspoken command, Romada kept her arms in place even after Neiara released her.

Neiara slid saliva-soaked fingers into Romada, coaxing her open. Her palm rubbed against Romada's clit, sending up a convulsion of pleasure. It was clear from the gleam in Neiara's eye that she expected Romada to remain still—*an impossible task. You ask too much*—so she tried desperately not to move, though she couldn't help the moan that escaped her mouth.

Romada tensed as Neiara's hot breath tickled her neck, foreplay for the fangs that sank into her, a tongue drawing, branding patterns onto her skin to elicit groans of pleasure. Neiara's lips brushed the edge of her gills, and Romada forced herself to relax under her lover's control.

Always, Neiara's fingers moved within her, massaging that most tender part deep inside her cunt. Romada let out a guttural sound—half moan, half Neiara's name—and panted through the torture. Her touch was fire, scorching her, consuming her, and Romada couldn't fight the addiction even if she wanted, gluttonous for the burn.

"Come for me," Neiara commanded, kissing her neck.

Unable to disobey, Romada spasmed around Neiara's fingers, euphoria gripping her to pieces; a hoarse cry rang in the air as she came apart. Neiara shifted down to kiss Romada's swollen clit and smell her victory. A groan rang out from Romada again as Neiara's tongue flicked out; instinctively, Romada broke her invisible bonds to hold Neiara's head close as she lapped at the cum, tongue pushing throbbing lips apart to drink from deep inside. Desperate to taste herself, Romada pulled Neiara up to kiss her, to lick her own cum from Neiara's lips, to revel in their shared desire.

A moment, an hour, a lifetime later, Romada fell asleep in Neiara's arms, the smell of sex a weighted blanket, the rocking of the ship cradling the couple in their slumber.

\*\*\*

The beams from the rising sun sneaking past the edges of the curtains fell on Romada's closed eyes, turning the darkness into a vermillion blanket. She shifted, still pressed up against Neiara, and breathed in the comforting and arousing smell of sex and citrus before rolling over and sitting on the edge of the bed.

Neiara stirred, shifting into the patch of warmth Romada had left behind, and blinked in quick succession. "Morning already?"

"Mm. You hungry?" Romada asked, standing and stretching her limbs. A yawn exploded from her, the sound pulling one from Neiara as well.

"Ah… My stomach is still queasy. Maybe just a coffee?"

"Seasick as ever," Romada teased, bending down to nibble Neiara's nose. "I swear, you're only a pirate, so you can be with me."

"Well, of course. It's not the glamor that pulled me in." Neiara winked and then looked Romada up and down, eyes settling on her ass. "Well, maybe it was…"

"Oh, shush," Romada said, pulling a loose-fitting shirt over her fins. Underwear came next; she didn't usually bother with it, but it was Worship Day, after all. Pants belted at the waist, and then she laced up her boots.

"Always dressing in a hurry," Neiara sighed. "Let me admire you for once."

Romada planted a kiss on her temple. "I'll be back."

Yaya stood over the oven range cooking up a storm when Romada got down to the galley kitchen. She snagged a plate of fried fish and eggs, as well as a mug of cinnamon coffee, before heading back to the cabin. Neiara sipped her coffee and watched Romada tuck in breakfast, a dreamy look on her face.

"What's on your mind?" Romada asked between bites.

"Thinking about my worship goals for today."

"And?"

"I want to work on my contemplation and gratitude. I have a lot to be thankful for, and I don't think about it enough. You?"

Romada mulled over that as she munched on a bite of flaky fish. "Mm, I want to lose myself in the experience of the sea and purge myself of stress."

"Sounds relaxing," Neiara said.

"Well, it is Rest Day." Romada finished off her last bite of egg and wiped her mouth. A crisp beer would have been the perfect drink to wash it all down. Too bad they hadn't had time to restock before leaving Celestinia.

"Are you going now?" Neiara asked as Romada stood up with her plate.

"It was a large breakfast, *deshani*," Romada said, patting her belly. "I'll give it a bit to settle. I'll be on deck soon to watch you and Inja worship."

"Is he out there already?" she asked, incredulous. "He's always so early!"

"Well, he didn't have anyone keeping him up late last night," Romada pointed out.

Neiara gave her a wicked grin. "Oh yeah. Poor Inja."

"Love you," Romada said, heading to the galley, but not before catching the kiss Neiara blew at her.

Yaya had migrated to the sinks and was washing a large pan when Romada entered the galley kitchen. "You're back," they said, huffing as they scrubbed. "I thought I would have to track down those dishes."

"I decided to be nice today and help out. Look, I'll even help you with the rest of the dishes."

"How kind," they said with a smile, still intent on the pan.

They washed the dishes together in silence, finishing the task within minutes. After the last dish was placed on the drying rack, Yaya turned to her with a question.

"Shall we?"

"I'd like to watch Neiara and Injago for a bit and rest up my stomach for a little while longer."

"Then I'll meet you up there," they said, heading toward the stern of the ship.

Up on deck, she breathed in the briny sea air and settled on a barrel to watch. Neiara, Injago, and a couple other pixies sat before the large, burnished altar. A statue of The Harvester stood in the center, and a handful of black candles in glass jars burned before them. A statue of Ajakin, king of the pixie gods, stood to one side. A single blue candle burned before him.

As one, the group had bowed their heads and closed their eyes. Breathing evenly, nearly in a meditative state, they sat to worship their gods.

Most pixie pirates naturally gravitated to worshiping The Harvester, seeing as they were the pixie god of death, journeys, and the unknown. Neiara, being a siren and having no gods of her own, had adopted The Harvester as her god when she joined the crew. Siren religion had been purged from all records several millennia ago, back when they had lost their homeland due to The Great War. Neiara had never hinted that she mourned the loss—Romada wasn't even sure she would consider it a loss since she never had it to begin with—but that didn't keep Romada from wondering if Neiara wished for a god fashioned of herself.

Romada watched them for a time, enjoying the gentle crash of waves against the hull, the wind sweeping over the deck, and the salty taste of the air. When Yaya popped up on deck and waggled their head fin at her, she nodded, ready. Together, they walked to the side of the ship and stripped to their underwear. Careful so as not to make any noises to disturb the worshippers, they climbed onto the banister and dove into the sea.

Peace flooded through Romada as water rushed through her gills, flooding her lungs. She closed her eyes and floated beneath the waves, listening to the sounds of the ocean. The merfae pod splashed somewhere nearby, and farther out, a whale called, low and powerful.

Romada opened her eyes and saw the ship had drifted a little ways away. She swam for it, Yaya beside her, and hummed to herself, feeling bubbles escape her gills. When she glanced back, she saw a trail of them in her wake. A grin split her face as she reveled in the ecstasy of worship.

This was happiness in its purest form: skin free in the water, being cradled by the loving embrace of the sea. The sea was her goddess, and Romada was Her child, vulnerable to Her whims. Despite Her destructive tendencies, She could not drown Romada; they were an intrinsic part of one another, no more able to be parted than the sea from the sky. The sea could wreck her ship, could destroy all she held dear as easily as a faerie could blink, but this wasn't a reason to spurn Her. So long as Romada cherished and worshiped Her properly, she knew her safety was ensured.

Romada came up for air beside the ship, coughing up water before floating on her back, looking up at the azure sky. Water tickled the edges of her gills, but she sealed them shut and closed her eyes, feeling the warmth of the sun on her upturned face. Her head fin moved with the current as the waves pushed against her body.

"Beautiful day for worship," Yaya called out from behind her.

She rolled over to face them, treading water. "It's always a beautiful day for worship! It's too bad we can't spend every day doing nothing but swimming."

"Well, thank the goddess for Rest Day. It has to be my favorite day of the week."

"Is it really a Rest Day if you still have to cook?"

They looked aghast. "What, and should I let all you lovelies starve because it's a Rest Day?"

Romada snorted. "I'm sure we would survive, Yaya."

They didn't look convinced. "I did manage to cook the entire day's meals this morning, though, so the remainder of the day is mine."

"That explains the mountain of dishes."

They nodded, humming to themself before launching their body backward and flipping below the water. Peering in the depths for them, Romada nearly missed seeing Fayne appear around the end of the ship. Romada waved and swam over to them.

"Worship?" Fayne signed.

"Yep. Every week."

They waved their hand at the word 'week' as if to dismiss it.

"Days like waves, eternal, not single. Cannot count waves. Why count days?"

Romada laughed. "I'm not sure! But I do know this: worship once a week keeps my sea goddess happy, which means she doesn't sink my ship."

Fayne tapped their head. "Smart."

Yaya breached the surface behind them, and they both turned to watch. Fayne leapt to them, their tail throwing a crescendo of water at Yaya's unsuspecting face. Yaya sputtered in indignation before splashing back. Romada giggled at the sight of them chasing each other in a mock war before she noticed what looked like storm clouds far out in the distance. Though the day was all sunshine and calm now, who knew when the storm would hit? She sent a quick prayer to her goddess to harbor them before she joined Fayne and Yaya.

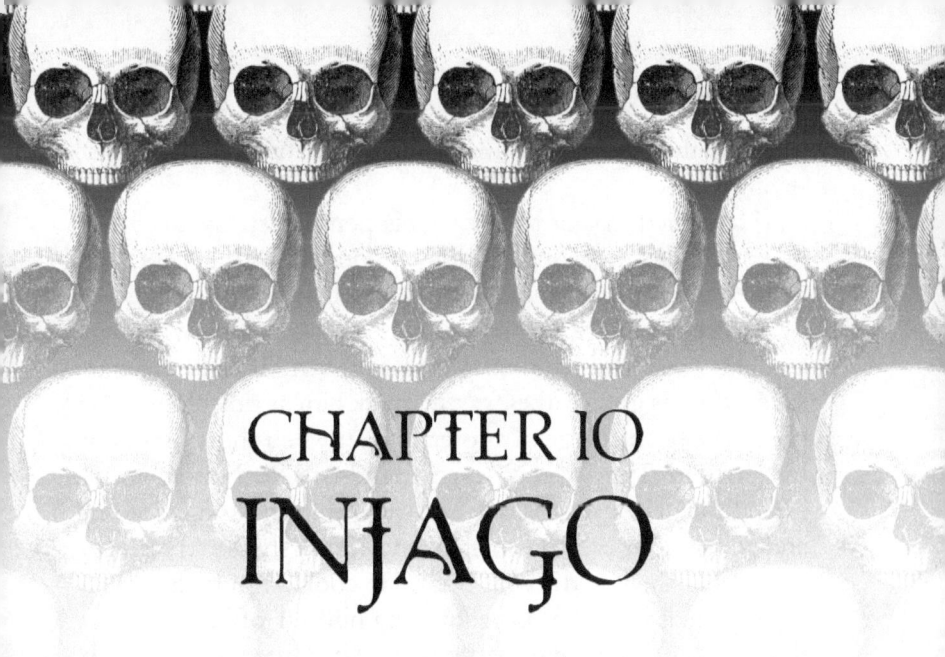

# CHAPTER 10
# INJAGO

**EYES CLOSED AND BREATHING EVENLY, INJAGO** meditated on The Harvester.

Or rather, he tried to. His thoughts kept getting pulled from the god and toward his faceless lover. Toward the masc-fae who would one day hold him and know him. The tall, dark, and handsome faerie who would sweep him off his feet. He was out there…right? Frustrated with himself, Injago attempted to push his thoughts back to his god but found he didn't even know what to think about. When was the last time his god had helped him with anything?

The Harvester was the god of journeys, of the unknown. They were the perfect god for a pirate. So when and why did worshiping become so difficult?

Injago thought of their journey toward Tilt Town, how the outcome was largely unknown. Would they find the map? Even if they located it, would they be able to get it back? And if they got the map, would they find riches in the abandoned mine? If they found treasure, would it be enough to build their dream house?

He sighed, trying to release his pent-up stress. Maybe if he could relax, he would be able to connect with his god. He worked to empty his mind, to let himself become a vessel.

**Protect Neiara.**

The words startled him. Was that his own thought or a message from his god? Either way, it struck him as ridiculous. Why should he be in charge of protecting her when she wasn't even his partner? They weren't even friends, really. Not anymore. Even though he used to go to her, wallowing and asking for pity and advice after each one night stand…as if she could fix it for him. As if she could fix his body. He couldn't pinpoint when it happened, when he started closing himself off from her. It didn't matter. What did matter is that, if anyone should be in charge of protecting Neiara, it should be Romada. Wrinkling his brow, he fought to figure out why this message upset him so much. All he could come up with was the fact that Neiara wasn't his responsibility in the first place, so why was his god tasking him with this? If it even *was* a message from his god.

But just in case it was, he should take it seriously, right? What was the best way to protect Neiara? She probably shouldn't go ashore in Tilt Town, even if it was a lawless town, a safe haven for vagrants. She would just be a liability. Again. They would be begging for trouble by letting her leave the ship.

Now, how to convince stubborn-headed Romada of that? What could he possibly say to override Romada's own desires and keep Neiara safe? He couldn't just say he thought it would be best because she would say he was worrying too much again.

Maybe he could bring up that it was a direct message from The Harvester. Would she respect his god enough to go along with it? Sighing, he decided there really wasn't a better course of action.

When he opened his eyes, Neiara was staring at her candle, the reflection of the flame in her eyes making them glow. He watched her, wondering if she had an easy time worshiping their god. Did she connect with Them? They weren't even a siren god in the first place. Did that make it harder to worship? What did she meditate on anyway? Was she selfish like Injago, ruminating on things she wanted and hoping her god granted her wishes?

Neiara glanced over at him and smiled. "Did you have a good worship?"

He pondered how to answer that. Should he tell her about the message? If he told her, maybe she could help him convince Romada.

"My god told me to keep you safe."

She beamed, eyes crinkling. "My god cares for me. I know They are always watching out for my safety. I trust you to obey Them and keep me safe, Inja."

That didn't go how he meant it to. Working to keep his frustration hidden, he forced a smile and asked, "What did you meditate on?"

"I thought of how thankful I am for the wonderful things in my life. I'm surrounded by loved ones. I have a home. I have food in abundance. I have Romada." Her voice grew soft toward the end.

Resentment blazed in his chest. While he dreamt of a lover, she was thanking his god for giving her everything she had, everything she had ever wanted, everything she had ever dreamt of. How was she so good? Always smiling. Always joyous. Always making everyone fall head-over-heels for her. And, most importantly, why was he so bitter about it?

Neiara leaned forward and blew out her candle. Realizing that everyone else had also ended their worship, Injago hurriedly followed suit. With his candle jar in hand, he went to the Worship Day chest and placed his candle in a hollow carved into the bottom of the chest. Neiara placed her candle beside his and nestled the statue of The Harvester in its bed of velvet.

Opening the Rest Day chest, Injago pulled out a hammock and started stringing it up. Neiara grabbed the double hammock and did the same, tying it from the railing to the mizzenmast. Injago settled into his hammock, a handkerchief over his eyes to block out the sun, and went back to daydreaming.

He heard a splash and a thud as someone came up onto the deck, and then Romada's voice reached his ears as she spoke to Neiara. The two spoke in hushed tones as they got into their hammock, voices fading as they presumably went to sleep in each other's arms. Injago wanted that. He wanted a strong pair of arms to hold him. He pictured him in his mind: strong and steady, with eyes like fire and hair that begged to be tousled. Lips that looked perpetually kiss-swollen. A smile that made Injago burn for him.

Where was he?

A squeal woke him, and he jumped, nearly upending himself from the hammock. At some point, his daydreaming had shifted to full dreaming, and waking from sleep to the sound of Neiara's excitement wasn't exactly ideal. The face in his mind faded fast, nothing more than vapor now. Scowling, he slung his legs over the side to see what the commotion was.

Neiara stood at the banister clapping, along with some of the other crew members, signaling the arrival of the sunset show. Every Worship Day, the merfolk—if they were with the ship—performed a dance at sunset for the crew's viewing pleasure. Neiara continued squealing and clapping as the merfolk got into formation, but when Fayne turned to the ship and took a bow, everyone fell silent.

As one, the merfolk slapped the water with their hands—*slap, slap, slap*—drumming up a beat. With each beat, a body part moved. Arms undulated in a uniquely disjointed fashion. Heads cocked, throwing their tendrils to and fro. Tails swished through the water and spun in the air, flinging drops of water in tall arcs.

*Slap, slap, slap.* The pounding of the rhythm was intoxicating. The crew joined in, stomping and clapping in otherwise reverent silence.

*Slap, slap, slap.* Twist, splash, flip.

Injago's attention diverted as he realized someone wasn't watching the show. Romada, rather than gazing at the enticing merfolk, was watching Neiara, watching *her* watch the show. A slight smile graced her lips.

As beautiful as the merfolk were, Injago begrudgingly understood Romada's intense fascination with Neiara. She was the most gorgeous fem-fae he had ever seen, with her dusky skin, chaotic curls, and bright green eyes. Those eyes could ensnare someone without her ever using her voice…which is exactly what happened with Romada. Again, Injago wondered if anyone would ever look at him the way Romada looked at Neiara. Envious, he tore his eyes away from the loving couple to watch the rest of the performance.

The show ended with a jettison of water from the flourishing of their tails, a cascading fountain in the middle of the ocean. The falling droplets held the colors of the sunset.

Neiara clapped the loudest, cheering as the merfolk bowed before they disappeared beneath the waves. "They never fail to amaze me!" she gushed, turning to Romada.

The crowd dispersed, allowing Injago to step closer to them.

Despite not watching a second of the dance, Romada nodded in agreement. "They always put on such a wonderful show. Fayne really likes us."

Neiara snorted. "Fayne likes *you*, silly."

"It's true. Everyone knows Fayne has a crush on you," Injago said.

"You're both being ridiculous. Stop it."

Injago held his hands up in surrender. "Whatever you say, Rome."

Neiara giggled but wouldn't meet Romada's eye. "Yeah. What he said."

The moon crept over the horizon, swapping places with the sun, its glow lighting up the ship. He watched both Romada and Neiara turn to watch its slow ascent. Like moonflowers, their faces followed its path.

"Time for worship," Injago said, his voice low. With a sigh, he left them to it and headed down to his bunk for another lonely night.

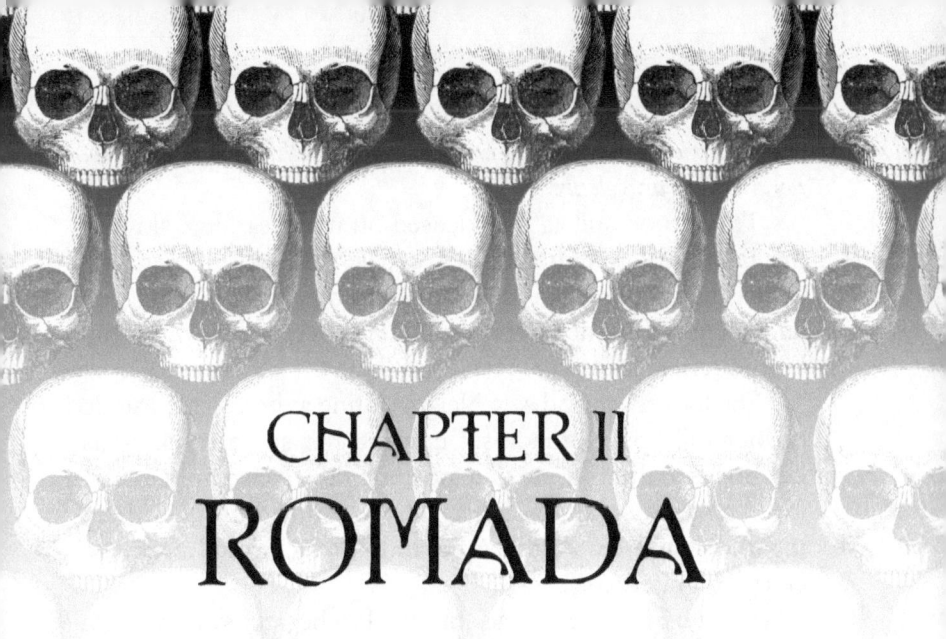

# CHAPTER II
# ROMADA

**THE WANING MOON AT HER ZENITH CAST HER** light upon the deck, illuminating everything as if it were daylight but with a haunting glow. Neiara's upturned face was awash in the pale lambency, her freckles standing out in stark relief.

Reaching out, Romada took her hand, caressing her with her thumb. "It's time," she whispered.

Together, they went to the altar, stripping off their clothes. Naked in the moonlight, they each lit a white candle before prostrating themselves.

Romada's skin prickled in the night chill, and she cast aside all thoughts of her physical being to focus on the love in her life. She breathed deeply. In…and out. In…and out. The only sounds were the lap of water against the hull and Neiara's hushed breathing beside her. She felt the blood rush to her head as she bowed further, deepening her stretch.

*Oh goddess, on this dark night, you have found me. You have embraced me as your own. You surround me with love and point me toward my heart's desire.*

Time stood still as she focused on her breathing, slowing her inhale and lengthening her exhale. The world started to spin as her body began to acclimate to the increase in oxygen, and when she opened her eyes, blackness crept into her vision before retreating.

She looked up and saw Neiara staring at her, a small smile on her full lips. Romada sat upright, her spine cracking as her bones shifted to the new position. She gazed at her siren lover, amazed at her existence. The moon had brought them together in more ways than one, and Romada would always be eternally grateful.

She closed her eyes and hummed to herself, swaying with the ship, basking in the effulgence of the moon, and reminiscing on how they had first met.

*The full moon shone bright overhead, and Romada itched for an adventure.*

*"Let's explore the town! Find someplace new!" she said to Injago and Yaya as they walked down the pier. "I want to see something I've never seen before."*

*"I heard there are dancers at this new bar over on the north side of town," Yaya suggested.*

*A long walk, for sure. The water horse trolleys had all retired for the night. But for the chance to see some beautiful dancers? "Let's do it."*

*They made the trek in good time and went to sit outside by the fire pit, the flames flickering at Romada's back, the warmth soaking into her bones. The stage was before her, waiting for its dancer. The music started right as the barmaid brought over her drink, and her eyes lingered on her lithe form before noticing the fem-fae who stepped onto the stage.*

*She wore an emerald-hued scarf over a black brassier and a short black handkerchief skirt: green eyes, perfectly matching her scarf, glowed from beneath high arching brows. Her dusky brown skin gleamed in the light of the fire, and Romada could see freckles covering every visible inch of her. Curly black hair was cut in a short halo, which bounced slightly as she danced.*

*And how she danced… Scintillating movements of the arms drew Romada in. Her hips shimmied to the beat of a drum that Romada heard distantly as though from underwater. Her stomach undulated hypnotically, and on her fingers were tiny bells that tinkled as she passed them down her thighs and then up to grab her hair. Her eyes met Romada's and smoldered.*

*"Holy moon. I need a drink," Romada said, tearing her eyes away.*

*Injago chuckled. "Someone caught your eye?"*

*"She could catch more than that," Romada murmured, eliciting a burst of laughter from both Yaya and Injago. Romada turned back to the dance right as the dancer spun, revealing a delicately pointed spine.*

*A siren.*

*"She damn sure doesn't need to use her voice to enchant me," Romada gasped. She physically couldn't handle the amount of sexual tension strumming through her; she shifted in her seat so she could face the flames instead. Maybe they would cool her down.*

*"You might get lucky," Injago said as the drumbeat stopped.*

*"As if someone as stunning as her would go for someone like me. Filthy pirates don't get so lucky."*

*"You're a pirate?" A delightfully lilting voice, accentuated by a delicate tinkling of bells, came from beside her. Romada looked up into the greenest pair of eyes she had ever seen.*

*As if by magic, Romada's mouth had become a desert, her parched tongue as dry and rough as sand. In a desperate move, she gulped half her drink. "Yes," she croaked.*

*"She's being modest," Injago piped up, ever the wing-fae. "She's the captain of our ship."*

*"A pirate captain," the dancer purred. Sliding gracefully into the seat beside Romada, she tapped a tinny tune with her fingers. "Tell me more."*

Romada hadn't understood why she had been singled out in the crowd. Maybe Neiara could smell the wanderlust on her and knew she was a surefire ticket out of town. Maybe she had spotted an easy partner for the night. Or maybe she was curious about why a water nymph dressed like a walking trash heap was drinking at her bar. Whatever the reason, Romada liked to think it was the moon that drew her to Neiara in the first place. It was the moon who deserved her unending gratitude for gifting her with the love of her life.

If worshiping the sea was happiness, worshiping the moon was love. And every Worship Day, Romada fell more and more in love with herself, with her goddess, and with Neiara.

When she opened her eyes, Neiara's were closed, her face alight with devotion. Romada waited patiently, and a moment later, Neiara looked at her.

"I chose a wonderful goddess to worship," she whispered.

"The goddess of lovers?"

Neiara nodded.

"I think so, too."

"How was your meditation?" Neiara asked.

"I thought of the night we met. I wondered what you possibly saw in me."

Neiara cocked her head to the side. "Only the most beautiful fem-fae I had ever seen."

Heat crept up Romada's neck. "But that's impossible because you're the most beautiful fem-fae."

"I guess we'll have to agree to disagree," Neiara crooned, reaching over to caress Romada's leg.

"Anything to make you happy," Romada replied, breathless.

"Ready to worship our goddess in the best possible way?" Neiara had lust in her eyes, and Romada's heart began to beat faster, thundering in her chest.

"Always, *deshani*."

Standing, Neiara took Romada's hand and led her to the cabin, where their bodies met in quiet and passionate worship.

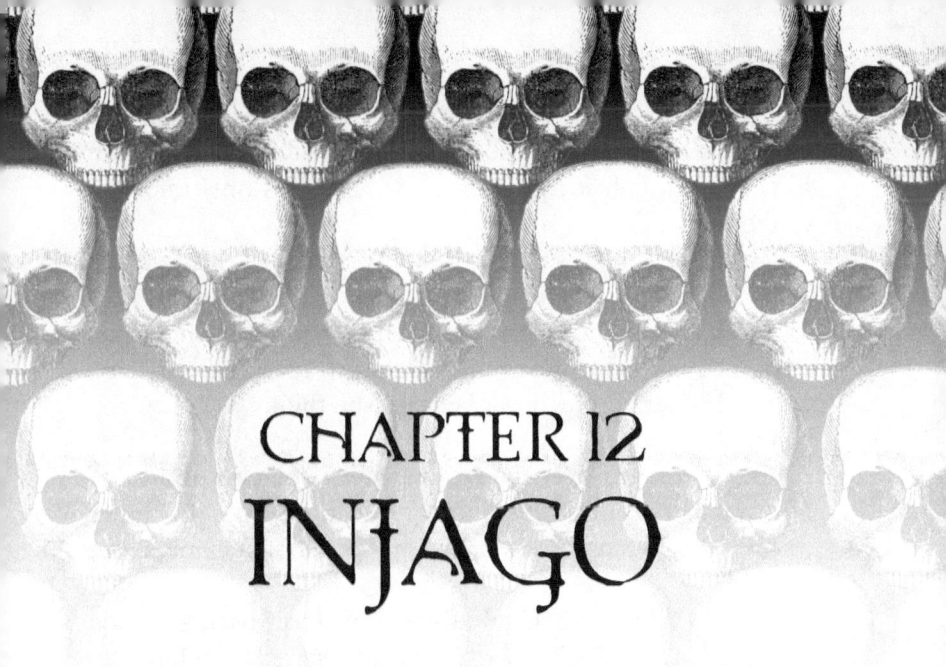

# CHAPTER 12
## INJAGO

**"I'M JUST WORRIED ABOUT HER," INJAGO SAID** in between bites of fried fish and potatoes.

Yaya nodded and swallowed before saying, "I agree. This kingdom is a dangerous place for sirens right now. I can't imagine losing Neiara and what that would mean for the crew and morale."

Injago resisted the urge to roll his eyes. Life on the ship had been fine before Neiara joined them, and it would be fine when she and Romada eventually retired as well. Besides, his concern wasn't for any effect that her potential loss might or might not have on the crew; he was worried what losing Neiara would mean for Romada.

"Romada is blatantly refusing to see how dangerous this is. I know it's because she's so damn optimistic and fearless, but still. You'd think she would see past her confidence and the so-called 'goodness' of faeries and realize that we need to do something to keep Neiara safe."

Yaya's brow ridges raised. "Have you talked to her about this? In a straightforward way? Or have you only said that you're worried?"

Injago did roll his eyes at that. "What does it matter? She won't listen."

Yaya whistled through their teeth. "You really should be talking to her instead of complaining to me. The last thing we need is her getting upset because she thinks you're talking behind her back."

Injago mulled over the rebuke while worrying at a piece of food between his teeth. Yaya was right though. Romada got very defensive when it came to people talking about her.

"Fine. I'll talk to her." He shoved his chair back and took his plate to the sinks. His sudsy reflection stared up at him, petulant. He started scrubbing at his dish, destroying his pathetic face and the remnants of his meal in one go. Yaya joined him a second later.

"I don't mind you complaining," they said, their voice gentle. "I'm here for you. But I think it's best if you talk to her instead of me. Who knows? You might get somewhere with it."

Injago clapped Yaya on the back before heading up to the helm. Ceta was at the wheel and gave him a hesitant smile when he came up the steps.

"Tilt Town is visible," she said, handing him the spyglass.

Holding it up to his eye, Injago could see the harbor entrance on the horizon. "Great. I'll go tell the captain."

"Injago?"

He stopped and turned back to face her.

"The storm is catching up."

Dark clouds were indeed creeping closer behind them. Injago wondered when it would hit and hoped they wouldn't take any damage. Nodding, he headed for the cabin. Hopefully, Romada was in a listening mood.

Giving the door a quick rap before opening it, he was greeted by a pair of blushing faces, one red and one purple, as the two lovebirds untangled from each other.

"Hi," Romada said, clearing her throat and straightening her clothes.

"I didn't mean to barge in," he said.

"And yet you did," Romada said, arms crossed. She stood a scant handbreadth away from Neiara, waiting for him to speak, but he was suddenly at a loss for words.

"Something on your mind?" Neiara asked, moving to sit on the edge of the bed.

"Yes. I'm worried."

Romada rolled her eyes. "Yes, Inja, we know. You're always worried."

This was off to a great start. "Okay, but this worry isn't unfounded." He rubbed the back of his neck before blurting out, "I think we should leave the kingdom."

Two dumbfounded faces stared at him.

"Why on Faerth would we do that?" Romada asked.

"It's not safe here! This kingdom is out for blood, and Neiara won't be safe anywhere. We shouldn't be going to Tilt Town. We should be leaving."

"If we leave now, we'll never get the map back," Neiara said quietly. "We'll be giving up on our dreams."

"Isn't your life more important than a map? Than a dream house?" He looked to Romada, hoping she was listening. She had a pained expression on her face but stayed silent.

"This map is our future! We deserve a future together, all of us. Pirating isn't a forever thing. I want to retire, and so does Romada," Neiara said, crossing her arms and looking pointedly at her girlfriend.

Romada still didn't say anything.

Injago swallowed a scream of frustration. "Well, at least tell me that you'll stay onboard while we're in Tilt Town. That way, no one knows a siren is in town. Rome and I can deal with Otandar."

"Actually," Romada finally spoke up, tapping her foot on the floor, "we were just talking about it, and we think it would be smart to find a healer who can perform a spine-flattening procedure for her."

He couldn't believe his ears. "You want to do that in Tilt Town? Of all places?"

"Why not? It's a pirate town. No one will bat an eye at me being there. They just want to get paid."

"Exactly! And guess who pays a lot? The fucking crown guards!"

"You're overthinking this, Injago," Neiara said.

Romada stepped up to Injago and put a hand on his shoulder. It was probably supposed to be comforting, but instead, it felt placating.

"We'll be fine. All of us. We will be diligent in our security, and we will keep Neiara safe. I trust everyone here to protect her."

"Tell her what our god said."

Injago grimaced, regretting telling Neiara. Through gritted teeth, he said, "My god told me to protect Neiara."

Romada raised a brow ridge. "See? Even They know. Believe in your god."

Injago shook her hand off his shoulder. "Fine."

"Anything else?"

"Tilt Town is on the horizon."

Romada's face lit up. "That's great! I'll be out there soon to come look."

Taking that as the dismissal it was, Injago left, shutting the door behind him. He stood for a moment in the eave, not wanting to see anyone, before remembering he had to relieve Ceta so she could eat. Sighing, he headed back up to the helm.

Ceta looked him up and down and asked, "Gods, what did you talk about in there? You look like shit."

"Thanks," he said dryly.

She held up her hands. "Hey, no offense. We all know you have the looks of a god—which is wasted since you won't even date anyone—so when I say you look like shit, I mean it in the kindest way."

Injago bit his tongue for a moment before answering. It wasn't *his* fault no one would date him. Why did it feel like he was the one being judged?

"We talked about personal stuff."

"Okay. Well, get well soon, I guess?"

He laughed. "Thanks Ceta."

She relaxed, then, and he wondered if she had been walking on eggshells around him since that night they had almost kissed. He felt bad for a moment before remembering it was her fault anyway.

"You want to take over? I'm starving."

"Sure," he said, stepping over and grabbing the wheel.

"Have fun," she called over her shoulder.

"Yeah," he muttered, staring toward the landmass ahead.

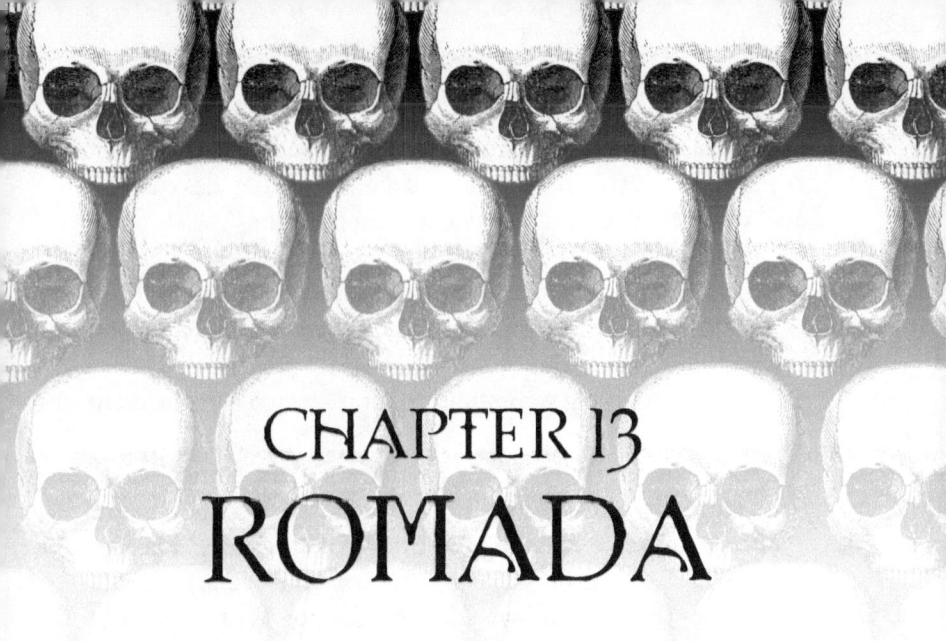

# CHAPTER 13
# ROMADA

**THE CABIN WAS SILENT FOR A MOMENT AFTER** Injago left, like they were both afraid to breathe. Romada glanced at Neiara only to find her staring down at the floor. Romada leaned against the desk and sighed.

"You know, he has a point."

Neiara didn't respond.

"What if something happens? I can't imagine losing you."

"You won't lose me," Neiara huffed. "And, who knows, maybe if you did, you would finally have some motivation to step up and do something about the situation."

Romada frowned. "What situation?"

Neiara threw her hands in the air. "Oh gods, Romada! The siren captives! We should be, I don't know, protesting! Or something."

"We can't protest. You're very clearly a siren," Romada pointed out.

"Okay, then after I get the spine flattening procedure."

"Why is this so important to you?" Romada reached down to finger the leaves of the tiny succulent on her desk as the ship shifted. "You don't even know these sirens."

"Because they're faeries just like us, Rome! They deserve freedom. Who knows what they are doing to them in those camps." She shivered, holding herself. "Besides, it's our moral obligation to care about others."

"Caring and doing something about it are two very different things."

"So you're choosing apathy? Where is your compassion?" Tears welled in Neiara's eyes as she spoke in earnest.

Romada sighed, rubbing the bridge of her nose. "Darling, I love you. I would do anything for you. But we are pirates! Not heroes. You fell in love with me, for me. Why is that not enough now?"

"I fell in love with a good faerie," she snapped. "And now I'm wondering where she went."

Tears stung Romada's eyes, and she blinked them away. "Okay."

Neiara began to cry into her hands. "I'm sorry," she said, words muffled by her sleeves. "I didn't mean that."

"I think you did," Romada said, striding for the door. "I'll be back."

Outside, she took a deep breath to calm herself, the salty sea breeze tickling her nose. It did nothing to soothe the pain in her chest at what felt like a rejection from her love. Maybe she should eat. Food always made her think clearer. It might even be able to lift her mood, though she was skeptical. She made her way to the galley, eager for some of Yaya's cooking.

Oblivious to her approach, Yaya stood at the sinks, washing dishes.

"Can I beg some bread off you?" she asked, tapping them on the shoulder.

They jumped and laughed as they turned to her. "Of course, Captain! There's leftover potatoes if you don't mind waiting for some fish."

Romada glanced at the freshly washed frying pan and shook her head. "Potatoes are more than fine."

She grabbed a plate off the rack and heaped the rest of the potatoes onto it before heading to sit at a table. Digging in, she savored the flavor of the herbs and spices that Yaya always used on their fried potatoes. The food actually was making her feel a bit better.

"Have you talked to Injago?" Yaya asked, coming over to her table.

She nodded and swallowed her bite. "Why?"

"Good. He was complaining earlier. I told him to talk to you. Better you having to listen to him than me!"

Romada's precarious mental state turned dark as her head fin bristled, and she glared at them. "What did he say about me?"

"Whoa, it wasn't like that," they said, taking a step back. "He was just worried about Neiara."

"Uh-huh," she said, finishing her food and standing.

"He didn't say anything bad. I swear," Yaya said, standing in her way and wringing their hands.

"Sure he didn't," she deadpanned, stepping around them and taking her dish to the sink.

"You know how he worries."

"I know." She stabbed at the plate with a rag. Her fingers slipped, and with a crash, the plate fell to the floor and shattered. "Fuck!"

"I'll clean that up," Yaya said in a hurry.

Romada stomped away, heading for the stairs. Injago stood alone at the helm, looking out over the water. The bastard looked peaceful. Romada climbed the steps to him, seething.

"Talking about me behind my back, Injago?" she hissed.

He jerked his head to look at her. "No."

"That's not what Yaya said."

"Yaya likes to complain about me," he said, not meeting her eye. "You know how they are."

Romada grimaced as she thought about it. Yaya did like to gossip. "So you weren't saying anything bad about me?"

"No! Gods, no."

"Because you know what happened the last time someone tried to start shit."

Injago paled. "I would never try to start a mutiny, Romada. I love you, and I respect you as my captain."

She sighed and scratched her head fin. Injago wasn't the person she was upset with in the first place, and taking her frustration out on him didn't seem fair. Plus, she could hear the sincerity in his words. "I know. I get so defensive now when I think about it… I guess I worry too, huh, Inja?"

He visibly relaxed when she used his nickname, and she felt a twinge of guilt for putting him on edge in the first place. She should have thought before reacting.

Injago turned to study her for a moment, scrunching his brow. "Are you okay? I mean, aside from the misunderstanding."

"Yeah. Fine."

He didn't look convinced.

"I'll be fine," she insisted.

"Okay… Want to see Tilt Town?" He handed her the spy-glass.

Popping it open, she looked through to see the harbor entrance. "When will we arrive?"

"Should be a little after nightfall," he said.

"Perfect. We can head out once we get there and be less suspicious."

"Newcomers at night? Totally not suspicious," he teased.

"Whatever. I'm going to go take a nap. You should, too," she said, leaning against the banister. His eyes had bags beneath them like he hadn't slept the night before.

He frowned. "I don't want to be belowdecks right now. I want to be alone."

"I understand. See you later," she said, patting him on the shoulder.

Neiara was pacing the cabin when Romada opened the door. Hearing her, Neiara turned to her with wide eyes. "Romada, I—"

"It's fine," Romada said, cutting her off with the wave of a hand. "I'm over it." The lie clogged Romada's throat, but she couldn't bear to fight with Neiara.

Neiara's eyes swam with tears as Romada sat on the edge of the bed and began pulling her boots off.

"We're going to reach Tilt Town tonight, and I want to rest so we aren't tired. Come nap with me?" Romada patted the bed.

With a small grin, Neiara rushed over and jumped onto the bed. "Can we cuddle?"

Romada smiled and snuggled under the covers, pulling Neiara close. "Of course, *deshani*," she said, placing a kiss on her temple. Maybe sleep would ease the sting of Neiara's words. The last thing she needed was bitterness toward Neiara during their shore time.

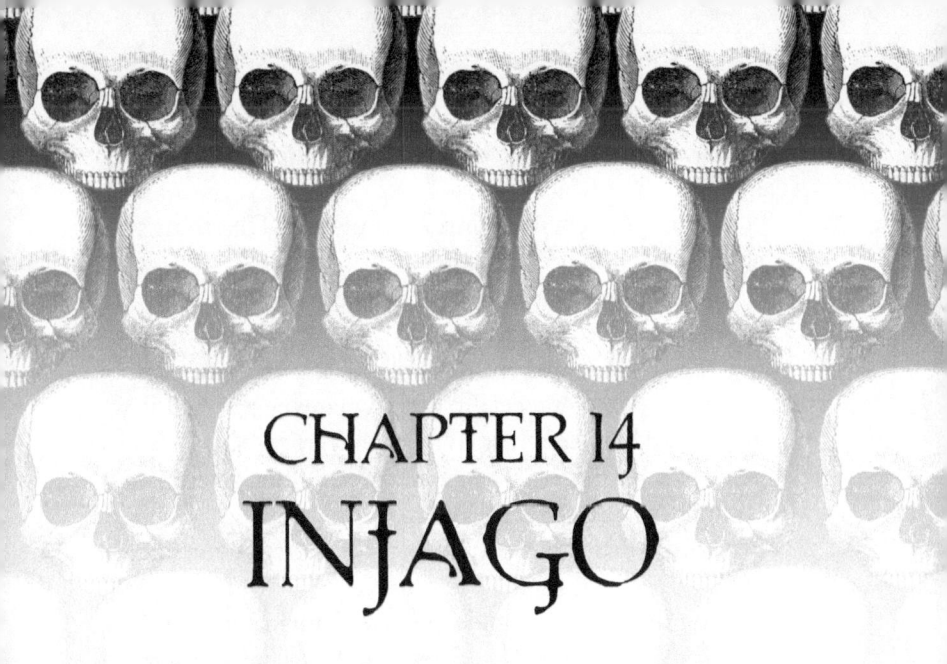

# CHAPTER 14
# INJAGO

**THE SHIP PULLED UP TO THE QUAY RIGHT AS** dusk fell. Injago and several other pixies flew down with ropes and began securing the ship to the bollards. Once the ship was tied down, he flew back up to the deck.

"Drop anchor!" he called and heard a distant splash in response. Ceta and another pixie worked to get the gangway in place, and once it was secured, he yelled, "Moored!" A small cheer went up on deck.

In small groups of twos and threes, the crew began filing off the deck and heading for Tilt Town. Injago hung back, waiting for Romada and Neiara to emerge from the cabin. When they did, he noticed a thin dagger belted over Neiara's tunic. She had wound a scarf around her head and neck, effectively hiding her head and spine. Romada had donned her full weapons belt, her sword and her curved dagger on opposite hips. Knowing her, she also had a stiletto dagger at the small of her back.

"We should take the blitz," Injago said in a hushed voice.

Romada seemed to be a second away from agreeing, but Neiara shook her head.

"A blitz in public will kill innocent people. That thing takes out ships; what will it do to a bar?"

Injago groaned. She was right, of course.

Romada nodded in agreement. "It's too dangerous."

Injago rolled his eyes. Romada might be all too comfortable yielding to Neiara—especially after whatever the hell it was that happened between the two of them earlier—but he wasn't about to just let this go. "So you would rather go into town with a siren instead. That's not dangerous at all."

Frowning, Romada said, "I don't appreciate your sarcasm, Injago."

Injago reined in his attitude. No use riling Romada up. They all needed to be in a good headspace if they were going to stay safe and alert. "Are you both ready to go?"

Neiara and Romada exchanged a look before grabbing each other's hands. If the motion was supposed to bring them comfort, it didn't show. If anything, Neiara seemed to tremble slightly. Or maybe it was a trick of the lantern light.

"Let's go!" Neiara said, tugging at her scarf.

They walked in silence toward the east side of town, where the more lively pirate bars were located. As they got closer to downtown, the streets grew more crowded. Even late at night, Tilt Town didn't sleep.

A rowdy group of elves stood outside Tapped Out—the bar where Otandar liked to frequent—blocking the entrance. After an exaggerated huff, Injago buzzed his wings to get their attention.

"Do you mind?" he asked, stepping forward.

With slack jaws, they cleared a path. Before Injago could enter, a drunk elf stumbled out of the bar and crashed into Neiara. She clung to her scarf while he apologized. He listed to the side as he peered at her face with a growing smile.

"You're a dancer!"

Neiara blushed. "N-no," she lied.

"Yeah! On the north side of town. What's that bar called?"

She shook her head. "I think you're thinking of someone else."

"Well, you look just like her. Pretty little thing with the voice of an angel."

"I can't sing," Neiara said through gritted teeth.

"Come on," Injago said, grabbing her hand and hauling her into the dimly lit bar.

The bar top spanned the entire left side of the room, adorned with glittering bottles of booze and glasses resting while their drinkers mingled and partied. Booths lined the left wall, though most remained empty, and tables filled the center. Nearly every space of the floor was filled with drunk elves, pixies, and the occasional water nymph. They found Otandar in the back corner booth, his wide girth filling one side.

"Friends!" he boomed as he pulled himself to his feet. Towering over the others, he pulled them into a giant, four-faerie hug, squeezing the breath from Injago. He wheezed when Otandar released them all, swaying on his feet. He forgot that Otandar liked hugs.

"How are you, Otandar?" Injago asked, rubbing the small of his back as they all slid into the booth.

Otandar grinned and took a gulp from his mug. "I'm great! Living the life! So good to see you all again. But uh..." He leaned in, looking at Romada, avoiding Neiara's direction. "Aren't you a bit worried bringing *her* here?"

Neiara huffed. "I'm quite fine, thank *you*. Shall we get to business?"

Otandar blushed and ran a hand through his long black hair, still not meeting her gaze. "Right you are. What is it you folks are looking for?"

"We're looking for a map that was...misplaced from my safe. It's a map to an old abandoned elven mine," Romada said.

"Misplaced, eh? Well, lucky for you, Otandar knows all the ins and outs of the current underground market." He chuckled before continuing, "And I just so happen to have heard of a map exactly like your lost one."

Injago's skin prickled, and he looked up to see two elves at the bar staring at him. No, not at him. At Neiara. Did they recognize her? He began to sweat. This was all a horrible idea.

"Where can we find it?" Neiara asked.

"Well, there's a fella by the name of Unkan who is going on and on about just such a map. I thought he was a bit too on the scotch to trust, but now, with you folks coming in here saying you lost this map... Well, now I'm interested." He winked at Romada. "Interested in acquiring it for you fine folks, of course."

"Of course," Romada said dryly. "We would love to get that line of inquiry going."

Injago glanced back at the bar and noticed a small group of elves now all talking furtively and occasionally glancing in his direction. This couldn't be good.

"Rome," he whispered. She shushed him as Otandar started speaking.

"Where are you staying? I'll send a boyo over to talk to him and have him meet you at your inn tomorrow." Otandar looked over at the bar, and something flickered in his eyes. "If you'll excuse me, I'm empty," he said, lumbering to his feet with his mug in hand.

Injago shoved Romada. "Listen to me! We need to leave."

"Right now? We're about to set up a contact."

Injago looked up at the bar again; Otandar was nowhere to be seen. There was no way to miss that hulking form. "He's gone."

"What?" Romada leaned over to search the room. "Blast."

Neiara let out a whimper, the first real sign that she might understand the situation they were in—that they had put themselves in. "Are we in danger?"

Injago didn't have the heart to answer. "Let's go," he said.

For once, Romada agreed without a word. They got to their feet, and Injago let out a pent-up breath when he noticed the group from the bar was no longer there. Maybe it had been a weird coincidence that they were looking in that corner. Maybe they would get back to the ship in one piece. Maybe he was worrying all for nothing. Again.

Injago had barely stepped out of the bar before he was shoved to the side. In a state of panic, he realized the group hadn't left after all; they had moved outside to wait for them. A gods damned ambush. Eight or nine elves—it could have been twenty —circled them, taunting them, hands and words assaulting them. Not willing to go down without a fight, Injago set his eyes on an elf at random and slammed his fist into their jaw. The elf went down—*an opening!*—and Injago instinctively yanked Romada by the arm, pulling her from the fray. He winced as her nails slashed his arm, as she shrieked in her ear, but kept his grip. Patrons of the bar had scrambled in all directions, but no one stopped him. They were going to make it! Feeling victorious, he looked back—

*Protect Neiara.*

Except he hadn't. He hadn't even thought of grabbing her, focused only on making sure Romada was okay. Neiara was being dragged away, the scarf discarded on the ground. Her mouth was open in a scream that ended just as quickly as it began when someone shoved a rag into her mouth. Terror filled her eyes. Romada wailed Neiara's name and drew her sword, but one of the elves turned back to face her with a...a blitz? Why was it so small? With the weapon aimed at their faces, Injago knew what they had to do.

"Run!" he shouted, hauling Romada in the opposite direction. Away from danger. Away from Neiara. Away from the faerie his god told him to protect.

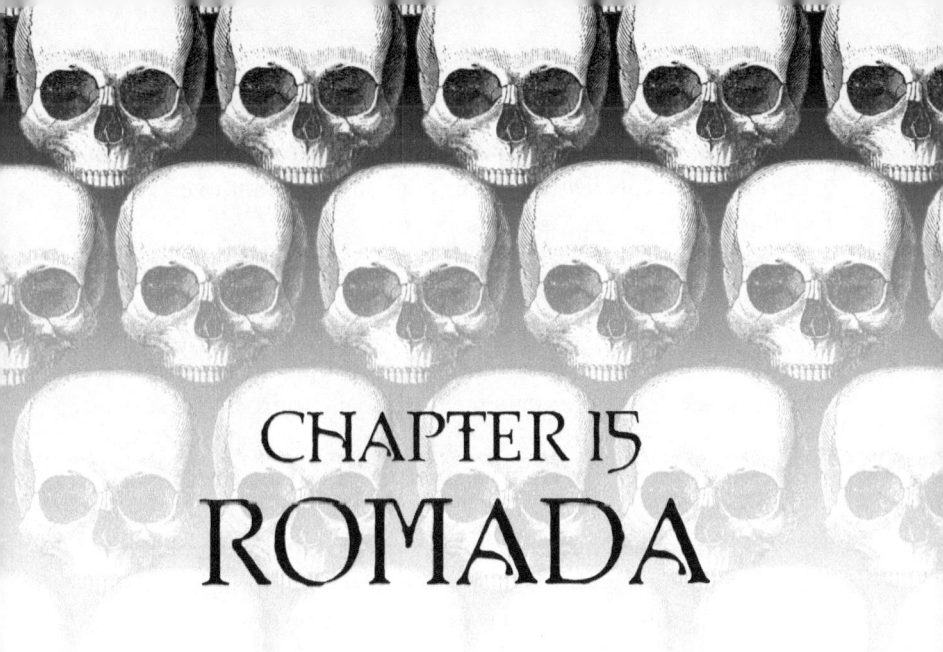

# CHAPTER 15
# ROMADA

**AS IF IN SLOW MOTION, THE MUZZLE OF A...A** blitz—or at least it looked like one—began to flash a sickly neon green. Romada stood frozen to the spot until Injago jerked her to the side and yelled, "Run!"

Faced with the choice of being dragged by a dislocated arm socket or running, so not much of a choice at all, she chose to run.

The image of Neiara's face as they abandoned her burned bright in Romada's mind as she raced through darkened streets back toward the ship. Neiara's eyes, as wide as Romada had ever seen them, fear shining out like a beacon. Her mouth agape, ready to scream, before a cloth was pressed between her lips, gagging her. Her hands held at her sides by her captors. Helpless. Forsaken. Gone. A sob tore through Romada's throat, cutting into her breathing. Tears blurred her vision while her chest burned.

What had they done?

She didn't slow until the plank was beneath her boots; Injago released his death grip on her arm and bent over, hands on his knees as he gasped for breath.

Legs like jelly, she fell to the deck and keened for her lost love.

*Neiara is gone!*

The strangled sounds coming from her throat surprised her, but she couldn't stop herself. Animalistic groans of sorrow scraped their way out of her, thick in the air, palpable. Black spots narrowed her vision as she turned to face Injago.

*Traitor!*

He had pulled her from Neiara's side, abandoning Neiara to a fate unknown without so much as a second thought. Neiara was lost because of him. He was the cause of Romada's misery and sorrow. And he would pay.

"What happened?" Ceta asked, helping Injago stand. "Where's Neiara?"

"She's gone," Injago panted.

Romada's stomach did a flip, and she sucked in air through her teeth, trying not to vomit. Ceta stared at her, a hand over her mouth in shock.

"Are you okay?" Injago asked, kneeling beside Romada.

"How could you?" she growled, the words forcing themselves from between bared teeth.

He shook his head, not meeting her eyes.

"How *could you!*" Romada screamed, launching herself at him.

Weakened by her misery and blinded by tears, it took little effort for Injago to subdue her. After a brief tussle, he straddled her, pinning her arms down as she wept. She screamed again—"TRAITOR!"—whipping her body from side to side, trying to get free. How dare he restrain her? Who did he think he was? Her dorsal fin bent beneath her, and her back began to spasm.

"Stop it!" Ceta yelled, hopping from one foot to the other.

Scrambling away from Romada, Injago looked at her warily. "I didn't think, Rome. I just acted."

"You didn't think," Romada spat, sitting up. "You didn't *think* about Neiara's safety?"

"I panicked! I'm sorry," his voice broke as he hung his head.

Romada stood, unsteady on her feet, and glared daggers at him. "You're a coward. We could have stayed and fought! We could have saved her!"

"They had a blitz, Rome! We stood no chance."

"I guess we'll never know," Romada said, her voice acidic.

"I'm sorry," he repeated, looking Romada in the eye. Some part of her realized that this was the first and second time he had ever said those words to her, but a bigger part knew that words weren't enough to fix this. His eyes shined with unshed tears as though he really felt remorse, but Romada wouldn't be moved by this...this *trick*.

"Sorry isn't good enough!" She lunged at him, letting her fist fly. Pain laced her knuckles as she connected with his jaw; his eyes rolled back, and he crumpled to the ground.

"What the fuck!" Ceta screeched, running to him.

*I hit him... I hit Injago.*

She had never hit him before, ever. Her hand was on fire, and when she looked down, her knuckles were split, blood seeping out of her wounds.

"Oh gods," she whispered, backing away. Struck with the urge to flee, she whirled around and ran off the ship, bolting into the night.

Her legs carried her into the western part of town, where only the dredges of pirate society dared to go. Thieves and murderers with no moral compass populated this area. A half-dressed pixie eyed her predatorily as she passed and shifted as if to proposition her. A prickle ran down Romada's spine, and she ran faster. She needed to get out of the open. She needed somewhere safe for the night. She wasn't sure at what point she had decided the ship wasn't safe for her—was it because Neiara was gone or because Romada had left Injago unconscious on the deck? Did it matter?

A dilapidated inn appeared in front of her as she turned a corner. She didn't see anything better in the immediate vicinity, so she hurried to it and pushed open the door. The harsh creak of the hinges announced her presence; two elves in the dining room looked up at her with blatant disinterest before continuing their drinking.

Romada scooted past the various mismatched tables and chairs to a spot in the corner. Settling herself down in the layer of dust and grime, she steepled her fingers and waited. A pixie barboy wandered out of the kitchens and over to her, his hair a tangled mess and dirt smeared on his cheeks.

"What you want?" he drawled.

"I need you to find someone for me," she said in a hushed tone.

He stared at her like she'd lost her mind.

Fishing out a silver coin, she held it up so it caught the light of the single lantern. "Find him, and I'll pay you."

He licked his lips and nodded. "Who you lookin' for?"

"An elf by the name of Otandar. Do you know him?"

"I'll find him," he grunted, rushing out of the inn with one backward glance at her coin.

She waited half an hour before Otandar lumbered into the inn, glancing around suspiciously. The barboy ran up to her, holding his hands out; she tossed him the coin, and he disappeared into the kitchen.

Otandar sat in the chair opposite Romada, looking her up and down. His eyes lingered on her knuckles. "What, uh, can I help you with, Romada."

"I'm not sure you'll be much help, honestly. You weren't any help back at the bar," she sneered.

He winced. "You know me. I'm a lover, not a fighter."

"Well, find me some information then, lover." The word left a bad taste in her mouth. She had only ever called Neiara that. Would she get the chance to call her that again?

"Information. I can do that. What do you need?"

"I need to find Neiara," she said through gritted teeth. "Where are all the sirens being taken? What's happening to them?" And what else could be more important than this?

He nodded, his throat working convulsively. "I happen to know of someone who has that information. Or, she should. There's a high-ranking City Official sailing past us any day now aboard the ship *Cherish*. Her name is Kalian. Word is she's one of the Officials in charge of the siren...relocation program. Find her, and she'll tell you what you want to know."

Romada reached for her coin purse, but he waved dismissively, a nervous smile on his face.

"No charge! Not after... Well, after what happened. Although, if you're still interested in the map, I'll take our usual fee to get in contact with Unkan for you."

Romada narrowed her eyes at him. "No thanks. I've got more pressing matters."

"Right, right. Of course. You have a good night, Romada." He made a hasty retreat, quick on his toes for someone so large.

Armed with the thought of being able to do something about finding Neiara, she went hunting for the barboy, intent on buying a room for the night. He eyed her coin purse and said it would be four silver coins. She knew he was raising the price just to gouge her, but she didn't have any fight left in her.

Her purse a little lighter, she followed him to a room. Inside, she found a desk, a chair, and a bed that looked like it hadn't been touched in years. At least the door had a lock on it, albeit a flimsy one. She dragged the chair to the door, hooking it under the handle as a precaution. She doubted she would sleep deeply, but just in case, she wanted some warning if someone tried to break in.

Exhausted, she flopped onto the bed. A small cloud of dust rose up, choking her, and she beat at the stiff blankets to get some sense of cleanliness. She huddled in a ball, still fully dressed, and wondered how she would ever get to sleep without Neiara in her arms. Would she dream of her?

The rattle of raindrops hitting the metal roof above her startled her as much as the sudden leak in the ceiling. As water seeped through a crack and splattered across the foot of the bed, Romada started to shiver. Soon, the shiver turned into full-body spasms. The tears came, hot and fast, as the sobs wracked her body. She remembered what it was like to be held captive, to be the prisoner of someone who hated her and tortured her. Was this Neiara's fate now? How could she sleep knowing this was her fault? Why hadn't she fought harder for Neiara? She could have thrown Injago off, rushed the guards. They didn't even know for sure that whatever the fuck that weapon had been was a blitz. She might have survived being shot by whatever it was. And now...

Regret filled her chest as she prayed. *Oh gods, please let her be safe.*

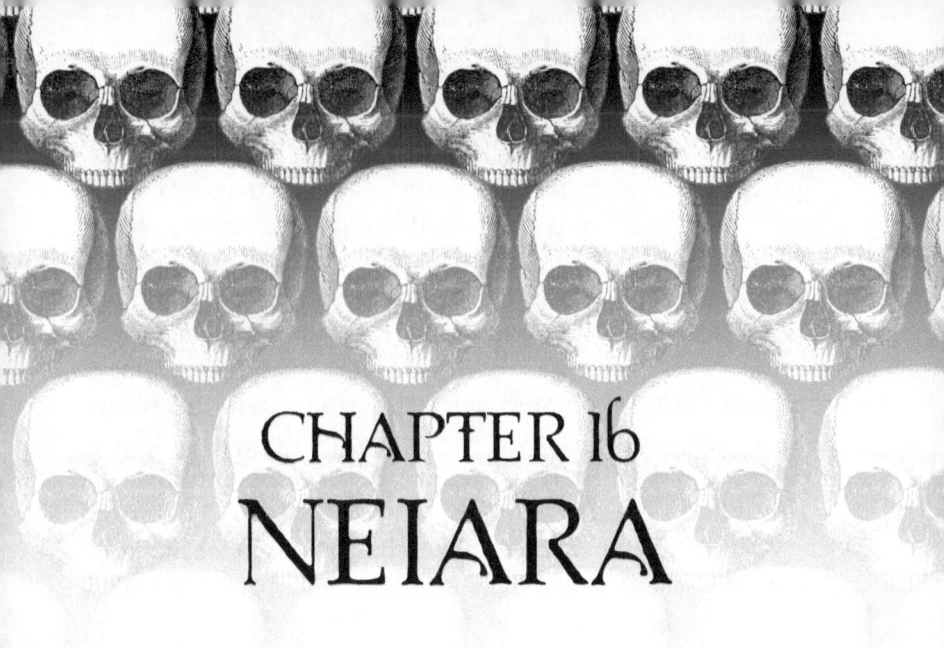

# CHAPTER 16
# NEIARA

**ROMADA WILL SAVE ME. ROMADA WILL SAVE ME.**
*Romada will s—*

Neiara tripped forward on the edge of a cobblestone, nearly falling on her face before righting herself. Silently cursing
herself for wearing sandals rather than boots, she marched on.

The group of elves had led her to the edge of town, where
they handed her over to a pair of royal guards in exchange for a
hefty bag of coins. She wondered how much a siren was worth.

This was useless thinking. She needed to focus on finding
a way to escape.

The mob had, of course, taken her dagger. She mourned
the loss; it had been a gift from Romada on their first anniver-
sary. How long ago that was.

They had also tied her wrists together, which made walking
difficult. She couldn't see her feet to know how to avoid the
dips and highs of the rough cobblestone streets. This wasn't
the first time she had tripped.

The worst thing, though, was the rag in her mouth. They had taken it from the barmaid to use as a gag, tied tightly behind her head. The sharp taste of stale alcohol threatened to recall the meager contents of her stomach. She breathed through her mouth, trying to lessen the stench; though breathing around the gag was difficult, it wasn't nearly as bad as smelling it.

Off in the distance, a light came into view, illuminating a street corner that she recognized. Her mind whirled. If she could slip past her guards, she knew how to reach a hiding place a couple alleys down. They'd never be able to find her. This was her chance.

Walking a little quicker, she reached up to scratch her head and peek behind herself to gauge the distance between her and the guards. She could make it. She had to.

As she reached the corner, she lunged to the side. She could taste freedom! As she took her first running step into the alley, the edge of her sandal caught on a stone, and she fell to the ground. Unable to catch herself properly, the breath was knocked from her.

*Curse these sandals!*

She wanted to scream! She wanted to cry. She wanted to get up and run, but the guards grabbed her, hauled her back to her feet, and pointed her back down the street. Breathing heavily, she resumed her trek toward the unknown. Where were they taking her?

And why had Romada and Injago left her? Everything happened so fast; one moment, they were there, and the next, she saw their backs as they fled. They were gone. Just…gone.

Now she was on her way to some terrifying camp… What did that even mean? What was going on? She couldn't breathe. She gulped air and choked on alcoholic fumes and silent sobs.

She noticed the raised cobblestone a second too late and fell again, this time landing hard on her knees. The skin broke, and she hissed in pain before realizing her sandal had broken, too, leaving her foot vulnerable to the jagged stone.

So now her foot was bleeding as well.

"Get *up*!" The guard grabbed a fistful of her hair and yanked her back onto her feet.

Scalp burning, foot and knees stinging… What next? Wincing, she kicked off her other sandal and began to walk on bruised feet, leaving a trail of bloody footprints behind her. Maybe they would be like macabre breadcrumbs, leading Romada on a quest to find her. She had to trust in Romada. Romada would never abandon her. Romada would save her.

A rumble of thunder rolled overhead, and a few fat raindrops sank into her curls, trickling down her scalp and down her spine. After that brief warning, the sky opened up and dumped what felt like the entire ocean onto the streets of Tilt Town. It seemed the storm had caught up after all.

*Romada will save me. Romada will save me. Romada will save me.*

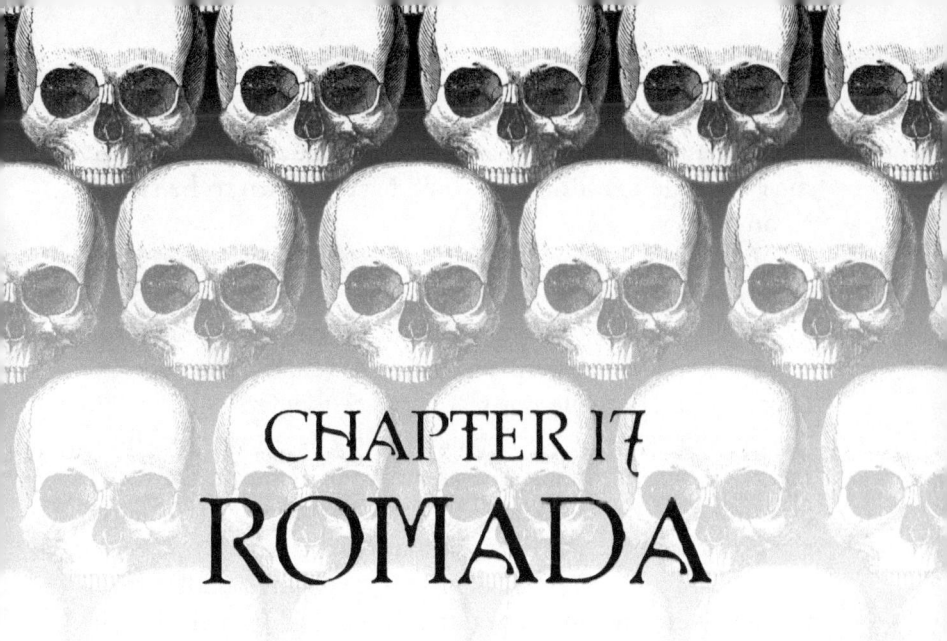

# CHAPTER 17
# ROMADA

**THE MUSTY SCENT OF DUST, MILDEW, AND** sweat permeated Romada's nostrils as she opened her eyes. Bewildered, she groped around the bed for Neiara. Where was she?

It hit her then as she stared at her surroundings: it wasn't a nightmare. Neiara was gone.

A sob wracked her chest, and she struggled to breathe. Oh gods—Neiara was really gone. Romada curled into a tighter ball and let the tears flow freely from her face, soaking the filthy pillow beneath her cheek. Would every morning hurt this much, waking up without her there? Without the curve of her smile, the sight of her freckles, the smell of her hair?

Romada was truly alone.

She quieted after a while, hating the fact that she was so weepy. When was the last time she had cried this much? Neiara loved to praise Romada for her strength. In her absence, Romada realized Neiara had been the source of that strength.

Ironic that it took losing her to see how much Neiara shaped their life together. Romada would have to learn to be strong all on her own.

"I'm coming for you, Neiara," she whispered. "I won't leave you to suffer."

Pulling herself together and straightening her clothes, she sniffled one last time before replacing the chair at the desk and opening the door. She was ready to face the day.

The dining room was populated by the same two elves from the night before; they stared at her as she entered the room. She strode to the door and yanked it open on its rusted hinges, eliciting a screech, and let it fall shut behind her.

A burst of sunlight glancing off of grimy puddles from the night's storm blinded her, and she blinked away fresh tears. Slowly, her vision came into focus; she saw an elf leaning against the outside wall, sneering at her.

"What are you looking at?" Romada growled, baring her fangs.

He stared at her for a moment before turning his attention elsewhere.

"That's what I thought," she muttered, setting out for the ship.

She knew there was an open-air market along the way and decided to walk through it rather than around it. The streets through the lower district often flooded when it rained, and she didn't feel like trekking through mud and silt. Maybe being surrounded by a crowd of anonymous faeries going about their day would help her feel normal again. Plus, it was a much shorter—and drier—walk back to the Guardian.

The sounds of the market reached her before she saw it, and she started to regret her decision. Was this much stimulation really what she needed? Stalls full of wares and food carts giving off the scent of cooking meat came into view, as did a sea of faeries. Taking a deep breath, Romada waded into the thick of it.

A flash of green caught her eye, and she twisted to stare at a scarf fluttering in the wind. It was wrapped around the neck of a slender pixie, her grey wings fidgeting behind her as she haggled with a candle maker. Romada tore her eyes away and caught sight of a coffee vendor a few steps ahead. He was standing in the way of the flow of foot traffic, holding a handful of beans and grinning at those passing him.

"Coffee! Roasted dark as can be! Coffee! Get it here!" His too-cheery voice punctured Romada's eardrums and reverberated in her head.

She made to move around him, but he stepped right up to her and held a bean to her lips; shocked, she opened her mouth to berate him, and before she knew it, he had popped the bean into her mouth.

"Best coffee around! You won't regret buying it!" he spoke directly in her face.

Unsure of whether to spit it out or bite it, she did the latter. Bitterness clawed its way across her tongue and down her throat, choking her. She gagged at the harshness.

His smile faded, and he whisked away to find his next victim, yelling, "Coffee! Get it here!"

Romada rushed away, trying not to spit out the remains of the coffee bean, when she was assailed by the overwhelming scent of cinnamon. A spice vendor stood in front of her, fanning a bowl of cinnamon sticks and wafting the smell into the crowd. Tears pricked her eyes as the combination of bitter coffee and spicy cinnamon jolted an image of Neiara into her mind.

*Her delicate hands wrapped around a mug of coffee, teasing Romada for not liking the flavor. Her laughter as Romada made a face.*

She whirled around, desperate to get away from the smell and the memory, and ran into another vendor.

"Lotion for your hair! High-quality ingredients!" The vendor looked up at Romada, eyes flitting past her, when she noticed her lack of hair. With a frown, she shifted to the side and continued her sales pitch.

Holding her breath and staring at the ground, Romada made her way to the edge of the market. A lump had formed in her throat, threatening to suffocate her as she ran toward the docks. Looking up, she let out a sigh of relief when she saw the ship moored in place. Some small part of her had wondered if Injago would leave without her after what she had done. He would never do that, though.

*Injago.*

She swallowed past the lump in her throat. Now she would have to face him, after what she did, after what *he* did. Would she be able to not only apologize but also forgive him?

Injago sat on a barrel up against the mast, watching the pier. His eyes met hers and followed her as she walked up the plank. A bruise had blossomed on his jawline, and Romada winced looking at it. Averting her eyes, she concentrated on the wood grain of the deck, waiting for him to say something. Anything. When he didn't, she peeked up at him. He was gazing off into the distance, out at the open sea.

She cleared her throat. What to say?

"Injago, I…"

He glanced over at her, and she realized she couldn't forgive him. Not yet. She couldn't because looking him in the eye brought back all her anger from the previous night. She was burning with it, aflame with fury, and she bit her tongue to keep from saying anything to ignite another fight.

"What?" he asked, his voice dull.

"There's a City Official passing by on a ship named *Cherish* today. She should have information on how to find Neiara."

His eyes held no emotion. "So we're going after her."

Romada scoffed. "Of course. I'll go to the ends of Faerth to find her. Nothing will stop me."

"Good." He stood, stretching his arms above his head. "Let's get the ship ready to go."

"Give the orders," Romada said, looking away.

"You look awful. Did you get any sleep?"

Ignoring his concern, she stumbled to the cabin and locked herself in. The sunlight piercing the room was too bright, illuminating the emptiness of it. She dug through a chest to find a quilt and threw it over the curtain rods, snuffing out the light.

Romada collapsed onto the bed, closing her eyes and breathing in the smell of coffee, cinnamon, and sex. Her eyes began to sting as tears formed; she swiped at her face, banishing them.

*Lying in bed, waiting. Footsteps in the dark. She huddled in bed, hoping she wouldn't come. Hoping she would leave her alone, for once.*

*But the footsteps stop at the end of her bed. They always do. Tears stream down her face as she waits for the hand to grab her, to lead her out of her room. To lead her to the office, where she will be disciplined. Beaten for the audacity to exist.*

*A voice whispers her name. "Romada..."*

Romada jerked up, panting violently. No. She was no longer a helpless child. She was a grown-ass adult, and she was in control of her life. The urge to throw something hit her, and she grabbed her pillow, lobbing it across the room. It struck the desk, knocking over the tiny succulent.

She jumped to her feet, lunging to pick it up. "I'm so sorry," she whispered.

The roots had become dislodged, and dirt was scattered across her desk. Scooping it up, Romada gently tucked the succulent back into the small, iridescent pot. It probably needed watering. Fetching her waterskin, she drizzled water over the fuzzy leaves.

"There you go," she murmured.

Hit with exhaustion, she fell back into bed in time to hear the crew working to get underway. To take them out to sea. To take them out to find Neiara.

She began to weep.

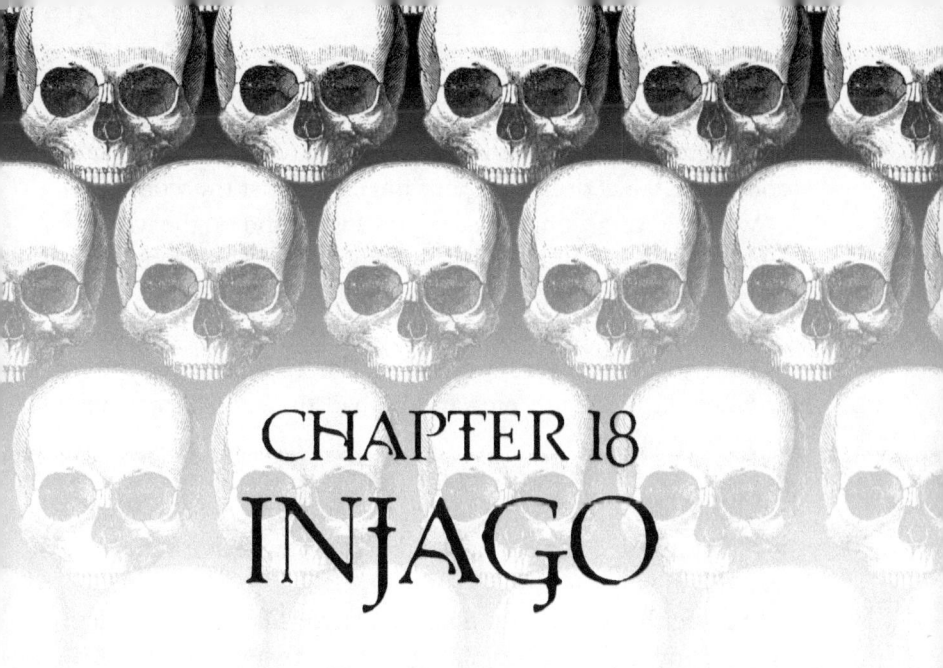

# CHAPTER 18
# INJAGO

**"WEIGH ANCHOR! LOOSE THE SHEETS! LET'S** get her moving!"

Pixies bustled about on deck, scrambling to follow Injago's orders. He stood still, staring at the cabin door Romada had disappeared behind.

She hadn't attacked him again, though there had been a telltale spark of violence in her eye for a moment. Her face had been swollen like she'd spent the night crying. He wondered where she had ended up for the night.

Clearly, she had been in touch with Otandar if she had information about a City Official, but who was to say how the meeting had gone? If Romada had been furious with Injago for abandoning Neiara, he was sure she had been angry at Otandar as well.

Ceta bumped into him and gave him a hasty apology. "Meet me at the helm?" she asked before rushing away.

Taking care not to interrupt the natural flow of faeries on

deck, he made his way to the stairs that led to the wheel. Ceta stood at the table, drumming her fingers against the wood.

"What's wrong?" Injago asked, resting a hand on the wheel.

Ceta turned to him, worry tightening her eyes. "Are you okay? You wouldn't talk to me last night."

"There was nothing to say."

"That doesn't answer my question. I'm worried about you." Her voice dripped with pity, and he had the sudden urge to tell her to shut up.

"I'm fine," he said, gritting his teeth.

"You look awful. I can't imagine how you're feeling right now." She pouted, staring at his bruised jaw from beneath lowered lashes.

Did she think she was being seductive? Did she think he was somehow going to be vulnerable to her wiles now that he was injured? He shifted, turning to face the bow of the ship, and watched the crew as they got the ship underway.

"You were attacked, Injago. Don't brush this off just because she's your sister. Romada is clearly not in her right mind."

"Romada is grieving. Her actions are understandable." He worked hard to keep his voice steady. Gods knew what he would have done if he lost the love of his life. Would he hit his own sister? He honestly wasn't sure. Of course, he would have to actually find the love of his life in order to someday lose him.

"She's gone off the deep end. Attacking you? And for what?"

"For what she sees as a horrible mistake on my part," Injago said, glancing over to see Ceta standing with her hands on her hips. Why was she so up in arms about this? Romada was her captain—their captain.

"Romada needs to get over it. There are plenty of pretty fem-fae she can fawn over. She's not acting like a responsible captain if you ask me."

"I didn't. And we're going after Neiara. That's final."

She paled. "Of course. Sorry. I'll leave you to it."

His insides clenched as he realized he agreed with Ceta to a certain extent. Obviously, no other fem-fae would be able to replace Neiara, and he would never even suggest that, but

Romada damn sure wasn't acting responsible about it. Running off in the middle of the night without telling them where she was going? What if she had never come back? What if she had been attacked and injured, left in a back alley to bleed out? He burned with fury at the fact that Romada couldn't even use her head to think straight.

A short pixie came up the steps. Injago could never remember his name. Eelan? Eetan?

His eyes lingered on Injago's bruise. "Anchor's aweigh, quartermaster. We're ready to cast off the lines."

"Do it," Injago said, looking out over the harbor.

"Cast off!" the pixie yelled as he stomped down the stairs.

Injago watched as the last line was freed, and he spun the wheel hard to starboard. The ship began to glide out into the harbor, a soft wind filling the sails. The breeze grew stronger the farther they got from the pier, sweeping over the deck and ruffling his hair, sending black curls across his vision. He breathed deeply, inhaling the salty air.

Once they got near the edge of the harbor, he called for the crew to secure the sails and drop anchor, keeping them in place. He could see clearly out across the open ocean and would have plenty of warning when the *Cherish* came into view.

He left the helm and made his way onto the deck, where he grabbed a passing pixie, Atar, and told him to be on the lookout for any ships. Atar nodded and flew up to the dragon's nest, the tallest point of the ship atop the mainmast. Satisfied that someone was on watch, Injago ventured down to the galley, where he found Yaya going through the latest provisions.

They looked at him and whistled through their teeth. "She got you good. What happened at the bar anyway?"

"A group of elves ambushed us outside and took Neiara away. I grabbed Romada, but I didn't even think about grabbing Neiara, too. I just…it all happened so fast. And now Neiara is gone and it's all my fault," Injago admitted, hanging his head.

Yaya clicked their tongue before responding. "I wouldn't say it's your fault. There's most likely an open bounty for sirens.

You had no idea there would be an ambush. You acted on your instincts to save Romada. It's no one's fault."

They rifled through a box of spices, pulling out various canisters and placing them on a shelf. When they grabbed a canister of cinnamon, they sighed.

"You know…" They tapped the canister against their chin. "It's probably more Romada's fault than yours. Neiara never should have left the ship. You warned her, and she didn't listen."

Injago tensed at their words and looked around. The galley was empty but for them, with no one to hear Yaya's words.

"And she definitely shouldn't have attacked you. I don't care how upset she was; you're family. And that bond should be stronger than anything else because you chose it." Yaya spoke in earnest, leaning closer to Injago with every word.

Injago almost asked why they were so adamant about Injago being innocent, but Yaya blushed purple and backed away.

"Anyway, I'm sorry you got hurt. And I'm sorry we lost Neiara," Yaya said, turning back to their box of spices.

"I'm sorry, too." And Injago couldn't help feeling sorry for himself as well. He really had tried everything to keep Neiara on the ship. He wasn't sure what else he could have done other than chain her to the mast. Why was Romada so sure this was all his fault? He hadn't done anything wrong, necessarily. Right? If anyone should have been responsible for grabbing Neiara, it would have been Romada.

But then he remembered the looks on Romada and Neiara's faces when they looked at each other. He remembered their eyes lighting up with love. He remembered the soft smiles they shared when they thought no one was looking. He remembered that his god spoke to him, told *him* to keep Neiara safe, not Romada.

Maybe it didn't matter that he tried his best. Maybe it didn't matter that he knew he hadn't done anything wrong. The end result was Romada losing Neiara. Would Romada ever forgive him? And could he forgive Romada for being so reckless and endangering not only Neiara but him as well? The two faeries closest to her, the two she loved the most… What had she been thinking? No house was worth this. And he knew he would never have pulled a stunt like that with the love of his life.

Yaya looked over at him, probably wondering why he was so quiet. "You okay?" they asked.

Injago stood, feeling the urge to be far away from anyone and everyone. "Sorry. I have to go," he said, leaving Yaya to their work. He made his way to his bunk and found the compartment free of any crew members.

Alone at last, he sank onto the mattress and allowed the motion of the ship to placate him. Pulling his blanket up to his chin, he closed his eyes and imagined his future lover again.

Tall, dark, and handsome. Eyes that shone with desire for him. Arms to hold him through any storm he weathered. Love strong enough to keep them together through whatever they faced. A reverence for who Injago was and disregard for everything he wasn't.

He was out there somewhere; Injago knew it. And Injago would find him. Romada would find Neiara, and he would find his love.

He had to believe that.

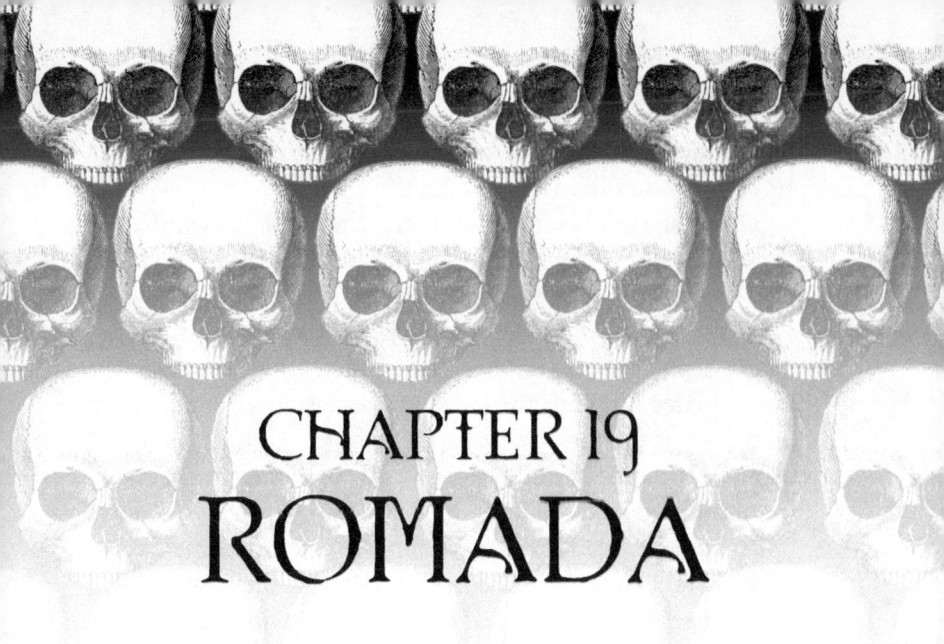

# CHAPTER 19
# ROMADA

**DRIFTING ON THE VERGE OF SWEET SLUMBER,** a call from beyond the cabin roused Romada: "Ship ho!"

She jumped up and struggled with the lock on the door before rushing out into the bright sunlight. Bolting to the banister, she gripped the wood beneath her fingers and saw it: a beautiful tall ship with three masts. The blue and green flag of the Ostranan Royal Naval Guard topped it, and Romada gave a feral grin.

"Step lively! Ready for a fight! Weigh anchor! Release the sails!" She turned to face the crew. "We've got a ship to catch."

A cheer went up on deck as everyone leapt about, readying the ship.

Taking the steps two at a time, she made her way to the wheel. Injago had reached it first, but he stepped back as she marched up and gave it a spin to point them in the same direction as the *Cherish*. The ship was fast approaching and would pass them soon, but Romada had no doubt they would be able to catch her. She was low in the water, laden with faeries and cargo, and would be an easy target.

Their sails billowed out, catching the swift sea winds, and propelled them forward. Digging her boots into the deck, Romada stood firm, angling them toward the *Cherish*.

"Hoist the colors!" she yelled, eliciting a wild cheer.

"Hoist the colors!" The call resounded about the deck as a pair of pixies dug into the chest at the base of the mainmast and drew out the massive black flag, hooking it to the line and raising it. It flapped wildly in the wind, and an alarm sounded on the other ship.

Romada grinned, baring her fangs. Time for some fun.

"Ballistae!" she screamed, and half the crew scrambled to obey her. Injago wound the mechanism with a fury, arms straining. Once it clicked into place, he hefted one of the bolts—tipped with a powerful spiked claw for maximum hull damage—over his head before placing it in the ballista. Up and down the deck, ballistae stood at the ready. The other half of the crew kept up their relentless torrent of noise, a sure-fire tactic to strike fear into the enemy.

As they drew nearer, Romada could see the faeries onboard the *Cherish* winding their own ballistae, though they had six total—three on each side—to the *Guardian*'s ten. She kept the ship aiming straight at them as they fired to lessen their target area before spinning the wheel hard to port. The *Guardian* pivoted in the water, presenting the ballistae with a perfect target.

"Fire!"

The ship lurched from the propulsion of the bolts; Romada heard several satisfying cracks as they broke through the other hull. She continued to spin the wheel until their other side faced the *Cherish* with five freshly loaded ballistae and gave the order to fire again. Five more solid hits, and then the *Cherish* raised a white flag.

"Prepare to board!"

The pirates' verbal barrage continued as she angled them closer before handing the wheel over to Ceta. Jumping down to the deck, Romada joined her crew as they stood at the banister, ready to board the other ship. The pixies spread their wings while she and Yaya held ropes in their hands.

"Now!" She jumped, flinging herself forward into the empty void between the ships. The gap was a maw threatening to consume her, but she sailed over it effortlessly and landed on the other deck.

Despite the flag of surrender, the *Cherish* guards were armed to the teeth and ready for a fight. Even better. Romada appreciated a fiery opponent.

An elf stood before her, holding his sword with steady hands. Letting out a wild scream, she charged at him, drawing her sword and dagger and feinting to the left before slashing down with her sword and clipping his right elbow. Blood spurted, and he dropped his sword from useless fingers, the tendons in his arm severed. She finished him off with a slice to the throat and kicked the corpse out of her way.

Fighting was easy when you were angry. And Romada was furious.

A pixie rushed at her, and Romada impaled her in the gut; she fell on the blade, and Romada had enough time to slide it out before another elf appeared, flourishing her sword. Romada slashed and parried and side-stepped, careful of the bodies on the deck and the slick pools of blood. Finally, she saw her opening, threw her dagger at the elf's stomach, and heard the satisfying squelch of flesh being pierced. The elf dropped her sword and grasped the dagger hilt in confusion. Romada slashed her across the neck, and the body fell.

The fight was over as swiftly as it began. Romada stood over a small mound of bodies, chest heaving. Adrenaline coursed through her veins, lighting her up and making her vision blur. She leaned against the banister, waiting as her crew searched the ship for Kalian.

Injago stepped up to her, bleeding from a shallow cut on his forearm. "We've searched everywhere but the cabin. She's locked herself in there."

"Find something to break down the door."

He nodded and came back a moment later with a sledge-hammer. Offering it to her first—she waved it away and gestured for him to go ahead—he slammed it against the hinges in turn. With a mighty groan, the door gave way.

Barging inside with blades drawn, Romada was confronted by an elderly elven fem-fae holding a dagger in shaking hands. Blue eyes looked wildly from Romada to Injago and back.

Romada feinted an attack, and the elf let out a cry, dropping the dagger and throwing her hands in the air.

"Don't hurt me!"

Holding his sword out, Injago stepped forward and retrieved the dagger, hooking it into his weapons belt before standing back behind Romada.

"Are you Kalian?" Romada asked, sheathing her blades.

The elf nodded, peeking at Romada from behind her fingers.

"We have some questions for you." Romada moved up inside what would have been a socially acceptable distance between strangers and crossed her arms, biceps flexing.

Kalian gulped and stared at the floor, shoulders twitching.

"Where are the sirens being taken?"

"They're being taken to holding camps. The children are being sold for labor, and the adults are... They're in the holding camps."

Romada couldn't believe her ears. Slavery? It had been outlawed on Faerth for over two millennia. Who was buying child slaves?

"The children are being transported elsewhere?" Injago asked. "Wouldn't they just enchant themselves free?"

"The sirens are being transported via ships bearing a red flag to mark them as containing hazardous cargo. And no—we have a new way of silencing the sirens. But I'm not telling you," Kalian said, jutting out her chin and glaring at Romada.

So the elf thought she had a spine... Romada chuckled darkly to herself.

"I can make you tell me," she said. Drawing her dagger, she inspected the tip. "Or you can be nice and tell me now."

Kalian paled. "I don't know, okay? They're using a new technique. It's experimental. But it's proving to be a useful way to solve our siren issue."

"Issue? Sirens are faeries. They aren't an issue." Romada's ears burned as she reined in her temper.

"Their voices are. They can coerce anyone to do anything! They're uncontrollable, and they don't deserve to use their voices."

Romada pinched the bridge of her nose, steadying herself. The hand clenching the dagger shook, so she replaced it on her weapons belt before continuing. "Sirens deserve to speak. It's a right."

"They are abominations! They don't even deserve the right to live."

Romada closed the distance between them in the blink of an eye, drawing her hand back and cracking her knuckles across Kalian's face.

Kalyan's head whipped to the side, and she gasped. A trickle of blood flowed from a split in her lip. Wincing, Kalian reached a finger up to press on the wound. A dangerous glimmer appeared in her eye.

"You won't find whoever you're looking for. They'll be long dead before you get to them."

With a howl of rage, Romada tackled Kalian to the ground. She only landed two punches before she found herself caged by Injago's arms as he pulled her away from the screaming elf. Romada considered fighting him to get free but decided against it; she shrugged him off instead, pacing over to the opposite side of the room.

The screaming cut off abruptly, and Romada turned back to see Injago wiping his dagger of blood, a fresh crimson seam splitting Kalian's neck in two.

"I could have done that," Romada protested, but he waved her words away.

"You weren't going to kill her. You were going to beat the pulp out of her and tire yourself out."

Romada grimaced. He was right. "We need to head to The

City and find the Official who runs this project. This new silencing technique doesn't sound good, and we still have no clue where the camps are located."

A painting on the wall caught Romada's eye. She walked up to it, dimly realizing that Injago was speaking but not hearing his words. The painting was of a merfae, their tail a stark coal black and their eyes a glowing white. She reached out to touch it and felt a jolt of static.

"I want this," she heard herself say. She turned to see Injago raising an eyebrow at her.

"Okay."

"Let's go. I'm sick of this ship." She stalked out of the cabin and into the fresh air.

"What do you want to do with it?" he asked, following her with the painting in his arms.

Romada looked around at the darkened oak deck, the magnificent masts, and the filigree carved into the banisters.

"Burn it."

They left the tragically beautiful ship in smoldering ruins and headed for The City.

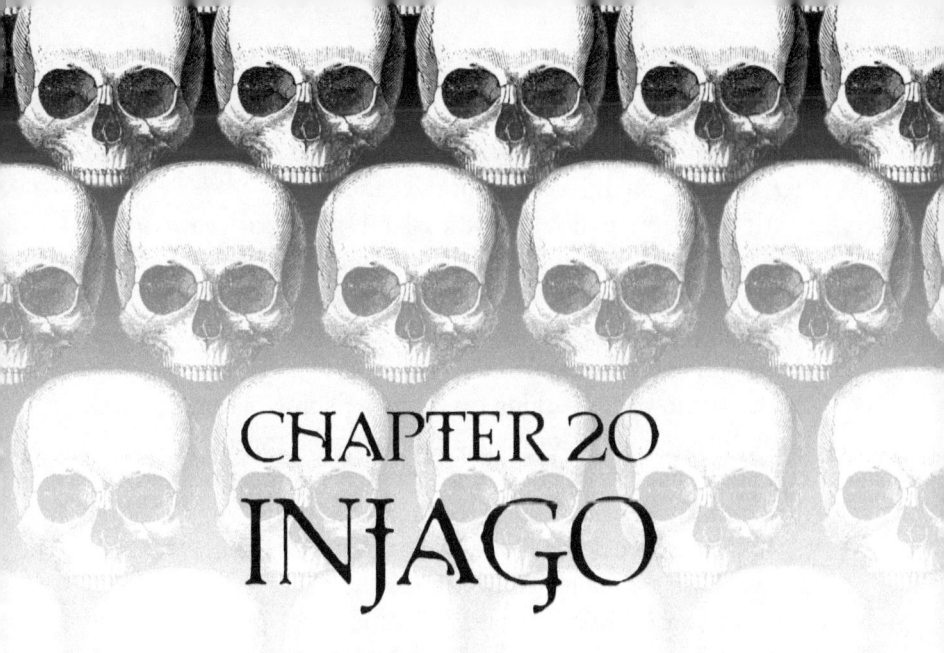

# CHAPTER 20
# INJAGO

**WITH ONE LAST BACKWARD GLANCE AT THE**
burning ship, Injago returned to the task at hand. Romada
stood with him at the helm, going over the map. He pointed
at an island in their path.

"We should go along the windward side to avoid the naval
base on the leeward side."

"Going around will take more time. Time we don't have.
We should go through the strait," Romada said.

"Yes, but dealing with the navy will take even longer, and it
has risks. We should go around."

"We're fast. They won't catch us," she insisted. Her fingers
curled into fists.

He wasn't sure if it was a subconscious move or whether
she was trying to threaten him, but he shifted back a step anyway, and she relaxed.

"We will take our chances," she said with finality.

Injago sighed. "Aye, aye, Captain."

Romada took control of the helm, and he stood behind her, both of them looking out over the water.

It took over an hour, but the island sprang into view on the horizon, a hazy green blob growing steadily larger and clearer the closer they got. Despite his hopes that she would change her mind, Romada aimed the ship toward the strait between the island and the mainland.

Ceta had been working on fixing a fishing net on the deck when Injago saw her look up and notice their trajectory. Frowning, she looked up at him and stared. He shrugged, and she dropped the net and ran up to the helm.

"What are we doing?" she asked under her breath. "There's a naval base on the leeward side."

"I'm aware," Romada said, her tone firm.

"Are you mad?" Ceta threw up her arms.

Romada turned to glare at her, fire in her blue eyes.

Ceta took a hesitant step back and nodded. "Aye, aye, Captain."

The jungles of the island began to take form, and Injago saw a flock of seadragons wheeling over one of the beaches. Long ago, a seadragon had adopted their ship. They had named her Terga, and she had been the pet of the crew, though she had slept only with Romada and had followed her everywhere. Injago smiled faintly at the memory. That had been before Neiara had joined them.

Despite the distance, the profile of the naval base came into view. Stone towers and walls were built into the side of the island, safe from the wind. Three ships were moored to their docks, and as the *Guardian* entered the strait proper, an alarm rang out.

Guards poured out of buildings and streamed toward one of the ships, and Injago watched as they began loosing the mooring lines and sails.

"They won't catch us," Romada said as they shot past the base.

The *Guardian* was boarded five minutes later.

\*\*\*

Injago fought in a haze, barely aware of the fights around him. He parried, he swung, and he slashed. When one elf went down, another took their place before him. It was an endless loop of blood, sweat, and steel, and he was tiring. His arm grew leaden, and his sword grew heavy. He hardly got it up in time to stop his latest adversary from cleaving him in two.

He whirled around in time to see Romada trip, drop her sword, and fall to her knees. An elf stood over her, blade raised. With a roar, Injago leapt forward and thrust his sword through the elf's body. With a jolt and a spasm, the elf died.

Injago let the body fall and held out a hand to Romada, who blinked up at him with confusion. When she realized she was on the deck, she pushed away his hand, grabbing her sword and using it to leverage herself back onto her feet.

All around, the fighting had stopped. Yaya held their hand to a cut on their arm, and someone else—Eegan? Eetan?—had a gash on his forehead, but everyone had survived. Injago's chest heaved as he gulped for air and gestured for everyone to get rid of the bodies. He clumsily sheathed his sword and grabbed the feet of one of the dead. Dragging the body to the side of the ship took monumental strength, and he gasped, holding onto the railing before shoving the body over the side. He stayed there, hugging the railing for who knew how long, watching the bodies fall, fade, and reappear on the surface.

Romada stood beside him, hanging onto the railing for dear life. She turned her head to look him in the eye, and he could feel the weariness emanating from her.

"You need sleep," he said.

"Can't," she whispered, looking away. "I just see her."

Injago knew the feeling. "What do you want to do with the ship?" He gazed at the magnificent rigging, wishing he had a ship as fine as this to his name.

"See if there are any provisions and then burn the rest."

Injago felt a flicker of sorrow for the destruction of such a beautiful vessel, but he relayed the message to the crew. He heard Romada mutter something before she swung back across onto the Guardian.

Yaya made to move past Injago, but he grabbed their uninjured arm and pulled them close. Their grip on their cut slipped, and blood began dripping from it, staining their pants blue.

Injago loosened the scarf at his waist and ripped a strip from it, binding the wound. Yaya flinched when he tightened the makeshift bandage, stemming the flow of blood.

"We don't have a healer onboard, so maybe don't get injured next time?"

Yaya let out a bark of laughter. "I should have thought of that." Their laughter faded when they noticed Injago's wound from the *Cherish*. "Maybe take your own advice, hm?"

"Go lie down," Injago said, tying off the ends. "You need rest."

Yaya blushed and gave him a jaunty salute.

Ceta came up to him, carrying a box that jangled in her arms. "I packed up the stuff in the cabin. There's jewelry and writing supplies."

"I'll take it." Hooking an arm around the bow, he flew back to the *Guardian* and headed for Romada's cabin. She would probably find it useful since she could often be found with her nose in a sketchbook. At least, she used to. He hadn't seen her touch her sketchbook since before they landed in Celestinia. With all the stress, and now with her muse gone, her artistic desire might have dried up.

Knocking on the door, he heard a muffled reply and pushed it open. He blinked at the sudden darkness; a blanket had been thrown over the curtain rod, leaving the cabin in shadows. The air was heavy and still with a slightly fetid smell. He hesitated a moment at the door, and a flame flickered into existence as Romada lit the lantern on her bedside table.

"I'm used to the darkness by now," she said, standing and walking to him.

Injago took in the sight of a tower of books by her bedside, stacked on top of each other. A slew of dishes covered her desk. Clothes littered the floor.

He cleared his throat, holding out the box. "Ceta found this for you."

"Give her my thanks," Romada murmured, taking the box and putting it on her desk without even looking through it. She hopped past the pile of books and flopped onto the bed.

"Rome..." He didn't know what to say.

"Close the door on your way out," she said, blowing out the lantern.

"Sweet dreams," he said, reaching for the door. He heard a noncommittal grunt as he swung it shut and then, a moment later, a soft sob.

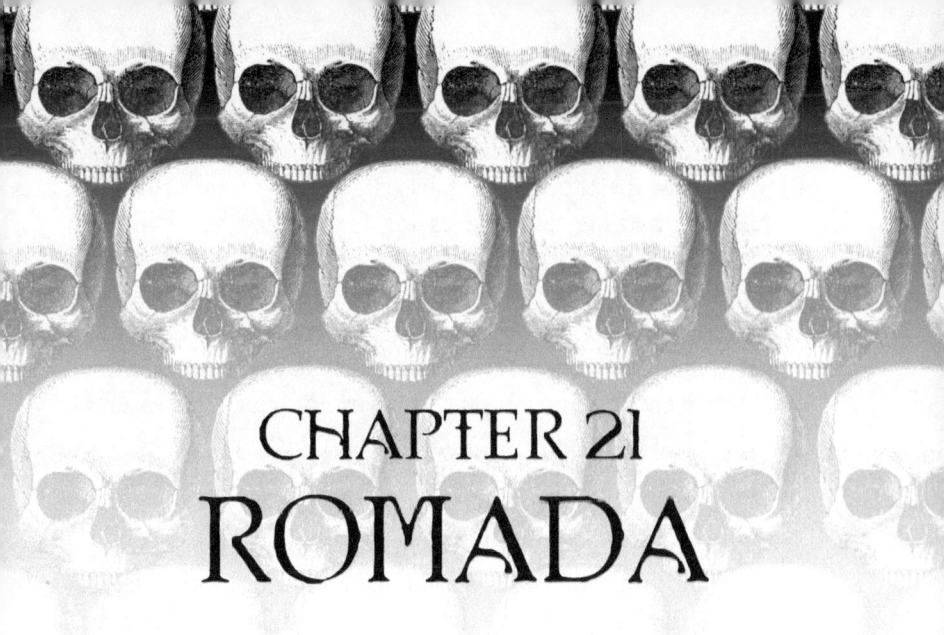

# CHAPTER 21
# ROMADA

**A HAND GRIPPED NEIARA'S THROAT; SHIMMER-***ing tears formed in the corners of her eyes as she choked on a scream of silence. Romada sobbed as she watched, as Delaini held her in place, forcing her to witness the death of her lover.*

Romada fell out of bed, tangled in sheets with a firm hold of her limbs. By the time she finished wrestling herself free, she could barely breathe from the exertion. She stood and tossed the sheets onto the bed.

The darkness of the cabin had shifted to a dimness as the sun rose. She watched the flickering pattern the sunlight made through the thin quilt, and her stomach sank as she realized what day it was.

It was Worship Day.

Her heart sat heavy in her chest, and she wondered if it would weigh her down all day, dragging her to the depths to be crushed by the weight of the entire ocean. How could she worship when her heart was dead?

She contemplated staying in bed all day—it was Rest Day, after all—but the thought of her sea goddess's wrath turning on her ship had her hastily dressing for the day. Trudging to her bathroom, she splashed cold water on her face and stared at her bloodshot eyes in the mirror. When had life become so exhausting? She knew the answer and scoffed at her reflection before lugging herself down to the galley in search of Yaya.

They weren't there. A pile of sparkling clean plates and covered dishes of food adorned the counters. Eetan sat at a table, sipping coffee. She asked him about Yaya's whereabouts.

"They're worshipping," he said.

So that was how it would be. Romada fought back a wave of ugly emotions and headed back to the cabin. Door locked, she stood in the middle of the room, the stillness of the air pressing in on her. She couldn't breathe. She tried to muster tears, but her eyes stayed dry, their reservoir of sadness used up in the night. Fuck. She couldn't even cry properly.

Resigning herself to a day of lonely worship, she stripped down to her underwear and walked out onto the deck. A handful of pixies sat at the altar—Injago was absent—but she headed straight for the banister. Peering over the side first, in case Yaya was there, she was momentarily mesmerized by the shimmering light on the wave caps. Yaya wasn't there, though; they must have been on the other side of the ship. She dove in.

The turbulence of the sea, not readily apparent from up on deck, thrashed against her as she sank below the surface. The ocean was anything but calm, and she felt her anxiety spike. Worship was supposed to be peaceful, not fearful. She gulped water into her lungs, trying to steady her breathing, but her chest seized, and she choked.

Romada shoved her arms back and kicked her legs, propelling herself back up to the surface, and coughed up the water from her lungs. The sea slapped her in the face as if chastising her; she wanted to scream in frustration.

She was a water nymph, caught halfway between being a faerie of the water and a faerie of the land. Never before had she felt so torn between those two identities as in that moment when the sea seemed to reject her and the ship held no comfort.

Working to slow her breaths, she closed her eyes, treading water just enough to float. When she felt calm again, she let herself sink below the waves, her gills pulling in water. This time, the transition was pleasant and soothing.

She drifted, eyes shut tight, for what felt like an eternity. Light flickered behind her eyelids, coaxing her to open them. She paid it no mind, lost in her own world.

A shadow fell across her face, and she opened her eyes in time to see the barnacle-covered hull of the ship crossing in front of her. With no warning, a sea current shoved her forward, bashing her body against the sharp edges.

Pain engulfed her, and she let out a soundless scream, bubbles flooding her vision. She pressed a palm to the hull and shoved off, pushing herself deeper and away. Blood seeped from several cuts up and down her body, and she laboriously made her over to the hand and footholds on the side of the ship.

With thick movements, she climbed back onto the ship, a trail of blood in her wake. She stood on deck for a moment, vision blurring and head in a haze, before—

*My wounds...*

—realizing she needed to stop the bleeding, disinfect the wounds. Vomit erupted from her throat, shoving its way out and splattering the deck. Not so much vomit as bile, the putrid neon yellow glowing in a growing puddle.

"Romada!" someone called out to her, but she turned and sprinted for the cabin, sealing herself back into isolation, back into the darkness. Shivering violently, she fumbled around for a cloth, a rag, anything, and splashed it with alcohol, pressing it to each cut she found, her pain blazing a trail along her body her fingers could follow without looking. The sting from the alcohol in each wound had her gasping, her vision a mess of dark spots and searing light, a greyscale kaleidoscope. She stumbled over to the lantern and managed to light it on the third try.

Light bloomed, and she looked down at her hands only to realize the 'rag' was anything but; she held a gossamer scarf of luscious silk. The beautiful green scarf which so perfectly matched Neiara's eyes. Now fittingly stained with Romada's blood.

Self-hatred spilled out of her in a wordless shriek as she threw the scarf in the back corner; it caught on the fern and lay draped across its leaves, bloody silken foliage. A mistake. So many mistakes in so little time. A roar filled her ears, worthless inner screaming as her fists beat against her thighs, gritting her teeth harder with each hit until they, too, shrieked under the pressure, threatening to shatter. She hoped they would.

How could she ruin something so precious? How could she be so careless?

Romada threw herself onto the bed, the pillow muffling her sobbing. It smelled like body odor, and she gagged, rolling over. Grabbing Neiara's pillow, she brought it to her face and breathed in the citrus scent of her hair lotion.

Feeling calmer, she replaced the pillow and sat up to grab one of Neiara's books from the pile beside her bed. Romada flipped through the pages, noticing where Neiara had made notes and underlined certain passages.

It brought her immense comfort to read Neiara's handwriting, to see the words that brought her joy. Romada had never understood how Neiara could be so enamored with words as to read an entire book in one sitting, but now that Neiara was gone, reading took up all Romada's time.

Not to say that she was reading the book so much as she was reading Neiara's commentary on the book. She couldn't have said what the book was truly about, but she could see how much Neiara loved it, and that was enough.

Romada lost track of time, skimming through the book and gleaning Neiara's insight. When she put the book down and rubbed her eyes, she noticed light no longer peeked around the edges of the blanket. She walked to the door and opened it a crack; darkness had enveloped the ocean, a shimmering sheet of stars twinkling overhead. A thin sliver of the moon hid behind a translucent layer of clouds; it was time to worship.

How could she worship the goddess of lovers without her lover?

Her chest felt empty and cold; looking down, she realized she was still naked. No wonder she was freezing. She closed the door again, locking it, and searched for her clothes. Pulling her shirt over her fins, she caught a glimpse of her pants and grimaced. There was no way she would want to wear those over her cuts.

Maybe a skirt? She had never owned any, not even in her youth at the Orphan Center, but Neiara had many. She found a long black skirt in Neiara's chest and pulled it on, tightening her belt over the waist.

It flowed over her legs, the soft material caressing her wounds. When she walked, it swished around her, rustling in the quiet of the night. Was this what it felt like to be feminine and pretty? To have your clothes sing delicate songs to the beat of your footsteps while kissing your skin?

She stood before the floor-length mirror, gazing at her reflection in the flickering light of the lantern. A tall and strikingly beautiful fem-fae stared back at her, cheekbones sharp enough to cut glass. Her muscular figure almost looked curvy in the loose-fitting skirt.

Romada twirled, enjoying the feel of the fabric against her legs.

When she looked again at the mirror, she saw the minute details she had missed before, like how her eyes had bags of exhaustion beneath them, how her mouth turned down in a perpetual frown. Beauty meant nothing to depression.

She was so very, very tired. Turning away from her haunting reflection, she sent a quick prayer to her goddess, asking for forgiveness. She had neither the energy nor the will for worship. Curling up in bed, she cuddled Neiara's pillow and drifted into a fitful sleep.

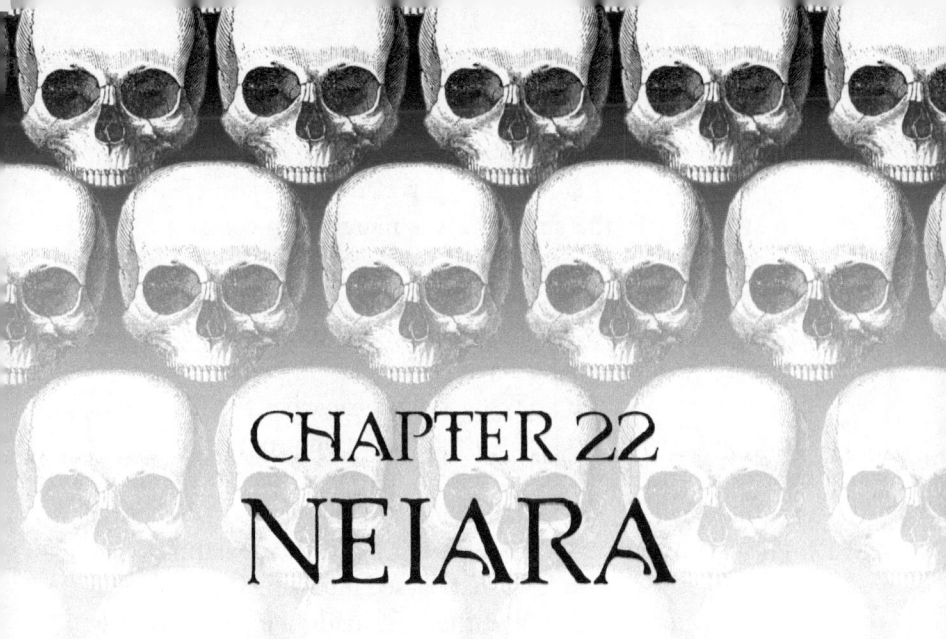

# CHAPTER 22
# NEIARA

**NEIARA WOKE WITH A START AS A GUARD SHOOK** her.

"Get up."

Attempting to get to her feet, her body a mess of painful joints and tender bruises, Neiara realized she was in the cargo hold of a ship, surrounded by sleeping sirens. She remembered walking toward the ship, two flags—one green and blue, and one red—waving high overhead. She remembered stepping onto the plank, swaying as the ship shifted beneath her. And then darkness.

Where was she now? And how long had she been asleep?

"I said, get up!" The guard hauled her to her feet and began dragging her toward the steps leading up and out of the cargo hold. Her joints creaked with every step, her muscles screaming at her in pain after being in disuse for who knew how long. Her back felt like one giant bruise.

Tripping up the stairs, she was led down a hallway and to

another set of stairs. At the top, she was assailed by sunlight bright enough to make her eyes water. Her vision cleared as she stepped off the ship and was marched into a stone fort. Once inside the massive walls, she saw a long line of sirens winding around the buildings, ending at what looked like a healing clinic. Or, at least, the faeries standing outside were in the maroon robes of healers.

Deposited in the line, she waited for what felt like hours, creeping forward every so often as the line moved. The sun beat down on her, the heat bringing sweat to her forehead and the small of her back. Her bare feet ached as she stood on gritty dirt; every tiny pebble felt like a thorn stabbing her tender soles. Every minute that passed intensified the gnawing hunger in her stomach, and the heat made the stench of her gag unbearable. Swaying on her feet, she waited and wondered what would become of her.

As she got closer to the clinic, she could finally see what the healers were doing. Each siren was being equipped with a collar. It looked like it was made of cloth, and it locked in the back.

When it was her turn, she stepped forward and attempted to swallow her nervousness. With gentle hands, a healer placed the cloth collar around her neck, smoothing it in place before using a round stone key to click it closed in the back. The collar was snug but not tight. Next, the healer removed the gag from her mouth.

Easing her jaw shut, Neiara breathed a sigh of relief. She licked her lips—what a glorious feeling!—and looked up at the healer to ask what the collars were for.

As soon as the words took form, agony struck her. She couldn't speak; she couldn't even breathe. The collar tightened like a vice, choking her into breathless silence. Her vision darkened as she fought for air.

"Relax your throat," the healer said softly.

Relax? How could she relax? She fell to her knees, heart pounding. Clutching her throat, she forced her neck muscles to relax under her fingers. Slowly, agonizingly slow, the collar loosened, and she gasped as air returned to her lungs. She expected the collar to tighten again at the sound, but it didn't. She looked up at the healer again, the question in her eyes.

"It will tighten when you use your vocal cords," the healer said.

"Get up," a guard barked, pulling her back to her feet. "Keep the line moving."

Neiara bleakly followed the line of sirens leaving the healers, wondering what fresh hell awaited her next.

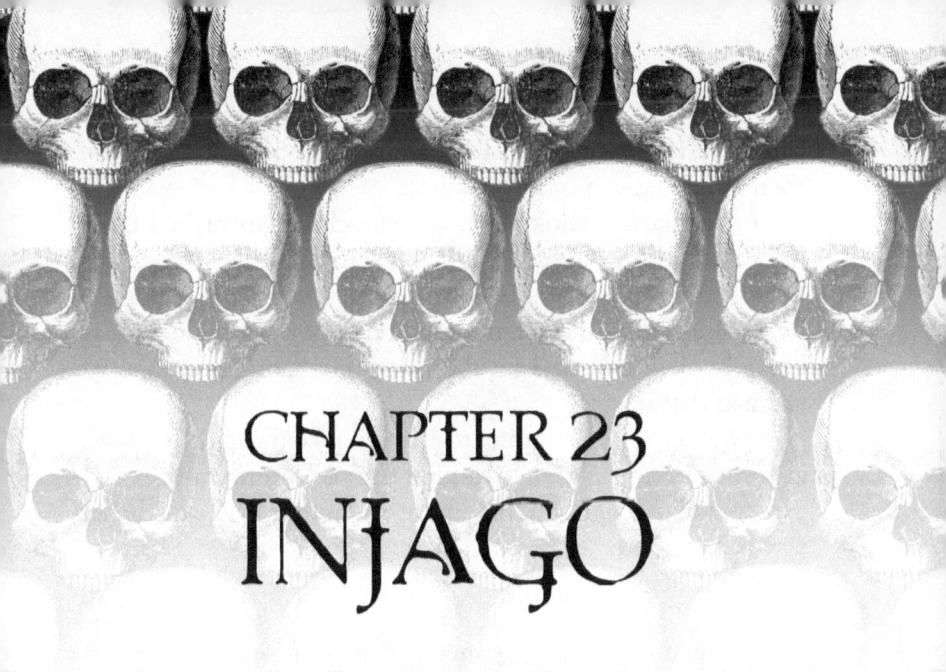

# CHAPTER 23
# INJAGO

**THE SHIP ROUNDED THE HEADLAND, AND THE**
City came into view, sprawling across the bay. The capital of
Ostrana was a magnificent sight, with towering buildings all
covered in glass, reflecting the ocean back out. Satisfied that
they would reach the pier within a couple hours, Injago went
to ask Romada what her plan was.

He knocked hesitantly on the cabin door. Romada had been
shut in there for days; the last time someone saw her, she had
climbed onto the ship bleeding. She hadn't even come out for
food; Yaya had expected her to sneak out at night, but they
had reported that no food had gone missing.

He knocked again and heard a faint groan.

"Go away."

"The City is in view," he said, raising his voice to be heard
through the door.

A thud reached his ears, followed by shuffling footsteps

and the click of the lock. Romada pulled open the door and then faded back into the darkness.

Injago nearly choked on the stench of unwashed body odor and rotting food. A light flickered into existence, and he stared at the small pile of dishes that had been sitting on her desk for days and the mountain of books by the bed. Was every book she owned on the floor? He hadn't even known she had that many.

"You know you're going to have to take those dishes back at some point," he said, breathing through his mouth.

Romada shrugged at his attempt at humor as she made her way back to bed. "I guess."

"Want help?"

"No."

"Okay. Well, we're here, at The City. What's the plan?"

She sat on the edge of the bed, hugging herself and rocking back and forth.

"Rome?"

"Don't call me that," she said in a flat tone.

"Talk to me. What are we doing?"

"I don't know," she whispered so lightly he strained to hear her.

His mind groped for an idea and landed on their old home. "What about going to see Delaini? She'll be so happy to see us. And she might have information."

"You just want to see her again and be reminded that you're her favorite."

"It's not my fault Delaini likes me better. Maybe you should have been better behaved." He smirked, expecting her to bring up any of the many, many times he had broken the rules.

Instead, Romada laid back on the bed, unresponsive. A long moment passed, and Injago began to wonder if he had said something wrong.

"Or do you have another idea?"

Silence. And then finally: "Fine. We'll go see Delaini."

"See you when we're moored?"

She gave a grunt of affirmation, and Injago shut the door, taking a deep breath of fresh air. How she managed to stay shut up in there all day was beyond his comprehension. Something was seriously wrong, but he wasn't sure how to help her. Not that she would accept his help. She had always been stubbornly independent. Even as a child, she never went to him or even Delaini for help, preferring to struggle through everything on her own. There was a nice sweet spot, right toward the end of their time together at the Orphan Center and into their first few decades of pirating, where she had leaned on him for help. Back when she told him everything, asked of his advice, and valued his opinions. Back before Neiara joined them.

They moored at the quay without any troubles, and Injago leaned against the railing to watch the crew leave the ship in twos and threes. Yaya had decided to be among the crew that stayed on the ship; they usually came to shore with Injago and Romada, but with the mission at hand, they felt more comfortable staying behind.

Injago whistled a little tune, watching the clouds overhead. After what felt like forever, Romada appeared in the doorway to the cabin, peeking her face out into the open and blinking her eyes at the light. She looked haggard, like she hadn't slept in a week.

"You sure you're up for this?" Injago asked.

She nodded, looking out over The City. "I have to. For Neiara."

"Okay. Let's go." He gestured for her to walk off the ship first and then followed her off the plank and down the quay. Four other ships were moored in the slips. Romada and Injago dodged faeries of all shapes and sizes as they walked toward the shore.

Once they got past the boardwalk of shops, they looked for a waterhorse trolley to take them farther into The City. The black velvet coats of a team of waterhorses shined in the sunlight as first Romada and then Injago jumped aboard. The waterhorses pulled the trolley at a leisurely pace, slow enough for passersby to jump on and fast enough that it was still quicker than walking. The water nymph handler lounged in the driver's seat and looked out over the crowds of faeries swarming the streets with a look of boredom.

The farther into The City they got, the more the street became a grid, wide lanes intersecting at right angles. They reached a busy crossroads, and the waterhorses stopped, allowing passengers to disembark and catch trolleys on the perpendicular street. Stepping off, Romada and Injago wandered over to the opposite corner to wait for a trolley heading in the new direction. It appeared a few minutes later, and they jumped on.

The sturdy spires of the Orphan Center soon came into view. They exited the trolley and climbed the wide steps to the massive double doors. Injago stood there for a moment, taking in the sight of his old home. The solid doors had always made him feel safe and secure at night. It had even been a game to see who could sneak out past Delaini to touch the street and get back without getting caught. This was made all the more difficult due to how damn heavy the doors were.

He glanced over at Romada to see a malevolent glare twisting her features as she stared at the doors. She shivered, and the look was gone, leaving Injago wondering if he had imagined it.

"Are you ready?" he asked.

"As I'll ever be," she answered cryptically, marching up to the doors and pushing one open.

Injago followed her in, shutting the door behind him. A spiral staircase took up the back of the foyer, leading up to the many rooms. A click of heels on the stone floor alerted him to Delaini's presence. A smile already on his lips, he turned to greet her.

Her pert lips held a matching smile, her thin eyebrows arching high under her signature blunt bangs. She wore a dark green pantsuit that hugged her tiny frame, and her eyes darted between him and Romada in recognition.

"My babies!" Delaini said in her high voice, holding her arms open for a hug.

Injago stepped into her embrace, breathing in the familiar scent of her floral perfume. Delaini placed a kiss on his cheek, no doubt leaving a mark of lipstick, and held him at arm's length to look him up and down.

"My, how you've grown! So tall—and so handsome!"

Injago blushed at the compliments. "Hello, Mama. I hope you don't mind us popping in to see you." He replied in Elvish out of respect for Delaini. While she could understand Pixish, she struggled to speak it well.

"Not at all," she said, releasing him and heading for Romada. Opening her arms again for a hug, she stopped when Romada flinched away. Instead, she put her hands on Romada's arms and patted her biceps. "How strong you are now, Romada."

Romada jutted her chin out in what Injago assumed was some sort of trace of her adolescent defiance, but Delaini smiled and stood on tiptoe to kiss her cheek. As soon as Delaini turned back to face Injago, Romada scrubbed at her face, erasing the lipstick mark.

Injago watched her quizzically. Why was she acting so strange? This was their mama, their only parent. She should be showing some sort of love rather than what felt like disgust.

"What brings my babies back to see me?" Delaini asked, stepping past Injago and gesturing for him to follow her to her office.

"We have some questions we hope you can answer," he said, stepping into the room and sitting on the sofa facing Delaini's desk.

Romada crept into the room behind him, but rather than joining him on the sofa, she stood beside the door, crossing her arms and scowling. Her blatant discomfort had him realizing that they had never come back to visit before, despite it being brought up several times in the last century.

Before he could try to figure out why Romada was acting so defensive, Delaini pulled his attention back by asking him what questions they had.

"You've heard of the sirens being taken," he said, resting his ankle on his knee.

Delaini nodded. "Dreadful, those camps. Or so I've heard. But we don't have any here in The City, oh no."

"That's good to hear. But we are looking for someone who is in charge. Someone who would know how to find someone."

"Well, now," Delaini said, tapping a finger to her chin. "I do happen to know the elf in charge of the whole program! His name is Anvargo, and he recently got promoted. He and his wife, lovely folks, adopted a pixie child from here last year. Ares still sends me drawings every few weeks. Such a sweet child."

"The elf's name is Anvargo?" Romada interrupted.

Delaini smiled. "Yes, dear. He lives just down the road."

Finally, they had a lead.

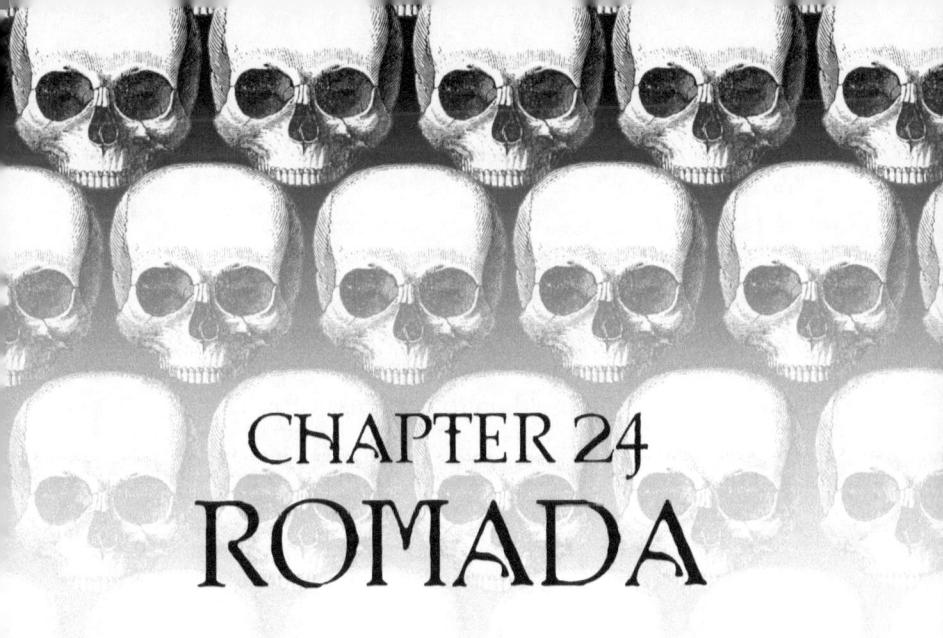

# CHAPTER 24
# ROMADA

**DELAINI SMILED, SHOWING A ROW OF STRAIGHT,** white teeth. Her fangs glinted in the light like unsheathed daggers as she spoke, and Romada struggled to repress a shiver.

*Don't look in the corner.*

But she did anyway. She knew she was imagining the hand-prints of sweat on the walls, spots where she had braced herself as Delaini whipped her with a belt.

*You'll never amount to anything. You're a worthless freak. No one wants you.*

Delaini's words hissed in her ears, a consistent susurrus punctuated by sobs. Romada's sobs.

"Yes, dear. He lives just down the road."

Injago brightened at her words. "You know where he lives?"

The room spun as Romada fought to control her breathing.

*I'm safe. No one can hurt me.*

The rationale was there, but so was the fear.

"He lives in the green building on the corner, top floor. You can't miss it."

*Useless. Worthless. No one will miss you.*

"Thank you, Mama."

*Kiss your Mama goodnight. Mama loves you.*

Romada ground her teeth together, the vein in her forehead threatening to pop. How much longer could she stand in this office, struggling to hold on to her sense of self?

"If I may ask, who are you looking for?"

The question yanked her back into her body.

*Neiara…*

Injago glanced up at her and cleared his throat. "We're looking for Rome's partner."

"Well, I hope you find him."

"Her," Romada snapped.

Injago shot her a look, but she stared at Delaini, daring her to make a move.

Delaini's eyebrow quirked up to the edge of her blunt bangs. "I hope you find her, then."

Letting out a shaky breath, Romada attempted to loosen her fists. Her palms had tiny triangular imprints of her claws embedded in them.

"We hope so, too," Injago said, standing and stretching.

Romada caught Delaini eyeing Injago with a look of rapture and realized that she probably found him attractive. Disgusted, Romada looked at Injago, studying his unruly ebony curls and piercing blue eyes. She knew objectively why fem-fae swooned over him, but seeing *her*—seeing Delaini, his self-proclaimed mama—doing it had her stomach flipping.

Injago walked up to Delaini and pressed a kiss to her forehead. Delaini fluttered her lashes at him. Sickening.

Before she could run out the door, Injago and Delaini had moved past her. Now Romada would be forced to pass Delaini to get free. Gritting her teeth, she made to slip by.

A hand shot out and gripped her arm, squeezing hard enough to bruise. Delaini pulled her close as if to embrace her.

"Don't forget that no one knows you like I do. Your siren partner? Of course you lost her. You have always been worthless and unwanted, my dear. Don't forget that."

Romada shuddered, and Delaini leaned closer to press a sticky kiss to her cheek before releasing her. Stumbling back, Romada whirled to follow Injago, words ringing in her ears.

*Worthless.*

Pushing past Injago, she shoved the front doors open.

*Unwanted.*

Tripping down the steps, she fell to her knees on the sidewalk.

*No one wants you.*

Tears blurred her vision as she convulsed on the cement, bruising her back and scraping her dorsal fin.

"Romada!"

Hands grabbed her and pulled her against a warm body.

*Don't hurt me!*

"I'm not going to hurt you."

Romada blinked up at Injago's sky blue eyes.

"Are you okay?"

"Get off me," she gasped, pushing him away and scrambling to her feet. Her breath came in gusts as she fanned herself. Sweat dripped down her forehead despite the cool breeze that swept down the street.

"You look green," Injago said, worry creasing his forehead. "What's wrong?"

"I'm fine."

He didn't look convinced, but he turned to face the street, giving her the appearance of privacy. Mopping her forehead with the neck of her shirt, Romada took a deep breath and steadied herself.

*I'm safe. No one can hurt me.*

The sky above had started to change colors; streaks of purple and magenta painted what little Romada could see of the horizon between buildings.

"We should go," she said, breaking the silence.

Injago nodded. "What's your plan?"

The green building Delaini had mentioned stood on the far corner of the block. It was one of the taller buildings in the area and looked about eight floors tall, though it was difficult to tell for sure given how each row of windows blended seamlessly with the ones of the next floor up. Sunlight reflected off the shiny glass, and a pair of fancily dressed guards stood at the entrance.

"It's nearly sunset. End of the work day. Anvargo will be heading home. We try and beat him there, hold the wife and kid hostage."

"Right, because he won't volunteer the information willingly."

"Exactly," Romada said, glancing both ways before crossing the street at a brisk pace.

They approached the guards nonchalantly, Romada with a slight smile on her face. Without a word, the guards allowed them inside.

"That was easy," Romada said under her breath. Injago grunted.

A lift was at the far end of a large and lavishly decorated lobby. Romada headed straight for it, dreading what would come next. A rune on the wall beside the closed metal doors glowed blue, and Romada pressed her hand to it, feeling it sap energy from her in order to call the lift.

"I hate lifts," she grumbled as the door opened. Once inside, she pressed the rune for the top floor, again feeling it feed on her. She swayed on her feet; a rush of adrenaline coursed through her from the sudden drop in energy.

Finding Anvargo's home was easy; it appeared to be the entire top floor of the building. When she exited the lift, Injago at her side, she faced a single door with the number 8 on it. She exchanged a look with Injago before knocking on it.

The elven fem-fae who answered was pretty, her bright eyes crinkling as she smiled at them in greeting.

"How can I help you?" Her voice was soft and lilted.

"We're looking for Anvargo. Does he live here?" Romada kept a cheery smile on her face while speaking.

The elf beamed. "He does! He's not home right now, though. Can I take a message?"

Romada glanced at Injago and nodded. Like a blur, he shot forward, pushing past the door and pinning the elf to the wall. She paled and let out a whimper, her eyes wide with fear.

"When will he be home?" Romada barked, getting up in the elf's face.

"I-in about ten minutes. Don't hurt us! I'll g-give you whatever you want!"

"Where's your son?" Injago asked softly as he held her wrists behind her back.

She started weeping. "P-please don't h-hurt him!"

"I won't hurt him," Romada growled, angry at the thought. "We want something from Anvargo, not from you. You just need to help us get it."

The elf bobbed her head, snot streaming from her nose. "O-of course!"

Romada did a quick sweep through the apartment and found Ares in a playroom. Bright blocks were strewn across the floor; his small hands delicately placed a block on top of a tower in front of him.

"Hi," Romada said, kneeling beside him.

He looked up at her, tilting his head to the side. "Who are you?"

"I need to talk to your papa, and to do that, I need to hold you real quick. Is that okay?"

He pondered this for a moment, his brows knitting together, before he nodded.

Romada gathered him into her arms, careful of his gossamer brown wings, and walked out to the family room. As soon as Ares saw Injago and his crying mother, he stiffened.

"Don't worry, we won't hurt you or your mama," Injago said.

Romada carefully pulled out her dagger and held it where Ares could see it. He eyed it but didn't move to touch it.

"I need to hold this where your papa can see it, okay? I won't hurt you."

Ares looked up at her and nodded, relaxing a bit in her arms.

"Okay. Anvargo will be home soon, yes?" Romada directed the question at the elf.

She nodded, lips quivering and tears shining on her cheeks. At that moment, the lock on the front door clicked and opened. An elf appeared before them, dressed in a tailored suit and holding a leather satchel. He wore a grin that vanished once he stepped inside.

"Kalar! Ares!" His voice shook, and he dropped the satchel. "Who are you? What do you want?"

"Easy now." Romada brandished the dagger. "Shut the door behind you. We just want some information."

Anvargo backed up, pushing the door shut with his hip while holding his hands in the air. "Anything! Don't hurt them!"

Kalar resumed her sobbing.

"We need to see a list of sirens who have been captured and what camps they've gone to."

His throat moved up and down as he swallowed, and he stammered, "But there isn't a list! I have a list of the camps, nothing more."

Romada stared at him in furious disbelief. They were rounding up sirens, tearing them from their homes and families and friends, and they didn't even know their names. Her blood boiled in her veins, and the hand holding the dagger started shaking. Anvargo must have noticed because he winced and held his hands up higher.

"I can give you the list of camps," he said slowly.

"Then give it!" Romada screamed. The dagger wobbled again, and Ares began trembling against her. She took a long, unsteady breath and asked in a calmer tone, "Where is the list?"

Anvargo pointed at the satchel.

Romada gestured to the satchel with the tip of the dagger. "Ares, go get the satchel—the bag, and bring it to me." She loosened her hold of him, letting him drop to the floor.

Ares crawled to the satchel and grabbed it. Standing, he looked from his papa to Romada, a question warring in his eyes. Anvargo smiled at his son.

"Go, give it to her."

Ares nodded and handed it to Romada before going back to stand beside his papa, his tiny hand reaching for Anvargo's. Anvargo pulled his son to his chest, though his eyes never left Romada.

"Walk over here, slowly, and back up all the way into the corner." Anvargo nodded and did as she said, his head bowed and eyes downcast. "We're going to leave now. Don't follow us." Romada's grip tightened on the smooth leather strap of the satchel as she motioned for Injago to move to the exit.

Anvargo stood still, holding Ares, as Kalar's crying continued. Injago dragged Kalar with him as he walked backward toward the front door, and Romada followed, wielding the dagger like a threat.

Injago took Kalar all the way to the lift, instructing her to press the rune. She obeyed with a shaking hand, and once the lift opened, he released her.

"Sorry," he said, pushing her back toward her home.

"Just get out!" she choked.

Romada and Injago rushed into the lift, and Injago slammed a finger against the rune for the ground floor.

"Out!" Kalar shrieked right before the lift doors slid shut.

"They'll have alerted the guards," Romada murmured, sheathing her dagger.

True enough, when the lift doors opened, the two guards from the front entrance stood waiting. Romada swung the briefcase at the head of one while Injago sucker-punched the other. The one Romada hit crumpled to the floor while Injago's guard howled in agony as they dashed past and out the front door.

Romada stood stock still for a moment, trying to get her bearings in the near dark of dusk.

"This way!" Injago shouted, and she took off after him.

"Halt!"

Romada looked over her shoulder and saw a guard running after them.

"Give me the satchel," Injago said, holding out his hands.

Romada hesitated for a moment before throwing it to him. Injago caught it and flung himself into the air, spreading his wings and flying in between the buildings and out of sight.

A quick glance behind herself showed the guard still hot on her trail, so she doubled her efforts and sprinted down the street, leaping out of the way of a trolley coming around the corner.

A crash and exclamations sounded behind her, letting her know the guard hadn't been so lucky. Grinning, heart pounding, she kept up her pace, heading for the ship.

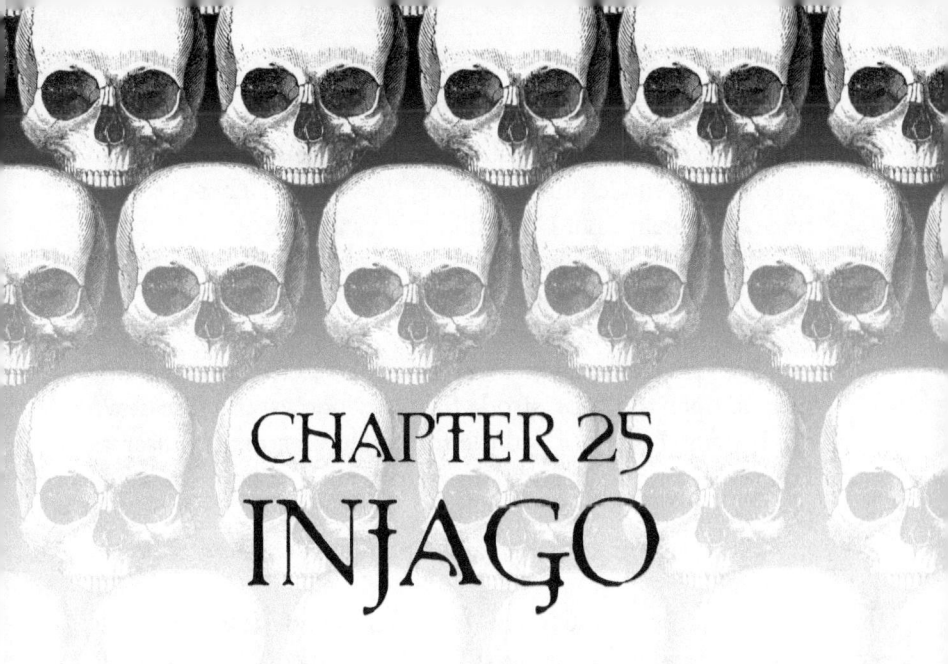

# CHAPTER 25
# INJAGO

**INJAGO LANDED ON THE QUAY AS HIS WINGS** gave out and stumbled forward as his legs tried to maintain his momentum. The ship was within reach, and he hadn't seen any guards trailing him. Once onboard, he turned, panting, to watch for Romada. Hopefully, she hadn't been caught.

A blur appeared at the entrance to the quay, all blue skin and brown leather. Had she run the whole way? Injago was tired from the long flight, but he couldn't imagine how exhausted she was from running through the streets.

Romada trudged up the plank, dragging her feet and gasping for breath. Her gills quivered as though trying to help her breathe, and her fins hung limp in fatigue.

"We...should get...underway," she wheezed, bending over with hands on her thighs. Every part of her trembled.

Ceta stepped over and eyed Romada as though wary of an attack. "Not everyone is back from shore time yet," she said, hands on her hips.

Romada straightened and gritted her teeth before taking a deep breath and letting out a long, slow exhale. There wasn't a trace of hostility, but Ceta still took a step back.

"Then let's make sure the ship is as ready as it can be for them when they get back," Romada said calmly.

Ceta nodded and hurried away.

"Let's check the satchel." Romada turned for the cabin. She pushed open the door, strode for the windows, and tore down the blanket. Light flooded the room, illuminating the disarray. Injago choked on the stench of rotting food and unwashed clothes.

"Gods, it stinks," she said, opening a window to let in fresh air.

Injago turned the satchel over in his hands. It was made of smooth, rigidly-formed leather, with a rune lock on its large clasp. He tried opening it with no luck.

"It's locked."

"Give it here," Romada said.

Injago handed it over and watched as she studied the lock for a moment before drawing her dagger. Hilt down, she slammed it onto the clasp. When the metal cracked, she used the dagger tip to pry it open.

"There!" she said triumphantly.

Inside was a mess of papers; Anvargo didn't appear to be the sort to organize anything. Injago couldn't help wondering why he had been put in charge of such an important program.

"Help me look," she said, grabbing half of the papers and shoving them at him.

Injago leafed through the papers slowly, looking for anything that might deal with the camps. He found several requisition forms for various camps but no names or locations. Sighing, he shifted through the last few sheets.

"Here!" Romada held a single page aloft. Haphazardly clearing a space on the desk, she smoothed it out on the surface.

"Five camps," Injago said, reading the list over a stack of dishes. "The nearest one is at Cape Guaraneau."

"We should go to the one out past Tilt Town." Romada stabbed her finger at the list.

Injago shook his head. "That would mean going back past the island and the naval base."

Romada's body tensed. "Neiara was taken in Tilt Town, though. She could be at that base."

"What's the harm in going to the closest one? Best case scenario, Neiara is there. We honestly don't know where they are taking the sirens that they find anyway. We don't know how it's organized. Worst case, Neiara isn't there, but we rescue a bunch of other sirens."

Injago knew he was being rational, but Romada might not listen to reason. He watched as emotions warred on her face, her fists clenched and her head fin rigid.

She stared hard at the page. What looked like a tear in her eye glistened, but she rubbed her eyes and sighed before he could know for sure.

"Okay, fine. We'll go to Cape Guaraneau."

Injago let out a pent-up breath. "I'll chart a course with Ceta."

Romada made a vague sound of agreement but didn't move. As he pulled the door shut, he heard a sniffle. She was probably going to cry again. It seemed like that's all she did since they had lost Neiara, since she no longer ate, socialized, or bathed.

He headed up to the helm, running into Ceta on the way. "Grab the map?" he asked, and she nodded as she continued on her way.

Up at the helm, he had the perfect vantage point to watch the bustling faeries on the quay. The gaslamps along the streets gave everyone immense shadows. He spotted a flash of bright purple wings and wondered which pixie aristo-fae House they belonged to.

Back at the Orphan Center, the pixie children had all dreamed of being adopted by an aristo-fae from some far-off land and going to live a life of luxury. In his entire time there, about 97 years, it had never happened. Which made sense since they lived in an elven kingdom. What foreign pixie would come to the capital of an elven kingdom to adopt a random common-fae child?

The drab grey of his wings marked him as a common-fae. He got them from his birth mother, who he couldn't remember. She had died when he was still in infancy, and he had never known a father. What he had known was the love of his mama, Delaini. It bothered him that Romada had been so rude to her during their visit.

It seemed so out of character for her. Romada was never hostile to faeries unless they had wronged her in some way. When had Delaini ever—

"You lost?" Ceta asked as she walked up to him, holding the map in her hands.

"Lost in thought," he answered, moving bottles around on the table so she could lay the map down.

"Where are we heading?" She smoothed out the edge of the map, putting bottles along the edge to hold it down.

"Cape Guaraneau." Looking at the map, he could see they had a straight shot to the cape once they got out of the harbor.

"It'll be faster to head straight there rather than follow the coast," Ceta said, making a line along the map with her finger.

"Find me a bearing."

She pulled out a compass and lined it up with the map. "There." After using chalk to mark the line, she handed it over, her fingers brushing his.

"Thanks."

"Any time," Ceta said, blushing and looking back at the map. Her chocolate brown hair fell in front of her face, hiding her red cheeks.

Injago huffed. When would she get over her crush?

"I'm gay, Ceta," he said dryly.

"I know that!" she snapped.

Injago pursed his lips and said nothing.

A pair of pixies came aboard, laughing raucously, and Ceta said, "That's the last of them."

"Let's get going then," Injago said. "Alright, boyos! Let's get this ship moving! Loose the ropes! Weigh anchor! Free the sheets!"

The crew scrambled to and fro, half of them flying to the quay to release the mooring lines and the others working on the anchor and the sails. Ceta stayed by Injago's side, rolling up the map and securing it in the rigid leather holding tube.

He looked out over the dark harbor. The light from the skyline of The City reflected on the black water. A thin sliver of moon glowed in the sky, and Injago wondered if, wherever she was, Neiara could see the moon too.

A thought hit him, and he chuckled. They were going to be heroes after all, rescuing the sirens just like Neiara had wanted.

"What's so funny?" Ceta asked.

"Thinking about how we're going to be heroes."

She snorted. "Who would have thought?"

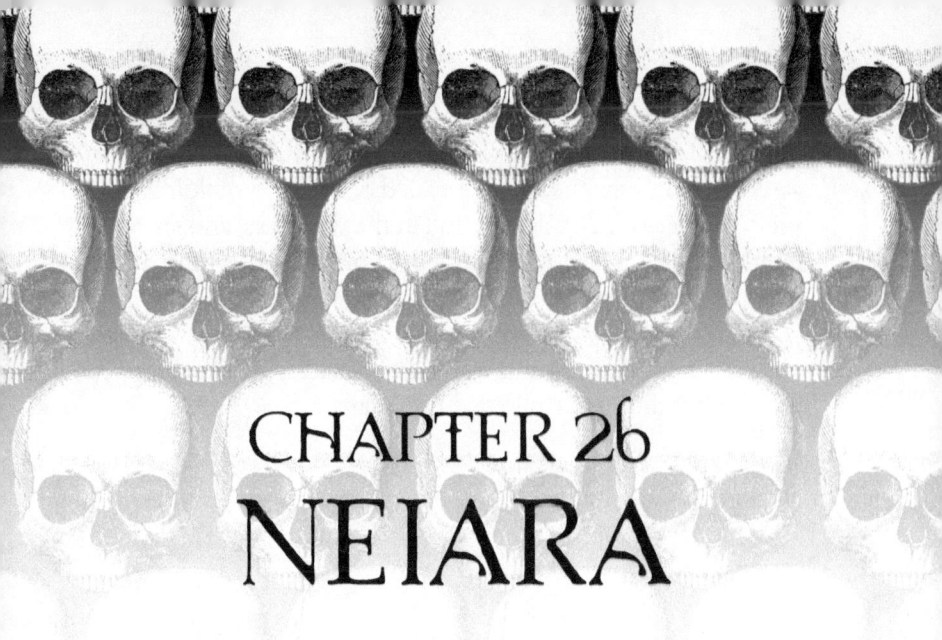

# CHAPTER 26
# NEIARA

**ROMADA WILL SAVE ME. ROMADA WILL SAVE ME.**
*Romada will save me.*

She couldn't remember the last time she had eaten, and yet she kept shitting herself. Her piss, what little of it there was, was dark and rank. Her eyes had trouble focusing on the shifting forms of sirens around her in the dark tent.

*Romada will save me. Romada will save me. Romada will save me.*

For some reason, the guards were moving her to a new location. Neiara sat on the ground patiently as the elven guard before her turned the key in the lock keeping her chained to the long line of sirens. Once he got her chain free, he hauled her to her feet and led her outside.

*Romada will save me. Romada will save me. Romada will save me.*

The fresh air caressed her face, and she gasped, breathing deeply. The night sky glowed with the feeble light of a crescent moon, and she gazed up at her goddess, silently praying for salvation.

*Romada will save me. Romada will save me. Romada will save me.*

Ahead of her, the guard headed for a lone building. The brick-and-mortar façade was dull in the darkness, and she wondered why the guard had decided to move her. Would a new torment await her? Or maybe food and water?

*Romada will save me. Romada will save me. Romada will save me.*

With aching joints and trembling muscles, Neiara stepped into the building and followed the guard.

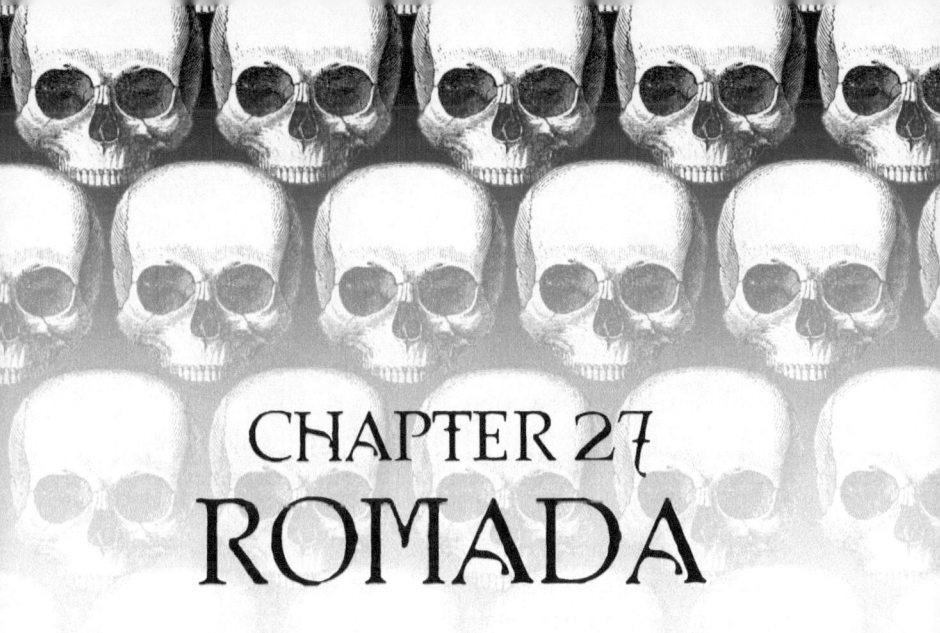

# CHAPTER 27
# ROMADA

**IT TOOK TWO LONG, EMPTY DAYS, BUT ROMADA**
finally heard the call that Cape Guaraneau was in sight. She
huddled under the covers, shaking violently as though from a
fever. The thought of finding Neiara—or worse, not finding
her—left her paralyzed with fear.

Someone knocked on the door again. The knocking, always
the knocking. Eventually, they went away; she just had to ignore
them long enough.

"Romada, please let me in," Injago said, his voice muffled
by the door.

"Go away," she croaked.

"We need to make a plan of attack."

Romada sighed in defeat. He was right, though she didn't
have to like it. Gathering the blanket around her, she stood
and shuffled to the door. She unlocked it and pulled it open
just wide enough for Injago to slip in before shutting it behind him.

157

"Thank you," he said, turning and taking in the state of her room, his gaze lingering on all of the dishes still stacked on her desk.

She hadn't left her room to take the dishes back to the galley, but then again, she hadn't been eating either, so it wasn't like the stacks were growing.

"What's the plan?" Romada asked, holding the blanket around herself and shivering.

"Well, all of us can fight. But I think we should leave some faeries behind in case we need to make a quick getaway."

She nodded.

"So, I say we take a team of ten and head to the camp. It's the newest camp, so it's not as well-established as the others yet. We may even surprise them."

Romada doubted that, but what was there to lose? Life without Neiara was quickly becoming meaningless, and every breath without her was a dying gasp of futility.

"Is that okay?" Injago asked, pulling Romada from the beginning of yet another depressing thought spiral.

"Oh, yeah, good," she stammered.

He looked relieved. "Great. And you know," he said, looking around, "if you keep hoarding dishes like this, Yaya is going to come up here and fight you for them."

Romada forced out a laugh, the harsh sound echoing in the stillness of the cabin. "That's so funny," she said, wincing at the tone in her own voice. "Okay, I'll see you out there."

Injago stared at her for a long moment before turning and leaving her in peace.

Alone again, she hugged herself tighter, wishing it was Neiara's arms around her instead of her own and the blanket. How long would Romada be tortured without Neiara's presence? Would they find her in the camp? Or was this just the beginning of a mad quest destined to end in tragedy and disappointment?

Romada dropped the blanket to the floor, grabbed her weapon's belt, and left the cabin.

\*\*\*

Walking through the town of Cape Guaraneau went by in a blur as Romada struggled to keep up with her crew. Perhaps starving herself for the last several days hadn't been the best idea, but hindsight was always clearer.

The group found the camp itself out past the town limits, nestled in the beginning of the forest. The dying sun's rays attempted to filter through the leafy canopy and failed, leaving them in relative darkness. They crept along on the cushioned ground, the dense undergrowth crowding the path. Ahead, Romada saw steel gates and a small guardhouse. No one was in sight.

"Plan?" Injago asked in a whisper.

Romada pointed at him and herself, then at the guardhouse. He nodded, drawing his sword and dagger. The two of them crept up past the guardhouse to the towering barbed wire-topped fence encircling the camp and flanked the guardhouse. Creeping up to the door, Injago nodded for Romada to take point.

Yanking open the door, Romada stormed the guardhouse with Injago on her heels. She slashed the throat of one of the two guards inside; blood gurgled from the wound, splashing her and Injago. Blood pounding and vision blurring, Romada spun to face the other guard in time to see her throw her weapon to the floor and her hands in the air.

"I surrender!"

Romada held the tip of her sword to the hollow on the center of the guard's collarbone. "What do you think, quartermaster?"

Injago stood in the doorway, his sword lazily pointed at the guard's gut. "What's another dead elf?" he drawled.

"I'm part siren. I can help you." The guard's voice was strong yet quiet, as though she didn't want to alert the rest of the camp.

Romada shifted on her feet. "Why should we believe you?"

"My cousin is in this camp. I sneak him food when I can. If you're attacking the camp, I want to be part of it."

It seemed too good to be true, but was it smart to turn down any offered help? "Search her," Romada said, taking a step back but keeping her sword trained on the guard's neck. If she proved false, she wouldn't live long enough to regret the deception.

Injago sheathed his sword and stepped up to the guard, kicking her sword away. His pat down revealed a dagger in her ankle sheath, which he snagged. Seemingly satisfied, he returned to Romada's side and shrugged.

"Can't hurt to have someone unlock the gate for us," he said in a low voice.

Romada admired the guard's courage and resolve in the face of the attack. No tears fell from her steely eyes; no quiver of her lip nor her hands could be seen. She was either a very good actor, or she really did care for someone in the camp. There was only one way to find out.

"I agree. Open the gate, and we'll see what happens," Romada said, gesturing with her sword for the guard to move.

Outside, Romada signaled to the rest of the party to advance to the gate while the guard pulled a ring of keys from her belt and examined them. Selecting one, she inserted it into the massive lock, twisting it and pulling open the gate.

Another guard popped up in the opening and snapped, "It's not shift change yet! Use the bushes."

The turncoat guard punched him in the nose, and he stumbled back, howling in pain.

"Now!"

Romada surged forward as the party rushed the gate. Someone stabbed the howling guard in the gut, and he fell on their blade, sliding to the ground in the throes of death. A third guard came running at the sound and engaged with Injago, who made quick work of her; she died without a sound.

The part-siren guard gave a tiny cheer as Romada took in the surroundings. A line of long tents took up most of the camp, with a building—the only building—off to the right and a rickety outhouse off to the far left.

"This way," the part-siren guard said, leading the group of

pirates to the building. "These are the barracks. I'm Falia, by the way."

"Nice to meet you, Falia," Injago said.

"Hush." Romada glared at them, and they both fell silent. She pushed in the barracks' front door and entered, her footfalls inaudible on the plush carpeting. The main room was vacant; it looked like a galley, with a kitchen off to the side and a bar counter with stools in the center. A small table with a deck of cards was off to the side; it was a cozy little eating and socializing space. Romada wondered if the sirens had anything similar but knew the answer was no.

A guard came waltzing out of a hallway and stopped in her tracks at the sight of the pirates. Romada leapt forward and slashed at her throat before she could speak. The guard's eyes opened wide as she died, slumping to the floor in a bath of her own blood.

"Rooms are through that hall, with the training room at the end," Falia said in a whisper.

"What's over there?" Romada pointed with her sword to the opposite hallway.

"That's the way to the healer's clinic, but we only have one healer, and he's always asleep by now. No one should be there."

"Okay. You and you, go check it out," Romada said, pointing to Yaya and Eetan. "The rest, with me."

The group crept down the hallway, stopping at each door and searching the rooms. Romada couldn't help but notice the comforts the guards had—two beds per room, two rooms per bathroom. Compared to her own stateroom, and by extension Neiara's, it was a tad cramped. Compared to the bunks of the rest of the crew, though? It looked comfortable and spacious. Romada couldn't help wondering how many beds the sirens had in their tents. Did they have blankets to keep warm? Neiara was a blanket hoarder, always burying herself under piles of furs and quilts. How would she fare with only one blanket? Or did she have to share with others? How many bathrooms did the sirens have at their disposal? Did they get to brush their teeth? Take baths? Was Neiara allowed to properly care for her hair? Those soft, luscious curls required a strict daily regimen even the most dedicated soldier would find daunting. And there was no chance that Neiara had access to her favorite curl cream, the one that smelled of citrus. The scent was so synonymous in Romada's mind with Neiara that she couldn't eat or even look at an orange without feeling a deep ache of emptiness in her heart.

*Where are you, deshani?*

They found several guards in their rooms and killed each one without a fuss. Romada's heartbeat sped up uncomfortably as they reached the end of the hall without having raised an alarm. The last room was the training room; she could hear dull thuds and grunts coming from past the door and could only assume the rest of the guards were inside, sparring with each other.

Injago broke down the door, and the pirates poured into the room; ten guards turned to face them with incredulous expressions. Without hesitation, three of the guards turned on the others, grappling them to the floor. The pirates had an easy time eliminating the seven guards who fought back.

Romada stood on shaking legs as she realized they had done it; the camp was theirs. Surely it couldn't be this easy? What laughable security. Blood dripped down the length of her sword, staining the wood floor, though the droplets were insignificant compared to the growing puddles beneath the dead guards.

The remaining guards huddled together. Romada suspected they were all part siren if they had turned on the elves. After a long moment, Falia broke away from the other guards and came toward Romada.

"Thank you for liberating the camp. We all have family here. It's why we each volunteered for this camp specifically. So it really means a lot to us that you came here. We're ready to follow your orders."

"I take it you're in charge now?" Romada asked, wiping her blade on the uniform of a dead guard before sheathing it.

"The rest of them picked me to lead them, though I defer to you."

"No need, Falia. We aren't going to be staying long. I'm here looking for someone."

Falia nodded. "And we can help you look."

A thought struck Romada. "Would you and the others be able to keep up pretenses that this is still an operational camp?"

"We thought of that too. The latest shipment of sirens arrived yesterday, and it should be a week before the next. By then, we should be able to have some of the sirens acting as guards, and we can set traps for any elves who suspect us."

"Perfect," Romada said. She clapped once, unable to help herself. Giddiness—or maybe panic?—lent energy to her step at the thought of seeing Neiara. "Let's go free the sirens!" She ignored the anxious quiver in her voice and hoped the others would as well.

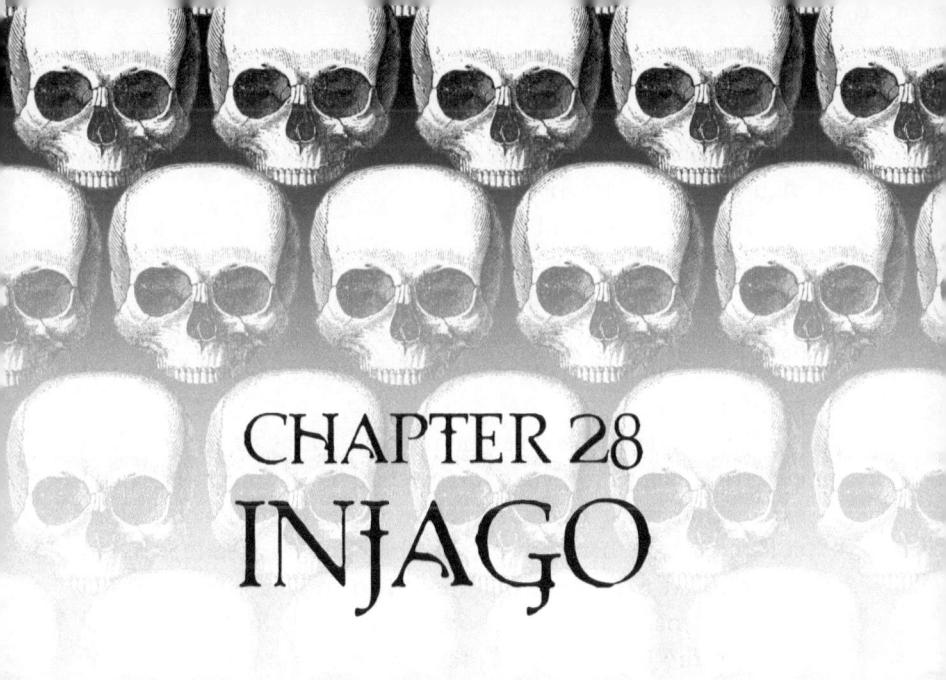

# CHAPTER 28
# INJAGO

**INJAGO WATCHED AS ROMADA SNAGGED A KEY** ring off a dead guard and marched off back down the hallway, a slight skip in her step. It almost looked like she had a shade of a smile on her lips. Injago followed her out of the building and toward the closest tent. The closer they got, the more the stench of urine and feces pervaded the air.

Romada grasped the tent flap and flung it open; the smell assaulted Injago, and he gagged. There was no light in the tent, so he backtracked to grab a lantern from the steps of the barracks and brought it to her.

Rather than taking it, she stood stock still, a mask of horror on her face, before abruptly turning and vomiting beside the tent. Her fins flinched as she retched, over and over again, bright yellow bile soaking the ground.

Injago stepped forward to look inside the tent and froze. Rows upon rows of cots lined the tent. On each cot, a barely

165

clothed siren lay still, matching collars around their necks and manacles on their wrists.

They were all children.

Row upon row of children stared at him out of the darkness, their eyes pinpricks of reflected light. Some were as young as teens—babies!—and all of them were bound to their cots, unable to touch each other, unable to offer each other physical comfort.

It was quiet. Too quiet, he realized. None of the children even so much as whispered. One child lay in a heap. It looked as though her throat had somehow been crushed by her cloth collar, a collar that each of the children was wearing. Blood had trickled from her open mouth to form a puddle on her cot. How many other such bodies would they find in the tents? He shut the flap, his mind grasping for reason in the face of this abject horror.

Romada continued dry heaving, her hands on her knees. "Why...didn't anyone...do anything?" she asked between gags

Falia shifted on her feet, her mouth contorted into a grimace. "We couldn't do anything. If we had, they would have locked us up too."

"That's unacceptable!" Romada straightened, a smear of slime on her lips. "I can't believe that, that we, we're pirates! Pirates are the first faeries to do something? Where are the good guys?" She wiped her mouth and glared at the siren guards in disgust.

"Rome, what matters is that we are here now." Injago held out a hand to her, as much offering as seeking comfort. "We are doing something."

"Shut up!" She grabbed the lantern from him and stomped off to the far end of the camp. Reaching the last tent, she peeked inside and, looking relieved, she went in.

"We need to start preparations for when they're all freed," Injago said. Facing the crew, he pointed at Yaya. "Go start cooking for everyone. Gods know when they last ate. Take whoever you need to help you."

Injago turned to Falia, who squared off her shoulders and lifted her chin.

"Send some of your guards to take care of the bodies in the barracks. We don't want the children to see that. Also, we should split up to free more of them at the same time."

Injago faced the rest of his crew. "Go back out to the guardhouse. Keep a watch on the path. We don't need any surprise visitors."

Everyone moved off to complete their assigned tasks. Injago took a deep breath to steady his nerves and realized Romada had taken the only lantern.

"Falia!" he called, and she turned back to face him from the barracks steps. "Do we have more lanterns? And keys?"

She nodded and loped off, returning with a lantern in each hand and two sets of keys. She handed one of each to him with a soft smile. "Need anything else?"

"Actually," he said, gesturing toward the tent full of siren children, "I was hoping you could answer a question for me."

Her smile slipped as she sighed. "The collars."

Injago nodded.

"They... I don't know what makes them work. Some sort of energy siphon. If they engage their vocal cords, the collar activates. It...tightens. They can't speak without—"

"Without having their throats crushed." Injago felt his stomach lurch. The child with the mangled throat must have been crying. Crying for help? For comfort? Did it matter? She died for it, gasping for air. Died for the audacity of using her voice.

Falia's lip trembled. "Exactly." Dropping her gaze to the ground, she turned and headed for a tent farther down the line.

Taking one more breath of relatively clean air, Injago reopened the tent flap and stepped inside. Some of the children had sat up, and they were staring at him. He walked over to the closest child and knelt down to examine her wrists. They were raw and pustulous; dried blood crusted her wounds. She flinched when he reached for her.

"I'm here to help you," he said in as soothing a voice as he could muster. "I'm not going to hurt you." When her brow wrinkled, still holding herself away from him, he realized he had defaulted to speaking Pixish. When he repeated himself in Elvish she relaxed enough for him to take hold of her manacles. As gently as possible, he inserted the key into the lock and twisted; the cuffs fell open with a clunk, and the child held up her hands, looking at them with wonder in her large brown eyes.

A smile split her dry lips as she looked up at Injago, and he saw that her two front teeth were missing. His heart melted a bit as he smiled back.

"Want to hold the lantern for me so I can see?" he asked, sticking to Elvish.

She held out her hands and grasped the lantern, holding it in her lap.

Injago moved across the aisle to the next child, an adorable young boyo with jet black hair and shockingly pale eyes. He held up his hands, manacles clinking, for Injago to unlock and gave a wide smile when they opened and fell to the floor.

One at a time, child by child, Injago unlocked the manacles, their jangling echoing in the unnatural silence of the tent. He wasn't sure how he was supposed to get the collars off; there didn't seem to be any sort of lock, only a flat clasp at the back that didn't have any visible way of opening.

Finally, after what felt like an hour, he had released all of the children. They had naturally formed small groups, hugging and holding hands. Smiles adorned their faces as they watched him move through the tent.

Injago cleared his throat, startled by the loudness. "We're going to have food ready for everyone soon in the barracks. You can follow me."

He turned and exited the tent, the crowd of children trailing behind him. The night air felt cool on his skin, and he took a deep breath, cleansing his lungs of the foul odor of the tent.

They entered the barracks building, the children filling the main room. Some sat on chairs and stools, bouncing in their seats.

Yaya and another pixie—Eegan? Eekan? Injago needed to remember to ask his name—were busy in the kitchen, cooking up a modest feast. The smell of cooking meat and baking bread flooded the space, and several of the children had growling stomachs. He would have to make sure none of them ate too quickly. The last thing any of them needed was falling ill from eating too much food on a starving stomach.

It was still too quiet.

Romada came in and stood beside him, looking at the children. "Is this all of them?"

"All of the children? I think so." He didn't mention the bodies still in the tent, their throats crushed by the strangling collars, the children who had died choking on silent screams. "What about the other tents? Is everyone free?"

"Not yet. How do we get the collars off?" she asked.

Injago shrugged.

"I've got it!" Falia came into the room, brandishing a large glowing blue stone in her palm. She walked up to the nearest child and held the stone up to the clasp on the back of their collar; the stone glowed red for a second, and then the collar came apart, falling to the floor.

The silence was broken as the child let out a peal of delighted laughter. Falia smiled at them and moved to the next child. In a matter of moments, the room echoed with giggles as child after child took their first opportunity to make noise and decided to laugh.

Injago but his lip, intoxicating laughter bubbling in his chest even as tears blurred his vision. His heart swelled with emotion, and he looked over at Romada. Her wide blue eyes shone, and her lip quivered.

"You did this," Injago whispered.

"Excuse me," she said, backing up.

He watched as she fled the building.

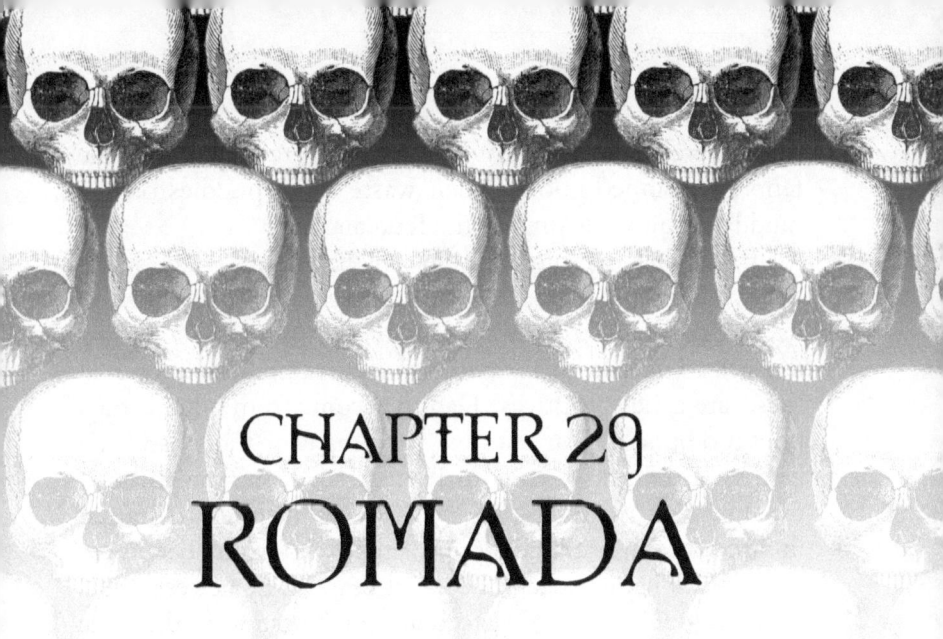

# CHAPTER 29
# ROMADA

**SIREN AFTER SIREN. LOCK AFTER LOCK. UN-**
trusting eyes met Romada's, wary of her potential to be a threat. Speaking Elvish in as soothing a voice as she could muster, she asked her hopeful questions.

"Have you seen a siren named Neiara?"

Vacant stare.

On to the next siren.

"Neiara? She's got dark skin and freckles, really short, curly black hair?"

Vacant stare.

On to the next siren.

"A siren named Neiara? She's got green eyes, like, really green."

Vacant stare.

On to the next siren.

Romada stood and stretched her taut back muscles in the stifling heat of the befouled tent. Unlike the children, the adult sirens weren't allotted a cot and instead were packed into the tents like canned goods. Their waste lay in puddles on the muddy ground, stinking up the fetid air.

It was only the third tent. She still had time to find Neiara. She would find Neiara. She had to. Every siren she spoke to had a dead look in their eyes, as though they had long lost the will to live. If this was the newest camp, how long had these sirens been captives? Had they come from other camps, ones too bursting at the seams? How many of them had been held for as long as Neiara? As Romada made her way through the throng of prisoners, freeing them one by one, she started finding faces that still held hope, sirens who hadn't been here as long and hadn't succumbed to defeat. These newest sirens were the ones she needed to question. These were the ones who would have seen Neiara.

"Were any of you taken from Tilt Town?"

Only head shakes. Siren by siren, she made her way through the tent, slowly losing her hope.

After several hours, she found a siren who had come to the camp only the day before. By then, someone had given Romada a blue lock stone for the collars, so she was able to free both their wrists and voices as she went. The newest siren gave a whoop of joy as Romada released her collar.

"Thank you so much! Oh gods, that was rough. I mean, I've only been here one day, but it was the *worst* day of my life, you know? I haven't eaten all day! I peed myself! And seriously, going that long without talking? Talk about torture!" She laughed, throwing back her head and slapping her knee.

Overwhelmed by the siren's enthusiasm, Romada gave her what she hoped was a smile before asking her about Neiara.

"I don't think I saw anyone like that on my ship. I would have remembered. Green is my favorite color, and I *always* notice green eyes. No green on my ship!"

Romada's face fell, and the siren looked abashed.

"I'm, um, I'm so, so sorry," she mumbled.

Romada turned, intending to free the next siren. As she took the first step, her legs gave out, and she fell to her knees, a sob wrenching from her chest. Filth coated her pants as she stared at the murky ground, throat convulsing and tears stinging her eyes.

"Hey, it's going to be okay! You'll find her."

The talkative siren got down on her knees with Romada and spread her arms as though to hug her; Romada flinched away, and the siren altered her movement to pat Romada on the back instead.

"I can't do this," Romada choked out.

"Yeah, I totally understand that. Here, let's give the keys to someone else, and they can keep going, yeah? Let's get you some fresh air."

The siren helped her to her feet, tossing the keys to someone, and helped Romada walk back to the tent entrance.

As soon as the cool night air hit her face, Romada took a deep breath, trying to cleanse her lungs. The stench of the adult tents was nothing compared to the children's tent—more body odor and urine than anything else—but it was still sickening.

"Anyway, I'm so positive you'll find Neiara. I'm Milla, by the way. So nice to meet you! And, like, you're not gonna stop just because she's not here, right? You're gonna keep going, and you're gonna find her." Milla babbled like a brook as Romada stood outside the tent, gulping for air like a fish out of water.

"I'd like to help you," said a dainty and mellifluous voice speaking fluent Pixish from behind Romada.

She turned to see a short, fat faerie with dimples in her cheeks; dark wavy hair complemented her golden brown skin. Who was this tiny fem-fae, and how could she help Romada?

"Uh, and you are?" Romada asked, also in Pixish.

"I'm Rehka," she said, smiling. "My twin brother and I were separated when they captured us, and I heard you're going to search the other camps. I'd love to tag along and help."

"Okay..." Romada paused, trying to find a way to let her down gently. "It's just, on a ship, it's very fast-paced and-"

"Oh, I'm a super quick learner," Rehka said, bouncing on the balls of her feet. "Also, you should know this." She turned and pulled at her shirt collar, revealing a smooth spine.

Romada bristled. How had they missed an elf?

"My brother and I had the spine flattening procedure decades ago, but our neighbors knew we were sirens and turned us in."

"How do I know you're really a siren?" Romada asked, eyeing Rehka with suspicion.

Rehka said a few words in a sing-song voice. Romada could recognize that the words were imbued with siren magic, but had no clue what they meant. Then, Romada's hand, of its own accord, rose in the air. She stared at it helplessly for a second before slapping herself across the face. She glowered at Rehka, rubbing the sting in her cheek.

"Do you believe me?"

"Yes," Romada grumbled. And then she really thought about it. Without Neiara's nightly singing sessions, the crew would have undoubtedly lost some morale. Not that she had taken the time to notice or check in on anyone... Having some entertainment onboard again could only help things.

Rehka stood before her, still smiling.

"Can you sing?" Romada asked.

"Without enchanting? Sure! I used to be in a choir."

"Perfect. You're hired," Romada said, holding out her hand.

Rehka took it and squealed, shaking Romada's hand up and down. "You won't regret this!" she said before bounding back toward the barracks building.

"Well, looks like I have a new crew member," Romada said in Elvish, turning back to Milla.

She had a slight, knowing smile on the corner of her lips. "And, maybe, a new friend."

Romada left her, feeling discomfited. She didn't want or need a new friend. Injago and Yaya were enough for her, always had been. Though, could she still call Injago a friend if she kept hating him? And Yaya wasn't too happy with her either, it seemed.

She sighed. When Neiara got back, everything would be fine again, back to the way it was before. Before she lost the comfort of her life partner. Maybe she could even forgive Injago for what he had done that night when he had abandoned Neiara to this fate. Romada's head fin twitched, and she gnashed her teeth together. Then again, maybe not.

Romada entered the barracks to find a gaggle of children eating and laughing and playing. It was mayhem but a joyous mayhem. She found her lips quirking up into a smile. Almost.

Injago turned, noticed her, and yelled, "There she is! The hero of Cape Guaraneau camp!"

A cheer went up, and the prickling of her neck and cheeks told her she had turned a bright shade of purple. She hadn't done any of this for praise or recognition. She wasn't a hero. She hadn't even wanted to come to this camp; it was Injago's idea. Children began to swarm around her, reaching their little hands and arms out to hug her arms and legs. One little lass grasped her hand, and Romada looked down into a pair of shockingly green eyes. Her breath left her, and her heart felt like it had torn in two.

The lass didn't look anything like Neiara apart from the eyes—her short hair was straight and red, and her skin was moon pale—but Romada broke apart from the group of children and fled outside, eyes burning and chest heaving. This wasn't how this was supposed to go. This wasn't what she had anticipated. How could not finding Neiara exist in the same space as saving and rescuing these children? How was she supposed to find joy or even contentment in this victory when Neiara wasn't here to see it? She rested against the outer wall and gulped fresh air, trying to calm herself. This didn't feel like a victory at all. It felt like she was drowning again, still stuck under the ship, flailing and praying for help. She swiped at the tears in her eyes as she heard the door creak open and someone step out.

"Are you okay?" Rehka asked in a hushed voice, concern written on her cherubic face.

"I'm fine," Romada grunted, wiping her hands on her pants. "If anyone asks, I'm heading back to the ship."

Not waiting for an answer, she set off, leaving the camp behind her.

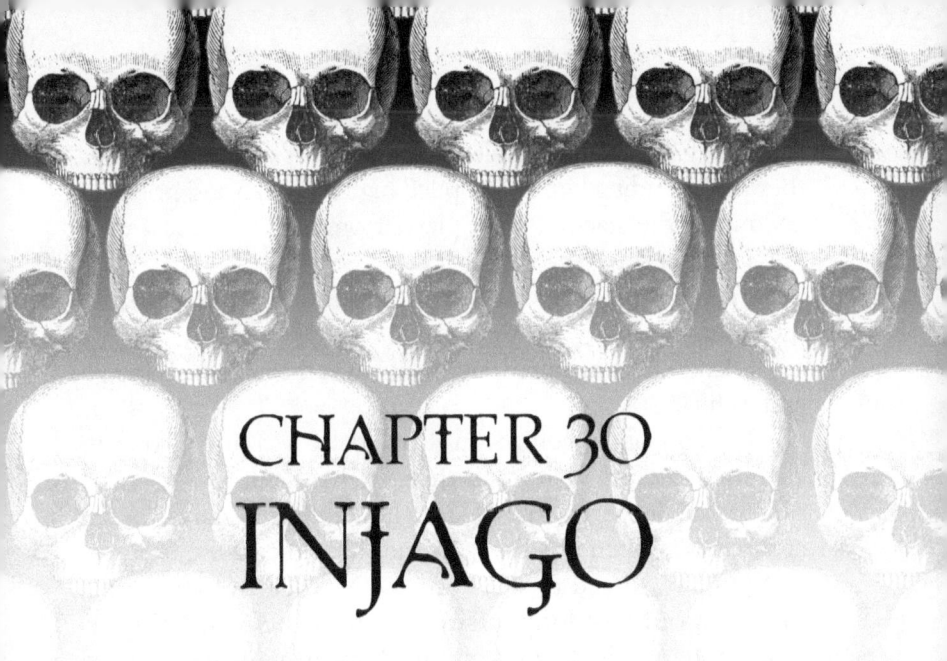

# CHAPTER 30
# INJAGO

**INJAGO TOOK A BITE OF POTATOES SOAKED IN**
egg yolk and tried not to laugh as Yaya told stories to Rehka.
The siren had wasted no time in charming everyone and had
begged Yaya to tell her about their most embarrassing moments.
Yaya had declined but decided telling her about Injago's most
embarrassing moments was just fine.

So now Injago had to choke down breakfast while trying
not to cringe and laugh in equal measures. He wasn't doing well.

Yaya stopped mid-sentence and stared past Injago's shoulder in shock. Injago turned to see Romada standing at the
entrance to the galley, a stack of dirty plates in hand. Her expression made it clear she would rather be anywhere but there.

"Romada! Good morning!" Rehka said, waving and grinning.

Yaya stood up and went to the kitchen to make up another
plate of food.

"Hey," Romada croaked before swiftly crossing the space
with lengthy steps to stand beside Yaya. "I brought some plates."

They gave her a wry smile. "I see that. Let's do an exchange," they said, handing her a plate piled high with fish and potatoes and taking the stack of dirty plates from her.

"I have more," she said.

"You eat first. You can help me do dishes before worship," they said.

"Okay," she murmured, sitting down at the table with Injago and Rehka.

"I'm so glad I caught you, Romada! I was just talking to Yaya about your worship schedule," Rehka said.

Romada began to shovel food in her mouth, staring down at the table. When was the last time she had eaten?

"Anyway, I used to worship The Mother, but after what this kingdom has done to sirens, I'm loathe to worship an elven god. Could I join you and Yaya in your worship of the sea?"

Romada choked on her food, looking up first at Injago, then at Rehka. Everyone waited in silence as Romada grappled with a conversation none of them were privy to. Finally, she replied, "Um, sure."

"Great!" Rehka beamed at her. "I'm so excited! I'm really hoping some merfolk show up. Wouldn't that be grand? I've never seen one up close before! I hear they're good luck."

"They are," Injago said, tipping back in his chair. "Not only that, but one of the local pod leaders has a crush on Romada, so they're always paying us visits."

"Ooh, Romada! Lucky you!"

Romada grunted and continued eating her food, polishing it off in minutes. Injago wasn't surprised. She was probably starving. Her face had become gaunt beneath her cheekbones, her breathing always slightly uneven. During their fight at the camp, he had noticed her faltering footwork and shaking sword arm. If he hadn't been sure that the rest of them could protect her, he wouldn't have let her leave the ship.

"Dishes!" Yaya called as Romada stood up.

She stuck her tongue out at them.

"Go get them," they said.

Romada made a noncommittal noise, and Yaya laughed. She ran off and returned with another stack of dishes, her breathing labored.

"There we go!" Yaya clapped her on the back. "Let's get this done."

"I'll help!" Rehka said, bouncing out of her chair and over to the sinks.

Injago leaned back in his seat and watched as the three worked in harmony, Rehka humming something under her breath. For the second time, it hit him that he wouldn't have Neiara at his side during worship. It wasn't much of a loss to him, but he couldn't imagine how painful it would be for Romada to worship the moon alone. It was the goddess of lovers, after all.

Would he ever worship with his love? The one he pined for with all of his heart? The one he prayed for every day?

Rehka giggled, breaking the relative silence. "Yaya, you've got bubbles on your chin."

Yaya laughed in response, then brought up a handful of bubbles to their mouth and blew them across the room at Injago. Romada's lips quirked up into the ghost of a smile before she ducked her head and began scrubbing even more vigorously than before.

"Don't break the plates, please, Captain," Yaya teased. Romada said nothing, but she slowed anyway.

They finished soon after, and everyone headed up to the deck. As Romada passed Injago, he reached out a hand to touch her shoulder, but she shied away from him and hurried up the steps.

Would she ever forgive him?

The other pixies who worshipped The Harvester had already started, their black candles lit on the altar. Injago didn't much feel like he had anything to say to his god that day. What could he say that he hadn't already? Worshiping every single week was exhausting. He ended up daydreaming about his imaginary lover more often than not anyway.

Deciding to forgo worship, he went to rest against the

banister and watch Yaya, Romada, and Rehka worship. After all, Romada used to watch him and Neiara. How was this any different?

After diving in, Rehka and Yaya surfaced, splashing water against the hull of the ship. Romada must have gone deeper because he couldn't see her. After a moment, Rehka dove back in.

Injago watched Yaya lazily float on their back, watched the bubble trail from Rehka begin to fade… He realized Rehka had been underwater too long right when Yaya looked up at him with concern.

"Where's Rehka?"

Injago pointed. "She followed Romada."

Yaya cursed and dove underwater.

Injago waited for what felt like forever. What had happened to Rehka? Finally, the three emerged, Romada dragging Rehka's body. Rehka coughed and feebly choked on water.

"What were you thinking?" Romada screeched. "You could have died!"

"I was following you," Rehka said in a meek voice. "I thought we were worshipping."

"That… You thought… " Romada shook her head, eyes squeezed shut as she grit her teeth. "That was me playing around, Rehka. I was seeing how deep I could go."

"Oh."

"I can breathe underwater, so I can do that. *You* cannot!"

"Can I still worship with you?" Rehka asked in a small voice.

Romada took a deep breath. Injago could see her fins shaking even from aboard the ship. "Fine. Just don't die."

Rehka broke into a teary smile. "Thank you, Romada!"

"I'll…stay up here on the surface. Just in case," Romada said before rolling onto her back.

Injago exchanged glances with Yaya. They shrugged and rolled over onto their stomach. It must have felt nice to have the water on your belly and the sun on your back. Eager for some sun himself, Injago stripped off his shirt and stretched. He never bound his chest on Rest Day. The heat of the midmorning sun crept over the swell of his chest, and the gentle sea breeze flicked over his nipples. Ordinarily, he wouldn't have bared his unbound chest on deck so casually, least of all in front of a stranger, but there was something disarming about the new siren. And his lungs and ribcage thanked him for the rare freedom. He leaned on the banister, careful not to pinch himself, and looked out over the water.

The ocean was a mess of waves, all in constant motion, slapping the hull and splashing the trio. Injago admired how the sun beat down on the shining surface. Guilt twinged in his throat as he looked over at the altar, where he should have been worshipping. Maybe his god would forgive him for taking one day away? He wasn't in the water himself, but it sure felt like he was worshipping the sea, so at least he was still worshipping.

Oh, what could it hurt? Injago stripped off his pants as well and climbed over the railing. The wake of his splash hit Yaya, startling them awake. They spit up water and blinked over at Injago.

"Were you asleep?" Romada asked, swimming up to Yaya and poking their waist.

"Maybe," they said, side-eyeing her.

Romada let out a burst of laughter, and Injago stared at her in wonder.

"I knew you could still laugh," Yaya said softly.

Romada gave them a small smile. "I guess so."

"Your laugh is wonderful! It brings joy to those who hear it," Rehka said with a grin.

Romada looked unsettled. "You think so?"

"I know so."

For a moment, Romada looked to Injago as if for confirmation, like she would have before everything happened, like she still valued his thoughts and opinions. Then, she quickly ducked her head, disappearing beneath the surface as if the embarrassment of Rehka's statement was too much.

Rehka shrugged. "You two think so, too, right?"

Injago thought about it in silence and realized she was right. When their captain was happy, the crew was happy.

And it felt like no one had been happy in weeks.

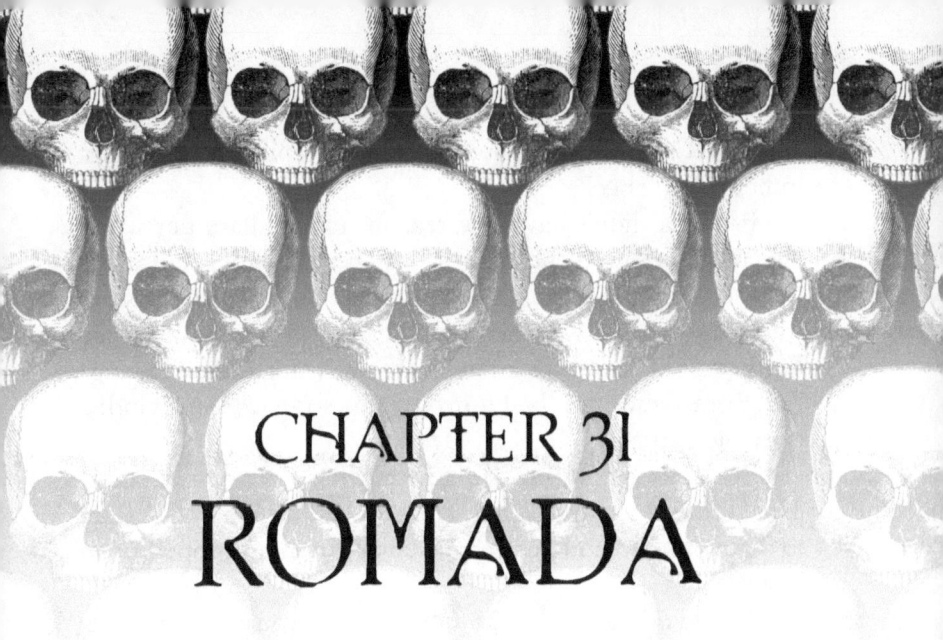

# CHAPTER 31
# ROMADA

**A SOFT SEA BREEZE RUFFLED ROMADA'S FINS** as she strung her hammock up on the deck. She had found a single hammock at the bottom of the chest; using the double hammock without Neiara seemed sacrilegious. But with nothing else to do and feeling in better spirits than she had in weeks—who knew that eating and getting fresh air and sunshine could help with mood?—Romada decided to break out her drawing supplies. She found herself bursting with creative energy and needed to release it before she burned with it.

She settled down with her pad and charcoal and stared at the page, waiting for inspiration to strike.

"You draw?" Rehka asked, sidling up to her.

Romada looked at her from beneath lowered lashes. She wasn't sure why Rehka was so friendly when Romada had all but bitten her head off earlier.

"Sometimes."

"Can I see?" Rehka gave her a broad smile, dimples stark in her round cheeks.

Romada didn't have any reason not to share her work; she always allowed the crew to watch her when she drew if they so wished. But still, she hesitated. This was an outsider. Allowing Rehka to see her drawings felt overly familiar, like Rehka would be able to know her from seeing these drawings. Did Romada want to be known by this stranger? She handed over the pad.

Rehka thumbed through it with care so as not to smudge any of the drawings. When she stopped on one of Neiara lounging in bed and laughing, Rehka's mouth dropped open in awe.

"She's so beautiful," she whispered. "You're an amazing artist."

Romada's neck blossomed a deep purple. "Thank you."

Whistling low through her teeth, Rehka finished flipping through the sketches and handed the pad back.

"What are you going to draw?"

Romada shrugged. "I haven't decided yet."

A splash from over the side of the ship captured her attention, and she hurried to the banister, Rehka at her heels. A mottled red and gold tail disappeared beneath the surface.

"Merfolk!" Rehka squealed. "Oh, my stars! Do you think they'll let me swim with them?" She turned to Romada, her big brown eyes sparkling with joy.

"I don't see why not."

Fayne resurfaced, and Romada waved to them, earning a grin. "Come swim," they signed.

Romada shook her head, and Fayne gave her a dejected look.

"This is Rehka," Romada said, gesturing to the siren with her drawing pad. "She wants to meet you."

Fayne waved and beckoned for her to come down.

Rehka bounced on the balls of her feet, making noises of excitement as she stripped off her clothes. Taking a running start, she leapt over the railing and dove in.

"Be nice to her. She's new," Romada said.

Fayne rolled their eyes. "I will be nice and not bite."

Romada laughed lightly. "Thank you." The laughter felt good in her belly, and she let a soft smile settle on her lips as she watched the two.

With a sly look, Fayne splashed Rehka right as she surfaced.

"Hey!" Rehka sputtered, wiping her face. "No fair! I need to breathe!"

Fayne made a hissing sound deep in their throat—which the crew had collectively decided was their form of laughter—and splashed Rehka again before launching themself out of the water and into the air, raining droplets down on Rehka's awestruck face.

"Wow," Rehka sighed.

Romada made herself comfortable against the banister and began to draw, the image of Fayne flying through the air engraved in her mind. With soft, smooth strokes, she sketched their form: the long tendrils coming from their head, trailing behind them, and their strong tail bowing back in a graceful arc.

Her fingers worked over the paper, adding details and smudging lines. She lost herself in it; the charcoal spread across the page of its own accord, and soon, she held a picture of Fayne's magnificent leap.

Romada's chest glowed with warmth as she stared at it, studying every detail of the mottled pattern and the expression of mischievous glee on their face. Content with the finished product, she called down to Fayne.

They swam closer, and Romada held the pad up for them to see. After scrutinizing the picture for a moment, they beamed.

"I look beautiful," they signed.

"That's because you are beautiful," Romada said.

They blushed, a crimson stain spreading across their high cheekbones, and did a backflip into the ocean.

"I think you embarrassed them," Rehka said, climbing back onto the ship.

Fayne didn't resurface, so Romada had to agree.

"Hey, I wanted to ask you something," Rehka said, squeezing the water from her long hair.

"What is it?" Romada asked as she reclined into her hammock and shut her eyes.

"Can I worship the moon with you tonight?"

Romada's eyes flew open. "The goddess of lovers?" she blurted out, sitting up and nearly upending herself.

Rehka looked mortified. "I mean! But she's also the goddess of time, change, and purpose, right? I feel like I'm finding my purpose by going on this journey with you and your crew."

Romada stared at her.

Wringing her hands, Rehka continued. "I just...I've never felt like I fit in anywhere. In life. But now, I'm doing something, you know? I'm going to help you find Neiara. I'm going to rescue my brother. And I'm going to help other sirens."

It made sense. And who was Romada to stop someone from worshipping her goddess? The moon deserved all the adoration given to Her and more. That wouldn't make any of it easier. It wouldn't make it feel right. Nothing felt right without Neiara.

"Yeah, okay." Romada laid back down.

"You don't mind?"

"No. Wake me up when the dance starts," Romada said, rolling over.

"The what?"

***

Fayne and their pod put on a spectacular show for the crew, garnering thunderous applause. Romada looked over at Rehka, her lips twitching into the semblance of a smile. Rehka's excitement reminded her of Neiara's.

Her heart ached as she wondered when Neiara would be able to see the merfolk dance again. Would they find her by the next Worship Day? Or would it take—gods forbid—months?

*Where are you, my love?*

The sun drifted lazily below the waves as though loathe to leave, and the relative darkness that ensued highlighted the thin slice of moon as She moved through the sky. Romada followed Her slow trek with her face, basking in Her meager light.

Much like the reluctant sun, she wished time could stop for a moment. She wanted to stay still, stay standing, stay looking at her goddess and not have to think about whether Neiara could feel the moonlight.

"Is it time?" Rehka asked in a whisper.

Romada nodded.

The crescent lent barely any light, but they sat at the altar and lit their candles to meditate anyway. Romada reminisced about Neiara and her tender touches. The wounds on her legs and stomach from last Worship Day were still healing and, at this point, Romada was sure they would scar due to her lack of healing ministrations. Neiara had always been better at that, knowing exactly which salve to use and how often to change bandages. She would have been horrified that Romada had disinfected them with alcohol.

Romada's thoughts drifted to the siren beside her. What was Rehka thinking of? It felt weird to be worshiping with someone who she wouldn't be intimate with after. She had never worshiped the moon with anyone but Neiara. In fact, she hadn't even worshiped the moon until Neiara had come into her life.

She prostrated herself further, feeling the deep stretch in her lower back, and imagined Neiara's hands touching her there, massaging the tense muscles. Did this even count as worship if she was so wrapped up in thoughts of her lover rather than her goddess? But She was the goddess of love, after all; surely, She would forgive Romada for being preoccupied with it.

How lonely her life had been before Neiara. Even with Injago at her side, she had felt adrift. Incomplete. Neiara was her sun, her anchor, her guiding star. Her life had meaning with Neiara in it. Her life had joy and warmth. She could share anything with Neiara. She could bare her soul, with all its scars and bruises, and know that Neiara would gather the tatters into her hands and kiss each one. She was never alone, so long as she had Neiara.

Giving up on her worship and ready to move to somewhere more comfortable, Romada sat back up and looked to her left, expecting to see Neiara's smoldering eyes. Instead, she saw Rehka, her head bowed and her lips moving around silent words. Romada's heart cracked open at the thought of going to bed alone and forgoing that most intimate worship. Alone, in a cold bed, in a dusty room, devoid of life.

Rehka's eyes flew open when the first sob spilled from Romada's throat. As Romada was wracked with grief, Rehka came to her, first placing a hand on her back and then enveloping her in a full embrace.

"Shh," she sighed, her breath hot against Romada's skin. "You're going to be okay. We're going to find her, and you're both going to be okay."

Romada nodded, relaxing into the first physical contact she had had in weeks. Rehka smelled like flowers and honey. It wasn't anything like Neiara's smell, but it oddly enough brought Romada comfort. She rested her head against Rehka's ample bosom as Rehka stroked her head fin with the gentlest of touches and murmured positive aspirations in her ear. Romada held onto her like a lifeline, breathing in her scent, afraid to let go.

Maybe this was worship, after all, because it sure felt like love.

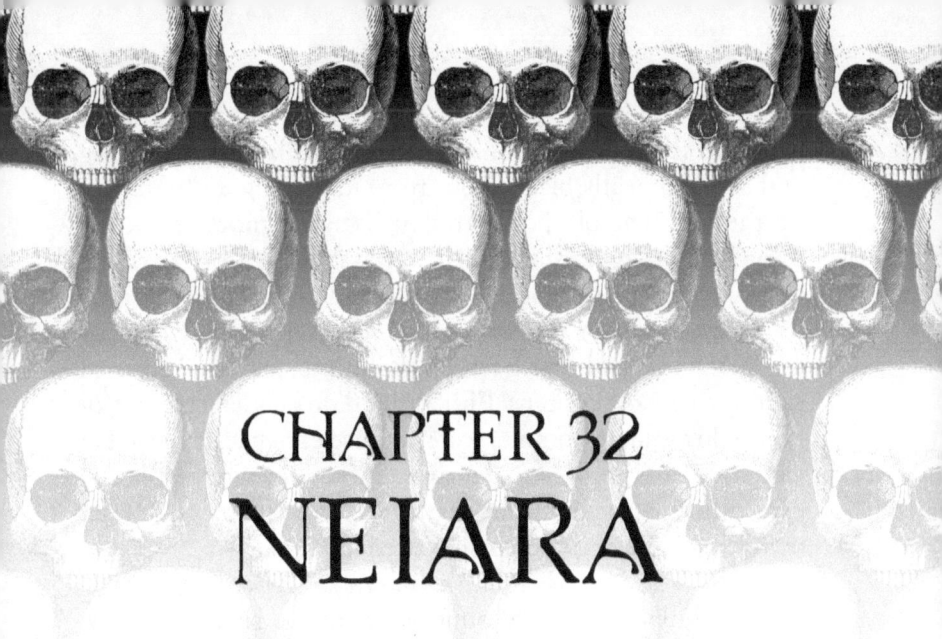

# CHAPTER 32
# NEIARA

**ROMADA WILL SAVE ME. ROMADA WILL SAVE ME.**
*Romada will save me.*

Neiara repeated the mantra in her head, day in and day out. Though whether it was day or night was impossible to tell. She hadn't seen sunlight in who knew how many days. The slimy stone walls of her prison cell kept her in darkness; the only source of light was the flickering of a torch in the hallway, desperately snaking through the slatted window in the door. Every now and then, the torch would go out, leaving her in inky blackness. Then it would be lit again, lending her and the three other sirens in the room—each bolted to a different wall—dancing shadows.

*Romada will save me. Romada will save me. Romada will save me.*

She wasn't shitting or peeing anymore. The last time she had felt a bowel movement, it had lodged like a stone in her ass, and she had used her fingers, straining against the length of chain holding her to the wall, to dig the feces out, bit by bit,

189

until she could finally void it. The pain had been excruciating, and she had nearly blacked out from it, panting in the silence of the cell. The old Neiara might have felt mortified at the thought of digging shit out of her asshole in front of three other faeries, but this Neiara was relieved to finally be free of it.

*Romada will save me. Romada will save me. Romada will save me.*

When she had first been placed in the cell, she had tried signing to the other sirens. Either they didn't understand her, or they didn't want to communicate because each had stared at her with dead eyes before looking away. Now, they rarely looked at each other, instead focusing on the walls, the shadows, or their own hands. Neiara's were still coated in feces.

*Romada will save me. Romada will save me. Romada will save me.*

The only thing more ominous than the silence was the periodic piercing screams that occasionally echoed along the outside corridor. Who could possibly be screaming? How were they able to scream? What kind of fate had they met? Was it Neiara's fate to bring forth screams on her dying day?

*Romada will save me. Romada will save me. Romada will save me. Romada…please save me.*

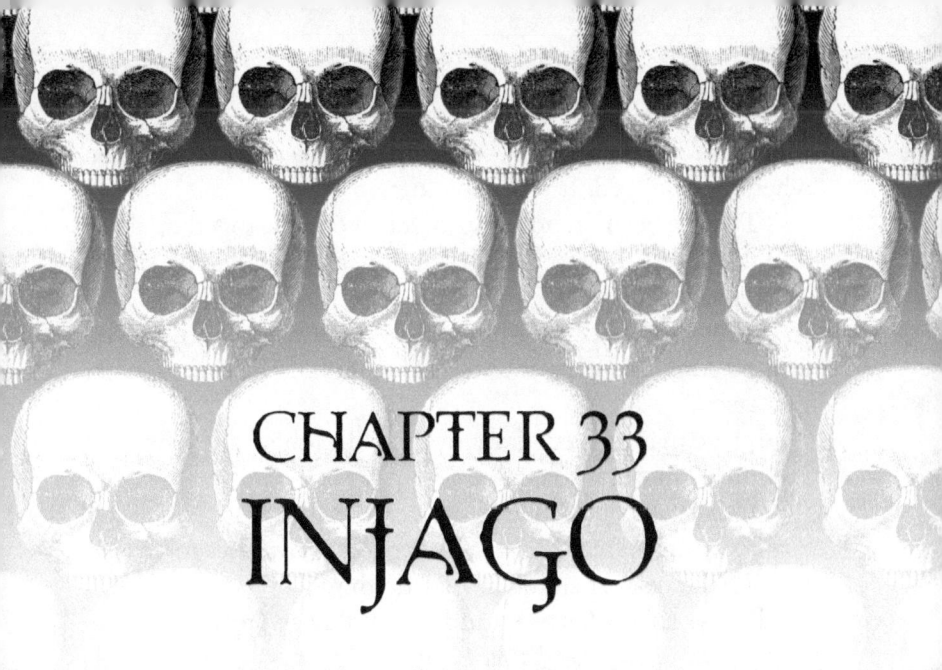

# CHAPTER 33
# INJAGO

**THREE DAYS WITH REHKA ONBOARD, AND IN-**
jago realized he hadn't seen Romada smile this much since
before Neiara was taken. In fact, he hadn't seen this much of
Romada at all since that night in Tilt Town. Rehka and Romada
were joined at the hip, their arms usually linked and heads together as they laughed over some joke or whatever it was they
were talking about. Rehka would randomly embrace Romada,
earning a fond smile.

When would Injago be the recipient of those smiles again?
When would he be the one giving and receiving those hugs? It
wasn't fair. Rehka wasn't family. She wasn't even a real member
of the crew. And yet, she was the sole recipient of Romada's
love and attention. The only one allowed to touch her, tease
her, and make her laugh.

Not only did it feel like Rehka had taken his spot in
Romada's life, but Neiara's as well. Their touches were intimate
and personal. Romada gave shy smiles to the siren as though

they shared secrets. Rehka ruffled Romada's fins and squealed when they hugged. It was nauseating to watch.

"They've been spending an awful lot of time together, that's all I'm saying," Injago said to Yaya over a breakfast of scrambled eggs and fruit.

"So what if Romada has a new friend? She needs to be around someone who doesn't remind her of the night Neiara was taken."

Injago made a face of annoyance. "But they're so close! All the time! They're inseparable."

With a twinkle in their eye, Yaya leaned in close and asked, "Are you jealous, Inja?" Their breath ghosted over Injago's cheek, making the teasing all the more irritating.

Injago rolled his eyes and shoved away from the table. "Whatever. I don't need this from you."

Yaya chuckled as they grabbed the dirty plates. "I'm giving you a hard time, boyo. Let Romada have some fun with her new friend. If it really bothers you that much, talk to them about it."

That did not sound like a conversation Injago wanted to have.

He joined Yaya at the sinks, scrubbing their plates and handing them over for Yaya to dry. His thoughts were a jumble as he tried to make sense of his feelings. Was he overreacting? Seeing things when there was nothing there? Would bringing it up directly to them actually help at all? It had such a potential to backfire, but then again...could things get any worse? Romada already ignored his presence. What more could go wrong?

Thanking Yaya for the food, he made his way up to the helm to give Ceta a break.

Ceta smiled when she saw him and shifted a step over so he could take the wheel. With a lazy hand, she gestured down at the deck where Romada and Rehka were sitting together, giggling over Romada's sketch pad.

"Looks like it wasn't hard to replace Neiara after all."

Anger quickened in Injago, and he glared at her. "She is *not* replacing Neiara."

"Oh, please. Look at them!"

"You don't know anything, Ceta!" Thunder rumbled on his voice even as he worked to keep his volume down.

She took a step back, looking shaken, and clenched her jaw. "Fine. I won't say it. But I'm thinking it."

"Noted."

They stood in awkward, stormy silence for a moment, swaying with the motion of the ship, before she sighed.

"I'm sorry for saying anything," she mumbled.

"You're free to go." If Injago gritted his teeth any harder, his jaw was sure to shatter.

Nodding once, she took the steps two at a time and then disappeared belowdecks.

Turning his ire to Rehka, he eyed her with suspicion. Was she trying to worm her way into Romada's heart? Neiara was still alive for all they knew. How dare she try to replace the love of Romada's life?

Romada said something inaudible to her, and Rehka let out a peal of laughter, throwing her head back. For such a small faerie, she sure was loud.

And insufferable.

Rehka glanced up at him and saw his glare. She stood, murmured something to Romada, and then made her way to the steps. She climbed them slowly, wobbling, still working on getting her sea legs. Eventually, she made it to his side.

"Something wrong?" she asked in a delicately soft voice.

"Yes, as a matter of fact." He refused to meet her gaze, instead looking out over the ocean ahead.

They stood in silence, Rehka drumming her fingers on the mahogany banister, tapping out a little tune. Gods, she was annoying. He wanted to smack her. Why was she so infuriating? Why did she bring out such violence in his heart?

"Is it something I did?" she finally asked.

"Just who do you think you are? You really think you can walk in here and replace the faeries that Romada loves most? You think you can replace me? Replace Neiara?" He turned to her in time to see her blanch, her normally golden-brown skin turning grey.

"I would never try to replace either of you," she said. It was the quietest thing she had ever said, and somehow that made him even angrier.

Injago fumed, his chest burning. His cloth bindings suddenly felt like they were strangling him. He knew he was no longer acting rationally, but this was his little sister! If he didn't protect Romada, who would? She was in a vulnerable state right now. And the audacity of this stranger to take his place. How could Romada be so oblivious to Rehka's obvious and predatory advances?

"Injago, can I tell you something?" Rehka asked, breaking the silence.

He huffed. "What?"

She ruffled her hair, looking nervous. "I don't feel romantic or sexual attraction. To anyone. I never have."

Injago stared at her as that sank in. "Oh... You don't... Ever?"

"Never. So... I understand why you might think I'm trying to replace Neiara, and I can tell you're trying to protect Romada, but she knows about me already. She knows we're just friends."

"That's good," he croaked, embarrassed.

"And I hope that's not what the others are thinking about us. And if they are, I would hope someone would set the record straight, for Romada's sake. She needs the respect of her crew." Rehka gave him a long, pointed look—long enough for him to start sweating.

"Yeah. I mean, I hope so, too. Of course."

"Good." She nodded, then gave him a broad smile, dimples appearing in her cheeks. "Say, I could be your friend too! If you're interested in having another one."

Injago blushed. He certainly hadn't expected this conversation to go this way. How was she so disarmingly charming? He had been horrible to her, and she still wanted to be his friend. Gods, what was wrong with him?

"I'd like that," he said, staring at the whorls on the wooden wheel. He couldn't look at her.

She stepped closer anyway and gave his shoulder a quick

squeeze. "Keep up the good work. Romada is going to forgive you any day now; I'm sure of it."

Injago couldn't help the surge of hope that cut through him. "You think so?" He peeked at her out of the corner of his eye.

"I know so." She winked.

They stood in companionable silence for a moment longer, both looking out at the ocean. Injago couldn't remember the last time he felt so relaxed.

"Thanks, Rehka."

"Any time." She patted him on the back and then left with a skip in her step, settling back at her place at Romada's side. Romada glanced up at him, and for a moment, traces of a smile still lit up her eyes before they hardened.

He sighed and turned his attention back to the sea. He hoped Rehka was right about Romada forgiving him soon. He wasn't sure how much more estrangement he could handle from his best friend and little sister.

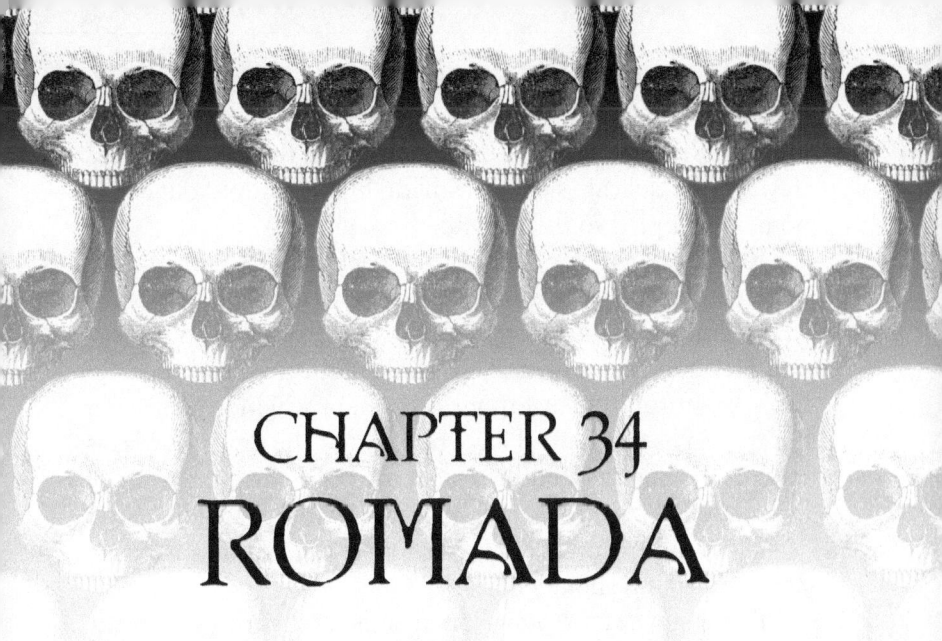

# CHAPTER 34
# ROMADA

**ROMADA CROUCHED IN THE UNDERGROWTH,**
ferns hiding her from her prey as she kept a close eye on Rehka.
The siren crept up the path toward the guardhouse, a rock in her
hand. The second camp had been just as easy to locate as the
first, though it had taken a hike out past Tilt Town to reach it.

Rehka assured the crew that the Song she had created would
only work on elves, but Romada had made sure they all had
earplugs just in case. She wasn't about to have any mishaps.

Stopping a few paces from the guardhouse, Rehka tossed
the rock at the door. It hit with a resounding **thud** that even
Romada could hear, and then the door swung open. Two guards
rushed out, swords drawn.

Rehka opened her mouth and began to Sing.

The elven guards stopped in their tracks as though held
by invisible restraints. Bewilderment twisted their features as
they both dropped their swords from twitching fingers and
mechanically grasped the daggers at their belts. In one smooth

motion, they brought the daggers to their throats and sliced through the delicate skin. Vermillion blood sprayed out as the bodies crumpled to the ground.

Rehka backed away and turned back toward Romada and the rest of the crew, gesturing for them to come out. Romada stepped through the foliage to meet Rehka, pulling an earplug out. Her concern spiked as she noticed the grey pallor of Rehka's beautiful golden-brown skin. Rehka held a hand over her mouth as she looked anywhere but at the dead guards, as though she might vomit or faint at the sight. With the way she was trembling, she might do both even without looking.

"Good job," Romada said in a low voice, resting a hand on Rehka's shaking shoulder.

Rehka gave her a tight-lipped smile and bent to grab the keys off the closest guard, wincing when she caught a glimpse of the blood in the dirt. She took a deep breath and turned back to Romada.

"I should be able to handle all the guards in the camp but stay close? In case I need you."

"We have our earplugs, so we'll be right next to you the whole way. If something goes wrong, you run, okay? Run to safety and hide in the jungle until we come get you."

Rehka nodded, eyes wide and shining with unshed tears.

Romada's stomach twisted at the thought of making Rehka Sing again, but this was their best shot at getting all the guards at once. Rehka knew that. Rehka volunteered. And Rehka wasn't someone who would make this decision lightly. Romada grabbed the keys and walked up to the gate, blade at the ready. The lock clicked open with the twist of the key, and the gate creaked inward on its hinges, allowing them to file through the opening.

A large grey brick building—the only building in sight—was in the center of the camp, surrounded by rows of long tents. A brass bell hung in a tower atop the roof, and a guard peered down at them, mouth open in shock.

Coming to his senses, he ran to the bell and began to ring it; the thunderous rolling echoed throughout the camp and caused a flock of dragons to take to the skies from the jungle. The front door of the building opened, revealing a crowd of guards. One by one, they poured out of the building, rushing down the steps, all while Rehka stood trembling beside Romada.

Looking sickly pale, she began to Sing again.

The company of guards halted as one, fear evident in their eyes as the Song entranced them and controlled their bodies. Hands grabbed daggers and raised them to necks. More guards came out of the doorway; as soon as they heard the Song, they reached for their daggers, too. Blades glinted in the light of the midday sun as they slashed in unison; a torrent of blood splashed the steps and the ground, soaking the dirt. Bodies fell over each other and tumbled down the stairs in heaps.

Rehka's eyes were shut tight, and tears covered her cheeks. She kept Singing as a handful more guards came out. These ones stared at the carnage, unaffected by Rehka's siren magic. One clapped another on the back, and they all turned to Rehka, grim smiles on their faces.

Romada reached out to touch Rehka, who shivered violently. Rehka opened her eyes and let out a sob, turning to bury her face in Romada's chest. Romada pulled the plugs from her ears and held Rehka close, rocking her back and forth.

"I killed them all," Rehka choked out. Her breathing was dangerously close to hyperventilation.

"They would have done the same to you and the other sirens. Or worse," Romada whispered. The pool of blood crept closer to them, so Romada gently moved a couple steps to the side.

"I know," Rehka moaned, shaking uncontrollably. "That doesn't make it better. That doesn't make me any better."

"It makes you a damn hero," Romada growled, squeezing her until she yelped. "I'm so proud of you."

"Thank you." Romada's shirt muffled Rehka's tearful voice.

Romada pressed a quick kiss to Rehka's forehead and released her; turning to the guards who still lived, she gestured for them to approach.

"They have to be part siren," Rehka murmured.

"Who is in charge?" Romada asked in Elvish.

A tall guard with bright blue eyes stepped forward, holding out her hand. "I'm Lagra. And you are?"

"I'm Romada," she said, grasping Lagra's hand and giving it a firm shake.

"And our savior?" Lag ra turned to Rehka.

Rehka's cheeks blazed crimson, and she held out her hand to Lagra as well. "I'm Rehka. Without Romada and her crew, though, I never would have been rescued from my camp. They're the real heroes."

"Crew?" Lagra looked back at Romada. "Are you part of the Royal Naval Guard?"

Romada laughed. "Oh gods no. We're pirates."

Lagra's smile froze as she looked them up and down as though wondering whether they were better or worse than the elven guards.

"We're looking for a siren named Neiara," Romada continued.

"And another named Imber," Rehka added.

"Well, you're welcome to look for them. We'll need help freeing the prisoners. And we should probably dig more outhouses."

Romada gestured for Injago to step up beside her. "This is Injago, my quartermaster. He'll make sure you get the help you need while we're here."

Lagra looked at Injago with wide eyes and fluttering lashes. "Oh, wow. Quartermaster? That's important, isn't it?" she asked in a sultry voice.

Romada rolled her eyes. Taking Rehka's hand, she snagged a key ring off a dead guard and began walking toward the tents on the far side of the camp. A thought hit her, and she stopped.

"Are there any children at this camp?" she asked over her shoulder.

Rehka gave her hand a reassuring squeeze.

"No. They all got picked up yesterday," Lagra called out.

Thank the gods. Romada wasn't sure she would have been able to handle seeing any more babies locked up in their own filth. She made a mental note to talk to Injago about tracking down the ship.

After several hours of walking up and down the rows and rows of captive sirens, asking them if they had seen Neiara while unlocking their shackles, Rehka and Romada entered the last tent.

With a shriek loud enough to wake the gods, Rehka leapt forward, yanking Romada along with her.

"Ow!" Romada yelled, pulling her hand free.

Rehka ignored her and threw herself around a handsome siren. "Imber! Oh gods! We found you!"

Romada approached them slowly, taking in the sight of Rehka's twin. Even seated, she could tell he was tall. He would probably tower over her when standing. His features were chiseled into his skin like stone artwork; high sculpted cheekbones and deep-set eyes were framed by short, soft curls the same chocolate brown as Rehka's.

She worked on unlocking more sirens as Rehka talked Imber's ear off; words poured out of her like a torrent with barely a pause for breath between them. When Romada had unlocked the last siren, she turned back to the twins, trying not to let the fact that they hadn't found Neiara mar the happy reunion. After everything Rehka had done for them, she deserved this. Not everything had to be about Romada. Despite not finding Neiara, there had still been a victory.

"Ready to go introduce Imber to everyone?" Romada asked.

Twin sets of beautiful brown eyes met Romada's, and Rehka grinned.

"Oh, gods! Introductions! Imber, this is Romada. She's the pirate captain who rescued me! We're going on a quest to find her girlfriend, who was captured a few weeks ago. Romada, this is my brother Imber!" She beamed up at Romada, who couldn't help but chuckle.

"Yeah, I gathered that," Romada said. "Pleased to meet you, Imber."

Imber nodded stiffly, and Romada couldn't help wondering if he would be a faerie of many or few words once his collar was off. She guessed it was probably the latter.

"Let's get out of this tent and find the others!" Rehka grabbed Imber's hand and rushed off, dragging her hulking brother behind her as though he were as small as her. Romada couldn't help noticing the tiny smile cropping up at the corner of Imber's mouth as he followed his enthusiastic sister.

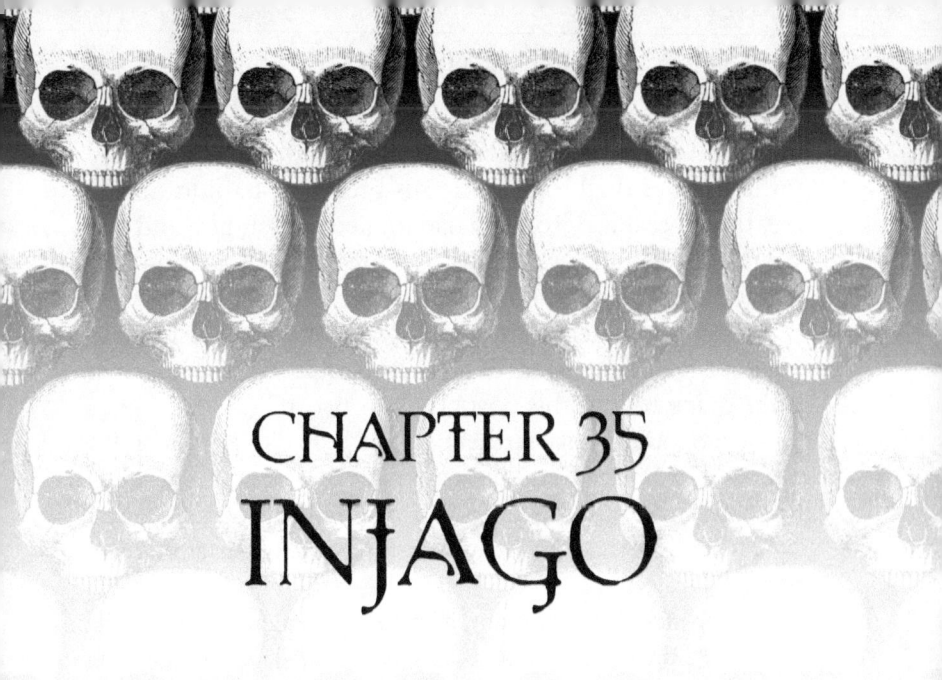

# CHAPTER 35
# INJAGO

**ROUNDING THE BUILDING IN TIME TO SEE RO-**
mada and Rehka exit a tent, Injago's jaw dropped at the sight of
Rehka's arms entwined with those of a tall, dark, and handsome
masc-fae. Was *that* Imber? He was…gorgeous. He looked like
he had been carved from marble by the steady hands of an
artist depicting perfection or a god. Was he even real?

Injago struggled to stand on suddenly weak legs when
the siren's piercing brown eyes met his. Imber's broad golden
brown chest rippled with muscles, and his brown curls fell
across his brow in a way that made Injago ache to brush them
aside. Full lips set in a hard line made Injago wonder how often
the siren smiled. It would be devastating if he did.

The heat of a powerful blush rapidly spread across Injago's face, and he tore his eyes from Imber to look at Romada
instead. Her eyes were downcast even as she maintained a
smile for Rehka. The trio walked up to him, Rehka chatting
endlessly and seemingly aware of nothing but this beauti-

ful masc-fae. Injago could understand that. He too wanted nothing more than to stand in his presence, bask in it. Too late, Injago realized Romada had looked over at him and was regarding him quizzically. She was probably wondering why his face was on fire.

"Injagoooo!" Rehka gave him a giant smile and gestured to the masc-fae in her arms. "This is Imber, my twin! Oh, Imber, you're going to love this boyo. He's so sweet!"

Injago looked up—farther up than he had to even with Romada—into Imber's eyes, noticing the flecks of gold speckling his brown irises and the deep furrow of his powerful brow.

"H-hey," he said, his wings rustling behind in embarrassment.

Imber stood there, silent, and Injago realized he still had his collar on. Would he be as chatty as his sister? He looked more like the brooding type: strong and quiet. What would his voice sound like?

Injago imagined being enveloped in those rugged arms.

"Injago?" Rehka looked down pointedly at his hand, and Injago realized he was holding a collar keystone.

"Oh! Here, let me get your collar," Injago said, tripping over himself to stand behind Imber. He held the stone up to the clasp and waited until it flashed red.

The collar came apart and fell into Imber's large hands; he dropped it in the dust and turned to Rehka, croaking her name in a voice rusty from disuse.

Her eyes lit up, and she threw her arms around his neck. "My *deshani!*"

Imber twisted in her embrace, freeing himself with a scowl. "Never call me that!" he spat in a low voice. "I am not some filthy elven word."

Rehka's eyes widened as she nodded, a tear forming in the corner of her eye. "Never," she agreed.

Injago exchanged a look with Romada. Would she have realized the significance of calling a siren by an elven term of endearment? Even though they spoke Pixish onboard the *Guardian*, Romada was always calling Neiara *deshani*.

Imber pulled Rehka back into the embrace and looked over at Injago. "Thank you. For coming to this camp." His voice was dark honey. Injago could have sunk into it and never come up for breath.

Injago nodded jerkily and stammered, "I'm glad to—happy to help. And that we got to reunite you, too. The two of you. Um, I need to talk to Romada about... Please excuse us."

Romada's brow ridge shot up, but she obliged him and walked a couple steps away from the twins.

"What?"

Injago took a breath, ready to gush about Imber, before deciding he wasn't ready to bring that up yet. "Did you find Neiara?"

Romada's face crumbled. "No."

"I'm sorry, Romada. But I promise we will find her."

She shrugged. "If you say so."

Yaya had set up a food station next to the building, and sirens were filing past, leaving with plates of food. Imber had to hold his plate as well as Rehka's because Rehka couldn't stand still and was doing some sort of little tiptoe dance around him.

Injago looked back at Romada in time to see a soft smile on her lips.

"Why were you so awkward back there?" she asked, nodding at the twins.

Injago's blush came back in full force, and he rubbed the back of his neck. "Ah... Imber is...very attractive, right? I've often dreamed of someone who looks exactly like him." At the admission, he gave a self-deprecating chuckle. Why was he saying this now, and why to Romada when she still wanted nothing to do with him? What did she care about his infatuations and dreams?

Romada burst into laughter, tears forming in her eyes. "Oh, gods! That's adorable, actually. And he *is* the epitome of tall, dark, and handsome."

"I know, right?" Injago gave her a sheepish smile.

"And honestly, he's not what I was expecting when Rehka

said she had a twin brother. I was expecting someone… I don't know. Shorter?"

"Me too. But I'm not complaining!"

Romada and Injago shared another moment of laughter before Romada stopped, looking at him with an indiscernible look. Injago could actually see the second she decided to close herself off again; the light in her eyes switched off, and her mouth set into a grim line.

"I have to go," she said in a rush before walking off, leaving him standing alone.

Injago looked around for the twins and spotted them off beside one of the tents. He loped over, eager to talk to Imber some more.

"Injago!" Rehka gave him a dimpled smile. "Where's Romada?"

"She took off. She's upset about not finding Neiara."

Rehka grimaced. "I was so happy to find Imber that I completely forgot about Neiara. Oh, poor Romada! I feel awful. Should I go find her?"

"I think some alone time will be okay," Injago assured her. "She won't be upset that you're spending time with your brother."

He peered over at Imber through lowered lashes; he truly was a marble statue brought to life, his face made of powerful angles and straight lines. Injago marveled at his beauty.

"So what now?" Rehka asked, snapping him from his reverie.

That was a good question. "What are you two planning to do? Will you be joining us or going your own way?"

Rehka put her hand on his arm and gave him a gentle squeeze. "You all helped me find my brother. The least I can do is help you find Neiara."

"Where Rehka goes, I go," Imber said in that deliciously deep voice.

Injago suppressed a shiver.

"Well, I'm happy to have you! Both. For the journey. With us. Happy you're both joining us."

Rehka gave him a knowing look as she looked between him

and Imber. "Then it's settled! You get to have us both for the rest of this venture."

"I should go," Injago said, backing away. "See you back on the ship." He was pretty sure that's where Romada had hidden. Time to face her and make sure she was doing okay.

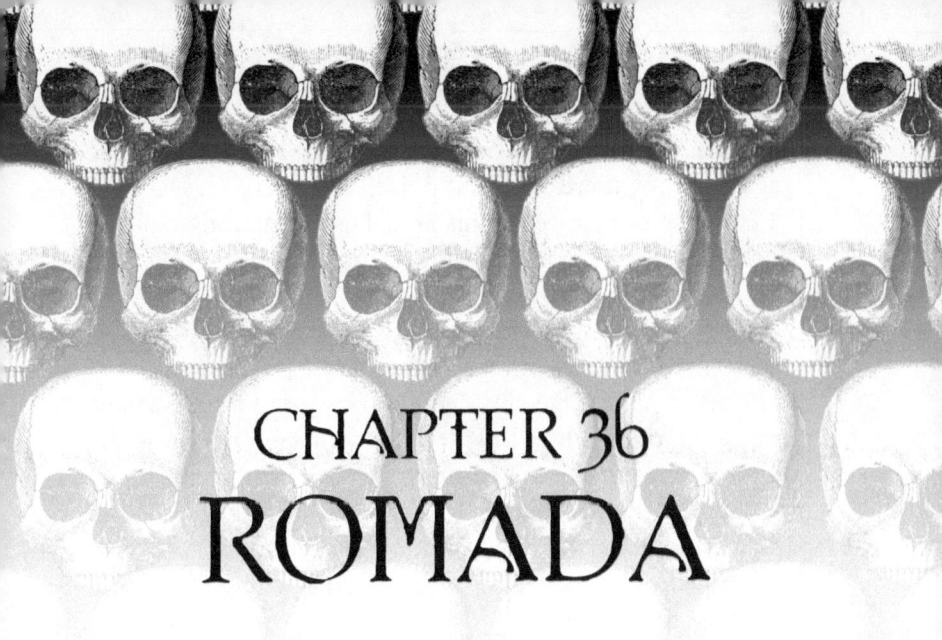

# CHAPTER 36
# ROMADA

**LAUGHING WITH INJAGO HAD FELT...GOOD.**
Right. It felt like coming home and being wrapped in a warm
hug. That's why she couldn't be around him. How could she
share a moment with Injago when she still blamed him for
everything? Romada stomped back through the jungle, ready
to be back onboard and safely locked away in her cabin. Maybe
then she would stop thinking about how, maybe, it wasn't all
Injago's fault.

Maybe it was hers.

***

After a couple hours lying in bed, Romada could no longer
ignore the angry rumbling and cramping from her empty stomach. Hoping that Yaya had something edible down in the galley,
she lugged herself out of bed and made her way to the door.

When she opened it, she was confronted with the sight of Injago standing there, his hand poised to knock.

"Hey," he said, lowering his arm. His entire body radiated discomfort, a stark contrast to how easily he had stood with her earlier, sharing laughter.

"Hey."

"I wanted to make sure you were okay."

Romada pursed her lips. This was as good a time as any to make up, right? Or at least try? How much longer was she going to deny herself the company of her best friend? How much longer could she keep holding him at arm's length? His patience and understanding wouldn't last forever.

"I'm really not," she said, sighing and opening the door a little wider to let him in.

He hesitated for a moment, wariness in his blue eyes, before stepping in and surveying the room. Though the stacks of dishes were gone, the quilt had once more been thrown haphazardly over the curtain rod, blocking most of the incoming sunlight.

The cabin had been too bright; it illuminated and highlighted the emptiness of the room. Romada's heart had enough aches without being reminded so harshly that she was alone. It was easier to lie in darkness.

Picking his way through the clothes and books on the floor, Injago made his way to Neiara's clothes chest and sat on it. He turned his full concern on Romada then.

"I'm worried about you, Rome."

The tears that had been held at bay by her feeble resolve came flooding out when he said her nickname. Romada knew there was no way she could continue holding this grudge. It was time to stop pushing her brother away and admit that she needed him; she needed his comfort and strength.

In an instant, he was up and cradling her in his arms as sobs tore at the walls of her throat.

"Talk to me," he murmured in her finned ear.

Taking a deep and shaking breath, she met his questioning eyes. "I fucked up, Inja. I fucked it all up, and I blamed you."

He pulled back slightly as if to interrupt her, but she held him all the tighter. She wasn't ready to let go. She couldn't stop now.

"I put Neiara in danger. I put all of us in danger. And I didn't, didn't think about the risks. I didn't think about taking precautions. It's m-my fault that Neiara got captured. And I blamed you."

Tears rimmed her eyes, blurring her vision but not enough for her to miss the kindness in his face. His arms held her close as she wept, one hand reaching up to smooth down her fins.

"Hey, Rome, it isn't your fault. We all messed up. Neiara too. She wanted to go ashore. She wanted to. Are you going to blame Neiara? Don't blame yourself then," he added when she shook her head.

"B-but I did this!"

His shushing was accompanied by gentle rocking, mimicking the motion of the sea. "We all did this. Say it with me. We all did this."

"We all did this," she mumbled.

"And we can fix it."

"We can fix it."

"We will find Neiara."

She took a shuddering breath. "We will find Neiara."

His eyes were alight with determination. She would have drowned in it if he wasn't holding her in place. Then he smiled and stretched up to press a kiss to her forehead.

"I'm sorry," she whispered, head bowed. When had she said those words before and meant them? Maybe never.

"We're good, Rome."

"Yeah?" She blinked down at him, clearing the tears.

"Yeah."

Romada sighed, relaxing in his embrace. "Good. Love you, Inja."

"I love you," he said with a smile in his voice.

Romada sniffled, wrinkling her nose. "I'm bloody starving."

"Let's go find some food then."

Hand in hand, they made their way to the galley. Holding his warm hand in hers…it felt good. It felt right. Why had she denied herself Injago's comfort for so long? He was family.

Yaya glanced up from some boxes when Romada and Injago walked in. A wide grin spread across their face as they noticed the interlocked hands.

"I knew it! I knew you two would make up!" they exclaimed, running up to the siblings and pulling them into a tight group hug.

Romada laughed, the tension from the last few weeks draining out of her. It was the three of them against the world again. With these two at her side, she knew they would find Neiara. She only had to survive until then.

"Okay, I don't need super specific details, but I want to know what prompted this," Yaya said. "But first, a toast!"

"With what?" Injago pouted. "Isn't all the alcohol gone?"

A conspiratorial glimmer flashed in Yaya's eyes, and they disappeared into the storage room before emerging with a small keg. Injago let out a whoop of excitement.

"Beer! Oh, Yaya, you've been holding out!"

They chuckled. "I was saving it for a special occasion. This seems like it counts!"

"It totally counts," Romada agreed, grabbing glasses from the cupboards and joining the other two at a table. "Okay, what's the toast?"

The frothy beer was dark as night, and Romada's mouth watered as it filled the glasses. It had been so long since she enjoyed a good beer.

"To friendship," Yaya said, raising their glass.

"To friendship!"

"And to family," Romada said softly.

Three glasses clinked before each faerie took a hearty quaff. When Romada looked at her two best friends and saw their matching foam mustaches, she couldn't help but laugh again. The stress of their quest seemed so much more manageable with friends at her side. Feeling a bit misty-eyed, she looked over at Injago and saw his concern.

"I just miss Neiara so damn much," she said, taking another drink.

Yaya nodded. "We all miss her, but I can't imagine how you're feeling."

"We will find her, Rome," Injago said, clapping her on the shoulder.

"I know. We won't stop until she's safe."

"Damn right!" Injago said, raising his glass. "To finding love!"

Romada thought of Imber's dark eyes and how Injago had melted when he saw him. She couldn't help the sad smile that spread over her face.

"To finding love."

Injago's eyes met hers, and she knew he was thinking of Imber as well. Injago had been looking for love since they first took to the seas together. Through all of the heartache and rejection, he stayed strong. He never stopped looking. It was long past time for him to finally find it; Injago, of all the faeries she knew, deserved it.

She hoped that, for his sake, Imber might one day return those feelings.

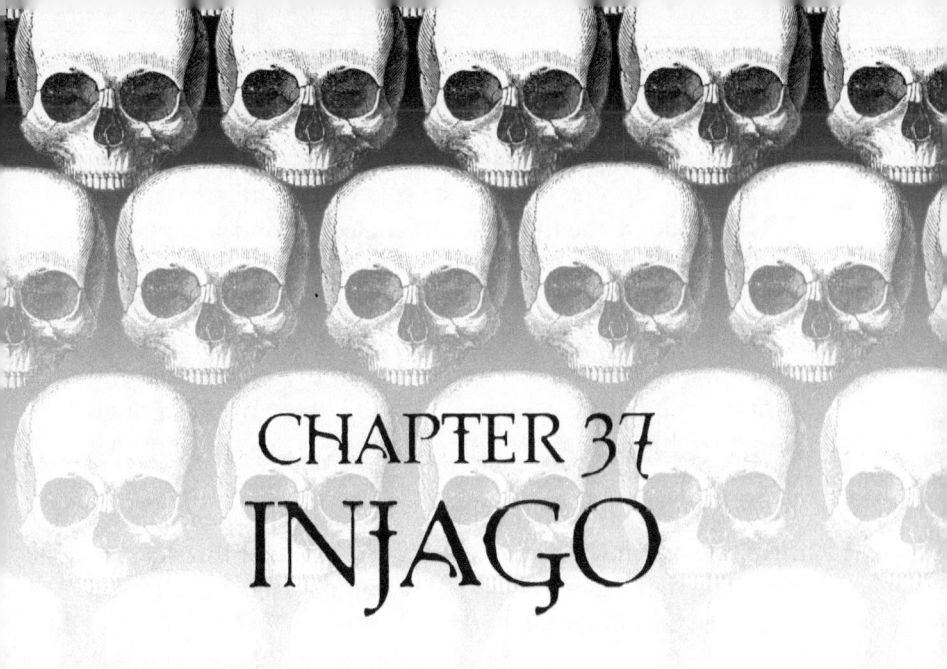

# CHAPTER 37
# INJAGO

**THE BODIES SHOWED UP THE NEXT DAY.**

Someone spotted the pod of merfolk when they were still a ways from the ship; Injago gave the order to stow the sails, and the ship came to a gentle stop. As the merfolk got closer, the crew could see them dragging three burlap sacks.

Fayne motioned for them to bring up the bags.

"Put your backs into it!" Romada yelled, hauling them onboard with the rest of the crew.

The first sack hit the deck with an unsettling squelch, and the scent of decay spread over the deck. Someone slit the bag open, and the partially decomposed body of a naked siren fell out.

Injago gagged at the onslaught of smells: putrid flesh, slime mold, and brined organs. The sea had done its best to preserve the body, but it had done a bad job; the disjointed limbs were held to the torso with the barest of stringy ligaments.

The neck had been mutilated with some kind of surgical instrument if the precision of the cuts were anything to go off of. The inside of the throat was mangled beyond recognition, and the haunting stare of pain permanently set in the dead eyes would absolutely be a source of nightmares to come.

Someone vomited over the side, and in a lightheaded daze, Injago realized it was Rehka. Imber stood still and silent over the body, his eyes betraying no emotion, though the set of his lips made Injago wonder if he had known the siren.

Injago held his breath as the other bags were opened. They held sirens in similar states: all of them had their throats torn open. The only relief Injago felt was in the fact that none of the bodies were Neiara's.

"Where… Where are these coming from?" Romada asked, looking green. "Someone get the map."

Ceta came hurrying over a minute later with it and held it open for Fayne to look at.

They studied the map for a moment before pointing at the area of the third camp.

Romada's eyes dimmed, and she excused herself, heading for the cabin. The door shut with a resounding **thud**, and then Injago heard a crash from inside the room.

Followed by another crash.

And another.

Injago exchanged concerned glances with Ceta and Rehka but decided it would be wise to wait until no more sounds came from the cabin. The crew stood in uneasy silence as they waited for Romada to stop her tirade.

When she had settled down, or at least was no longer making any audible noises of destruction, Injago gave the cabin door a hesitant knock. A muffled 'come in' came from inside, and he opened the door.

The entire cabin was wrecked. Ink dripped from a stain on the wall; the shattered inkwell lay in pieces on the floor. The fern had been upended, and dirt was strewn across the safe and desk. The lantern had been smashed on the floor; Romada would need to clean up the oil so they didn't have a fire hazard. That was the last thing they needed.

Romada sat on the bed, cradling a tiny succulent in her hands. It had been a gift from Neiara if Injago remembered correctly. It alone had been left unscathed. She held it tenderly, as if it was a baby, and she gazed at it with a mix of despair and adoration. Maybe it was her last piece of hope.

"We need to ready the bodies for burial," she said, standing and placing the plant back on the desk.

"We await your command," he heard himself say.

She nodded and brushed past him, striding out onto the deck.

"We are going to give them a proper burial," she said, hands on her hips as she projected her voice to the crew. "Drop the anchor. Yaya, find someone to help you rig some weighted shrouds. Injago, Eetan, help me clean the bodies."

Injago looked over at Eetan. So that was his name.

They worked in silence, scrubbing the bodies free of slime and mold and patting them dry. Yaya brought up weighted shrouds, and they wrapped the bodies in them. When preparations were done, the crew gathered near the bow where Romada stood, back straight and head held high. A slight breeze blew over the deck, gently clearing away the scent of death.

Romada raised her hands in the air. "Oh goddess," she prayed, "we bequeath to you these three souls. May you embrace them and carry them into the afterlife safely. May you bring forth their souls back into three beautiful merfolk to populate your depths. They didn't deserve this end, but this is what life gave them. May their next life hold better days than what they saw at the end of this one. May they have peace and happiness to make up for the horrors they witnessed."

She bowed her head and closed her eyes. "And goddess, as you hold them dear, please give us the strength and courage to find their captors, their torturers, their murderers, and bring them to justice. Bless them and bless us."

"Bless them and bless us," Injago murmured with the rest of the crew.

One by one, they lowered the shrouds into the sea. Slowly, they began their descent, bubbles floating up from them as they sank. Injago watched Romada watch the bodies fall out of sight; the wind ruffled her fins as she turned her attention to the sky and sighed. Her lips formed words he couldn't hear, and he wondered whether she was praying for them to find Neiara at the third camp or praying for them not to. Which would be worse?

The crew stayed silent out of respect for the dead and watched Romada for their cue to get back to work. Injago's thoughts strayed back to Neiara, though. Where was she? On the one hand, if she was at the third camp, they would find her sooner rather than later. On the other hand, that was where death and mutilation were being dealt, and he hoped with all his heart that she was safe from that at least. If that meant they didn't find her at the third camp, he hoped Romada could accept that. It would be best for all their stress levels if they found Neiara as quickly as possible but not at the expense of her life. And he wasn't sure his captain would survive seeing Neiara's dead body. He wasn't sure if any of them could.

Finally, Romada turned to the crew.

"Look lively!" she yelled, face animated with determination. "Raise the anchor! Loose the sheets!" She looked out at the distant horizon, and the crew looked with her. A fierce smile twisted her lips as the wind picked up, whipping at her head fin. "Let's follow the wind, mates!"

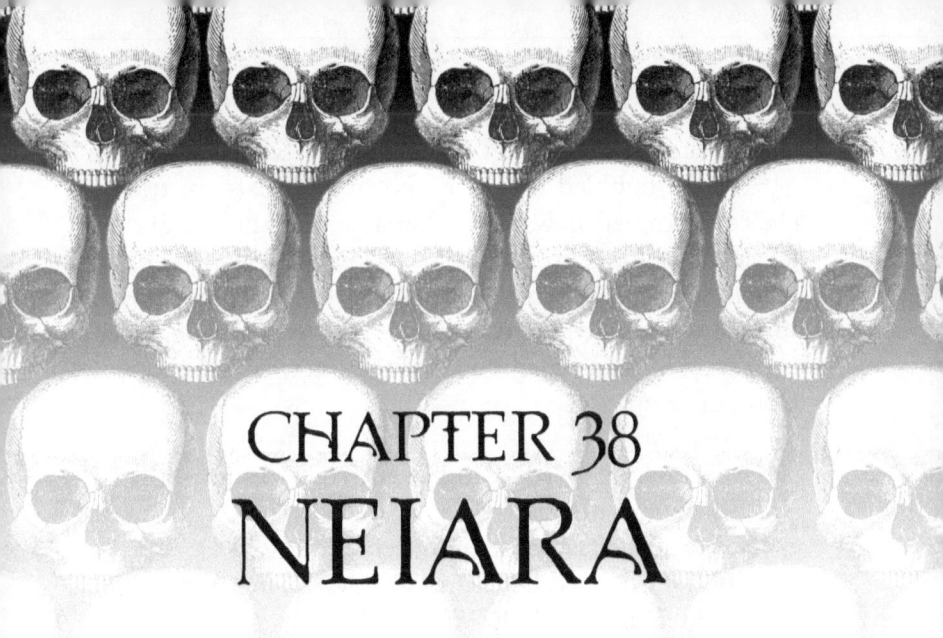

# CHAPTER 38
# NEIARA

**NEIARA OFTEN DOZED TO PASS THE TIME; IT** was always fitful rest, but it was better than staring at the slimy walls while trying to avoid looking at the other sirens. One of them had been dead for a while; the stench of rotting flesh was somehow even worse than the smell of putrid piss and feces.

When she woke from one of her naps, she noticed a new siren had taken the place of the dead body. The siren stared at her as she stirred, as though waiting for her to do something. Neiara averted her eyes.

A soft clinking sound echoed in the cell and drew Neiara's gaze back to the new siren. She was signing!

"Hello."

Neiara couldn't stop a smile from spreading across her face. Finally, someone who knew how to speak with their hands! "Hello."

"How are you?" she asked.

Neiara made a face. "I feel like shit."

The siren grinned, fangs on full display. "Smell like shit too."

A laugh bubbled up out of Neiara's throat—or tried to. The collar immediately choked her as soon as her vocal cords activated, the pressure against her windpipe leaving her gasping and seeing stars before it abated. As her vision returned to normal, she realized the two other sirens were staring at her.

Neiara looked straight ahead at the new siren, who wore a look of contrition.

"Sorry."

She shook her head. "I'm happy to talk to someone."

"What's your name?"

Neiara spelled it out, letter by letter.

The siren formed her name silently, smiling. She pointed to herself. "I am M A D R A."

Madra. What a pretty name. Neiara mouthed it, trying to remember what it felt like to roll her Rs. She glanced at the other two sirens, who were staring at her with open mouths and concern. Too bad they couldn't join the conversation.

A guard walked by, banging against the cell door as they passed. The sound boomed against the stone walls, making Neiara's ears ring. She winced, shutting her eyes tight, and waited for the echoes to end.

When she opened her eyes, the dead siren lolled against the wall, eyes cloudy and jaw agape. Maggots crawled through the flesh, and Neiara fought to control her nausea. She looked back at the other two sirens and saw bodies slumped in death as well. Tears stung her eyes as she bit her lip, drawing blood from cracks of dehydration, and wondered how long she had been alone. How long had she been stuck in here with corpses for companions? She squeezed her eyes shut again, willing the corpses to go away, for Madra to come back. To not be alone.

Opening her eyes, she looked at Madra's smiling face. Her eyes were a bright blue, just like the ocean. They almost glowed in the dim light. She was so beautiful, ethereal even. Like she had stepped out of a painting.

Madra stuck her tongue out, and Neiara laughed silently, the sound of it only in her mind. How nice to have a cell companion who knew how to sign, someone to help while away the days. And it would be nice to not be reminded of how many more days she could endure before Romada saved her.

If Romada ever did.

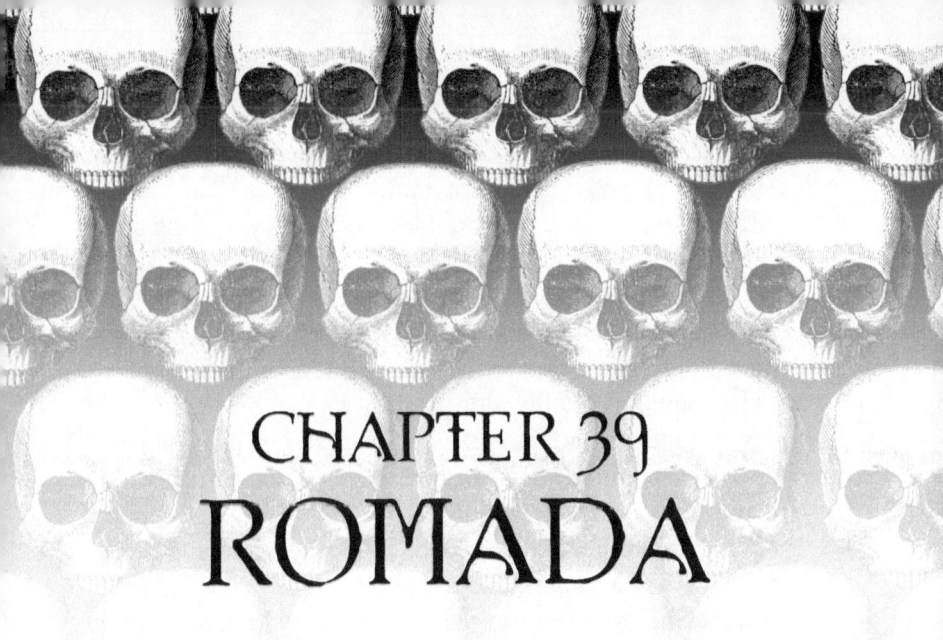

# CHAPTER 39
# ROMADA

**ROMADA SMUDGED A CHARCOAL LINE WITH** her finger, smoothing the edge. Rehka lay in a hammock, watching her over her shoulder.

"What do you think she's doing right now?" Rehka asked.

The outline of Neiara's form on the page, drawn from memory, made it easy to know who Rehka spoke of. Romada sighed as she drew another line and then tapped the charcoal stick against her lower lip.

"I don't know…eating? Gods, I hope they're feeding her. At sea, she was always seasick. Throwing up every morning. I'd make sure she ate enough food every day to make up for it. But now…"

Rehka rolled over onto her stomach, arms and legs flopping over the sides of the hammock. "You're worried about her health."

Romada nodded. The conversation lapsed into silence as

Romada studied her partial drawing and tried not to think about Neiara starving in some rotting tent.

Rehka poked her in the shoulder. "What do you think she'll eat first once we rescue her?"

Romada smiled to herself and smudged another line. "Coffee." A burst of laughter came from near the helm, and she glanced up; Injago stood at the wheel, Imber at his side with a smoking pipe held to his mouth. Imber had a hint of a smile on his lips, and Romada found herself wondering if he had ever grinned before. Surely, as a young boyo, he had been cheerful? Or had he always been brooding?

"What was Imber like as a child?" she asked, nudging Rehka.

"Oh, he was a total prankster! He was always playing jokes on Mama. She would swat his hands and scold him, but I know she thought he was funny."

Romada looked back up at the imposing and stony masc-fae before her and tried to imagine him playing a prank on someone.

And failed. Her imagination had limits. She turned back to her drawing, lining the slope of Neiara's shoulders. Imber had been hanging out around Injago a lot the past few days. The connection between them was magnetic, with Imber following Injago like a compass needle follows North.

Injago seemed happier, too. His attitude was more carefree, though Romada wondered how much of that was due to them making up and how much was because he had the attention of a handsome masc-fae. Ceta had been making herself scarce lately; seeing Imber beside Injago always brought a scowl to her face. It's not like she had ever had a chance with him anyway. Romada rolled her eyes at the thought of Ceta fantasizing about a gay faerie.

Speaking of gay…

"What's Imber's sexuality?" Romada asked in a low voice. Even if Imber was gay, seeing Injago for who he was and what he did and didn't have was a potential complication. Many masc-fae in the past hadn't minded for the night, but in the morning, Injago would find himself alone. Romada's heart had felt for him each time.

"Sexuality? He's… Oh, I don't know the word. He doesn't care about gender? He sees faeries as faeries and likes who he likes."

Romada nodded and tried to contain the grin that threatened to split her in two. So Injago did have a shot after all. She hummed to herself, more as a way to keep her lips in a straight line than anything else, as she shaded Neiara's collarbone.

"Why do you ask?" Rehka tapped her on the head.

"It looks like Imber and Injago are getting along really well." She couldn't risk saying anything more than that.

Rehka gave her a conspiratorial wink. "Well, that's nice! They would make a cute couple."

Romada couldn't help but agree. Injago's inky black hair and fair skin were a beautiful contrast to Imber's various shades of rich brown and gold. Together, they made a handsome pair.

She nearly jumped out of her skin when an obnoxious giggle echoed over the deck. Looking up, she caught Injago in the throes of laughter, eyes only for Imber. He noticed her looking a second later and covered his mouth, his cheeks turning a harsh red.

Had Romada ever heard him giggle before? Maybe as a child, but not as an adult. What had Imber said to him?

Rehka had succumbed to the giggles herself, rolling around in her hammock. "That was the most adorable thing ever!" she cackled.

Imber's face was, as usual, devoid of any emotions, though Romada could have sworn she saw a trace of mirth in his dark eyes as he released a swirling lungful of smoke.

Injago, on the other hand, looked like a strangled tomato.

Averting her eyes to give him some semblance of privacy, Romada turned her attention back to her drawing. This was the first time she had attempted to draw Neiara without using her as a real-life reference, and the exercise felt useful in aiding Romada in solidifying her memory. Of course, she would never truly forget her beloved's face, but sometimes, when she pictured Neiara in her mind, she got all hazy.

It frustrated Romada to no end. She loved Neiara! Why was she forgetting her?

So she hemmed and hawed and pored over the drawing pad, determined to draw her from memory only. A line here, a smudge there… Neiara was beginning to take shape.

Rehka jumped down from the hammock. "I'm thirsty! Want anything?"

"Some fruit, if Yaya has any," Romada said before Rehka skipped over to the hatch and disappeared belowdecks.

Her drawing was still missing something, some essential part of Neiara that she couldn't put her finger on. If only Neiara was there, emerald eyes shining, fangs glinting in the sunlight as she laughed. Romada took a deep breath and sighed. This was as close as she could get.

Whistling, she held the pad up for Injago to see. He looked at it for a moment before smiling and giving her a thumbs-up.

Romada hummed again, pleased with herself. Injago often teased her about taking too much artistic license with her drawings, so if he thought it was good, it was.

Rehka popped back up on deck and headed for her hammock, an orange in one hand and a waterskin in the other. "Catch!" she said, tossing the orange at Romada.

Romada caught it smoothly, though she nearly missed seeing the tender touch between Imber and Injago. Imber reached out and tucked a wayward curl behind Injago's ear tip, causing a deep flush to creep up Injago's neck.

How many times would this boyo blush? Romada hid a snicker behind her hand. Once she felt calm again, she set to peeling the orange as the ship began the process of slingshotting around the edge of a cape. With the right angle of the rudder and the sails, and with the help of the wind, of course, they could shoot around the curve ahead and get back on course with less effort. Every second wasted at sea was another second that Neiara spent in captivity, another second that Romada ached from the loss of her in her chest.

The orange fell from her fingers as the ship jolted to the side, throwing her across the deck and into the banister. Head spinning from the impact, she dimly heard Injago yell out to hold fast. She lurched to her feet to see a ship heading straight past them, barely slipping by without a collision. The danger of slingshotting past a cape was, of course, that a ship from the other side could be doing the same thing. But what were the odds? The royal blue and green flag waving in the brisk wind at the top of their mainmast marked it as an official ship of the Royal Naval Guard, but the small red flag below it snared Romada's full attention.

*A slaver ship!*

Romada's chest vibrated with fury as she screamed, "PRE-PARE TO BOARD!"

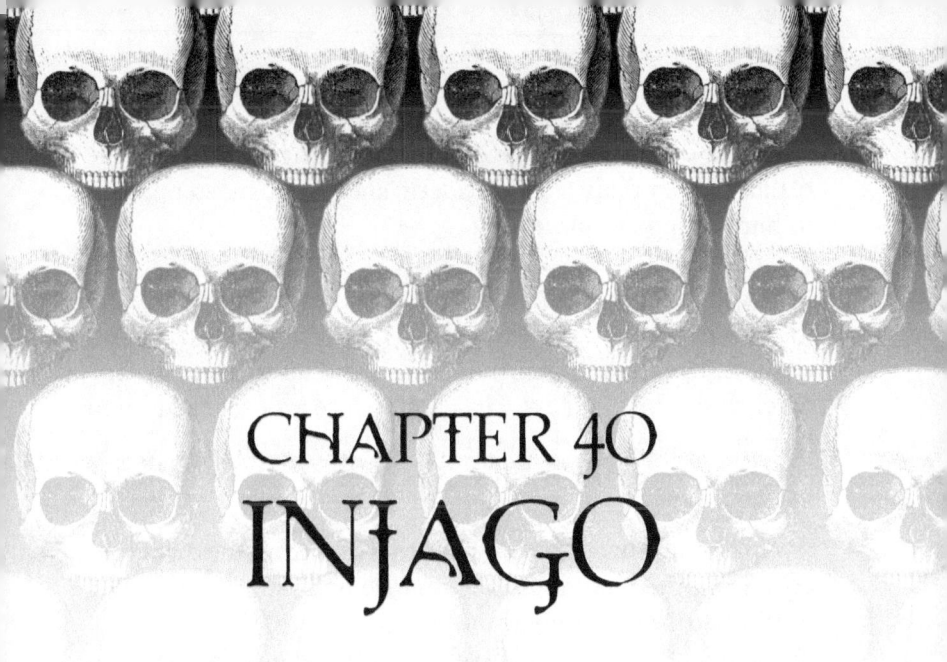

# CHAPTER 40
# INJAGO

**INJAGO SWERVED AGAIN, THIS TIME MANAGING** to scrape the hull of the other ship. The sound of splintering wood filled the air, and Injago winced. The poor ships! But this was their chance to free sirens—and children at that. Some collateral damage was fine, so long as the captives weren't injured by it.

Ceta came running up to the helm, out of breath. "Go," she panted, grabbing the wheel.

Unsheathing his sword, Injago flung himself into the air and flew across to the slaver ship. He landed heavily as the ship lurched to the side and readied himself for a fight.

And what a glorious fight! His first opponent was nimble, her blade flashing forward again and again. He parried, feinted, and thrust before pulling back in time to avoid certain death. Romada's war cry pierced the air, and his opponent's eyes shifted; swift as the wind, Injago lunged in and slashed her throat.

Wide eyes stared up at him as limp fingers dropped the blade, and her body fell to the deck; another guard stepped up to him, taking her place.

There was always another guard.

Injago fought mindlessly, his movements flowing faster than his thoughts, his reflexes saving him again and again. Parry, slash, thrust. Repeat. Another elf stepped up to him, this one barely older than a child. His chubby face was screwed up in fear, and he held his blade in front of him as though unsure of whether it would save him.

It didn't.

All around Injago, chaos reigned. Cries from the dying and cries from the victorious rang out. Behind him was a trail of death. Before him: Imber?

Imber crushed the skull of an elf, blood gushing between his fingers, and then whirled around, reaching for another opponent. Over and over, he pulverized the guards to death with his powerful, bare hands.

Injago stared at him, mesmerized. It was only after another second that he realized Imber was Singing under his breath, a low croon for his opponents that rendered them incapable of defending themselves. Injago couldn't have moved even if he had wanted to.

He couldn't imagine fighting while also Singing. The lung capacity required must have been enormous, just like the rest of Imber. Glancing over at Injago, Imber tumbled forward toward him, tucking his knees beneath his chin, and came up in a crouch with a sword in his hand. The tip of the sword was embedded in the guard who had been about to impale Injago.

Shivering, Injago wondered whether it was the tension between them or the near-death experience that had his nerves rattled. He genuinely couldn't tell. A scream of rage drew his attention, and he tore his eyes away from Imber's. An elven guard was charging him from across the ship.

It was easy to sidestep and thrust his blade into her heart without putting himself in danger; he kicked the body away from himself and turned back into the fray.

The fight was over within a matter of minutes, and again, he found himself drawn back to Imber. The sight of his chest gleaming beneath his loosely tied shirt was intoxicating. Sweat beaded and slipped over the panes of muscle… Injago wanted to taste Imber.

He wanted Imber to taste him.

A hand clapped him on the shoulder, and he startled before realizing it was Romada. She grinned.

"We did it!"

"Of course we did." Injago puffed out his chest in pride.

"You know… this ship is in good condition. Minus the hull scratches," she amended, side-eyeing him.

"That's true…" he said, wondering where she was going with that statement.

"We might as well add it to our collection. Start our own fleet. We've talked about it for years, and here's our chance."

Injago stared at her in disbelief. "Really?"

"And, well, a ship needs a captain."

"Yes…" He couldn't breathe. Was this really happening? Was she…

"Congratulations on the ship, Captain Injago," she said, grabbing his hand and giving it a firm shake. Too shocked to match her movement, his arm and body bobbed limply from side to side. He would have fallen if she hadn't held on.

"Captain Injago," he whispered in awe.

Imber came to stand beside him and placed a hand on his back. "Congratulations, Captain."

"I don't know what to say." He felt tears forming in his eyes and blinked hard to clear them. He had known this day was coming, but so soon? He had expected at least another decade before this dream was realized.

"I supposed you'll be wanting half of my crew," Romada said with a sigh. "And of course, I'll need a new quarter-master."

"Ceta will be an amazing quartermaster," Injago said, glancing over at the *Guardian* to see her figure at the helm. "She'll rule your crew with an iron fist."

Romada nodded. "I call Yaya, of course. But you can have Eetan since he's a decent cook as well."

So that's what Eetan did on the ship? Injago realized belatedly that he wasn't a very observant quartermaster. He would need to shape up now that he was captain.

"I call Imber," he blurted out. Had he really said that? Gods, what if he didn't want to come with him, though?

"I will gladly follow you." Imber's deep voice cut through Injago, leaving him feeling further unbalanced.

Romada frowned. "But Rehka will stay with me. Are you sure you're fine being separated again?"

Imber nodded. "This is not the same as being split up by camps. I know she is safe, and I can see her across the way." Rehka was indeed waving and smiling, all dimples and teeth, over on the *Guardian*. Imber had a fond look on his face as he raised a hand back. "Plus, I look forward to getting to know Injago better," he said, glancing at Injago out of the corner of his eye.

Injago felt a blush heat his face. How many damn times was he going to blush? Imber was a hazard to his poise.

"What now?" Injago asked, looking to Romada for guidance.

"First order of business is freeing the children," she said, ducking down to rifle through the pockets of the dead guards. After a few tries, she found a keystone and held it in the palm of her hand. It glittered in the midday sun.

"You don't have to go down there," Injago said in a low voice just for her. He took the keystone.

Romada trembled for a moment and nodded. "Divide everything up how you see fit. I trust you," she said, backing up.

With a heavy sigh, Injago turned toward the hatch, ready for the task at hand. He had freed children once; he could do it again. But gods help him if these children were in worse conditions than the ones back at Cape Guaraneau.

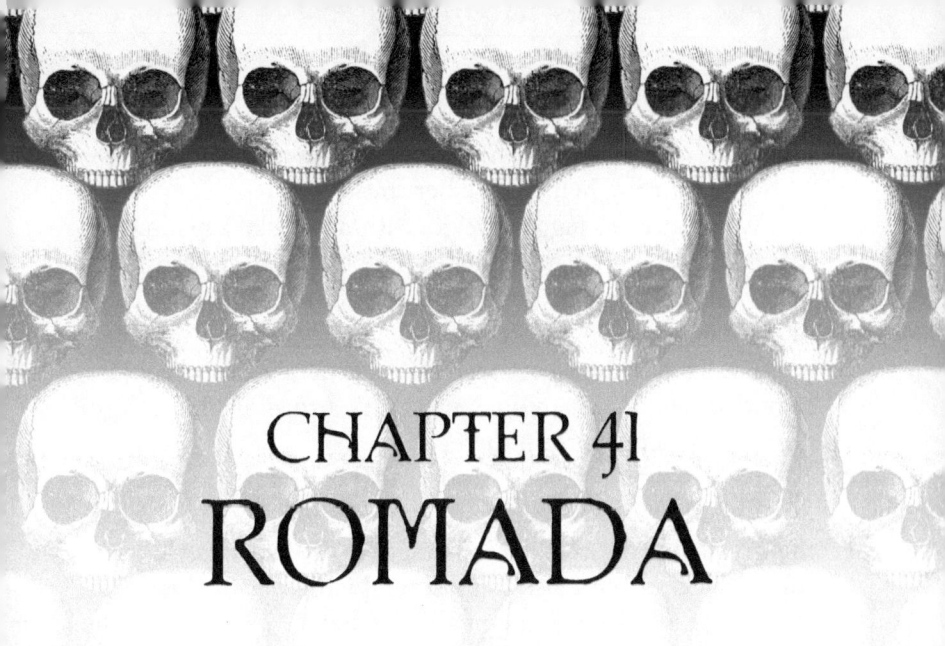

# CHAPTER 41
# ROMADA

**INJAGO MADE QUICK WORK OF DIVIDING CHIL-**
dren and goods between the two ships. Romada hadn't had to
lift a finger, and it was all set. Ceta effortlessly took control
of the *Guardian*, turning them back toward their destination.
Romada stood with her at the helm, watching the halved crew
working on deck.

"Captain, if I may?" Ceta's pale brown wings were folded
tight at her back as she stood ramrod straight. Romada wasn't
sure how long Ceta would stay so formal, but it was better than
when they were butting heads.

"What is it?"

"I suggest we refuel as soon as possible. With so many more
mouths to feed, we'll be lucky to have our supplies last another
three days. The food they were feeding the children was little
better than animal feed."

Romada's heart ached for the children and all that they

endured, but the sight of them running up and down the deck, whooping for joy, helped ease her spirit.

"Where do you suggest we go?" Romada asked, resting her hands on the mahogany banister. The map was stowed in its place belowdecks, but Ceta knew the shoreline like the back of her hand.

"You've heard of Ferendalf?" Ceta rotated the wheel just a smidge, keeping them on course. "It's a small fishing village nearby. I'm actually from there."

"I know of the place. It's populated entirely by pixies?"

"Yes. They've got very anarchist views and live entirely off the grid from the rest of the kingdom. I know they'll have supplies for us, but I also think several families would jump at the chance to take in some of the children."

Romada pondered that for a moment. It would be wonderful to find homes for the children, especially the younger ones. Pirates weren't exactly equipped to raise babies. But giving them away inside the kingdom... It was a risk they would have to assess when the time came. Not to mention the children would eventually need to be reunited with their own families, and how much harder would that be if they grew emotional attachments with these pixies?

"We'll sit down with the families and talk about it. See if they give off any warning signs."

Ceta nodded. "I'll set a course for Ferendalf then."

"Thank you, Ceta." Romada wasn't sure she had ever thanked her for anything, but it felt like the proper thing to do.

Ceta looked over at her with wide, mortified eyes. "You're welcome, Captain," she stammered, looking back ahead.

Injago's ship, now named *Freedom*, pulled alongside the *Guardian*, and Romada looked over to see him standing at the helm and waving wildly. She cracked a grin and waved back.

The children on each ship began to screech back and forth at each other, as children are wont to do, and Romada's spirits raised even more. They sounded like a flock of seadragons, and she couldn't help laughing.

Out of the corner of her eye, she saw Ceta staring at her.

Rehka stood on the deck, waving and blowing kisses to the other ship as it passed. Imber raised a hand, though he didn't wave it, his solemn expression never wavering.

Romada wasn't sure what Injago saw in him aside from his good looks. He was quite handsome in a brooding way, but what did they talk about? Clearly a good amount of it was humorous, if Injago's giggles were anything to go by. But what did they have in common? What was Imber's passion? It didn't seem like he got excited about anything. Then again, she had never been interested in masc-fae, so who was she to judge Injago's taste in them? She only hoped he would be happy.

Rehka made her way up to the helm and stood at the rear banister, gazing out over the ship's wake in the water. She sighed, a soft musical note. Romada hoped she was happy, too. In the short time she had known Rehka, the siren had become dear to her. She couldn't imagine not having Rehka at her side. But then, was that something Rehka wanted? They had never talked about Rehka staying on with the crew after finding Neiara. Romada hoped Rehka would stay, but then again, it wasn't the life for everyone. She had to respect that. Even she and Neiara wanted out of the pirate's life.

Neiara. Romada's heart welled with surreal sadness as she watched the children's joyous scamperings across the deck. "I wish Neiara was here to see this," she said.

Rehka turned to her. "She would be proud of you."

"You think so?"

"Of course! I mean, I don't know Neiara, but I know you. You've changed, Romada. Everyone can see it," she said, looking pointedly at Ceta.

The pixie cleared her throat and stared straight ahead, ignoring Rehka, though she did throw a cautious glance at Romada.

"What do you think, Ceta?" Romada asked, feeling uneasy.

"You have changed, Captain. For the better, I think."

Romada mulled over that. She had said thank you to Ceta for the first time ever. She had apologized to Injago, finally admitting blame when it would have been easy—had been much too easy—to blame him instead. She was starting to recognize and acknowledge her own limitations and realizing when she needed help from others.

Which, mortifyingly, was often.

"You're a great captain, Romada," Rehka continued.

"Well, all our efforts would mean nothing if it wasn't for you," Romada said, trying to shift the attention off herself.

Rehka stiffened, her expression darkening. "I did what I had to. I'm not proud of it."

"Oh," Romada said, abashed. "I didn't mean it like that. I'm just grateful."

"I know, and I'll do whatever it takes to help you find Neiara. You know this. But I don't want to think about it."

"O-of course," Romada stammered, her stomach twisting in knots. "Forget I said anything."

"No, I can't." Rehka sighed, staring out at the rolling waves behind the ship. "Because you're right. What I did was crucial to our success. The next camp will be bigger, and we need my Song to deal with it."

She was silent for a long moment. Romada stood beside her awkwardly, wondering what on Faerth she could even say to make the conversation feel less awful.

"Maybe I should teach the Song to the children. You know, just in case."

Romada gulped, a lump in her throat nearly choking her. "You would do that?"

Rehka's eyes tightened as she turned to look at the children frolicking on the deck. "I want them to be prepared for anything."

Romada looked at her, realizing that despite her delicate and warm exterior, she had nerves of steel and a will strong enough to crush anything in her path. She was ruthless and angry. And she had every right to be. Bloodletting wasn't always the answer, but violence didn't stop just because one asked nicely. Sometimes, one had to fight back. And Romada hoped that if the children were ever faced with the possibility of re-enslavement, they would use the Song rather than go quietly.

"I think that's for the best," Romada said in a small voice.

Rehka nodded, looking away. Her shoulder shook almost imperceptibly. Was she crying? Romada felt monstrous for bringing all of this up in the first place. How could she have been so crass?

A thought came to mind; she wouldn't normally offer physical comfort to anyone other than Neiara, but this was Rehka, and she was hurting. And she was hurting because of Romada's big mouth.

Taking a deep breath, Romada asked, "Can I give you a hug?"

Rehka turned, eyes shining bright with tears. "Please."

Romada enveloped her short frame in a tender embrace, webbed fingers flexing against the soft fabric of Rehka's tunic as the familiar honey and floral scent tickled her nose. She felt the telltale prickle of tears in her eyes and wanted to laugh. When had she become so emotional?

Rehka relaxed in her arms, humming a happy little tune.

"We're going to be okay," she said, the inflection making it sound almost like a question.

"Of course we are," Romada said, rocking her back and forth.

Ceta cleared her throat again, and Romada released Rehka, facing the wheel.

"What is it?" Romada asked, irritated that her hug had been cut short.

"Nothing! Sorry! I just wanted to point out that we are about to pass the *Freedom*."

Romada looked over and saw that they were indeed gaining on the other ship and would overtake them in a few seconds. As they passed, Injago waved, a grin lighting his face as he noticed Romada watching.

Rehka and Romada waved back, smiling through their tears.

"We're going to be okay," Romada said. She reached over to grasp Rehka's hand, interlocking their fingers. "I promise."

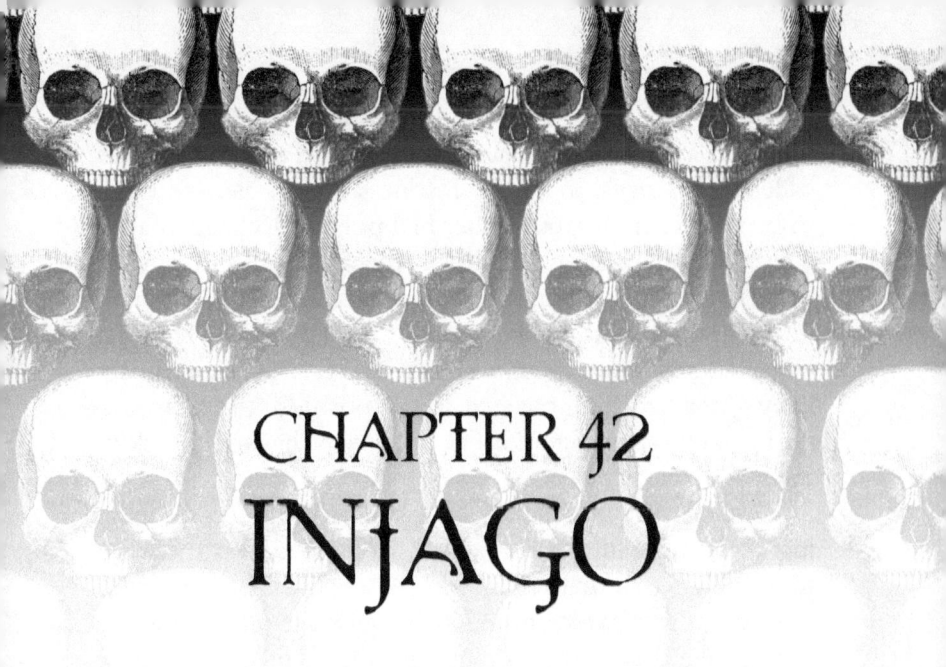

# CHAPTER 42
# INJAGO

**NIGHT FELL, AND WITH IT, LANTERNS WERE**
lit about the ship. Stars appeared overhead in the dark sky,
though no moon was visible. No matter; Injago knew how
to use the stars to navigate. Careful to keep the ship slightly
angled away from the *Guardian*, Injago steered the ship—*his*
ship—through black waters. He wished he was sharing the
moment with Romada but took comfort in the fact that she
was probably holed up with Rehka, enjoying her company.

How funny that where once he was jealous of the little siren,
now he was happy Romada had her friendship. Of course, he
didn't have much time for jealousy now that he had Imber's
attention. Or, rather, that Imber had all of Injago's attention.

He had told Injago of his time spent in the Royal Naval
Guard, which explained why he knew his way around a ship.
Despite being one of the best sailors stationed on his vessel,
he was never promoted up the ranks, simply because he was a
siren. After a decade of disillusionment, Imber left the Guard

to pursue a career as a freelance sailor aboard a merchant vessel called the *Horizon*. In a fit of madness, Injago had asked him to be quartermaster, but Imber had politely declined, making a cryptic remark about schedules. Injago wasn't sure what to make of that other than the obvious fact that he had to pick a different quartermaster. He picked Atar, a pixie who had been with the crew since the *Guardian*'s very first port call. Injago knew Atar had long coveted Ceta's position as quartermaster-in-training and figured that this meant he would pick up the tasks quickly.

The real test, though: would he still have a ship come morning? After hesitating for a second, he handed over the wheel to his new quartermaster and headed for the cabin. *His* cabin.

The lantern, which normally hung by the cabin door, was out, leaving the entire area dimly lit by the lantern at the mainmast. Fumbling for the door latch, Injago didn't notice the figure beside him until a hand reached out and touched him.

"Wha—" Injago attempted to call out, but the figure placed a finger against his lips, gently shushing him.

Squinting at the darkness, Injago made out the shape of a tall masc-fae with messy hair and dark, gleaming eyes.

"I did not mean to startle you," came Imber's rough voice in a whisper. "I merely wanted to wish you a good night."

Injago nodded and saw the moment Imber realized his finger was still touching Injago's mouth; Imber flushed and averted his eyes as he removed it.

"Apologies," he said, rubbing the back of his neck.

"No apology needed," Injago said, breathless. "Thank you for coming to see me. Do you want to come in?"

Imber studied the door impassively before shaking his head. "I should not."

"Why not?" Injago stepped closer. Imber's eyes met his; Injago's loins stirred in response.

"Because I might not be able to control myself," Imber said, voice hoarse.

Injago's heart pounded in his chest so loudly he knew the whole ship could hear it. "What if I don't want you to control yourself?" He took a step closer, close enough to smell Imber's musk, close enough to feel him trembling. With a smirk, he took one more step, pressing Imber back to the wall.

With a low moan, Imber closed the gap between them and pressed his lips to Injago's, hands tangling in his hair as he held Injago still. As if Injago dared to move. As if he dared to even breathe.

Imber tasted like citrus and smoke, like happiness and desire. His arms held Injago close, cradled him, made him feel safe. This was everything Injago had dreamt about, everything he could have hoped for from the tall, dark, and handsome stranger. A fire lit within Injago, pooling between his legs. He pressed up against Imber's thigh, rutting on the hard muscles, barely containing a moan as he felt his cunt clench.

With a gasp, Imber tore himself away and was gone in the night before Injago could even open his eyes.

Injago swayed and leaned against the door for support, wondering if he had imagined it. But no, the smell of Imber's musk still lingered in the air, and his lips were swollen from the kiss. He pressed his fingers to his mouth, wishing it had been more than one. His other hand went to his groin. He could feel himself throbbing through his pants, and his breathing hitched.

Dazed, he entered the cabin and began to undress in the dark, not wanting to see the empty cabin, not wanting to see how alone he was. He unwound his bindings slowly, thumbing a nipple as the last layer came undone. He was still throbbing, still aching. Still empty. Lying in bed, he worked his fingers through the slickness between his legs, panting until his release crested through him, until his mind quieted enough to fall asleep.

*** 

Injago woke from a dream and blinked at his surroundings, confused. Why was he in the cabin?

Leaping up, he let out a whoop; this was his cabin! On his ship! He was the captain!

Dressing with enthusiasm, he had to catch himself from

leaving the cabin without boots; he was so damn excited to get up to the helm. But first: breakfast. How would Eetan's cooking compare to Yaya's?

He headed down to the galley to find out, passing Atar on the way. Realizing who he had just seen, he stopped and called out to him.

"Atar! Who's at the helm?"

"Oh, that siren, Imber? I needed a quick break, and he said he didn't mind."

Injago's mind swirled with questions. Imber had turned down quartermaster. Why was he at the helm? Had he changed his mind?

His stomach growled, reminding him of his priorities. Shaking his head, he decided to deal with Imber later. He snagged a plate of fried fish and fried potatoes from Eetan—which looked and smelled incredible—and shoveled it all into his mouth, still steaming hot. Chasing it down with a mug of coffee, he stood, ready to face the day. And Imber.

The stoic siren was still at the helm when Injago made his way up the steps, looking out over the horizon and occasionally shifting the wheel to one side or the other. He glanced down at Injago, his expression revealing nothing about how he might have felt about their kiss.

"Where's Atar?" Injago asked, looking out over the deck. Despite their brief, passionate familiarity the night before, he suddenly felt unsure of where they stood. Was that all there would be? Was Imber regretting it? Would they be able to get back to that easy, lighthearted rapport?

"I said I would wait for you, and he went to bed," Imber answered, his voice deep and husky.

A shiver raced down Injago's spine. "Ah, okay. I can take it from here. Thank you."

Imber stepped aside, releasing the wheel, and Injago took it, relishing in the smoothness of the wood. It wasn't mahogany like the *Guardian*'s but it was a lovely burnished oak. The worn wood felt like silk beneath his hands.

And it was his. All his.

One hand on the wheel and one hand on his hip, Injago surveyed the ocean before him. Being captain was an entirely new adventure, and he couldn't wait to see where it took him.

A rough hand slid into his, and Injago jumped before realizing Imber still stood beside him, his impassive face betraying no sign that he was holding Injago's hand. Or wait, was that a twinkle in his eye? Injago wondered if anyone down on the deck could tell what was happening up at the helm. He wondered if he cared.

He cleared his throat. "Lovely weather today." He couldn't have said what the weather was, exactly, but any weather was lovely when Imber was touching him.

Imber nodded, his finger tracing Injago's palm. "A great day for sailing."

"Do you miss Rehka?" Injago's face glowed beet red from the stimulation, and he swore at himself for having such an expressive face. Hopefully, no one was looking.

"I do, but it is a comfort to be able to see her across the way. And I know she is happy."

"I guess that makes all the difference. If Romada knew Neiara was happy, maybe she wouldn't be so worried either," Injago mused.

"We will find her," Imber said.

Injago stared up at Imber's chiseled jaw and wished he could trail kisses along it. He wanted to run his hands through those tousled curls. He wanted to pull Imber's shirt open and lick the massive expanse of bare chest.

Imber's eyes met his, and Injago looked away. He wasn't sure if his thoughts had been well concealed or plain on his face. Imber chuckled, a deep rumble. Injago's ear tips burned with embarrassment. Was Imber laughing at him? He hadn't said anything funny. Or was this more flirting? When had he become so bad at recognizing flirting? And why was he so sweaty all of a sudden?

"You seem uneasy," Imber said, pulling his hand away. "Have I misread your desire?"

*No!*

"Not at all," Injago stammered. "I very much, um, desire… you." As Imber continued to stare, Injago felt he had to offer an explanation. "I'm nervous."

Imber chuckled again. Even as Injago watched, he couldn't see any traces of mirth on Imber's face. He really needed to learn this trick. Each time Imber made him laugh, the sound carried over the entire deck. The red splotches on his cheeks betrayed him just as much as his laughter.

"Why are you nervous?" Imber placed his hand back in Injago's.

"I'm just not…"

Not what? What was he supposed to say? That he couldn't believe this beautiful masc-fae was actually interested in him? That he wasn't sure Imber wouldn't turn away once he saw what Injago hid under his clothes? Or even worse, that he wouldn't care in the moment but change his mind after?

"I haven't been with many others," Injago said in a rush. It was a lie; he had been with plenty of masc-fae before. They all left as soon as they got what they wanted from him, though. A hole was a hole, after all. When presented with a willing one, most masc-fae—even the gay ones—didn't turn it down. That didn't remove the disgust on their faces after, when they reverted to thinking with their brain rather than lust. Would Imber be any different? He couldn't know for sure.

"I do not mind inexperience," Imber said.

Injago gave Imber's fingers a gentle squeeze and smiled when he squeezed back.

"I'm a fast learner," Injago said, not looking at him. Hoping. Wishing.

"Good." Imber had that hint of laughter in his voice.

"So if there's anything you want to teach me tonight…" It would be better to get it over with sooner than later. Would he be able to handle the crushing weight of this going wrong, even now? Certainly not if they spent forever in the before phase, just to have it all come crashing down.

Imber gave his hand another squeeze. "We will go slow."

"Slow. Okay. Slow is good," Injago said, working not to pout. Maybe acting inexperienced wasn't the way to go. He wasn't sure what the right thing to do was. Though if their future kisses were anything like their first, Injago wasn't sure how much he could handle before he burst. He only hoped Imber fell with him.

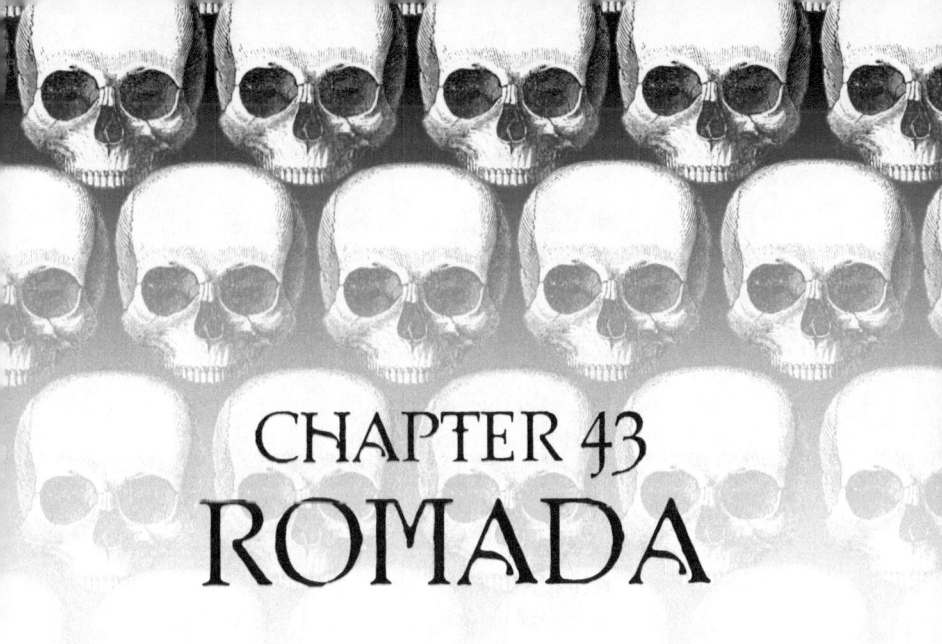

# CHAPTER 43
# ROMADA

**"SHIP ON THE HORIZON!"**

Romada heard the call from inside the cabin, where she had slipped into a light doze following a spectacular meal from Yaya. Leaping from the bed, she tripped over her blankets in her haste, upending herself onto the floor. Finding her boots, she pulled them on and raced outside.

Taking the steps to the helm two at a time, she gasped, "Is it a slaver ship?"

Ceta had the burnished copper spyglass to her eye and nodded, lowering it and handing it to Romada.

Peering through it, Romada studied the blue and green flag of the Royal Naval Guard flying above the smaller red flag for sirens.

Beside them, the *Freedom* matched their speed. Romada watched as Injago jumped into the air and flew over to the *Guardian*, landing beside her and Ceta.

"Our plan?" he asked, out of breath.

"We can run along both sides and hit with the ballistae," Ceta offered.

"That might hit the children," Romada pointed out.

"Oh yeah…" Ceta shook her head, lips pursed in thought.

"Wait! I've got it." Romada leapt down to the deck and grabbed the nearest child. "Go find Rehka," she said.

Injago and Ceta stared at her as she walked back up to them.

"What's the plan, exactly?" Ceta asked, keeping them on a steady course toward the oncoming ship.

"The sirens will use their killing Song on the guards, and then we will board and rescue the children."

Ceta raised an eyebrow but remained silent. Injago rubbed his chin as he stared at the slaver ship.

"What if it doesn't work?" he asked in a low voice.

"You called for me?" Rehka came up beside Romada.

"Yes! Did you teach the children the Song?"

Pain lurked in her tightened eyes, but she nodded. "They know it."

Romada turned her to face the approaching ship. "We need to use it on the guards so we can save the sirens onboard."

Rehka straightened her shoulder and lifted her chin high. "We can do this," she said with steely resolve.

"Go, gather the children."

"I hope this works," Injago muttered after Rehka left. "We'll have our ballistae armed and ready just in case."

"Good idea," Romada said.

Injago gave her a wry smile before leaping in the air and flying back to the *Freedom*.

"Raise the colors!" Romada yelled over the deck.

"Raise the colors!" The shout rang out as a pair of pixies ran to the chest and pulled out the black flag. Together, they clipped it to the mast and began to hoist it high.

The slaver ship sounded an alarm and began to turn around. Their attempt to evade the pirates would be laughable at best. The heavily armored and overloaded ship was too low in the water to make much headway. Soon, the pirate ships were but a ship's length away and gaining.

"Rehka! Sing the Song!"

Rehka nodded and faced the group of children, speaking to them before they all turned to face the other ship. Their voices raised in Song, and Romada's body shuddered from the first notes until her mind recognized that she wasn't being enchanted. She watched as the guards on the ship stopped in their tracks and turned toward the *Guardian*, their hands reaching for their weapons...

With a flourish, the elf who must have been their leader thrust their sword in the air and shouted. The rest of the elves joined in the battle cry, unsheathing and brandishing their weapons, before they all rushed belowdecks. Romada stared at the ship in bewilderment. What was going on?

Soon, the guards returned, siren children in tow. Romada couldn't grasp what was happening until the first body fell over the side, throat slit from a guard's dagger. Over and over, blades drew across slender necks, and blood poured out across the railing as the guards slaughtered the children, tossing them over the side of the ship, their bodies sinking as their chains dragged them down into the abyss.

A scream of outrage pierced the air. Through a red haze of fury, Romada realized it was coming from her own throat.

The once steady rhythm of the Song faltered as the sirens saw what was happening on the slaver ship. Cries of horror and despair resounded around Romada as the children dropped to the deck and hid their faces from the massacre.

Still screaming, Romada stomped down the stairs and into the cabin, slamming the door against the wall. She yanked open drawers in her desk, searching for it...and found the blitz in the bottom drawer. "For extreme cases only," Otandar had said when he sold it to them. "It's volatile and uncontrollable."

Volatile and uncontrollable was exactly what she needed. She strode to the bow, her battle cry still emanating from her now raw throat, and took aim at the hull of the slaver ship, down by the waterline. She wanted the ship to sink, to carry all of those heartless elven guards into the crushing depths of the sea. Planting her feet wide, she squeezed the trigger. A green beam of heat blew open a hole large enough for a rowboat to fit through. The fiery backdraft singed her fins. There were a few siren children still in the hold, but from how their bodies were strewn, she doubted they had been alive.

Screaming through the sorrow clogging her throat, she squeezed again, and a second hole blew open. Water began to swirl like a vortex around the holes, flooding the inside of the ship. Dragging it down.

*Good fucking riddance.*

"Fire!" Injago shrieked from onboard the *Freedom* on the other side of the slaver ship. The deep **twang** of the ballistae strings reverberated over the water, as did the splintering sounds of wood as the bolts hit the hull.

Dimly, Romada realized she had stopped screaming, that she couldn't have screamed any more even if she had mustered the energy. Her voice was completely shredded. She sobbed silently, choking on her grief and horror, watching as the smoking ship groaned and sank below the surface, leaving a swath of bubbles and bodies. This was her fault. If she hadn't trusted so much in the Song, those children, those poor babies, would have lived. They should have done what Injago suggested. They should have boarded the ship like normal, like pirates did. They were pirates after all, not heroes. They didn't swoop in to save the day. How was she supposed to live with herself, knowing she was responsible for so many innocent lives lost?

Soon, the only sign left of the devastation was the blood spreading across the surface, a million crimson wave caps decorating the sea. It reminded her of the blood that she knew was staining her own hands, blood she would never be able to wash away.

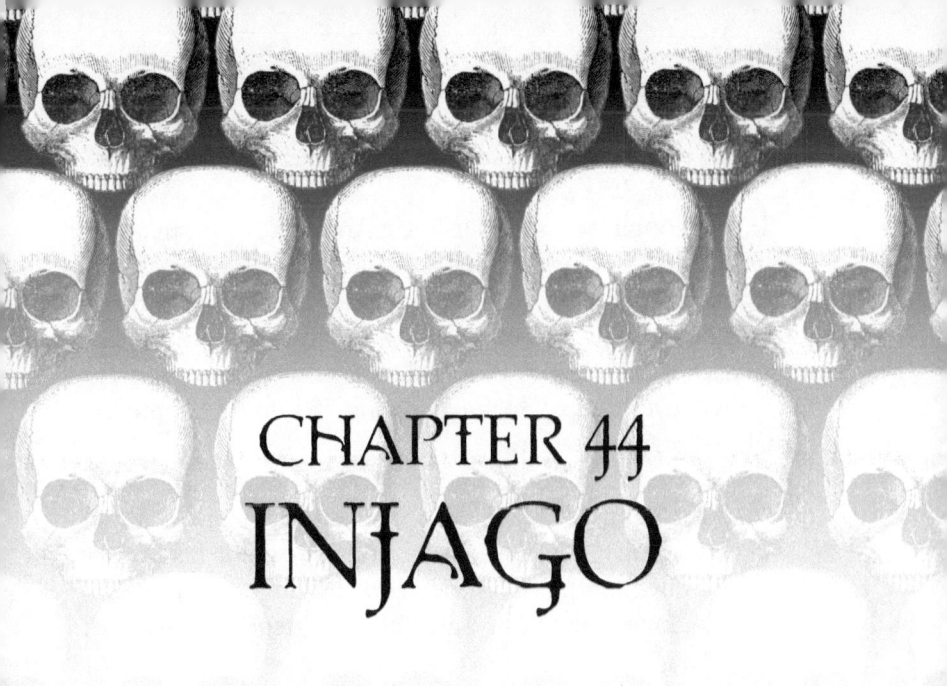

# CHAPTER 44
# INJAGO

**EVERY TIME HE CLOSED HIS EYES, ALL HE** could see was red.

Red. Roiling red. Red bubbles bursting and splattering all over him. He couldn't see anything else, he couldn't feel, he couldn't breathe. The roaring in his ears shattered the red with an image of a child's bloodstained face.

Injago tore his eyes open, gasping for air; it took him a moment to realize he still stood at the helm, though the ship had started listing toward the *Guardian*. He quickly corrected his course. No need for another bloodbath.

His eyes were drawn to movement on deck as a pixie named Anavi emerged from belowdecks. Injago called out to him, and Anavi headed for the helm.

"Captain? Is there something you need?"

"Yes," Injago said, working to keep his voice from shaking. "I need you to watch the helm for me for just a bit until Atar wakes up."

Anavi scowled. "Why are you asking me to do this? Why don't we wake Atar early?"

Injago contained a sigh. He knew Anavi wasn't particularly self-motivated, but he *was* opportunistic. Injago took a gamble.

"Remember how Ceta worked under me as quartermaster-in-training? She helped with my shifts, took care of the map, charted courses. Now look: she's her own quartermaster."

Anavi's eyes lit up. "So you're saying, if I do this, someday I might be quartermaster?"

Injago clapped him on the back as he moved back, relinquishing the helm. "Anything is possible if you work hard."

Heading down the stairs two at a time, he made his way to the cabin. Flinging the door open and shutting it behind him, he at last allowed himself to give in to his tears. He sobbed, choking on guilt.

"Oh, gods... All those children." His whisper was broken by a hiccup. He couldn't breathe. His lungs... Yanking his shirt over his head, he stared down at his bindings. Damned things! Frantic, he tore at them, stripping them from himself. He stood, bared, chest heaving, and took his first deep breath of the day. And sobbed all the louder.

Every time he closed his eyes, he saw red. He saw the sea boiling with their innocent blood. *Children!* He saw faces above gaping neck wounds as they drowned. *Babies!* He wept for them, all of them.

"They didn't have to die," he hissed at no one. But who was to blame? Romada had done what she thought best. Rehka and the children had done their part. It wasn't anyone's fault that the Singing hadn't been loud enough to enchant the guards.

That didn't mean he felt any better about it.

He longed to sleep, to lie down on the comfort of his new bed and let the darkness fall around him. He wanted to blot out the faces, the tiny hands waving in the water.

But every time he closed his eyes, he saw red.

A knock sounded on the door, and he scrubbed his face free of tears. "Who is it?" he asked, silently cursing the shakiness of his voice. The captain didn't cry over babies.

"It's Imber," came a deep voice.

Injago pulled his shirt back over his head and rushed to the door, pulling it open only enough to see Imber's face. His chiseled jaw and high cheekbones could cut glass, but his face gave Injago a sense of security and stability, especially given his perpetual stoic expression.

"Can I come in?"

Realizing he was standing in the doorway staring, Injago flushed and stepped aside to let him in. "Of course," he said.

Imber's long strides carried him to the center of the cabin as Injago shut the door and leaned against it. Now what? Imber had never seen him without his bindings. Most of the crew had, but it was never something anyone remarked on. He had no clue if Imber had known before now. Weakly, Injago crossed his arms over his chest, hoping it would be enough. Turning to face Injago, Imber raised his arms.

"Would I be remiss to think you would enjoy a hug?"

Injago hesitated. He would have loved a hug, had longed for such an offer. But he was struck with the nagging feeling that Imber was only giving him physical attention because he felt like he had to. He wanted Imber to want to do it. And...maybe he was scared. Scared of what Imber would say, what his face would look like, when Injago removed his arms from his chest.

"Why do you like me?" Injago regretted the words as soon as they left his mouth. They hung in the silence between the two, shaking the space into something with the potential to be emotionally damaging. Why hadn't he just said yes?

Imber dropped his arms. "I sense that you would not believe me no matter what I say," he murmured, his voice so low it was nearly inaudible.

"I'm pitying myself," Injago said, raking his fingers through his curls as he looked Imber in the eye. "It was rude of me to ask."

Imber crossed his muscled arms and pursed his lips, his eyes dropping to Injago's chest.

Injago mirrored him, covering himself once more. Neither of them said a word. It looked like neither of them even dared to breathe. Finally, Imber looked back up, making eye contact again. Injago could have cried in relief that Imber's face hadn't twisted, hadn't shown disgust. He looked sad. Was that better or worse?

"I'll believe you. Promise." Injago begged behind closed lips for Imber to come back into the conversation.

Imber nodded, though he still didn't speak. After long enough that Injago had broken a sweat in nervousness, he spoke.

"You exude a kindness. I can tell you are a good faerie."

Injago was pleased to hear this, but he snorted derisively. "I'm a pirate."

"Pirates do not venture out to save others from harm, and certainly not faeries they do not even know."

Injago didn't have a retort for that, but he didn't want to argue anyway. He wanted to be thought of as a good faerie. He wanted to believe he was good. And it was validating to hear it from someone he was so attracted to.

"You saved my life, Injago. I will always feel a debt to you. I think that is why you do not want to believe that I can also like you."

Shrugging, Injago finally looked away. The thought of Imber being indebted to him was...disturbing. Not because Imber might be attracted to him because of it, but because he actually liked the fact that Imber felt like there was a debt. And *that* made Injago uncomfortable. What did that say about him?

"But I did not become enamored with everyone in your crew. Only you. You are the one who drew me in. You and your kind eyes that have seen so much and yet still look for the goodness in others."

Injago struggled not to make a face. That assessment didn't sound like him. Was Imber seeing what he wanted to see? Was Injago wearing a mask to attract Imber? And if he was, and it was working, did he really want to correct Imber?

He covered his face with his hands to avoid looking at Imber. His chest hung heavy, making him realize hiding his face rather than his breasts made him feel even more vulnerable.

Everything felt like such a mess. How was he supposed to go forward with wooing Imber now? This was all a farce. Imber was painting him with false compliments, a truth that twisted him into something he wasn't. He hadn't remembered to save Neiara. Everything since then had been a course correction. How kind and good of a faerie could he truly be?

"If you knew half the things I have done, you would feel differently," Injago said, his voice raspy with emotion.

Imber stepped closer, and Injago dropped his hands to look up at him. Pain hollowed Imber's face.

"I am a siren. Do not presume to think my hands are cleaner than yours."

Injago swallowed around the lump in his throat. There was a buzzing in his ears as Imber stepped even closer.

"You say that like being a siren is a bad thing."

"It can be." Imber's eyes hardened. "I could make you love me. I could force you to love me, and you would never know. I'm despicable."

"You don't need to force me," Injago said, breathless.

Imber's eyes melted into a pool of amber. "You do not know what you are saying," he said. His usually smooth voice was gruff.

Injago took a step forward, keeping eye contact. Imber was a finger's breadth away; Injago could feel the heat radiating off his body.

"I know what I want. I want you to want it, too."

He saw the moment Imber's control wavered; with a gasp, he jerked forward and caught Injago's mouth with his. Heat and desire spread through Injago's bones, making him light as air; he would have floated away if he hadn't fisted his hand in Imber's hair, holding to him like an anchor.

A knock sounded on the door, and they leapt apart from each other. Imber's golden brown skin was blotched red. It was nice to see his composure wasn't ironclad.

Injago went to the door, opening it a crack.

Anavi stood in the doorway. "Atar came and relieved me," he said, shuffling his wings. "I was hoping I could take the map from you and start caring for it like Ceta did. If that's really a responsibility you think I can take on."

Injago nodded, still flustered. "One moment."

Shutting the door, he strode to the desk and opened the top drawer, pulling out the map. It was the backup copy that Romada had kept in her cabin; she had gifted it to him along with the ship.

"Here," he said, opening the door just enough to pass it through.

Anavi took it, his eyes lighting up as he held it with reverence. "Oh, wow. You won't regret this! I'll be the best quartermaster-in-training ever!"

Injago smiled. "I don't doubt it."

Anavi headed off with a skip in his step, his brown wings fluttering behind him.

Injago shut the door again and turned back to Imber, who stood over in the doorway to the bathroom, out of sight from the main door.

"Where were we?" Injago asked in a playful tone.

Imber shook his head. "I should leave."

"Oh. Of course." Injago tried to keep disappointment from coloring his voice and failed.

After letting Imber out, he stood in the center of the cabin, wondering what on Faerth had just happened. He and Imber had had a moment, right? It felt like a breakthrough. And yet… Why was he now alone?

He lay down in bed and closed his eyes. All he saw was red.

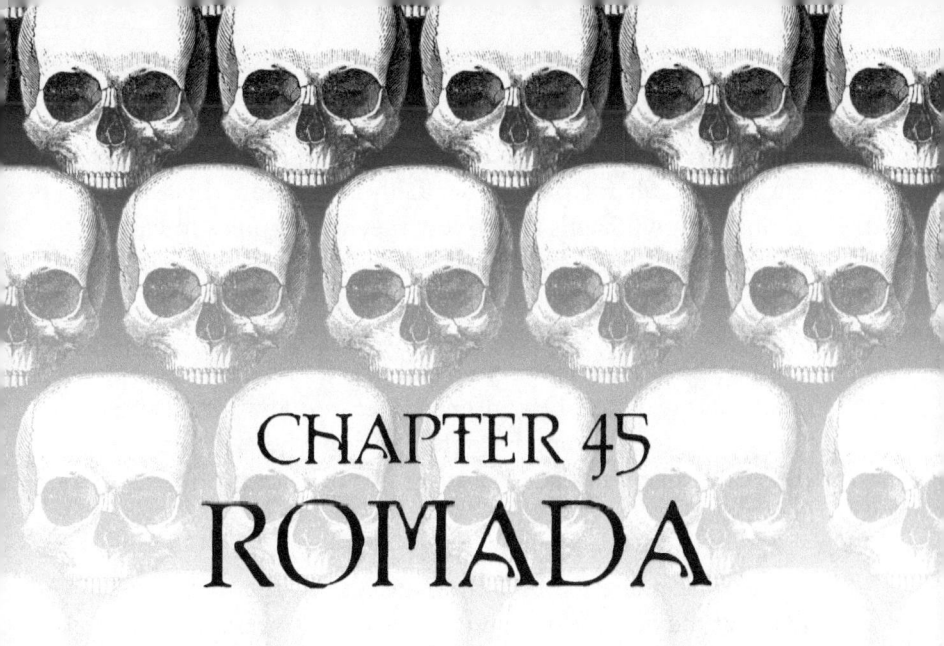

# CHAPTER 45
# ROMADA

**ROMADA JOLTED AWAKE FROM A DREAM OF** drowned children pulling her into the depths of the ocean. Those grasping, clinging hands, cold as ice, had gripped her with steely strength. She sat upright, chest heaving as she realized she wasn't in the water; she was in bed, she was alone, and she was safe.

But not absolved of her guilt.

It crushed her, sapping the life from her limbs and tore chunks from her heart, leaving holes that flooded with sorrow. A void of anguish lived in her now, consuming her will to live as though it was a delicacy, as though it was desperate for more. She couldn't let it win.

She tried to look on the bright side: the children were no longer living as slaves, and their souls would be reborn as beautiful merfolk, populating the seas, bearing good luck and fortune to all those who saw them in their travels. This should have been a comfort, and yet…

257

And yet, it was her fault they had died in the first place. It was her fault for placing her faith in the Song instead of getting her own hands dirty. Now they were ironically stained with innocent blood that dripped from her fingers even as she stared at them. She would never be free of this loss.

Groaning and rolling over, she wrapped the blankets around her like a cocoon with full intentions of going back to sleep. It was Rest Day, after all. Her goddess would surely forgive her for sleeping in, right? And maybe, with any luck, she could sleep all day, drowning her despair in dreams of better days.

Days when she hadn't failed everyone.

A knock pulled her back from the edge of slumber, and she glared at the door. Who dared disturb her depression?

"Rome?" Rehka's soft voice floated through the door, and Romada knew she had no choice but to drag herself out of bed for worship. She could deal with disappointing her goddess, but not Rehka. Pulling open the door revealed a haggard siren. Sadness peered out of dim eyes. Rehka gave her a halfhearted smile, one Romada attempted to return. And failed, again. That's all she was: a failure.

"Do you want to eat first?" Rehka asked, her voice low and dull.

"No, I…I don't think I can." Romada hugged herself, shivering with nausea at the thought.

Rehka nodded. "I understand. I was sick after dinner last night."

"I didn't eat," Romada admitted.

"Probably for the best."

They walked out onto the deck and peeled off their clothes under a pale, foggy sky. Clouds hovered over the water, obscuring half of the *Freedom*, though it was anchored only a ship's length away.

Romada gritted her teeth as the chilly air enveloped her. "Let's get this over with," she said, throwing one leg over the banister.

"Are you allowed to say that?" Rehka asked.

"Wait!" Yaya emerged from belowdecks, panting. "I'm here." They peeled off their pants and shirt, tossing them on the deck.

They jumped together, a triplet of splashes echoing over the water. Romada's gills burned from the cold and she gasped underwater, struggling to accept the water into her shuddering lungs. The frigid water raked her insides, and she choked and thrashed, trying to get back to the surface. She wasn't sure what drowning felt like, but if she had to guess, it would be like breathing ice-cold water.

Erupting from beneath the waves, Romada coughed up the icy liquid, vision blurring and shifting as she tread water.

Rehka was beside her, shivering. "Are you okay?"

"I can't breathe," Romada answered. Tears stung the corners of her eyes.

"I'm not sure how much longer I can last either," Rehka said, teeth chattering.

Yaya popped up beside them. "Fayne is here," they said, pointing.

Romada looked and saw the pod in between the ships; Fayne led them, a smile on their face and a large spiral shell brandished in their webbed hand.

"That's a pretty shell," Rehka said once Fayne reached them.

With a grin, Fayne brought it to their lips and blew into it. Romada clapped her hands over her ears at the enormous bellow that boomed from the end, echoing over the still water.

"Wow!" Rehka said, uncovering her own ears after Fayne stopped. "How does it do that?"

Fayne pointed at the spiral and then moved it to the crook of their elbow so they could say, "Spirals, small to big. Make sound small to big."

Rehka and Romada gasped, grabbing each other.

"If we can make something like this—"

"But bigger! We could—"

"Make our Song heard—"

"Across the water!"

Yaya looked between the two of them, confusion wrinkling their face. "What are you two saying?"

"We need to make one of our own!" Rehka clapped her hands giddily. "We make one, and then our Song will work!"

"Obviously, it will need to be much bigger, so all of you can Sing into it, and so it can be heard at a longer distance," Romada said, excited. She turned to Fayne. "Thank you!"

Fayne blushed and bowed their head before flipping head over tail and vanishing beneath the waves. With the disappearance of their resident merfae, their spirits once more sank down to dismal heights. The cold sapped at Romada once more, reminding her that she couldn't handle it for much longer.

"Let's get out of here? I'm freezing," Yaya chattered.

"I can't feel my toes!" Rehka said, making her way to the side of the ship.

"Wait, you still have toes?" Romada asked.

Rehka's answering peal of laughter was a balm; Romada couldn't stop the smile that spread across her face as she climbed the ship.

They dried off and dressed in a rush, eager to be warm, before stringing up their hammocks. Romada lounged in hers, a blanket loosely draped over her middle, and swayed with the gentle motion of the ship. She watched the fat clouds above as they drifted by.

A call rang out over the water, and Rehka ran to the railing.

"It's Injago and Imber in a rowboat! How silly; Injago could have flown over," she said, waving at the two.

"And leave Imber all on his lonesome in a rowboat?" Romada clutched her chest in mock dismay. Rehka snickered.

A length of rope was tossed up and over the banister and Rehka caught it, tying it off. Even from afar, Romada was impressed by the quick and tight knot she made. Rehka had learned a lot in the short amount of time she had been onboard. Had it really only been a week since they had rescued her?

The boyos climbed up the side of the ship and onto the deck, receiving hugs from Rehka. Imber also got a peck on the cheek, which he had to bend down to accept. Hand in hand, the twins meandered away to the other end of the deck, heads together in conversation. Rehka's expression was somber, at odds with her playful demeanor only seconds before. Romada's grief and guilt, which had been held at bay, came crashing down around her again.

"Hey." Injago stood at the end of her hammock, hands in his pockets and shoulders hunched. "How are you doing?"

"I've been better," Romada said, aiming for a light tone and instead choking on a sob.

"Want a hug?"

She stood without hesitation and stepped into his steady arms. The tension drained away.

*Who knew hugs could help so much with stress?*

"I'm starving," she said after a few seconds. "I didn't eat last night."

"Me either."

"Someone's hungry?" Yaya asked, coming up to them. "Come on, I'll get some food cooking for you two."

Together, they traipsed down to the galley, where Injago and Romada settled down at a table while Yaya banged pots and pans around in the kitchen.

"I miss having you here," Romada said quietly. She traced a pattern along the wood grain of the tabletop. "I'm glad you came over for the day."

"We've been spending our Rest Days together for centuries," he said with a gentle smile. "I wasn't going to break that tradition now."

Romada returned the smile. "Thanks, Inja."

"Love you, Rome."

In his words, Romada heard his forgiveness, and knew he didn't blame her for the tragedy. It didn't make any difference in how much she blamed herself.

"I love you, too," she whispered, not daring to speak any louder for fear of breaking the dam holding back her tears.

He reached over to grip her hand, giving it a squeeze. "We'll get through this."

"Yeah."

*Gods, please let that be true.*

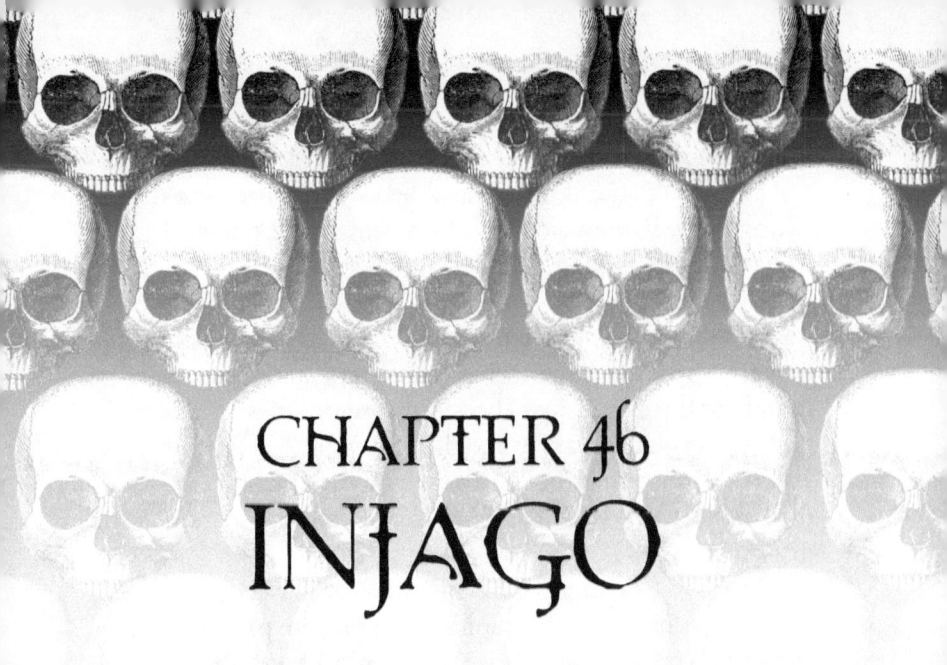

# CHAPTER 46
# INJAGO

**DESPITE THE CHILL IN THE AIR, MOST OF THE**
crew was up on deck, lounging and relaxing. Rehka and Yaya
were bundled up in sweaters, sipping steaming mugs of coffee.
Romada was in her usual halter top, prickles on the skin of her
arms and chest.

"Put a shirt on," Injago said. He leaned over the edge of
his hammock to watch her sketch on her large drawing pad.

"I'm fine," she said, not losing her focus on the contraption
she was drawing.

"What is that?"

She shrugged. "We don't have a name for it yet, but it's
going to be our saving grace."

"What does it do?"

"It's going to be like a horn, but for voices. The voices will
be louder and carry clearer and farther over the water."

It clicked in Injago's mind then. "You're going to attempt
to use the Song again."

"It's a precaution."

He wasn't sure if that was a lie or not. How was it their saving grace if they didn't plan on using it? "I guess it's good to have a backup plan," he said slowly.

"Exactly."

She didn't look like she wanted to say anything else on the subject, so he lay back in his hammock, staring up past the rigging at the clouds just above the dragon's nest.

"We haven't had a day like this in a while," he said absently.

"It's almost time for the change of the season."

"I'm not looking forward to the monsoon rains," he grumped.

"Scared of getting your wings wet?" she asked, giving him a wicked grin. Even when smiling, he saw the pain in her eyes, the grief and the guilt. But what could he do about it? He played along with her joke.

"Hey now! Pixies don't like wet wings, okay? Wet wings can't fly!"

She snorted and turned back to her drawing. "Bring on the rain. I'm not afraid of water."

"You're a water nymph, for gods' sake! Hush."

Chuckling, she lifted a leg to kick his hammock, sending him swinging.

"Rude," he said, hunkering down low so as not to fall out.

When his hammock finally settled, only moving with the gentle sway of the ship, he turned to look at Imber. He was deep in conversation with Rehka, their faces mirroring each other in somberness. Injago knew how hard it was to accept the tragic loss of life—death was an inevitability after pirating as long as he had—but he couldn't imagine how Imber and Rehka felt, seeing their own kind heartlessly slaughtered. At least as pirates, they chose their fate. They knew the risks. But those children... Squeezing his eyes shut tight, he saw red.

He must have fallen asleep because the next thing he knew, Imber was shaking him awake.

"It is starting to get dark," he said in that deliciously deep voice. "We should head back."

"Of course." Injago yawned, sitting up to stretch. "Yes, let's go."

Rehka gave each of them a goodbye hug. As Injago swung his leg over the banister, he looked back up at her. Catching his eye, she gave him a wink. Flustered, Injago nearly slipped on the damp handholds on the way down to the rowboat.

The silence was punctured by the splash of the oars as Imber rowed; his muscles rippled under golden brown skin. Injago found himself mesmerized until the image of Rehka winking came back to the front of his mind.

In a low voice so as not to carry through the still night, Injago asked, "Why did Rehka wink at me?"

It was difficult to tell in the dying light of the sun, but he could have sworn Imber blushed. "I may or may not have told her of my infatuation," Imber murmured, not meeting Injago's gaze.

"Are you ashamed of it?" Injago was curious and yet not altogether ready to hear the answer.

Imber shook his head. "Not at all. I am merely unsure of the protocols when it comes to romantically pursuing your captain."

Injago let out a quiet laugh over Imber being more concerned about crew etiquette than the fact that Injago was built differently. "I don't know either. But as captain, I think whatever I say goes."

With a slight smile, Imber nodded. "This is the way."

The diluted glow of the moon filtered through the clouds overhead, lighting their path back to the *Freedom*.

"Will you worship the moon tonight?" Imber asked. "I would welcome your company."

*The moon? I'm not a water nymph. Why on Faerth would I worship the moon?*

He considered his words carefully. Neiara wasn't a water nymph either, but she had worshipped the moon. Maybe sirens liked the moon goddess.

"The moon is a water nymph goddess," he said slowly. "I've never worshipped her."

"I wish I could be so cut and dry with who I worship," Imber said, a hardness in his voice.

"Why don't you worship any siren gods?"

Imber gave him an indiscernible look and said, "Our gods were all stricken from record several millennia ago. Back when sirens were slaves of other races, before slavery was abolished, all records of our gods were destroyed to keep us from being able to worship on Rest Days so we could keep working."

Injago's jaw dropped. "That's horrifying," he said, stumbling over the words. Horrifying didn't even begin to describe it.

He had earned terrible scores in history class when he was a child and couldn't have recited the history of his own species. He didn't even know all the kingdoms that were native lands for pixies, other than Dradour. To carry such knowledge, to know that history was repeating itself... He was beginning to understand why Imber was so solemn.

They reached the *Freedom* and called out to someone to help them tie off the rowboat. After they were secured, Injago turned to Imber.

"You know," he said in a murmur, "I'd love to worship the moon with you if you'll still have me."

Imber's eyes shone in the moonlight. "I would like that."

After all, worshipping the goddess of lovers with someone who Injago hoped would become a lover made sense. And if it brought him closer to Imber faster, even better.

They climbed onboard and worked together to raise the rowboat to its stored position and then parted ways to go ready for worship. Injago had never watched Neiara and Romada worship the moon, but he supposed it had to be similar to how he worshiped—used to worship—The Harvester, though their moon worship always ended in lovemaking. He knew that wouldn't be the case with him and Imber, at least not yet. Imber wanted to go slow, and though every bit of Injago was against that, he couldn't rush Imber or change his mind. Pushing the issue might push him away altogether.

Besides, the longer they had before they slept together, the more time Injago could enjoy the feeling of someone longing for him. And the longer it would be before Imber inevitably lost interest, as all the masc-faes he had slept with did.

*Don't think like that. Give him a chance.*

Selecting a white candle from his desk, Injago headed for the altar below the foremast where Imber waited with a candle of his own. "Ready?" Injago asked with a shiver of anticipation. Whatever did or didn't happen between himself and Imber, he wanted to wait for it with an open heart, rather than a reserved one. He was tired of grieving before he even experienced the loss.

"Let us worship," Imber said, holding out a hand to Injago.

Injago took it and settled before the altar, ready to accept the light of the moon into his life.

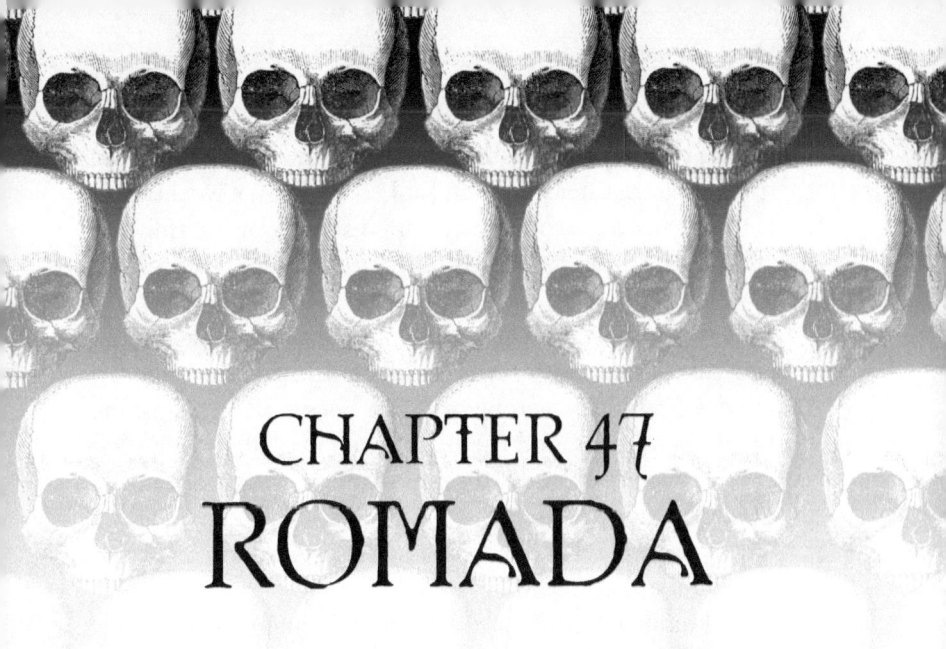

# CHAPTER 47
# ROMADA

**AFTER ANCHORING OFFSHORE OF THE VIL-**
lage of Ferendalf, a handful of the two crews headed for shore.
Rehka, Ceta, and Romada headed straight for the metalsmith to
talk to her about their plans. Ceta had grown up helping her in
the shop and was a veritable bubble fountain of conversation
as they walked. Romada couldn't remember the last time Ceta
had said so many words. Or maybe she couldn't remember the
last time she had paid enough attention to care.

"She made all the door handles in the village! Some of them
are custom designs, but not all of them, of course. Though
I guess just from the fact that she made all of them by hand
means they're all custom, right? I've got to show you the handle
she made for my parents' front door; the spiral work is amazing.
Oh, and the one for the mayor's front door!"

Ceta chatted their ears off the whole way, stopping only
once she threw open the shop's front door and exclaimed,
"Sinta!"

A tall, willowy pixie with cropped red hair and a plethora of freckles across her pale skin looked up from a workbench. "Ceta?" She strode across the cramped shop, a broad smile on her face and her arms outstretched for a hug. "I've missed you!"

The two pixies embraced, gushing affection for each other. It wasn't until they both turned to face Romada that she saw the obvious familial resemblance. The shape of their lips, the curve of their noses, and the tilt of their eyes all looked identical. They even had the exact same shade of wings: a beautiful pale brown, nearly golden.

"Are you two related?" Romada asked, looking back and forth between them.

"Oh, I didn't tell you? Sinta is my aunt!" Ceta said with a soft smile as she looked up at Sinta. "I was so lucky to have such a cool aunt growing up. Other kids had relatives who taught them fishing or farming. Bo-ring!"

Sinta's laughter was the sound of tinkling bells, eerily similar to Neiara's. Romada's chest was hit with a pang of sorrow.

"I was lucky to have such a hardworking niece," Sinta said. She gave Ceta's cheek an affectionate squeeze. "Now, what can I do for you? Don't think I know you didn't just swing by to say hi to your dear old aunt."

Ceta gestured to Romada.

Clearing her throat, Romada offered the sheets of paper with her sketches. "We'd like to commission something from you."

Sinta took the pages and rifled through them, hemming and hawing. "What are you going to call this thing?"

Romada glanced at Rehka, lost for words.

"The megasound," Rehka said, nodding her head with finality.

"Megasound... I quite like that. How big do you need this to be?"

Rehka held out her arms, and Sinta's eyes widened.

"We need several faeries to be able to talk into it at once if that means anything," Romada said, looking around the shop. A huge bellows was attached to the hearth, and various tools hung from hooks all around the perimeter of the room. Metalwork projects in different stages of completion lay on benches in the back.

Sinta muttered to herself as she moved over to a rack of metal sheets. Walking her fingers on a couple of them, she counted under her breath before snapping her fingers and smiling.

"I should be able to have this done for you in a couple days."

Rehka and Romada exchanged looks.

"We kind of need a rush job," Romada said with a grimace as a means of apology.

Sinta sighed. "So you need it by tomorrow."

Romada nodded.

Sighing again, Sinta said, "Well, in that case, give me three strong bodies to help, and I'll see what we can do."

"Ooh! I volunteer!" Ceta said, jumping up and down.

"I volunteer Imber," Rehka said. "I mean, with those muscles, he's gotta be helpful, right?"

Romada grinned. "Then I volunteer Injago. He may be small, but we all know he won't want to leave Imber's side."

Rehka let out a giggle, and Ceta rolled her eyes. Romada noticed though that her smile hadn't dropped. Maybe she had finally given up on her futile crush.

"Great!" Sinta clapped her hands together twice. "Send them here as soon as possible and we'll get this thing, this megasound, done lickety split."

***

Rehka and Romada sat at a table set up at the far end of the great room in the village's Community Center, staring at a list of names Ceta had scrawled onto a torn sheet of paper. They were families who Ceta was sure would be interested in fostering or adopting some of the siren children.

"That's so many families," Rehka said, reading the list again.

"I think the more important thing is that we don't even know if the children want to be adopted. They might be holding out on finding their families if they have them."

Rehka nodded, pursing her lips. "That's a fair point! We can't give these children out like they're candy. They deserve to have a choice."

A line of pixies slowly assembled before them, no doubt the families that Ceta had written down. Romada felt daunted. Was this the right thing to do? How did they even find good families for the children in the first place?

"What's the plan?" Rehka asked in a whisper.

"I guess we interview them? Ask questions about their family and what kind of home they're offering? I don't know."

"What kind of questions would you have asked if this was you back when you were a child waiting to be adopted?"

Romada's eyes tightened in pain as she turned inward, memories of countless adopting parents-to-be refusing her again and again. She had always thought it was because she wasn't pretty enough, or smart enough, good enough…everything that Delaini reminded her of again and again. As an adult, she couldn't help wondering how much of it had actually been Delaini working behind the scenes to keep her favorite punching bag close and silent.

"I…don't think I can think about that," Romada said, voice breaking.

Rehka reached over to rub her back. "Hey, it's okay! You don't have to think about it. We'll figure this out."

"Okay," Romada said. She shuddered as she fought through the nausea that struck her at the thought of being on the adoption block again. Looking at the line of parents waiting, she knew that, once again, she would be a disappointment. Who would pick her? Who wanted her?

No one ever did. No one but Neiara.

*And Rehka.*

Romada swallowed her pain. She wasn't alone. Rehka was with her and would help her through all of this. She had been helping since the moment they met. And Rehka would be there when they finally found Neiara. Holding onto the hope of finding Neiara, her shining light, Romada settled in for a long session of painful memories, endless questions, and a perpetual yearning to feel like she belonged.

***

After several hours of interviews, Rehka called for a break. Romada knew it was because she could no longer speak clearly and kept forgetting what she was saying, and she was grateful Rehka recognized that the stress was getting to be too much. They stood and exited the village Community Center to go stretch their legs.

Collectively, the crews had decided to let the siren children loose to run, play, and screech so long as they stayed in sight of a crew member at all times. Yaya and Eetan had volunteered to watch them all at the park in the center of the village, so that's where Rehka and Romada headed.

They walked arm in arm down the main road of the neighborhood, pointing out little things to each other, like the menagerie of dragons beside one house and how another house was nearly overgrown with creeping ivy. The fresh air helped Romada relax, the stress draining away the farther they got from the Community Center.

The sound of the park reached her ears before she saw it; the shrill laughter of children hard at play brought a smile to her lips even as she worked to wipe the traumatizing memories of her own childhood from her mind. She had always prided herself on being strong, both physically and emotionally. This time without Neiara was showing her though that Neiara had been the source of that strength; learning how to cope without her was exhausting.

They rounded a bend in the road and the park came into view; a gentle rolling hill stood in the center, crowned with a playground complete with slides, swings, and a seesaw. Children giggled as they chased each other, weaving among the play equipment and running down the hillside. Surrounding the park were a dozen houses with front yards ranging from 'well-manicured' to 'wildflower garden.'

"This is precious," Rehka said.

Romada nodded, humming to herself as she took it all in. "I want this."

Rehka looked up at her. "You want children?"

"Yes, but more than that, I want community and stability. Safety and happiness. I've only been a pirate for a century, but it's tiring. I want a home."

"Traveling the seas is a grand adventure," Rehka said as she surveyed the park.

"Neiara is all the adventure I need."

Rehka smiled and rested her head against Romada's arm. "I like that."

Together, they looped around the park before heading back to the Community Center to finish finding homes for the children.

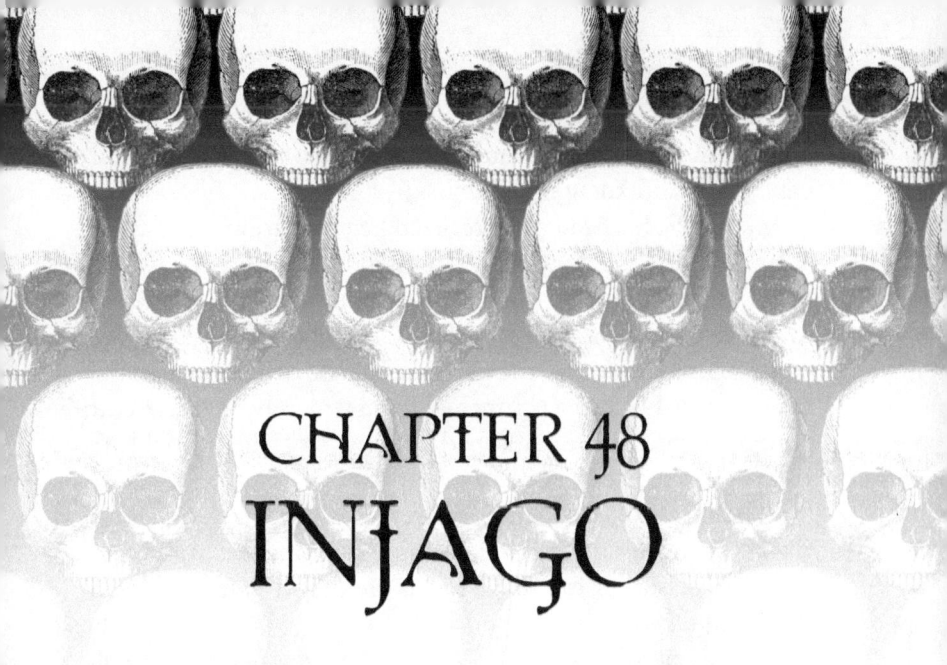

# CHAPTER 48
# INJAGO

**INJAGO COULDN'T KEEP HIS EYES OFF IMBER.**
Sweat gleamed on Imber's bare back, his skin glistening in the glow of the furnace as he worked with Sinta to bend the metal into the correct shape.

"Get back to work," Ceta huffed, making Injago wonder how long he had been staring.

"Sorry," he mumbled, chastised. Being bossed around by Ceta was a new feeling but she knew her way around the shop better than he did. She very impressively knew what she was doing too. He had never thought to ask her what she had done before she took to pirating.

He turned back to his task of warping the spiral infrastructure of the device, which involved heating the metal strips with a blowtorch and bending them while they glowed cherry red. It was tough work, and he often had to stop to catch his breath, both from the physical exertion and the intense heat.

Which led to him staring at the target of his lustful infatuation for who knew how long.

He shook his head as he realized he was staring, once again, at Imber's rippling deltoids and instead focused on the twisted metal before him. The work was mind-numbing; he found his thoughts drifting far away. To The City, in fact. The red of the metal reminded him of the particular shade of lipstick Delaini always wore. His brow scrunched as he remembered their visit, how disrespectful Romada had been, wiping the lipstick off with a glare at Delaini's back.

The metal sparked, and he threw his hand up to block his vision. The resulting flash caused him to momentarily go blind everywhere but for the shape of his hand, and a face appeared in his mind.

It was the blue face of a young Romada, her cheeks still rounded and full and her eyes a bit too large. A bruise marred her cheek in the form of a handprint, and he had asked her who had slapped her.

"No one," she had said in a haughty voice. "I don't know what you're talking about."

He had chalked it up to her feeling embarrassed that someone had gotten the better of her.

The next week, she sported tiny pairs of bruises on her arms. He had asked who had pinched her. "No one," she had huffed, pulling at her sleeves. "I don't know what you're talking about."

The next week, she refused to sit down in class, complaining that her butt hurt. He had jokingly asked who had spanked her, or if she had slipped and fallen. She always had been clumsy.

"No one!" she had yelled, tears in her eyes. "I don't know what you're talking about!"

When everyone else snuck out of bed to play, Romada would already be gone, though they had never found where she went off to. She would slink back to bed long after the rest of the children returned from their fun and had gone to sleep.

Injago saw in his memories how she had flinched when Delaini touched her, how she followed every rule to the T, and how even the mention of Delaini, or the click of a heel on the tile, would change her whole demeanor from tough, bossy warrior to small, cowering child. He saw again how Romada glared daggers at Delaini when they had visited her, how she smeared off the lipstick as quickly as possible, how she had looked sick the entire time they were in Delaini's office. How tough, warrior Romada had been reduced to a glowering, quaking child once more.

He stared into the red-hot metal sparks, realization dawning on him.

How could he have been blind to the abuse for so long? All the signs had been there. Romada had always been loud, boisterous, and carefree. The moment Delaini showed up, that all crumbled away. The day Injago had aged out of the Orphan Center had been the first time he had ever seen Romada cry.

"Take me with you," she begged. He had hugged her, telling her that she had less than 15 years left, and he would be waiting for her. She said it wasn't enough knowing he was out there. She needed him to be with her. He had jokingly said she would find him overbearing, and she had yelled, "That's what big brothers are for!"

The last words he heard her say until they were reunited as adults.

He couldn't believe he had missed it. Her cry for help. Her pain. How dare Delaini lay a hand on Romada? Innocent Romada. Precious Romada. She had been a child!

But Romada wasn't a child any longer. She was still his little sister, but she didn't need his protection or his pity. It was too little, too late after all. Should he say something? Or would talking about it dig up old, festering wounds?

Did Neiara know? He grunted as he worked over the metal. Of course she did. Romada shared everything with Neiara. He thought she had shared everything with him at one point, that Neiara had stolen something from him when she entered Romada's life. Now, he wasn't so sure. Maybe Romada had always closed him off from the pain she carried. Maybe he didn't know her at all.

Anger and regret blossomed in him, fueling his metal-bending rage.

***

Injago stood in the shop, shoulders weak and chest heaving, and stared at the finished contraption. Soot marked his brow, and sweat dripped down his back, but it was done. He was thoroughly exhausted.

"We did it," Ceta panted.

Sinta let out a gusty sigh. "Not my finest work. But it'll do."

Ceta and Sinta embraced, their identical noses touching in a familial kiss.

"Thank you for your help," Sinta said, slinging an arm over Ceta's shoulder.

Ceta was all smiles. "It was an honor to work for you again."

Injago glanced at Imber, wishing he would put an arm over his shoulder, pull him into a hug. Not that he could reach that high. Maybe if he hovered. Which would look ridiculous. Gods, he couldn't stop staring. Imber caught his eyes and blushed, looking away.

*How long will this infernal tip-toeing continue?*

The door to the shop flung open, letting in a stream of sunlight and a breath of fresh air.

"Good morning!" Rehka said in a cheery tone. Romada stood at her side.

Romada's gaze turned to the device. "Oh, wow," she breathed.

"That is the most ugly, amazing thing I have ever seen!" Rehka ran up to it, awe in her eyes.

The giant hunk of polished metal gleamed in the mid morning light. "Yeah it's…terrifying," Injago said. The metal had been twisted and crushed into shape, its lack of cooperation through the process evident in its hideous appearance. It looked like death. Which Injago supposed it was.

"What's the name of this thing?" he asked.

"The megasound," chimed Sinta, Rehka, and Romada at once.

Injago blinked in surprise at the quick answer. "The mega-sound... Who came up with that?"

Rehka raised a small hand in the air, a proud grin on her face. "It's fitting, isn't it?"

"Does it work?" Romada asked.

Already standing at the speaking end, Ceta shouted into it. The resulting noise had Injago quaking in his boots, his ears ringing violently. Shaking his head, he looked up to see Ceta laughing, though he couldn't hear it.

"Great!" he said in what he knew was a too-loud voice, though he could barely hear himself. "So it works!"

The ringing faded away, and he sighed in relief.

"Next time, let's make sure our enemies are the only ones on the loud end," Rehka said with a giggle.

The corner of Imber's lips quirked up, and Injago stared at him in astonishment. Had he almost laughed? Outloud? In public?

"How are we getting this onto the ship?" Romada asked, gesturing at the sheer size of it.

"And which ship?" Injago asked.

Rehka rubbed her chin. "That's a good point. We should consolidate the rest of the sirens on one ship."

"I'll take the sirens," Romada said. "Minus Imber, of course."

Injago felt his cheeks heat. "So we just have to get this thing, this megasound, onto your ship."

"What if we rope it off and fly it on?" Ceta suggested.

"That could work," Sinta said, looking Injago up and down, then turning to Imber. "Too bad this one doesn't have wings."

Imber's golden brown skin darkened as he scowled.

"I'm sure you've got plenty of strong pixies here in the village," Injago said hurriedly. Imber gave him a look that Injago could only assume was gratitude.

"You're right! Ceta's father is husky. Let's go find him," Sinta said, grabbing Ceta's hand. The two exited the shop.

"If only I was so lucky to have been born something other than a siren," Imber said in a low voice, disgust marring his attractive face.

"You quit that," Rehka said, folding her arms and glaring at her brother. Injago couldn't remember ever seeing Rehka look angry before.

"Why? Why shouldn't I wish I had been born anything other than what I am?"

"You're pitying yourself. We don't do that." Rehka stepped right up to Imber, standing toe to toe with him. "We make the best of what we've got." Imber cast his eyes to the floor.

"Of course," he rumbled, looking properly chastised.

Rehka smiled and patted Imber's arm. Injago realized he wanted to be anywhere other than there and looked to Romada for help. She saw his expression and nodded, motioning for him to come with her.

"Let's go find some of our pixie crew and get them to help," she said, tugging his arm when he got close enough.

Injago and Romada stepped into the sunlight, leaving the twins behind.

# CHAPTER 49
# ROMADA

**AFTER A FULL DAY AND NIGHT SPENT IN**
Ferendalf—mostly spent getting a dozen siren children
sest up with families and restocking their ships—Romada
was relieved to be back on the ship, sailing the open seas
and heading toward Neiara. The rotting sirens they had
found the week before still haunted her dreams, and she
often found herself wishing Neiara wouldn't be found at
the third camp if it meant she wasn't near whatever had
killed the sirens.

*Please be safe.*

And yet she did hold out hope that Neiara would be
found soon, safe and well, waiting in the third camp. What
would they do after she found her? Part of Romada wanted
to continue the journey toward freeing the rest of the sirens.
There were only two more camps, after all. Someone needed to free them. It wouldn't be enough to simply liberate
the remaining camps, however. Someone needed to start a

revolution against the kingdom to stop the oppression at its source. Someone, but was Romada up to the task?

Rehka stood beside her, chatting about the siren children as Romada turned the wheel, keeping the *Guardian* on course. Having spent so much time with the children, Rehka was a fount of knowledge when it came to their lives and interests. She shared all of it with Romada as she kept her company at the helm.

"Little Surrell collects seashells! I told you she lived by the coast, right? She's been watching ships sail past her home her whole life and is so excited to be on a real ship now! Oh, and Orikk! He's so sweet. He loves to paint. He paints mostly landscapes—his favorite ones are coastlines—and he's really missing his paint set. Maybe we can find some paints somewhere?"

Romada nodded—hemming and hawing in all the right spots—listening to Rehka ramble but not focused enough to actually take it all in. There was no point in becoming close to the children; they were all going to leave as soon as they found their families, either blood relatives or an adoptive family. And that would be the end of the relationship.

There was a reason Romada didn't have many friends. Injago would say it was because she was too reserved with her emotional connections and who she trusted, but really, it was because she didn't see any reason to invest in a relationship that was bound to end. Injago aging out of the Orphan Center before her had nearly killed her. Even though he had promised to be there when she got out, the pain of loss and abandonment had been there. She couldn't go through that again.

Children came and went from the Orphan Center the entire time she had been there. Injago had received several adoption offers during his childhood, though he turned them all down. He never said why, but she liked to think it was because he didn't want to leave her. He had adopted her as his little sister when she had been too young to even know what a brother was. Romada would always be grateful for his decision to wait for her on the outside; who knew how her life would have gone if she had aged out of the Orphan Center alone?

"And Patya, the redhead? She has the sweetest singing voice. I really think she could be a professional singer someday. Oh!" Rehka gasped as Ceta burst up from belowdecks, panic written across her face as she leapt up the stairs to reach Romada.

"The camp, the next camp—oh gods," she panted, bending over to rest her hands on her thighs. "I didn't realize. But the next camp is at th-the fully operational Naval garrison base."

Romada stared at her in horror. "A fully staffed garrison? *The* Naval Garrison? How did we miss that?"

"I'm not sure!" Ceta wailed, throwing her hands in the air. "What do we do? We can't take on a whole garrison! That's— that's hundreds of guards! Maybe a thousand."

Romada's heart galloped through her chest, rattling her and stealing her breath. Her knuckles whitened as she tightened her grip on the wheel.

"Let's think about this logically," Rehka said in a soothing voice. "We have the megasound." She gestured at the metal contraption near the bow, covered with a sheet of fabric.

Ceta squinted at her in confusion. "And?"

"So we go right up to the base, taunt them into coming out, and then the children and I will Sing the killing Song. We'll kill them all." Rehka's voice was flinty and harsh. Romada knew Rehka hated the idea despite it being her own suggestion.

"You really want to do that?" Romada asked. Would Rehka be able to live with those scars on her soul? Would the children?

Rehka looked away, focusing on the water rushing past the ship. "It is what it is. We will do it."

Romada glanced back at Ceta in time to see her hide a look of revulsion behind an expressionless mask. Romada didn't blame her; she was also loathe to turn the children into murderers, particularly mass murderers, though her disgust was more directed at herself for going along with the plan. She held no contempt for the sirens. They didn't choose to be monsters; a violent reaction in response to the cruelty inflicted on them was entirely justified.

"I'm going to practice with the children again," Rehka said, turning away and stomping down the stairs, her long, wavy hair tumbling over her shoulders as she walked to the hatch. Romada watched her disappear belowdecks, angry with herself for not being able to comfort her friend. If there was ever a time Rehka needed emotional support, it was now.

She turned to Ceta with a sigh. "Shouldn't you be asleep?"

Ceta gazed out at the horizon and shrugged. "I'm having a hard time adjusting to my new sleep schedule, especially since I slept last night." Shaking her head, she gave Romada a wry smile. "Want a little break before I try to sleep again?"

Romada wasn't about to turn that offer down. Releasing the wheel, she stepped back and said, "Come get me when you're tired."

With a jaunty salute, Ceta said, "Aye, aye, Captain!"

Taking the steps two at a time, Romada headed for the cabin, eager to have some alone time so she could marinate in her own awful feelings. She loved Rehka, but having her as a friend meant never having a moment of silence. When Romada was avoiding her feelings, this was perfect, but right now, she needed to soak in her misery and let her emotions loose.

Kicking off her boots and flopping down on the bed, Romada absently scratched her scalp and pictured Neiara in her mind. Would Neiara approve of the plan? Would her blood run cold at the thought of the children becoming killers? Would she have come up with a better plan in the first place?

"Help me," Romada whispered to the stillness of the room. "I don't know what to do."

The ship creaked beneath her, but no one spoke back to offer aid. No one was going to help her this time. Romada had never before admitted that she was at a loss for action, but rather than feeling dismayed at the confession, she felt a moment of peace wash over her. Maybe Neiara was reaching through the nether separating them to tell her it would all be okay. That it was okay not to know, okay to be conflicted, okay to hesitate.

If anything, it showed her sense of compassion, right? Wasn't that something to cherish?

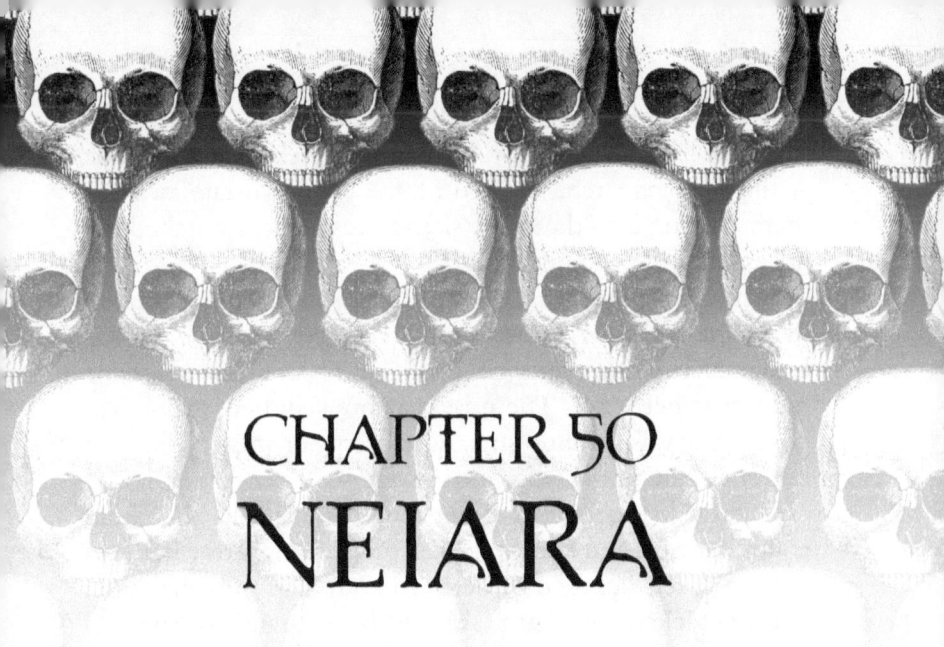

# CHAPTER 50
# NEIARA

**THREE NEW, ALIVE SIRENS KEPT NEIARA COM-**
pany in the cell. These ones looked fresh off the boat; hope
still shone out their eyes. One of them had mastered the art of
crying silently, and she wept constantly. Neiara had long since
lost the ability to cry. She was probably too dehydrated at this
point. Most of her time was spent sleeping since it was the only
way she escaped the pain in her limbs, in her gut, in her head.

The guards came for them, one by one. The siren to Neiara's right was taken first. Neiara heard her screams shortly
after she was taken. She never came back, and no new siren
took her place.

The siren across from Neiara was next. She fought the
guards as they dragged her from the cell, surprising Neiara with
the explosive strength coiled in her skinny limbs. Neiara never
heard her scream. She wasn't sure if that was a sign of strength
or a sign that she died before they could take her collar off.

That siren didn't come back either.

Then it was just the two of them left. Neiara dared to look at the weeping siren, terrified of the unknown fate awaiting them. Staring into the other siren's eyes, Neiara watched her cry and memorized her face.

She couldn't tell what color the siren's skin had been before the grime and muck coated it, but her eyes were the darkest brown Neiara had ever seen. Lank hair of an unknown shade hung past her waist. The nose was hooked; her jawline was strong. She was a plump siren, with plenty of meat still on her bones despite not having eaten in who knew how long.

Neiara looked down at her own skeletal self. She could count her ribs, and her hip bones threatened to tear her skin open. She felt sickened by her own body. Did the other siren find her sickening? Once, she had been beautiful. She had commanded attention when she danced, when she moved. Now, she was a breath from death.

The guards came for the weeping siren next. She went with them, docile as a domesticated animal. Neiara could only assume they led her to slaughter, as her screams were the loudest sound she had ever heard.

Neiara slept fitfully, waking at each tiny sound, sure the guards had come back.

*Romada will save me. Romada will save me. Romada... Please...*

They came for her, piling into the cramped cell to lead her to her fate. She stood on weak limbs, barely able to carry her own weight. Grasping her arms, they led her out of the cell, down a corridor, and to a door that opened to reveal an operating room. A table, covered by a cloth, held an impressive array of surgical tools, all shiny and deadly. A light, so bright it seared Neiara's eyes, hung above a gurney. They strapped her down, wrists and ankles attached to the sides of the railing.

As if she could have gone anywhere on her own.

The door swung open, and a healer walked in, followed by a group of elves wearing the green robes of apprentice healers. So, she was to be a lesson.

Holding out a collar keystone, the healer hissed, "Don't get any bright ideas, siren. We all have earplugs in." The keystone clicked against the back of her neck, unlocking her collar.

Glancing around at the group, Neiara realized the healer spoke truth. Every ear was plugged. She wasn't sure what she would have done if that wasn't the case, though. What could she do? Make them kill themselves? She wasn't a murderer.

After strapping Neiara's head into place, the healer picked up a scalpel. It gleamed, throwing off rays of light as it descended toward her neck.

*Romada, save me! PLEASE!*

Neiara's breathing sped up as a finger brushed her throat, and then the knife sliced through her skin. It was the coldest thing in the world. Stars erupted in her eyes as the pain spread through her body, lighting her nerves on fire. The world dropped away, and the only things that registered in her mind were the pain and the screams echoing in the room.

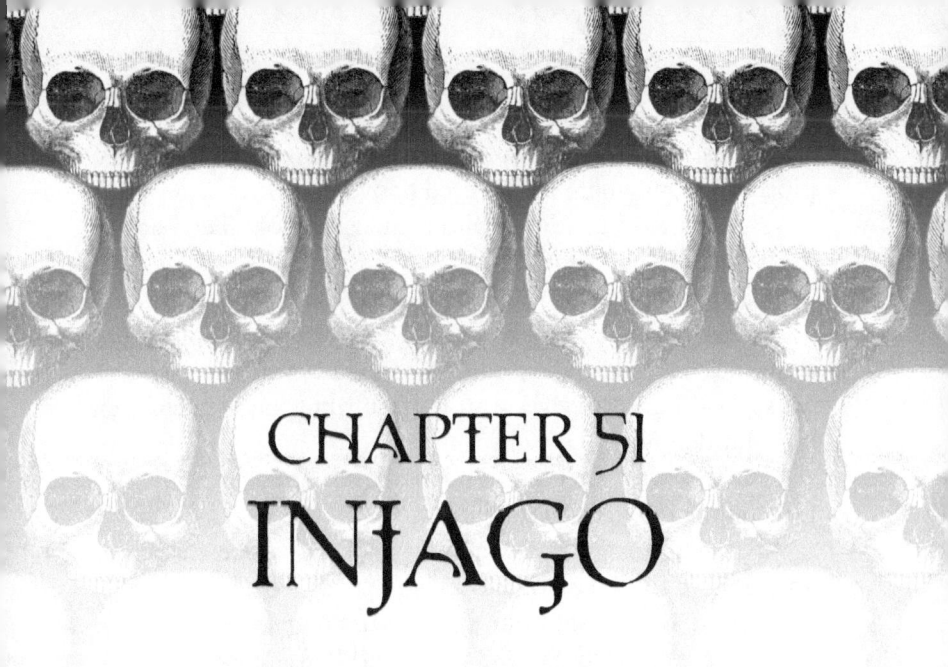

# CHAPTER 51
# INJAGO

**THE SHIPS WERE LESS THAN HALF A DAY'S**
travel from the third camp when a merfae pod swarmed the
*Guardian.* Both ships dropped anchor, and Injago flew over
to see if Fayne had any news for them. As he got closer, he
could see Romada and Yaya had both jumped in the water to
join the merfolk.

"So it turns out the next camp is also a naval garrison base,"
Romada said, splashing around.

"We attack the guards with claws and teeth," Fayne said. "If
you lure them out, we kill them."

Romada frowned. "I like that plan, though I worry about
you being in harm's way."

Fayne rolled their eyes, a habit they had picked up from
Romada, no doubt. "I call other pods to join us. We are strong.
We are not scared to fight."

"I know you're not scared! I want you to be careful, that's all."

"Does this mean we won't use the killing Song?" Injago piped up from where he hovered above the waves.

Fayne turned to Injago with a quizzical look, then back to Romada. "Killing song?"

Romada shot Injago a dirty look. "The sirens created a Song that makes elves kill themselves. We were going to use it on the guards at the base but"—she lowered her voice to a whisper—"I'm not really comfortable turning the siren children into murderers."

Fayne waved their hand in irritation before signing, "Merfolk kill the guards. Do not worry."

"Perfect," Injago said, clapping his hands once. "I say we anchor here for the night and finish the last leg of the journey at dawn. It should only take a few hours to get there."

Romada nodded. "Good plan. And Fayne, thank you."

Fayne blushed and sank beneath the waves.

"Always embarrassing our resident merfae leader," Injago chided.

Romada scoffed at him and began to climb back onto the *Guardian*, Yaya right behind her.

"You want some hot food before you fly back?" Yaya called out.

Injago gave them a mock grimace. "Now why would you tease me like that? I know it's too early for you to have finished cooking dinner."

Yaya chuckled. "Come on, you can watch me while I cook. I'll let you sample as I go."

Though his stomach rumbled at the suggestion, Injago said, "I shouldn't. If I don't fly back now, I know I won't have the strength to later."

Crestfallen, Yaya nodded.

"Celebratory dinner tomorrow, though?" Injago asked.

They gave him a small, sad smile. "Sure thing, Inja."

The crew had assembled on the deck of the *Freedom* by the time Injago landed. Dusk began to fall and someone had already lit the lanterns. The exhausted faces of the crew told him that they were probably hoping his news would be about resting for the night. Thank goodness it was.

"Good news, boyos! We're anchoring here and heading out at the crack of dawn," Injago said, projecting his voice.

A cheer went up, and a couple pixies broke into a pirate shanty, dancing together in the middle of the deck. The joyous song overtook the rest of the crew, and they began clapping their hands and stomping their feet. In stark contrast, Imber stood silent and still off to the side, gazing at Injago with those dark, indiscernible eyes. Injago walked up to him, stopping at a socially acceptable distance, and waited for him to voice his concerns.

"What is the new plan?" Imber asked after a long moment, his deep voice velvety smooth.

"The merfolk are going to attack the guards after we lure them out. This way, the children don't have to use the megasound or killing Song."

Imber's expression shifted slightly, and Injago questioned whether or not that was disappointment on his face.

"You don't like the new plan?" Injago asked haltingly.

Imber pursed his lips but said nothing. The silence was suffocatingly strong.

"Well, I'm glad the children won't be mass murderers," Injago finally added, rubbing the back of his neck.

"No one had concerns about the children Singing the Song until the megasound was made."

Injago couldn't find any words to refute him. He certainly hadn't told Romada not to try the Song on that slaver ship, though he wished he had.

"And there should be no limits to what must be done to save my siren brethren from the shackles of the kingdom," Imber continued.

Injago shook his head in bewilderment. "But turning your children into killers? Into child soldiers?" What was Imber saying?

"The kingdom must learn that what it is doing is wrong and that faeries will stand up and right their wrongs, even if they themselves will not. You and your crewmates have done this. The children deserve to strike back at their oppressors as much as the adults do."

Injago took a step back, head reeling. Of course the children deserved the right to fight back, but they didn't deserve to be scarred for life from it. To have those memories of their victims in their minds… To have that blood on their hands that could never be washed off. Injago still remembered the face of the first faerie he had ever killed. It wasn't something one could forget.

Injago was a pirate, the lowest of the low, and he still didn't believe children should be forced into killing. How could Imber be okay with this? Even the kingdom didn't hire children for their military.

*But they sold children into slavery…*

"I can't think," he gasped, taking another step back. The pirate shanty continued in the background as he looked at Imber with a confused conscience.

Imber's eyes tightened, and his mouth drew into a hard line.

Injago knew Imber was closing him off. He knew he had hurt Imber, but he couldn't handle the depth and complexity of the conversation at hand. He didn't have the right words or the delicate sensibility to convey his opinion without disrespecting Imber's or hurting him more. And Injago didn't want to do either. Taking a step away from it all was the best thing to do, right?

"We'll talk tomorrow?" Injago asked in a soft voice.

Imber nodded, a peculiar look in his eye before he turned and walked away. Injago couldn't help feeling like he had messed up somehow. Like every time he interacted with Imber, he took one step closer and two steps back. Soon, they would be so far apart, nothing could hold them together. His dreams of Imber felt like they were nightmares, foretelling their failure at a relationship rather than their unending love for each other. As much as he wanted to try and keep his heart open, keep waiting before calling it quits, nothing so far had proved to him that hoping was better than leaving.

And what did Injago know of love anyway? He wouldn't be able to feed it properly even if he had all the tools. He was cursed to be alone. He would probably even die alone.

Injago trudged to the cabin and shut the door behind him before falling onto the bed. Darkness was overtaking the room so he lit the lantern, removed his bindings, and made himself comfortable. Lying back on his pillow, soft as a cloud, he still couldn't untangle his thoughts. He chased them through the cabin, hoping for some clarity. The whorls on the wood panel ceiling above him turned into waves and whirlpools as he stared at them. He followed the grain to a spot that looked like a face. A small, stricken face.

Suddenly, the waves were blood red, and the face was a child sinking beneath them. He shut his eyes tight to drown out the image, but all he saw was red.

# CHAPTER 52
# ROMADA

**ROMADA STARED AT THE THIRD CAMP THROUGH** the spyglass. It was the first camp that actually looked like an intimidating and secure location; buildings were nestled in the cliff face, and a stone wall spanned the entire camp, with the only entrance a giant and solid metal gate leading to the docks. The docks were, thankfully, empty save for a handful of rowboats.

She let out a gusty sigh. "Well, there's definitely no way we are going to be able to sneak in like the last two times."

Ceta snorted derisively beside her. "That's for fucking sure."

"Good thing they're here to help," Rehka said, waving down at the merfolk surrounding the ship. There had to be at least fifty of them.

Romada had never seen so many merfolk in one place before. It was hard not to feel her spirits lift a bit when they were being escorted by a rainbow.

"I am glad they're here. But I still don't like it." Ceta said.

Romada turned to her. "You don't like what?"

"The plan."

Before she could control herself, Romada's blood heated, and she snapped, "Then figure something else out!"

Ceta held her hands up in mock surrender for a second before taking control of the wheel again.

"We can't do this if we're fighting ourselves," Rehka said quietly.

Romada pinched the bridge of her nose in exasperation. Rehka was right, of course. Ceta hadn't meant to insult her personally, or her leadership, or her judgment. And if Romada was being honest, she didn't like the plan either. But what was the alternative?

Taking a deep breath to steady herself, Romada said, "I'm sorry, Ceta. I shouldn't be snippy."

Ceta stared at Romada with bulging eyes. "Um, no worries, Captain. That was my fault. It's actually a good plan," she said, frowning. "It keeps us all safe."

"The children's safety and well-being is my priority," Romada said, looking down at the children frolicking about the deck. "I'll do whatever I can to make sure we don't lose them or"—her chest tightened—"scar them."

Ceta nodded. "I understand.

Rehka gave Romada's hand a gentle squeeze and interlaced their fingers. "We won't lose any more children, Rome."

Romada's throat convulsed at the thought. "Good," she said, voice breaking. Her soul couldn't handle the sight of any more dead children. The only bright side was remembering the merfolk who would soon be spawned, who would grace the seas and add to the rainbow.

"There's Fayne," Rehka said, pulling Romada from her thoughts.

"Okay," Romada said, releasing Rehka to look over the side. She looked back up at the camp and the imposing gate, a plan forming in her mind. "Ceta, I need you to fly over to the *Freedom* and tell Injago our new plan."

"What new plan?"

"We're going to use our ballistae to hit the gate and bring it down. I guarantee after the guards come out, that gate will be locked up tight with no way for us to get in."

Ceta gave her a curt nod and stepped up to the railing before flinging herself into the air. She flew quickly and landed on the *Freedom*, where she ran up to Injago.

Rehka nudged Romada. "You think this will work?"

Turning the wheel slightly to angle the ship better, Romada said, "It better. What else can we do?"

Rehka pursed her lips but stayed quiet. Romada knew she wanted to use the killing Song but also knew that she wouldn't bring it up unless it looked like all was lost. Hopefully, that moment wouldn't come.

Romada looked over to see Ceta flying back over. She landed beside Romada with a grim smile.

"They will follow us in and position themselves to take out the gates. I told them not to aim at the boats so they don't hit the merfolk."

"Good call. Let's hoist the colors and show them who we are."

"Hoist the colors!" Ceta yelled out.

"Hoist the colors!" The call spread across the deck as someone rushed to the chest and pulled out the black flag. It flapped in the wind as it rose in the air. Romada could hear the same call echoing over the water from the *Freedom* as they raised their flag as well.

A battle horn sounded from the garrison camp as the ships sailed closer, echoing in the small harbor. The gate began to rise, and troops poured out, streaming toward the boats. So, so many troops.

"Arm the ballistae!" Romada shrieked, and the crew jumped at her command. The sound of metal against metal rang out as the spears were loaded in. "Drop the anchor!"

The ship jerked as the anchor hit the ocean floor, pulling them to a sudden stop. Ceta spun the wheel to turn them broadside to the gate, giving the ballistae crew an easy target.

"Fire on the gate!" Romada shouted, and the deep **twang** of the ballistae strings reverberated on the ship. They weren't close enough to hear the impact over the sounds of the guards, but Romada could see the spears hitting the gate in multiple spots. Spears from the *Freedom* joined the onslaught.

Ferocious shouts from the oncoming guards reached Romada's ears as they rowed toward the ship; their shouts quickly turned into screams of terror as the merfolk attacked, overturning the boats and dragging the guards to the depths. It would only take one venomous bite from their fangs to kill, but Romada imagined it was more satisfying to drown them. After all, she knew that dancing with an opponent in a fight was more fun than killing them in one blow.

The screams continued to assault the crew, and Romada belatedly hoped there were no undercover sirens among them. Maybe the killing Song would have been a better option. It was too late, regardless.

"Fire!"

The ballistae crew shot the gate. It was buckling in certain spots now; Romada was sure it would come down in the next couple of volleys.

"Fire!"

An entire section of the gate had bent inward, causing it to warp in its tracks. So close, so close.

"FIRE!"

With a resounding crash that could be heard across the harbor, the gate fell to the ground in a twisted heap. A cheer went up on both ships as the crews witnessed this small victory. Rehka threw her arms around Romada, hugging her tight and laughing with joy. Romada allowed herself a tiny grin as the sounds of strangled screams continued.

"Captain," Ceta said in hushed horror. "Look."

Out in the open water, on the horizon, was an armada of ships. Romada grabbed the spyglass in a panic and brought it to her eye; every ship flew the green and blue flag of the Royal Naval Guard.

"They found us," Rehka choked out.

Romada's heart chilled as she realized what needed to be done. It had been inevitable; she had known the Song would be their saving grace. It was time.

*Gods, forgive us.*

"What do we do?" Rehka asked in a whimper, eyes wide as she shook from head to toe. Her breathing hitched even as Romada rubbed her arms to calm her down.

"Rehka, dear, we have a plan. Remember? We have the megasound." Tears formed in Romada's eyes.

Rehka looked up at her, focused on her slowly. "The mega-sound."

"Yes. We will use it on the armada. You're going to Sing."

"Sing. I can do that."

"I know you can," Romada said, her voice cracking as she suppressed her grief. "Go, gather the children."

Nodding, Rehka left to find them.

"Do you think this will work?" Ceta spoke so low, Romada strained to hear it.

"Pray to the gods it does." Romada's voice didn't betray her fear, but she had to clamp down on the banister to keep herself from shaking to pieces. She had to be strong.

The sirens emerged from belowdecks and, as a unit, headed for the megasound.

Rehka stood in front of the children. "Today, we stand up for what is right. We fight for our siren siblings. We take back our lives! Today, we say no more oppression! No more enslavement! Today, we fight to use our voices! NO MORE SILENCE!" she screamed.

"No more silence!" The children cheered, fists pumping in the air. The words made Romada shiver.

"Now, let's see what this thing can do," Rehka said, whipping the covering off of the megasound. It gleamed in the midday sun, a terrifying instrument of death wielded by those who would soon lose their innocence. Romada shut her eyes, unable to look at it without sobbing.

"Ready?"

"Ready!"

"Now, Sing."

The fine hairs on Romada's arms raised at the sound of the children's euphonious voices raised in Song. Her heart pumped madly as her body fought its own fight-or-flight response. She knew her body was still under her control, but every part of her screamed **run**.

The ancient language of the sirens boomed out from the end of the megasound, rattling Romada's bones. Her eyes flew open as she stared out at the approaching ships, waiting. At first, it looked like nothing was happening until the head ship began to turn.

And then another ship turned.

And another.

Within moments, every ship was turning off course and crashing into the other ships. Romada whipped out the spyglass and watched as elf after elf drew their daggers across their own throats, leaving the helms unattended. The sharp crack of wood splintering against wood met her ears, and the first ship sank, impaled by the bow of another ship.

Ship after ship sank.

Ship after ship after ship.

And still, the sirens Sang. Their voices melded together into the most hauntingly beautiful melody of destruction. The beatific expressions on the children's faces made Romada's bowels twist as she realized she was looking at a small army of the deadliest killers on Faerth.

Glancing back over at the camp, Romada saw the guards who had not been captured by merfolk had ended their lives as well. The merfolk milled around in bloody waters, watching the ship. Romada's stomach threatened to recall her breakfast, and she quickly turned away.

As the last ship sank beneath glittering waves, Romada called for them to stop. The sirens paid her no heed, Singing as though their lives depended on it. Which, Romada supposed, was true. Her head began to pound from the cacophony, and she made her way, step by agonizing step, to Rehka. As Romada moved to grasp Rehka's hand, Rehka whipped her head around and glared at Romada with withering malice.

Taking a deep breath, Romada looked her in the eye and said, "Rehka, it's okay. You did it." Careful not to make any sudden movements, Romada placed a kiss on her hand.

Rehka's voice faltered, and she stopped Singing. "It's over?" Tears gathered in her eyes.

Romada nodded, pulling her into a hug. "It's over."

Weeping, Rehka collapsed in Romada's arms.

"Did we win?" one of the children asked, tugging on Romada's shirt.

"Yes, we did. All thanks to you, my little hero," Romada said, smiling and trying not to vomit.

"Heroes! We're heroes!" the children said, jumping up and down. Romada squeezed her eyes shut, wishing she could block out the horrific sound of children laughing.

"It's time to look for Neiara," Rehka whispered.

Romada latched onto the image of Neiara like a lifeline. Hope blossomed in her chest.

*Please be here.*

"Romada?"

She opened her eyes to see the look of concern on Rehka's face. She forced herself to smile again, for Rehka's sake. "Yes. Let's go."

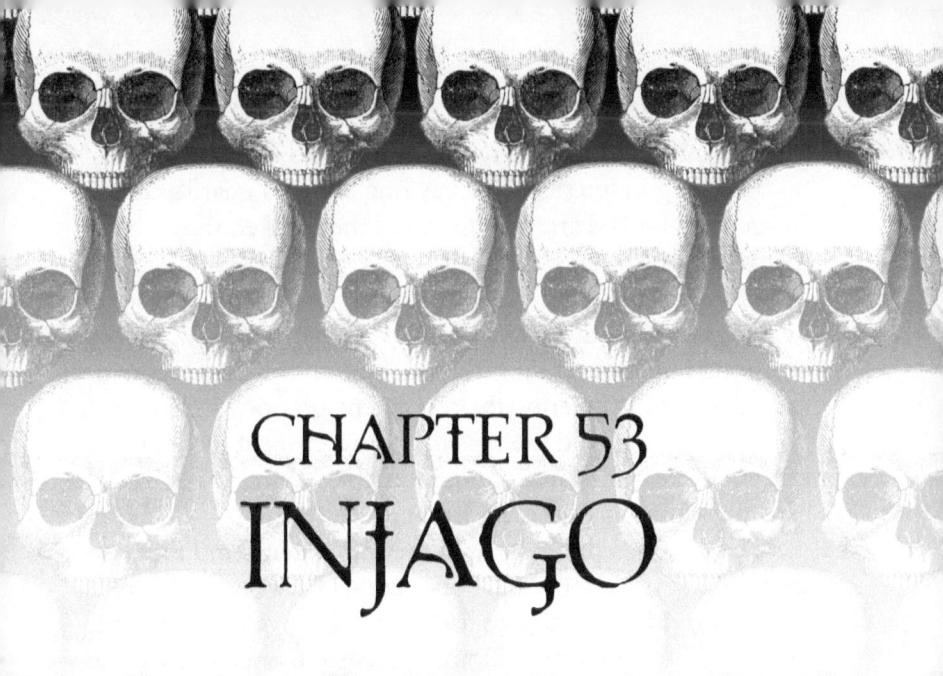

# CHAPTER 53
# INJAGO

**INJAGO AND HIS CREW ROWED TO THE DOCKS,** their oars dipping below the red waves and between floating corpses. The stench of death and the sharp tang of blood was heavy and oppressive. It dragged down Injago's mood, though he knew they had won.

*But at what cost?*

He glanced over at Imber, noticing the grim set of his lips as he surveyed the carnage. Did he feel differently about the children murdering everyone now that he was faced with the reality of the aftermath?

The boat bumped against the dock, and Atar jumped out to tie them off. The rest of them made their way over to join Romada and her crew. Injago clasped Romada's hand and pulled her in for a hug; her cheek rested on his forehead, and when he released her, he saw unshed tears in her eyes.

"You ready for this?" he asked in a low voice.

She sniffled once and nodded. "Let's go free the sirens."

Stopping first to snatch a key ring off of a guard's corpse, Injago then looked after the group as they walked through the mangled ruins of the iron gate.

The inside of the garrison was a tangle of brick and stone buildings without any tents in sight. A red flag hung on the door of a long building set into the cliff side on the right. Romada veered toward it, steering the rest of the group with her.

The building held the sickeningly sweet scent of decay. Rehka choked on the fumes for a moment, waving for everyone else to go ahead as she steadied herself.

The hall was dimly lit by flickering lanterns mounted on the walls at even intervals. Doors were set between the lanterns. The first room they came to had no windows or bars set in the door, but it was unlocked. Romada pushed it open and gasped. The room was dominated by a giant pile of bodies, all naked with pointed spines and torn throats. A pool of congealed blood and bodily fluids covered the floor. Someone vomited in the hallway.

Romada pulled the door shut. "We'll come back if we have to."

The next door was locked, and Injago fished through the key ring, trying key after key. The correct one slid in, and he twisted, swinging the door open.

Green eyes the color of dull emeralds set beneath a crown of curls stared at him from across the room, and a jolt of recognition went through him.

*She's alive.*

Except she wasn't. The slump of her neck, with her head against her shoulder, made it painfully obvious that her muscles—what little she had left—had started to decay. She sat on the floor, arms held straight up by chains bolted to the ceiling. Those alone were the only reason her body hadn't crumpled to the floor in a heap.

Injago looked at Romada. Tears poured from her eyes as she slowly crossed the room and knelt beside the corpse of her lover. Shaking hands reached out to touch Neiara's cheek with the barest of touches; even that slight pressure was enough to split her skin, oozing rotten fluids.

A howl of pain echoed in the silence of the room as Romada broke down, cradling Neiara's body. Rehka stepped up to place a hand on Romada's shoulder, but Romada wrenched herself away, weeping uncontrollably.

The room held at least a dozen other sirens—some alive, some dead—chained to the ceiling. The living ones stared at the pirates in confusion, probably wondering who on Faerth they were and why they were there.

Clearing his throat first, Injago said, "We have liberated the camp. All of the guards are dead. We will be freeing you all, but it will take time."

A couple of the siren prisoners exchanged glances before several started crying, though their cries were silent. When Injago looked again, he realized all of them had bandages on their throats.

Neiara had a similar bandage on hers as well. Injago moved to peel back the bandage as Romada lay on the filthy floor. An incision crossed Neiara's throat, held together by bloated stitches. The healers had ripped into her throat with precision instruments, searching for something. And based on the silent sirens surrounding him, he knew what it was.

"What is it?" Rehka asked in a hushed voice.

Fighting back nausea, Injago said, "They stole their voices."

Rehka gasped and covered her own neck as she looked around at the other sirens, grief on her face as though she felt their loss and pain. Maybe she did.

Injago turned to see Imber looking at him with a peculiar expression. Swallowing his trepidation, Injago said, "Let's get everyone else freed."

After handing his set of keys to Atar, Injago and several others of the crew filed out of the room to go look for more keys and explore the rest of the rooms in the building. Injago headed back outside for some fresh air and found another keyring on a dead guard. When he turned back, Imber was standing in the sunlight, face upturned to the sky. He looked peaceful for once. Injago almost hated to disturb him.

"We found Neiara," he said, walking up to the handsome faerie of his dreams.

Imber nodded without looking at him.

"What will you do now?" Injago asked.

Letting out a big sigh, Imber met his gaze. "I have thought about this day. I pledged to help you find Neiara. This has been done."

Injago couldn't breathe. Was Imber leaving? More importantly, did Injago want to make him stay?

"I do not know what to do with my life now. I could go anywhere, do anything. No one would know I am a siren."

Injago steeled himself for Imber to continue. Imber's eyes bored into Injago's with a ferocity that scared him. He felt the urge to kiss this beautiful masc-fae before him and beg him to stay. But the only way to be the good faerie that Imber saw... was to let him go.

*Please love me.*

Imber shrugged his broad shoulders. "What should I do, Captain?"

Injago couldn't find the words to admit who he really was without his mask, that he was a spiteful, jealous, and deeply flawed faerie who just wanted to be loved. That he was lonely and jaded. He didn't have the strength to crack the picture-perfect image Imber had of him.

With a sad smile, Injago said, " You deserve to be happy and free. You have no obligations to me or anyone here." Please don't leave me.

Imber closed his eyes and tilted his face back up to the sky. "Thank you, Injago."

"Can I ask you for something?"

"Anything."

Injago's heart constricted. "Can you hold me?"

In the blink of an eye, Injago was folded into Imber's strong embrace. Injago breathed in the scent of citrus and smoke, tears forming in his eyes as he fought to keep himself from kissing Imber one last time.

*Enjoy this moment.*

Imber squeezed him tighter before he abruptly released him and walked back into the building. Alone, Injago stood in the warmth of the sun, tears spilling down his cheeks. Imber deserved someone who was actually kind, actually good. He deserved a better faerie than him.

So why did he feel like he had made a terrible mistake?

*Neiara would know what to do.*

But Neiara was a corpse in a stone tomb. And there was no one left to help him.

Romada, Injago, Yaya, and Rehka will return in the sequel novel *The Healing Song* in Spring of 2026.

# ACKNOWLEDGMENTS

Thank you to Charlie Knight, my amazing editor, steadfast best friend, and now fellow author. To Joy, for always hyping me up when I felt like this book wouldn't ever be completed. To Shawna Barnett, author of sapphic pirate books *Seabird* and *Windfall*, for being an enthusiastic beta reader and giving me incredible feedback. To Dani, my middle school best friend, for first introducing me to *Pirates of the Caribbean: The Curse of the Black Pearl* in 2003 and kickstarting a life-long obsession. To Aunt Jen for buying me that cool pirate information book with the fold-out inserts and letters (iykyk). To Adik Graves, my baby brother, closest confidante, interior formatter, and unhinged critique partner, for always listening to my latest story idea and helping me figure out what the heck it's supposed to mean. And to you, dear reader, for taking a chance on Faerth and keeping my pirate crew company through their various tragedies and perils. Your support means the world to me.

# GLOSSARY

# SPECIES OF FAERIES

**Pixies:**
Winged humanoids with elongated and pointed ears, long fangs, and sharp nails. Able to fly though this is frowned upon in certain kingdoms/countries. The indigenous species of the kingdom of Dradour. Social caste is dependent on wing color which is determined by bloodline/distance from purebloods in the genetic pool.

**Elves:**
Wingless humanoids with pointed ears and small fangs. Enhanced sense of balance and rhythm. Excellent dancers and thieves. The indigenous and ruling species of the kingdom of Ostrana. In pixie- dominant kingdoms, they are sometimes considered second-rate citizens due to a stereotype of them having an inherent criminal nature.

**Sirens:**
Wingless humanoids with pointed ears, small fangs, and a spine with outwardly-spiked vertebrae. Can enchant people with the sound of their voice through Singing or talking, though talking is most often only felt as a strong suggestion rather than a command. Persecuted in certain kingdoms due to their powers. Were enslaved as a species for thousands of years and only recently are seen as citizens. If a siren has had the spine-flattening procedure done, they are physically indistinguishable from an elf. Called "thornback" and "spike" as slurs.

**Imps:**
Large, hulking humanoids, like small giants with comparably smaller heads in proportions to their bodies, tiny pointed ears, protruding fangs, and large razor sharp claws. Usually seen in manual labor jobs or hired as bodyguards. Seen as the lowest citizens in Cities and are often nomadic.

Glossary

**Water nymphs:**
Hairless amphibious humanoids who can breathe underwater using gills in their necks. Skin can be various shades of blue, green, or purple. Webbed hands and feet with sharp nails on their fingers. They have 1-3 fins running down their back, which can be flattened under their clothing but can also be flexed to look kind of like wings. Ears have spines with webbing on them so they can move their ears to hear better underwater. They can bond with waterhorses and therefore run the trolley systems in Cities.

**Merfolk:**
Singular: merfae. Hairless half-humanoids with long tails. Long, tactile tendrils on their heads act as lures when hunting fish. Webbed hands and ears, fangs and claws. Speak using sign language. One large fin runs from the base of their neck to the base of their torso. Including their tail—which is three times the length of their upper body—they are the size of an average elf, which makes them very petite. They are considered dangerous in groups as they can work together to overturn small boats and can deliver a paralyzing bite but are seen as harmless creatures of luck to those onboard ships. Merfolk are considered to be the reincarnated souls of those who died at sea. They do not have the capability to reproduce and do not have a concept of gender.

**Sprites:**
Tiny, winged humanoids about one third the size of an elf/pixie/siren. They generally stay in their own colonies which are considered off limits to other faeries due to their fierce territorial instincts and their venomous bite. As such, not much is known about them, though many faeries speculate they feed off the blood of other faeries.

# PIXIE CASTE SYSTEM

### Purebloods:

The original indigenous family of the area. Each pixie king-dom has a pureblood family who are usually the rulers of the kingdom. The purebloods of Dradour are umber-skinned with blood-red wings and black hair with a streak of white at the forehead; King Oberon, Queen Tatiana, and their son were the only pixies left of the original Dradourian Pureblood family. Purebloods are able to deliver a venomous bite with their fangs, which are elongated compared to other pixie castes. Purebloods have a hard time producing other pureblood children who aren't miscarried or stillbirths. They have an extended life span and can live for almost ten thousand years. They reach adulthood at roughly 100 years of age, which is average for most faerie species.

### Nobles:

Half-pureblood. These are children of a pureblood and some-one who either was not indigenous to the area or is a faerie of a different species. Due to a genetic quirk, Dradourian nobles all have albinism. Nobles inherit their wing color from their pureblood parent. They are seen as royalty, though they are all bastard children of the king or queen. If the rulers are unable to produce an heir before they die, the nobles are next in line for the throne.

### Aristo-fae:

These are the descendants of nobles. Over time, different wing colors emerged as nobles and children of nobles procreated with pixies from other areas of Faerth. All aristo-fae have bright, jewel-toned wings. In the kingdom of Dradour, each aristo-fae House is named after a different gem or precious metal that correlates to the dominant color of their wings. Higher-level aristo-fae Houses have lighter-colored wings, whereas low-er-level Houses, which are seen as being further from purebloods, have darker-colored wings. If all nobles were to die, the higher-level aristo-fae Houses would form a committee to choose one of their own to be ruler. This caste is generally upper working class, though some lower-level Houses might be middle to lower working class.

**Common-fae:**
These pixies are so many generations removed from purebloods that their wings are muted and dark. Most of their wings are a brown, black, or dark grey. These pixies do not have any call to royalty and will never be a candidate for ruling the kingdom. Pixies in this caste are middle to lower working class and form the general population of most pixie-dominated kingdoms as well as a large percentage of the immigrant population in elven kingdoms.

# RELIGIONS

**Pixie Pantheon:**
- **AJAKIN [AH-YUH-KIN],** the king of the gods: the god of strength, war and peace, and justice. Call on him for protection in your endeavors.
- **MAJAKIM [MAH-YUH-KIM],** the queen of the gods: the god of love, nurturing, home and hearth, buildings and structure. Call on her for blessings in the House.
- **ARDER [AHR-DUR],** the Reader: god of literature and arts. He is also a god of education, learning, and hard work. Call on him for aid in memory.
- **TALEAHA [TAH-LEE-UH],** the Healer: god of healing. God of childbirth and pregnancy, of gender transformation and sexuality. Call on her for fertility aid.
- **THE HARVESTER, AKA DEATH:** (agender) god of journeys and the unknown. Of winter and the harvest, of abundance and famine. The god of economics and resource manipulation. They cradle you in death and give you sweet rest.

**Elven Pantheon:**
- **DEATH** is the god of friendships, of journeys, of the unknown. Death greets everyone like an old friend.
- **FATHER** is the god of building, of structure, of outer strength. He is the roof over your head; he is your shelter.
- **MOTHER** is the god of love, of peace, of inner strength. She is the hearth in your home, the blanket of dreams.

**Water Nymph/Merfae Pantheon:**
- **THE SEA:** She is a goddess of chaos and destruc-

tion. She is the goddess of passion, trust, and emotional strength. She brings all to rest in the depths of her bosom and cradles them as her children.

- **THE MOON:** She is the goddess of time and change, of direction and purpose. She is the goddess of thieves and lovers. Her changing light shows both her reliability and her fickle nature as she vacillates between illuminating the soul and blanketing her followers in darkness.

**Siren Pantheon:**

Any teachings and texts of siren religion were eradicated when sirens were first enslaved. Since then, many sirens have chosen to worship the gods of the elves, pixies, or water nymphs, though many forgo religion altogether.

**Imp Pantheon:**

The imps are largely a nonreligious species, preferring to believe in hard work, the luck of chance, and the reward of effort. No gods answered when they called, so they quit calling to them. As such, imp religious texts do not exist, or if they do, no one knows where to find them.

# ABOUT THE AUTHOR

Felix Graves is a queer and disabled AAPI author of dark speculative fiction. Most of his writing involves tragedy, queer romance, and faerie-inspired creatures. His debut novel, Farzana's Spite (2024) is the first novel in the Stories of Faerth anthology series, with The Killing Song (2025) being the second. He has also published a handful of horror short stories including Color Unknown (2024) and Behind the Mask (2025). He prides himself on writing stories with a starkly honest ownvoice commentary on mental illness, disability, and queerness. When not writing, he can be found reading queer fiction, cooking elaborate meals, or gaming with his friends and family.

# CONTENT WARNINGS

The Killing Song is a dark fantasy horror novel and contains scenes and topics that may cause distress for certain readers. Please exercise caution when reading.

A non-exhaustive list of content warnings includes:

- depictions of symptoms of depression, anxiety, and panic disorders, including thoughts of despair, major depressive episodes, suicidal ideation, panic attacks, nightmares, disordered eating, dissociation, hallucinations, and intrusive thoughts
- references to past emotional, mental, and physical abuse of a child by a parental figure
- depictions of fantasy species-based racism toward adults and children, including hate crimes, use of slurs, rioting, physical assault, slavery, arrests/abductions, mass incarceration, genocide, medical experimentation, and internment camps
- depictions of extreme violence and gore
- depictions of vomit, urination, and defecation
- mass murders, including the murder of children
- multiple depictions of coerced suicide
- use of child soldiers
- multiple uses of a fantasy weapon of mass destruction
- on-page consensual sex scene
- on-page masturbation
- use of "cunt" to self-refer to a trans man's genitals
- death of a main character